Not a single person thought anything amiss until the clank of the shell announced its arrival in the weapon's chamber. Collectively, the ladies of the Hollywood Weight Watchers turned and witnessed firsthand the origin of their destruction. The ensuing explosion rocked the foundation of the Rite-Aid building. The projectile missed Ellen Peterson, ripping through the easel and detonating in the wall. The foundation was instantly reduced to a smoldering pile of rubble and set off the overhead sprinkler system. Survivors cowered, wailed, and screamed as they were showered with water and lethal chunks of concrete.

1st Printing
El Dorado Publishing
Copyright 2019

Son of Ravage

J.P. Linde

Cover Design by
Brett Vail

For Lori and Pacia

Special Thanks:
Lisa Wittman
Richard Melo
Brett Vail
Aaron Montes

To the crew:
Tom McComb
Glenn Holmes
Jerry Lambert
Ric Hart
Dan Sanders

And of course,
David Lawrence Anderson

1954

The combined rap sheet inside the stolen Buick totaled more than six pages and it was assumed the four hoodlums were more than capable of getting the job done. Surely one notorious armed burglar, one capo of the Costa Nostra and two low level, teenage street punks, recruited off the mean streets of Detroit, could ice one, lone middle-aged man.

The target was driving a black 53 Mercedes Sedan and the four had taken over the pursuit on an Interstate just outside Chicago. He had fled New York three days prior and his movements had been closely monitored. Whoever wanted the man dead, wanted it badly. Their orders were simple and direct: eliminate with extreme prejudice.

They saw their chance in a deserted gas station in the town of Glen Ellen. The four peered out the steamy windows of the Buick and watched their victim step out of his car, heading for the restroom inside the run-down building. He was not what any of them had expected. The middle-aged man while tall, appeared hunched and exhibited a discernible paunch. What little hair remained on top of his balding head was an unsettling mix of jet-black and snowy white.

The driver gunned the engine and the Buick roared, skidding to a halt and blocking the Mercedes from an easy escape. The thugs jumped out of the vehicle in a flash and fanned out around the Mercedes. They were now in a perfect position to collect the easy payday.

"May I help you, gentlemen?"

The hoodlums pivoted, a collection of ruddy faces snapping away from the building and toward the authoritative voice. It was him. Somehow, he'd managed to get the drop on them. He was unarmed but appeared more formidable up close. The target had somehow grown in both size and stature since disappearing inside the restroom. He was well over 6 feet tall and despite the extra weight appeared in better shape than any of them. The man clutched the handle of the gas pump, a steady stream of petrol gushing out the nozzle and pooling at their feet. In his other hand, he held a book of matches, his tan fingers poised to execute a one-handed flick and turn the entire service station into a fiery maelstrom.

"I bought him out," the man announced with a calm assurance. "I'm now the proud owner of this fine Texaco station. I'm thinking of renovating and starting from scratch. What do you think?"

The impetuous teens charged, coming at him from opposite directions. One pock-marked youth wielded a switchblade and tossed it from hand to hand as if he just stepped off the stage from a touring production of "West Side Story." "I'm going to cut ya," the teen cackled.

Not wishing to be outdone, the other delinquent grabbed onto a dripping squeegee. It was not the best of decisions, but the only weapon he could manage on such short notice.

The man's leg came up in a blur, the heel of his black leather jackboot smashing switchblade teen in the jaw. The knife dropped, clattering on the pavement and the punk stumbled back into a pump before dropping to the ground. He was the lucky one. The man answered squeegee with a half- gallon of premium to the face, the delinquent gagging and sputtering from the swallowed fuel. The man dropped the matches and reached out, snagging the pasty-faced punk and wrapping the hose around his scrawny neck, the black, rubber garland spilling liquid death onto the cold, gray concrete.

The adult assassins reached for their automatic weapons, concealed beneath gray trench coats. Before the steel had left their holsters, the man had aimed both teen and nozzle at the two

2

adults. The burglar and capo were drenched with gas, the man retrieving the book of matches off the ground in a flash, lighting one, and poised to flick the small flame at the two stunned hitmen.

Without a word, the two adult survivors backed off and fled, hightailing it to the open doors of the Buick. The failed enterprise was never reported to their bosses. This bungled job marked the four for life and they'd now be forced to disappear from the face of the earth. Before the doors of the Buick slammed shut, the two survivors swore they heard the hum from an intense vibration. The noise came from everywhere at once as if something or someone was quivering with such intensity that it produced actual noise. They didn't bother glancing back to identify the source. That would take precious time that neither criminal felt they had.

His pursuit and elimination had quickly turned into the preferred sport of the underworld. Given the lack of ability displayed by these particular assailants, the reward for his removal had dropped considerably. Every small-time criminal and hoodlum in the country was looking for him. Continuing by car was no longer an option. The middle-aged man with the receding hairline needed another plan. He glanced across the road at the deserted train station. The next scheduled train was still hours away, but it had given him an idea.

It had taken three states to achieve the confidence required to trust her fellow passenger. The anxious young mother was on her way to visit her husband stationed in Fort Lewis, Washington. Her brave soldier was part of the latest deployment to Korea and the young wife was willing to travel across the entire country to ensure her man spent time with his new family. She had purchased a brand-new dress for the reunion, her strawberry blonde hair recently cut and fashioned in the latest style. Very soon, she'd be back in his loving arms. Changing into her new frock along with quick application of make-up would only take a few minutes. The train was currently barreling through a heavily forested section of the northwest state with no scheduled stops until their final destination.

The brooding stranger had chosen to sit across from her the entire trip. They had exchanged only a few cursory words, and those were scattered between the man's long furtive looks out the passenger car window. Still, there was something comforting in his quiet, calm nature that made her trust him. He was older, uniquely handsome in a parental way and radiated an overall aura of protection. It was the same feeling the young mother experienced around a beat cop or fireman. It was only a few minutes and was a strong enough hunch to entrust her precious baby to his care.

"If it's not too much trouble," she said, accompanied by her most coquettish smile.

He turned his attention from the green terrain, rolling past at a speed of over 70 miles per and offered the faintest of smiles. He nodded, signaling he understood. It was all the answer she needed, and the young mother adjourned, leaving the stranger and her newborn son for a quick trip to the powder room.

The three Ninjas attacked without warning, shattering the two closest windows, and swinging themselves effortlessly into the deserted passenger car. They landed in the middle of the aisle, screaming at the top of their lungs and striking a threatening pose. The assassins were dressed entirely in black, their faces masked with matching balaclavas. They were armed with long bamboo shafts that the middle-aged man instantly recognized as the lethal weapon known as Shiani. The attackers held the weapons over their heads and waved them threateningly, waiting for the target to make the first move.

A chill wind blasted through the broken windows as the passenger rose to full height. He swung himself into the aisle as the three announced their first moves with a scream.

The man dropped to his knees as the bamboo weapons swooshed past, barely missing his balding head. He dropped onto his back and kicked, his legs trapping the first attacker and sending him tumbling into the others. The Ninjas had lost both the benefit of surprise and balance. The man was back on his feet

4

again and executed a vicious but controlled counter-attack. He grabbed the closest Ninja, snatching the bamboo weapon out of gloved hands. The man wielded the stick with an expertise that guaranteed real damage and had no qualms about showing his ability. With several thwaps of the stick, the first attacker dropped, and the highly skilled passenger moved onto the others. He crouched, launching his paunchy frame into the air while at the same time swinging the bamboo shaft in a wide, sweeping arc. The weapon connected with both masked heads, propelling them backwards into the seats closest to the broken windows. As the attackers rose, the man landed and using the backs of two seats, lifted himself and kicked out both legs. Jackboots met startled Ninjas in the midsection, sending both attackers tumbling through the very same shattered windows that announced their arrival.

The man grabbed the remaining Ninja by the seat of his trousers, lifting him out of the aisle and launching him through the window. The battle had taken days to prepare and had been thwarted in less than two minutes. Crisis averted, the man returned to his seat, covering the sleeping baby with his leather flight jacket to protect him from the onslaught of cold air. He sat down in his seat and returned to his sullen brooding as if nothing out of the ordinary had ever taken place.

The baby awoke unexpectedly and wailed. It had managed to sleep through the entire assault and now, sensing abandonment by his mother, proceeded to summon a full-scale tantrum. When a few quiet words didn't bring satisfactory results, the passenger's body commenced to vibrate, emitting a slight hum that returned the infant to a state of cooing serenity.

"The days of the hero are gone," the man announced unexpectedly. "Like the ancient Greeks who abandoned their own gods and heroes, the American people have rejected me."

It was an odd conversation starter and the wide-eyed innocent did not know what to make of it.

"I moved out of my penthouse offices in New York." The man leaned in as if the next statement revealed some hidden truth.

5

"Leased the entire floor to the Chairman of the Board of Pepsi Cola. Didn't do it for the money. I'm worth millions."

The baby sneezed and followed this with a wide-eyed coo.

"The first of my crew quit after my expedition to the center of the earth," the man explained. "Three years later, the last retired. He was the most loyal of the five and his departure stung the most. The anthropologist gave up adventuring for a life in the suburbs. Like the physicist, the mathematician, the architect and the Certified Public Accountant before him, he left me."

It was the strangest bedtime story the baby ever heard. He didn't comprehend a single word but there remained something in the haunted, hunted voice that held his attention.

"Family and friends are not the only ones deserting me," the man continued. "My tan skin is taking on the withered look of a discarded wallet." He patted his stomach to emphasize the next point. "I'm at least seventy pounds overweight and what little hair I have left is abandoning my scalp and taking up residence in the shower drain."

The baby's face crinkled as if concentrating. The infant was either fully engrossed in the conversation or filling a diaper.

"And, to make matters worse," the stranger added. "There's a criminal mastermind who wants me dead."

"Portland," the portly conductor bellowed as he waddled through the passenger car. "Portland, Oregon. City of Roses." The uniformed employee paused briefly to study the broken windows before moving on. "Damn kids. They do this every time the train arrives in the city. It's a federal crime to throw rocks at a train."

The young wife, attired in her new dress, returned. She too paused at the site of the broken glass on the carpeted aisle. A rushing wind howled as it ricocheted about the car.

"What happened?" she asked incredulously.

"Darn kids," the passenger echoed in lieu of a more forthright explanation. "Apparently it's against the law to throw rocks at a moving train."

The young mother thanked the stranger and he smiled and shrugged, signaling with a dismissive wave that babysitting amidst all the broken glass had not been a problem. The infant had not only been a witness to an incredible battle but to an astonishing life. Unbeknownst to both mother and son, a legend had sat directly across from them.

The man turned his attention to the view outside the window. His time with the baby had given him another idea and all he needed now was an opportunity and enough time to execute it.

The rhythmic clacking of the tracks was joined by a whistle blast as the train rolled noisily through the urban landscape of the growing city. The sun had just settled over the western hills, and the passenger could still make out the darkening silhouettes of the countless warehouses, refineries and factories that kept the small population thriving. He retrieved his leather jacket, grabbed his satchel and waited between the cars, watching as the train slowed, approaching the brick station and signature clock tower of Union Station.

He had been on the run for six days. Keep moving, was what he once thought. Now he wasn't so sure. His new plan was a long-shot. The enemy was far too close for his liking.

He caught sight of the small diner as he meandered past the city's post office. The busy street was named Broadway and had little in common with the sister street of his beloved New York City. No neon lights or vibrant nightlife here. Street lamps flickered, attempting to ward off the encroaching night. The light inside the small eating establishment was a beacon, welcoming the weary traveler and he headed to it like a moth to a flame.

It reminded him of one of the eating joints his colleagues frequented during the years of the Great Depression. There were no booths, just one long counter with a dozen red leather stools. He entered and the bell above the glass door tinkled, announcing the arrival of another paying customer. He dropped his suitcase at the end of the counter and sat on the stool closest to his belongings.

The seat afforded him a perfect view of the kitchen and he arrived just in time to witness the growing cigarette ash of the fry

7

cook drop onto the unseen grill. Years ago, he'd have admonished the worker with a calm, but severe, lecture on hygiene and proper food preparation. Tonight, he watched the tobacco cinders drop and said nothing.

"What will it be, handsome?"

The waitress appeared out of nowhere. She was a redheaded Irish lass, Maureen O' Hara attractive, and appeared to be every bit as world weary as himself. He considered her frame healthy with striking green eyes that seemed to reach over the counter to welcome him.

"How are the cheeseburgers?" he asked.

"Do I look like the kind of person who frequents a joint like this?"

He liked her immediately and that was something. He hadn't been attracted to a woman in years.

"What the hell's that sound?" she asked, puzzling over a noise that seemed to come from everywhere. "Are you vibrating?"

"I'm sorry," he answered, surprised at his own candor. "Nasty habit."

"Well, stop it," she said with a wry smile. "We don't allow questionable bodily functions in here. It ain't that kind of place."

"Friends call me Rock."

"Devon," the waitress answered as she extended her hand across the counter.

The figure remained in shadow and watched as his prey and unexpected date left the diner. It was late, and the streets of the city were empty. Only the occasional truck, pulling in or out of the post office parking lot, dared to disturb the night. While he waited, a thick fog had rolled off the nearby Willamette River, slowly overtaking an unsuspecting city.

The couple were arm and arm and, if there was any doubt he had the wrong person, there was the unmistakable physical vibration. Harrison Thunder watched with the cool patience of a jungle cat as the couple turned south and proceeded up Broadway.

The end was finally in sight. He had cashed in so many favors to make this little surprise a reality and a small fortune had been paid to secure the result. The cost had been worth it. The villain was now in Downtown Portland, spying on the man he had pursued across an entire continent.

His previous battles with the crime-fighter had not prepared him for this. This middle-aged man posed no active threat and seemed blissfully unaware he was even being followed. Thunder tracked the couple from a safe distance, watching as they strolled past Mary's club, the Benson Hotel and the glimmering lights and neon of several marquee movie palaces. Half a mile later, the man and woman cut through the city's south park blocks, ending up in front of the Ione Plaza Apartment building.

Thunder hung back behind one of the many fir trees and watched. The woman would soon be gone, and he'd finally be alone with his lifelong adversary. After two decades, it was nearly over. He watched in amazement as a man known for his chasteness, pulled the redheaded waitress close and kissed her. This was no peck, no protective goodnight gesture from a golden age hero. This was Bogart and Bacall and the villain suddenly realized the night might not be ending for the couple. He watched as the waitress grabbed the hand of the prudish hero and led him into the lobby of her building.

He sat on a park bench and looked up, mesmerized by the sixth story window. The light flickered on minutes after the two left the lobby. He would now be forced to wait an entire night. As much as he wanted to leave, he couldn't. Somewhere in that upper level apartment, the puritanical hero was committing acts of carnality that would make his master criminal head spin. This proved that he was no better than the rest of us. Thunder felt a temporary pang of remorse and briefly considered not killing him. The feeling vanished quickly.

The sun crept over the western hills and cast first rays of light on the 12-story building. Thunder could now see the countless homes of old Portland money that dotted the western hills. He grinned. Inside these homes, an innocent public were leaving their beds, never realizing the history about to take place in their city.

His prey would awake soon, running through his rigorous daily physical and mental regimen. As long as Thunder knew him, the man had never missed a day. Most likely, he would conduct his calisthenics right here in the public park. It would be the perfect setting for his little surprise.

Several hours passed and the hunter continued to wait. He was growing impatient, something he prided himself in never being. But since last night, he had been proven wrong several times and this agitated his usual icy-cold demeanor. Sometime, after nine in the morning, Thunder drifted off asleep.

"Are you waiting for someone?"

Thunder woke with a start. He gasped, focusing his attention on the familiar voice.

"You," he managed. His wits were still several seconds away from returning.

"Thunder."

"Rock Ravage, known in crimefighting circles as the Ravager. I always thought your unique handle more suited for a character from a dime novel."

"Funny."

Thunder's light banter returned along with a number of unanswered questions. "A woman, Rock?" he said. "Doesn't that soil what little reputation you have left?"

"Never mind her. She has nothing to do with us."

Both men stared off toward the hills. It was now past ten and the city was fully awake. In the park blocks where the two great enemies sat, dogs were being walked and coffee consumed in the warming sunshine. Students from nearby Portland State University scurried from Lincoln to Smith Hall in a mad dash to make it to their next class. To the world at large, these two were nothing more than two middle-aged white men reminiscing on a park bench.

"Besides, you're too late," the prey added.

"To kill you? I think not. Damn near got you at the gas station. Not to mention my little surprise on the train. Five minutes, give or take, makes no difference."

"That's not what I was referring to," Rock answered. "You'll never win."

"My dear Rock. Our relationship was never about winning or losing," Thunder said. "It's way past that." The master villain leaned in before continuing. "Never underestimate the power of hatred. One day, such hatred will unite the entire planet."

Rock Ravage vibrated.

"Really?" Thunder complained. "Look at yourself. You're a joke. You're old, fat and in this condition, couldn't best one of my lowest lackeys."

"Care to try me?"

"I've wasted enough time. This is over."

The Ravager's vibration changed in intensity.

"Must you do that? You know it's unnatural for someone to be able to actually do that."

"Sorry." He wasn't. The subtle vibration was the Ravager's natural alarm, a warning that danger, excitement, or both were close at hand.

"I have to admit, seeing you in the embrace of an honest to goodness woman took me by surprise."

"She has nothing to do with you," he lied.

"It proves you're human. No better, or worse, than the rest of us." Thunder stood and stepped away. He looked off into the hills, nodded and raised his index finger. "That makes killing you so much more difficult. Goodbye, Rock."

The shots echoed off the surrounding buildings, joining the screams of a panicked public as they scrambled for cover.

There was nothing about the assassination in the city's two newspapers. Harrison Thunder had covered up the entire incident. His connections inside a corrupt Portland Police Bureau guaranteed the coldblooded murder of the world's greatest hero never made it to print.

1989

The air was a late-fall, early morning brisk and the stars dotting the night sky burned considerably brighter than the flickering street lamps closer to earth. The hour was late, and the middle-class neighborhood was asleep as the drunken figure cut through the side yard of the mid-sized ranch house. A series of canine boobytraps threatened his every step. In a sober state, he could have easily avoided them all. He slipped and stumbled over the dewy grass, taking an abrupt turn, leading away from a more conventional entrance through the front door. He halted at the east side of the house, concentrating his blurry vision on the cement well that housed the basement window. The idea for this unorthodox entryway was forged from necessity and would save him an unwelcome ambush with a more conventional approach.

A slight tap of the foot was all that was required to free the window from the semi-impenetrable lock of mossy sludge. During the simple execution, his heavy boot missed the frame and the pane of glass shattered. This was not the stealth he was hoping for. The shadow glanced over his shoulder and nearly passed out from the resulting dizziness. The second attempt was successful, and the window kicked free. The lean drunk dropped into the well, sliding through the small opening. He landed on a basement floor that had just been seasoned with broken glass. Above his head, the breached entry banged shut with a muffled thud. One click later, the entrance was locked and the drunk was finally alone.

He collapsed on a musty orange sofa and closed his eyes. The room was spinning, and he swung a leg over the end cushion, landing a boot on the floor to halt his vertigo. The nightly regime of alcohol and marijuana had done little to resolve any of the major issues in his life. He was thirty years old and there were just too damn many. He was unemployed, single and broke, and no amount of intoxicants, imbibed or inhaled, was going to change any of it.

His looks certainly wouldn't save him. In overall appearance, he was quite undistinguished. Hair, uncut in over a year, was styled in an unkempt Jewish fro. Somewhere beneath the shaggy brown locks, sleepy blue eyes possessed a cloudy dullness that only comes from perpetual inebriation. He did possess a crooked mouth that certain women, depending on how much they'd been drinking, sometimes found appealing. His unmuscular frame was thin, he was taller than average, and indistinct in every way.

Nestled in the comfort and security of his childhood home, he'd take stock, turn his life around and somehow get back on track. As consciousness faded, he vowed to come up with the first steps in overcoming his current life of not-so-quiet desperation. All he required was the reflective stillness the early morning hours in this basement would provide.

"Barry, did you break the basement window?"

The distinctly maternal call roused him from his thoughts, piercing through the basement ceiling and accessing the waxy recesses of his inner ear. It was the shrill voice of his sixty-two-year-old mother.

"Barry Steven Levitt, you don't live here anymore," she said. It was the opening salvo in the latest battle for the heart and soul of her only adoptive son.

"I'm in the middle of something," Barry growled from his prone position on the scratchy sofa. "Can we talk about this in the morning?"

"I'm calling the police."

"I'm pretty sure the Neighborhood Watch already beat you to it," he called back. His eyes remained tightly shut as if opening them would only escalate the confrontation. "I just came to get a few things."

He opened his eyes and glanced around the dark room. The only thing he hadn't removed or pawned was an old Hewlett Packard desktop resting on a rickety table. "I came for my computer," he yelled.

"Don't take the table. That's my sewing table."

Barry sat up, the ear-splitting din of his mother having successfully transported him from drunk to hung-over. He cupped his head with both hands and took a deep breath. "What do you want?"

"I've told you time and time again never to use that basement window. And now you've broke it and I'll have to call the glass people. I have a front door!"

"You changed the locks," Barry said. Even though he neglected to check, he knew it to be true. Hence, his need for the more unconventional and undignified mode of entry.

"I changed them for a reason," his mother countered. "It's a very bad world out there. Filled with all sorts of crime and violence perpetrated by fully-grown, adult sons that don't have jobs. You have until noon tomorrow to be out of my basement, Barry." The last statement had the rehearsed finality of words uttered more than once. "Good night."

Barry listened to his mother stomp back to her bedroom. Minutes later, a blissful unconsciousness seized him.

Due to the influx of new members and obligatory weigh-ins, Saturday's late morning meeting of the Hollywood District Weight Watches rarely started on time. The hour-long sessions were held in the musty and dank basement of the neighborhood Rite-Aid Building and despite the cavern-like atmosphere, it had become a favorite gathering place for the city's dietary challenged.

A frantic Ellen Peterson arrived five minutes before the meeting was scheduled to begin, snatched her card, and skipped the optional stop at the scales. The usually poised and dignified senior was fidgety, her nose running uncontrollably. Her flawless pink skin had broken out in a painful rash and every nerve in her body was currently under attack. The sixty-seven-year-old widow had mistakenly attributed the sudden onslaught of symptoms to the thrill of her upcoming announcement and had completely misdiagnosed the cause. Her body was suffering from a host of serious side effects that only accompanied prolonged exposure to a lethal drug or chemical. Without ever realizing it, A.A.R.P. member in good standing, Ellen Peterson, had a sizable, addictive monkey on her back.

Her discovery simply couldn't wait any longer. The quicker she shared her findings, the sooner she'd cure adult obesity once and for all. The first step was to present her results before this august body and to follow it by basking in the appreciative glow of her scientific achievement. There'd be plenty of time after to take the next bus home, drink another glass of her newly discovered miracle elixir and bathe her entire body in a bathtub filled with Calamine lotion.

"Where have you been, Ellen? I haven't seen you in weeks." The insincere query belonged to Jen Gassaway, Captain of the local Neighborhood Watch. Jen clearly didn't need Weight Watchers but somehow found a way to attend every meeting. Ellen was sure that Jen's presence and fit 120 pounds were only here to make all the other women in the neighborhood feel inferior. But with Ellen's upcoming announcement, all of that was about to change.

Several ladies followed Ellen and Jen to the metal folding chairs. Others remained standing, visiting, or browsing the shelves for the latest in over-priced, fat reducing delicacies. It was several minutes past eleven and it appeared that once again the meeting was going to start late.

Ellen was grinding her teeth as she considered the best way to reveal her findings. "Jen," she began. "In my lifetime, I've seen my share of scientific breakthroughs. I've lived long enough to watch a man walk on the moon and witnessed groundbreaking inventions revealed to an unsuspecting world by such giants as Ron Popeel and heavyweight champion of the world George Foreman."

"That's nice," Jen answered, clearly not caring one way or another.

"Never in my wildest dreams did I imagine that I'd be on the verge of my own scientific discovery."

Jen's eyes glazed over as she worked through a catalogue of scenarios needed to excuse herself. Ellen has clearly gone off the deep end, the neighbor thought. She has never recovered from the death of her husband and a heartbreaking desertion by her only daughter.

"Jen, this news is bigger than all of those put together," Ellen lectured. "Just think of it. No more tallying points in some journal. My weight loss supplement is a miracle, birthed into existence by precise scientific processes and exacting clinical detail."

"Good for you," Jen said with an insincerity that accompanied her biggest smile. The neighbor placed a hand on

Ellen's arm, squeezed gently and was instantly alarmed how frail her neighbor was.

Ellen sensed she was being judged and shook her arm free. A sudden hot flash raced through her body and she now suspected that Jen was attempting to steal her secret. Let her try, she seethed. She'd would only be guessing.

The secret ingredient was a crystalized substance Ellen had found in a plastic sugar container stored in back of the kitchen cabinet. She didn't recall purchasing any florescent green sugar products but she sure as hell wasn't going to let Jen know that. The paranoia subsided as quickly as it appeared, and Ellen took a deep breath.

"Mixing equal parts quinine water, a dash of Chamomile and a heaping teaspoon of my super, secret ingredient, I stumbled upon the greatest diet discovery since Atkins." Ellen was perspiring. It was as if each word was taxing dwindling physical resources. But it was too late to stop. It was time to present her findings to the world and finally put this nosy so and so in her place.

"I've documented my experiments with over thirteen hundred entries on the message boards of the World Wide Web. I discovered it quite by accident," she continued hurriedly. "I'd been receiving these free yellow and blue coasters in the mail. Somehow one of them found its way inside my daughter's computer."

"How is Tilly? It's been years since Ron, or I have even seen her."

Ellen flinched. "I need to share my findings with the world," she blurted. The mention of her only daughter had struck a nerve.

"That's great," Jen answered, patting her certifiable neighbor on the thigh.

"I came here because these are the people I really care about."

"Oh look," Jen stammered. "It's Dorothy!" Jen waved her hands, untangling herself from the uncomfortable conversation.

It was like ripping a Band-Aid off an open wound and once accomplished, she moved on quickly.

Ellen was once again alone, sitting abnormally erect in the uncomfortable metal chair. Good riddance to bad rubbish, she thought. She tasted the salty blood inside her mouth and ignored it. Obviously, her miracle still had a few bugs to work out. Ellen's dilated eyes darted about the basement meeting place, focusing on the two plus-sized matrons browsing the diet cookie shelves.

"It wouldn't hurt either of you to try my elixir," Ellen mumbled.

The two browsers were the first to spot the visitor. It was a brief glance, accomplished through four equally diminished eyes.

"He's a big fellow," the first lady commented, her attention riveted on the trademarked Weight Watcher points listed on a box of chocolate-flavored mints.

Her companion was busy inspecting her own carton, silently calculating if the artificial sweetener was safe for anyone suffering from stage-two diabetes. "Yes," the companion agreed. "And that big metal hat doesn't help."

The hat in question was steel-plated and weighed a quarter of a ton. The iron-clad headpiece was a fully functioning tank turret with an extending 35 MM barrel and was not something that could be purchased at a local haberdashery. The heavy turret completely covered the giant's head and rested on two massive shoulders.

"He should take that thing off before weighing in," the first browser commented.

Hidden gyros whirred, buzzed and clicked as the turret swiveled, the lethal barrel aiming directly at Ellen Peterson. Was she seeing things? Ellen wasn't entirely sure. She was shaking uncontrollably. She blinked, hoping it might clear the image of the steel-plated assassin from her mind.

"With the new point system," the oblivious leader droned, "you can eat all the fruit and vegetables you want. And that goes for everything except our starchy friend, the potato."

The audience of ladies remained focused on the skinny and exuberant leader, fully engaged in the spirited lecture on the differences between fruits, vegetables and starchy yams.

Not a single person thought anything amiss until the clank of the shell announced its arrival in the weapon's chamber. Collectively, the ladies of the Hollywood Weight Watchers turned and witnessed firsthand the origin of their destruction. The ensuing explosion rocked the foundation of the Rite-Aid building. The projectile missed Ellen Peterson, ripping through the easel and detonating in the wall. The foundation was reduced to a smoldering pile of rubble and set off the overhead sprinkler system. Survivors cowered, wailed, and screamed as they were showered with water and lethal chunks of concrete.

The smoke cleared and Tanktop surveyed the dead and dying with the aid of an elaborate electronic targeting system. He focused on the prone body of Ellen Peterson, identifying her by cross-referencing a profile found on American Online. The frail victim was covered in white plaster and a shopping cart from the Rite-Aid Pharmacy one floor above. The villain's internal imaging system noted the fading yellow of victim's dissipating body heat. She didn't have long to live. A pungent smoke trailed out his barrel as the steel-plated villain reached down and snatched Ellen's purse.

The wail of sirens reverberated through the tiny speakers inside his headpiece. He only had two shells remaining and it might not be enough to explode his way out of a tight spot. He was not overly concerned. He had what he came for and a meticulous escape plan was in place.

Tanktop lumbered through the water, dust and debris to the crumbling emergency stairs in the far corner of the basement. The stairs remained intact, and he ascended quickly, leaving the carnage, moans and pitiful cries for help behind.

Arriving on the parking lot roof, he watched the first responders arrive. Uniformed police, firemen and paramedics rushed into a dark, foreboding smoke. A flashing red chronograph inside his turret ticked down the time remaining until the whir of rotary blades confirmed his historic getaway was at hand. Within seconds, the roar of the military chopper overpowered the noisy panic on the street.

The Boeing CH 47 Chinook Helicopter descended out of a bright blue sky directly above the smoking roof. The belly of the military flying machine slid open, exposing a winch, cable and electro-magnet. It was 11:15 in the A.M. and the transportation had arrived exactly as scheduled.

The magnet lowered and activated several feet above the steel turret. Tanktop's 16 sized loafers levitated off the roof as steel headpiece met powerful magnet with a resounding clang. Without a moment to spare, the chopper made a wide circle, the prone body of the assassin swinging out over the crowd in a final farewell.

Horrified onlookers gawked upward and pointed. Even the emergency personal paused from their life-saving tasks to peer into the blue sky. The chopper and the dangling metal man were last seen heading west over the river and toward the nearby hills.

"Whoa!"

"What's that smell?"

"It's his boots! Get them off and we'll burn them in the fireplace."

They had been called on to dispose of a body. The carcass remained warm, was breathing and would not go willingly. Two people assigned to the task studied their unconscious friend, puzzling over the next step. Lately, watching out for him had become a full-time job.

Barry recognized the voices but refused to respond. He was in the blissful purgatory between drunkenness and consciousness. He had dozed fitfully into the latter half of the day and was not ready to face reality, family or friends.

"Go away," Barry mumbled, flopping on the sofa so that he now faced the back cushion. "I'm otherwise indisposed."

"Maybe he doesn't want to leave."

"We'll let the geniuses decide," the leaner of the two answered.

They called him Face, a nickname lifted off the character from his favorite television show, "The A-Team." The handsome blonde actor walked away from the sofa, over to the basement fireplace and sat on the brick stoop. He unfolded a copy of Daily Variety and began to read, leaving the task of removal to the reinforcements.

The subscription to the daily trade had not helped the actor's career. The primary cause of his failure was a reoccurring case of psoriasis that dampened his lifelong dream of becoming a hand model. To combat the affliction, the actor habitually lathered his hands in coal oil and kept them covered 24/7 in white, cotton gloves. Despite the lack of a real career, Face was a loyal reader of the periodical and renewed his subscription annually.

The other person remained, puzzling over an effective way of maneuvering the uncooperative body off the sofa. In the looks department, he was the polar opposite of the actor, making any friendship all the more unlikely. They called him Beast, and he did share more than one physical characteristic with a Neanderthal. This unsettling ape-like appearance was the result of an addiction to the cotton found inside Benadryl inhalers. The habit had long since passed but the physical effects lingered. Beast's long straggly hair was parted down the middle and he wore a stained white tee shirt that barely covered his barrel chest.

The brutish man bent and lifted the sofa effortlessly, his belt-less jeans revealing a full inch of butt crack. "We'll carry him out," Beast offered. "Grab an end."

"I'm good," Face commented, his face masked behind the distinctive green and black banner on the front page. "Don't forget to lift with your knees."

Beast grunted his response, released the end of the sofa and it banged onto the floor.

"And I say we tell him about the letter." A new voice announced from just outside the room.

The unseen response came in a droll monotone that was neither hushed nor urgent. "And I prefer we didn't. We need to find a way to remove him from this basement."

"And how do we do that?" Doc asked. The portly chemist entered the room wearing his customary white laboratory coat.

The rotund man was balding prematurely and his Benjamin Franklin hairstyle gave an impression of the chemist being much older than his thirty-three years. The round wire-rimmed glasses didn't help. Doc carried two mugs of coffee, a smoldering Camel cigarette dangling from his upper lip. A steady trail of tobacco smoke seemed to follow the man wherever he went.

22

His closest colleague waited for the smoke to dissipate before making his appearance. They called him Brain and his lean frame was attired entirely in black. Even the frames of his Buddy Holly glasses matched his preferred color choice. The perpetual thinker was pale, his dark hair combed over an oversized "This Island Earth" forehead. Beneath the distinctive haircut was a hyperactive cerebellum that housed billions of inconsequential facts.

Brain clutched his ornate walking stick. Like his friend's lab coat, the cane was an affectation that the eccentric was never without. In his free hand, he carried two folding lawn chairs. "I may have an idea," Brain offered.

"He won't budge," Beast reported. "I tried everything."

Doc rested both cups on the fireplace mantel and joined Beast at the opposite end of the sofa. The two lifted the back end of the couch and dumped the uncooperative body onto the floor.

Barry hit the ground hard. "What the hell?" he wailed.

"Your mother wants you out," Doc announced.

The disgruntled Barry picked himself off the floor and sat on the sofa. Brain retrieved the cup off the mantel and brought it to a person he considered one of his closest friends.

"Alice left me."

Beast unfolded both chairs and sat. He glared at Barry with deep-set brown eyes. "You could've crashed at my place."

Beast rented a small house that was infested with fleas and adopted cats.

"I'm fine," Barry muttered.

Face peered over the top of his paper. "Nothing wrong with his decision-making skills."

Brain removed a disk out of his shirt pocket and walked over to the old desktop computer. He switched on the machine and it took a small rodent's lifetime for the outdated technology to boot up. Brain slipped the disk into the drive and activated the Microsoft Power Point application with a sticky click of the mouse. The computer's fan whirred and clattered in noisy protest.

"Okay, you're all here," Barry said, taking a sip of coffee. "Who wants to start the intervention?"

Face folded the Variety and set it on the stoop. "No intervention for me today" he announced. "I have plans."

"Handling this device requires surgical gloves," Brain complained as he warily tapped the mouse.

"The stories that thing could tell," Barry answered. He fired up a roach he found digging through the coin pocket of his jeans. "Is this going to take long? I have a cyberdate with a nuclear physicist who just so happens to be Playboy playmate."

"You want me to get the forensic goggles out of the trunk?" Doc asked.

Brain shook his head. "And reveal his biological Jackson Pollock? I'd rather not."

"Is belittling my sexual appetites part of the intervention?" Barry asked. "If it is, you'll definitely want to check my browsing history. It's a doozy."

No one bothered to answer. As a group they were used to their friend's half-assed way of ignoring conflict or feedback. It was just who he was and despite it, they continued to appreciate his uniqueness.

"What are we doing here?" Face said, his handsome face set in a rehearsed glower. "I have an audition at three."

The audition was print media for a local department store. It was an easy hand modeling gig, showcasing inexpensive Timex Watches. The job paid well and required little work. The dried, flaky skin beneath the white cotton gloves all but guaranteed he'd never get the job.

"He has nowhere to go," Beast blurted. "Maybe he could stay with you, Face."

"Screw the audition," Face announced after considering the proposal. "What can I do to help?"

The opening slide flickered, the image passing through several months of accumulated dust and grime. The five studied the screen with various degrees of interest.

"Eleven hundred hours," Brain began, hovering the curser over the rubble that once was the Rite-Aid building. "The explosion originated in the basement, during the Saturday meeting of the Hollywood Weight Watchers."

Beast raised his hand. It wasn't required but he couldn't get past rules firmly established for him in the third grade.

"Yes, Beast?" Brain said.

"Black OPS blew that Rite-Aid back to the stone-age."

"You'd know all about the stone-age," Face commented. "Cave dwellers are your people."

Lacking a suitable comeback, Beast growled.

Brain grimaced and clicked into the next slide. The image was a single, grainy frame lifted from a local newscast. The military chopper was high in the sky, the steel-plated perpetrator dangling below the electro-magnet.

"Expensive way to move," Barry commented. "Why didn't he just call a friend with a pickup?"

"Zoom in," Doc requested.

Brain clicked the mouse several more times and the pixels magnified into a grainy fogginess. It was their first look at the turret-sporting villain and all, but one, remained silent. Face, never at a loss for words, gawked open-mouthed at the small screen.

"Dig that crazy hat," Barry said after the notable silence.

"Illuminati!" Beast declared.

"It's like trying to communicate with an ape," Face moaned, retreating back behind his periodical.

"Oh yeah?" Beast blustered. "You wouldn't say that if I was Koko."

"Koko the gorilla communicated by sign language and possesses a vocabulary of over one thousand words." Face fired back. "For the record, that's 900 more than you."

Doc ignored the chatter took a sip from his coffee. "I'd like the chance to examine that alloy," he said.

"Hmm," Brain noted. "Would have to be resilient enough to handle the heat and recoil of at a high-caliber shell."

Doc removed a slide-rule from his lab coat pocket and proceeded with calculations the others could only guess. He handled the device like a pro, the smoldering cigarette dangling from his lip only adding to the number-crunching spectacle.

Beast watched Doc with wide-eyed enthusiasm, nodding and grunting his approval at the mathematical magic happening before his eyes.

Face looked to Barry for a reprieve. The two were clearly taken aback at the strange course of the conversation. "I give up," Face said.

"So," Barry said, his mouth contorted into a vacuum hose and sucking up the last remnants of intoxicating smoke. "What does this have to do with me?"

Doc exchanged eye contact with his colleague. The man in black nodded.

"I'm sorry," Brain said. "I was unaware you had a previous engagement."

All eyes were on Barry and he was getting angry. The lazy grin was gone, replaced by a piercing stare that promised his patience with his friends had come to an end.

"There's only one non-military installation where one can find a Boeing Chinook chopper," Doc announced. "Brain and I want to check it out."

"And yet my simple query goes unanswered," Barry tried. "Why do I care?"

"We want to examine that helicopter," Brain said. "We thought you'd like to come along."

"It's not like you have plans," Doc snapped.

"That attitude isn't even going to get me into a pair of clean pants."

"Your mother has requested that you move out," Brain concluded.

"I'm in," Beast bellowed.

"What if Alice calls?" Barry uttered the statement without the slightest bit of confidence.

Face lowered his paper and rolled his eyes. It was the only fitting response.

"What? It could happen."

It wasn't happening, and they all knew it. Doc and Brain were willing to try anything to get their friend to leave. And they had one hell of an ulterior motive. The nighttime diversion was the perfect opportunity to confront Barry with the letter's startling revelation. Along with the mystery of the chopper and the man with the metal hat, it was all too much to pass up.

"Where would we be going?" Barry asked. "Because if it costs money, I'm tapped."

Face cleared his throat from behind the safety of his paper. They all were.

"We'll need gas money," Doc puzzled.

"We don't need money," Beast announced. "All we need is a length of garden hose and a dimly lit parking lot,"

Barry studied the faces of his closest friends through the intoxicating haze of his high. "I'm sorry, guys," he said. "The answer is no. And what gives any of you the right to tell me what to do? You think I have to stay here? There are plenty of places I can live." He stood and gestured wildly. "I can live in the Central Library during the day and hang out in the Blue Mouse Theatre at night."

"They switch to porn at nine," Face commented. His friends glanced at him with an annoyed curiosity. "I've heard that anyway. I have no proof because I've never set foot inside that place."

"Case closed," Barry said. "I don't want to hear another word."

Despite their best efforts, Doc and Brain had failed. Only Beast was on board and the big man didn't fully understand what was going on.

The shrill voice called from the top of the basement stairs, cutting through the friend's accumulated tension like a rusty knife. "Barry, I've decided to let you stay," his mother announced.

Barry grinned and sat. He waved off his friends with a dismissive hand. "I guess you'll have to go on this little adventure without me."

"I need you to drive me to Dr. Miller," his mother continued. "My colon's irritated. I also need to stop at Fred Meyer and pick up powdered doughnuts and a gallon of chocolate milk. After that you can mow the lawn, rake the leaves and we'll have a long talk about your future."

Barry glanced at the broken window above the worn sofa. "Maybe we should leave through the window," he offered quietly.

The nightclub was dark, and the stench remaining from last night's tobacco and cheap beer drifted over the venue like a toxic cloud. Tanktop found the singer on stage, the toothless frontman slumping atop a wooden stool. The villain's sophisticated imaging system immediately noted his handler's tremulous hands clutching the microphone stand. He seemed poised to either launch into a soulful ballad or plummet off the stool like an inebriated lemming.

"So, did you find it, bucko?" The accent was thick as a Dublin fog with each syllable slurred; affected as much by the speaker's country of origin as the open bottle of Jameson's nestled between his legs.

Curled up at the singer's feet was the latest casualty of the concert tour. She looked to be fifteen years old, (she was twenty-six) possessed long tangles of strawberry blond hair and was dressed in a white blouse and plaid Catholic girl's skirt. If the henchman had bothered to examine her, he'd have easily recognized the countless needle marks located on the back of her knees. She had either overdosed or nodded off. Either way, the metallic henchman didn't much care. He had important matters to attend to.

The Posers first U.S. tour in ten years had provided the perfect cover. No one would ever suspect the lead singer of the Ska band of anything other than constant drunkenness. The audience's perception of the falling rock star was a man who could hardly make it through a performance, let alone be mid-level management in a super-secret criminal enterprise.

With each expulsion from the band, the group's popularity dropped. Every time the singer returned, concerts sold out across Europe and the states. Legally ensconced in the U.S., IRA member, and recording artist, Shamus O' Hooligan, was free to carry out his employer's orders.

Tanktop's cover didn't fit as neatly into the rock-and-roll masquerade as his handler. For starters, there was his startling physical appearance. While brute strength provided him the ideal cover of roadie, there remained questions over his choice of hats. Most in the roadie profession preferred the backward baseball cap over a steel turret and cannon barrel. It was soon decided that the giant needed to remain out of sight and hidden from the public. Tanktop, a nickname given to him by members of the band, remained offstage during all performances. On the rare occasion he was spotted, the turret was explained as the medical appliance for a man who lost most of his face during a nasty brawl at CBGB's.

The henchman managed to translate the singer's request and the contents of Ellen Peterson's charred purse was dumped into his lap. Shamus fumbled with the lid of the plastic container before Tanktop snatched the receptacle, opened it effortlessly before returning it. Bloodshot eyes widened as the singer peered into the jar. Tanktop watched the Irish crooner insert an unwashed finger and wipe the inside. When Shamus removed the digit, it was covered in a fine green crystallized dust. He then inserted the digit into his right nostril and snorted. Dark, sleepy eyes blazed as the reward toggle, located in the brain's limbic system, rewarded him with a wave of crazed euphoria.

"Hard to believe this ain't what the shit's for," Shamus growled. "We'd be bloody billionaires."

Three months had passed since a significant part of the shipment had been stolen. Their employer had ordered it recovered no matter the cost. Shamus's services were requested and the metal man, known as Tanktop, was enlisted to ensure the investigation was conducted thoroughly.

"We're due in San Francisco Thursday night," Shamus grumbled. He hoisted the bottle of Jameson's and took a long slurp through three multiple-colored straws. "If we haven't retrieved them barrels by then we'll both be dead."

Tanktop nodded. He'd take care of it.

"Kill anyone who gets in your way."

The meeting had concluded. Tanktop watched the singer's bloodshot eyes roll into his forehead. Dark eyelids fluttered and slammed shut. Pale hands loosened their grip on the microphone stand and Shamus O'Hooligan teetered off the barstool and toppled onto the floor. The bottle of whiskey shattered, the unconscious girl sleeping through it all.

"Shite," Shamus managed before a total blackout seized him.

Face's hand appeared from the back seat and squeezed Beast's shoulder. "Don't force me to get the tranquilizer gun," he warned.

Barry sat in the front passenger seat, his brain clouded with the numbing haze of marijuana. He had convinced himself that the hour and a half joyride was a diversion, and that he was nothing more than a passive observer on one of his friends featherbrained ride-a-longs.

"What makes you think it's even here?" Face asked.

"It's the only helo of its kind in the entire state," Brain explained. The thinker was seldom wrong and, if he was, he never admitted it. "And if it's not been returned, we may find a clue as to who stole it."

Doc unfolded the colorful brochure and studied a map that included the location of the main attractions. He confirmed his friend's theory with a deep exhale of cigarette smoke. "The map says it should be in the southwest corner of the structure," he reported.

"Let's get this over with," Face said from the backseat. "The sooner we get started, the better I'll feel about all the bad decisions I'm making in my life." The actor slid off his jacket and exposed a security uniform and a tin badge of the minimum wage variety. He reached between his legs, grabbed a matching baseball cap and placed it over his well-coiffed blonde head. "How do I look?"

Beast studied his friend with an open-mouthed intensity. "Like a douche in a baseball cap," he answered. The big man sat in the driver's seat, removing his own jacket and revealing the exact same uniform. "While I, on the other hand, am perfect."

The plan was to convert the acres of Western Oregon cornfields into an aeronautical Disneyland, but the financial result was hardly what any of the investors expected. Once completed, there were planned additions of a movie theatre and water park. But, the anticipated throngs of tourists never arrived and the venue, without the benefit of a headline attraction, was a monetary disaster. If someone didn't think of something, the Pacific Northwest's only museum of its kind would be on the verge of bankruptcy. The magnificent lime-colored glass structure was badly in need of a miracle.

The Aeronautical Museum showcased a collection of outdated military aircraft, including one stolen, Boeing CH 47 Chinook helicopter. The aerial supporting acts needed a showstopper and one celebrated piece of engineering had just become available. The investors wasted no time in paying the exorbitant fees to secure ownership of the wooden miracle from Long Beach. It was a Chamber of Commerce coup and the only question remaining was how to get the headliner to McMinnville. One thing was certain; Howard Hughes' folly, The Spruce Goose, was not going to fly there.

The museum had been closed for six hours and was scheduled to reopen the following morning. The bright overhead lights remained on, passing travelers on Hwy 18 treated to a fleeting glimpse of the exhibits inside.

Beast fiddled with the driver's handle, the big man primed and ready to throw open a door and begin his signature brand of chaos. "We ready or what?" he growled.

They arrived in Beast's '66 Ford Galaxy 500, and it idled roughly, belching smoke and pollutants into the otherwise quiet night. The car was parked on a gravel shoulder across the highway. All peered out the windows at the vast, empty parking lot and the green structure beyond. The doors finally opened, the fraudulent security personnel piling out of the car and into the night. Only Barry remained inside.

Doc addressed the remaining passenger. "You coming?" he asked.

"Knock yourselves out," Barry answered. "Run along and have a good time."

"I'll let you hold the flashlight?" Beast offered.

"I'm good."

Beast refused to take no for an answer. He pushed Doc aside and leaned inside the car. "You can't sit in the backseat of life forever," he scolded. "You've got to grab each day by the balls."

"You go grab all the balls you want," Barry said. "I'll be right here in the car when you're done."

"You make it all sound so appealing," Face commented.

"Besides, since when does getting shot qualify as grabbing each day by the balls?" Barry asked, a resentful edge returning to his voice.

"Whoa," Face interjected. "Hold up a sec. Who said anything about getting shot? I thought we came all this way to peer through windows."

"Nobody's getting shot," Doc said. "Unless we decide to use you as a human shield."

"Something's going to happen tonight," Beast promised. "Something big!"

"Do you mind?" Barry complained. "You're letting the cold air in."

Face pondered the possibility of death by cop and was second-guessing his decision to tag along. Barry could be right, the actor reasoned. "Can we at least talk about this?"

Doc and Brain removed their jackets and now all four wore the signature security outfits of short-sleeved blue shirts, jeans and cheap, nylon baseball caps.

"I'm not taking another step until I know we have a plan." Face offered. "Gather up."

No one bothered. They left, leaving the nervous actor standing alone by the car. "I can't get shot," Face complained. "I don't have medical coverage."

Doc heeled the butt of his cigarette in the gravel as the three started across the highway.

"Beast, I want you to promise me you're not going to do anything stupid," Face pleaded, hurrying to catch up.

"What's that supposed to mean?"

Brain sighed. "He means no throwing anyone through a plate glass window."

Beast considered the statement, gazing over at the tempting walls of green glass. "Oh, yeah," Beast chuckled. "I'm not making any promises."

The four approached the structure with a confidence exhibited only in those with severe learning disabilities. Beast lumbered ahead of the rest and reached the entrance doors first.

"Check it out," Beast bellowed. "It's open!"

Beast opened the door without incident and gestured for all to enter. A quick-thinking Brain caught the door and closed it gently behind them.

"Keep an eye peeled for cameras," Brain warned.

"Cameras?" Face muttered. "Who said anything about cameras?" The actor pulled the bill of the cap over his eyes.

Doc had noticed the folded cardboard falling to the floor. It was the first official clue. He reached down and retrieved it.

Brain leaned in over his colleague's shoulder. "Obviously amateurs," he said.

"Yeah. Not like us," Doc whispered.

"Set-up?" Brain asked.

"A trap," Beast added. It was said much too loud for a clandestine visit.

"We're so screwed," Face muttered, attempting to steady an already failing resolve.

The glowing cherry abandoned the joint and scorched a scarring path through the crotch of Barry's jeans. As it burned through his well-worn apparel, it picked up in both speed and intensity. By the time the fireball reached bare skin, it possessed the heat of a small sun.

"Son of a bitch," Barry shrieked. He launched his entire body upward, his head colliding hard with the roof panel. "Shit!"

Barry threw open the car door and heaved his body into the night. It took a spirited and impromptu jig to finally separate himself from the offending ember. He took a deep breath and glared across the highway. The perpetrators of his misery were somewhere inside the green building. He held the trespassers accountable for everything currently wrong in his life. His failed relationship, his lack of financial resources, a possible first-degree burn and the lack of any decent travel snacks were all added to his hastily growing list of grievances.

A sudden urge to urinate overtook the need for revenge and Barry stepped to the other side of the car. His back was to the acres of corn stalks that bordered the highway and, as he unzipped, he noticed three sets of bright headlights approaching rapidly from the west. An unexpected paranoia seized him. Barry ducked, taking cover behind the old sedan. He watched as the vehicles slowed, switched off their high beams and glided into the western entrance of the museum.

Car doors flew open and a small army of men climbed out into the night, the imposing shadows gathering at the back of their respective vehicles. Trunks popped free and the men reached in, pulling out what Barry was sure were large automatic weapons. The sinister shadows conferred briefly, and Barry's attention once again focused on the museum. He saw no sign of his friends but did catch a glimpse of a fleeting shadow darting from a gray World War II Spitfire to a Sopwith Camel. He couldn't be sure, but the figure appeared to be a woman.

A panicked Barry desperately patted his pockets until he remembered that Beast was the keeper of the keys. This left him with only one choice, and this pissed the unwilling passenger off even more. Now he was forced to warn his friends and getting to the front entrance without being spotted wouldn't be easy. His mouth was bone-dry, and his heart thumped with an intensity he felt in his teeth. He also happened to be hyperventilating, feeling he might pass out at any second.

Using a crowbar pulled from the trunk of her yellow Triumph TR6, Tilly Peterson made short work of the museum door. She triggered no alarm and slipped a piece of cardboard between the lock and frame to guarantee a hasty retreat. Adrenaline pumped through her attractive, athletic frame. It fueled her rage but did little to heighten the most basic decision-making skills.

She slipped inside the museum, her first priority to seek cover and get her bearings. Across the hanger, the Spruce Goose. The wooden behemoth dwarfed all other exhibits. Tilly took a deep breath and commenced with a full sprint. Halfway across the room, she dropped into a baseball slide, slowing to a convenient stop behind the cover of an information kiosk. She popped up and glanced about for any sign of the getaway chopper that had played such a significant role in her mother's death.

"Okay, lady," the unseen voice commanded. "Get out of there. Nice and easy."

Tilly saw the barrel of the MAC 10 and the grimacing face of the thug who wielded it. He was a greasy, pocked-faced man, his nose caved in from a habitual dependence of cocaine.

"Drop the bag and kick it over here," nose-less ordered.

With no other choice, Tilly complied.

The emergency exit was locked and there was no visible way of getting in. Barry glanced over his shoulder for any sign of the shadowy assassins. He saw no-one and felt a sudden rush of relief. Maybe, he just imagined it; the effects of too much cannabis combined with an overactive sense of paranoia. Even if there was no immediate danger, he thought it a good idea to get his friends out before the authorities arrived. The four were amateurs. If they were caught, there'd be consequences.

He spotted Doc and Brain hiding behind metal stairs leading to the upper level of the museum. Without thinking, Barry rattled the glass door.

Three armed thugs leapt out from behind a Mercury Space Capsule and fired a short burst of machine gun fire. Barry jumped, diving out of the way before the flurry of lead exploded the glass.

Shattered glass hit concrete as another barrage of bullets blasted through another wall.

"Shit," Beast said, the oversized brute peering over the prop cargo crate where he and the actor had taken cover.

A significant portion of the south wall was now gone, and a squall of frigid fall wind whipped through the museum.

A fretful Face rose, looking anxiously over Beast's shoulder. "I need a new pair of underwear," he said fretfully.

"This was unexpected," Brain offered. Both he and Doc monitored events from their defensive position under the stairs.

Doc shrugged. Things were getting worse. He reached into his pocket and pulled out his pack of cigarettes.

"Now?" Brain asked. "Those things may just be the death of you."

Doc answered with a flustered grimace. "Discrimination," he muttered. As the last remaining cigarette smoker of the group, he held onto the habit as much from stubbornness as addiction. Society, in his mind, was writing off the smoker and he'd soon be as extinct as the Tecopa Pupfish and the Round Island

Burrowing Boa. Heels dug in, Doc flipped open and ignited his engraved Zippo. "Cheers," he muttered as he lit what he thought was the last cigarette of his life.

"Hey," a breathless Barry said, sneaking up behind his unsuspecting friends. "I hate to be a buttinski, but I'd say you got a little problem." It was virtually impossible for Barry to sneak up on anyone but somehow, he'd managed it. "I think these men out here want to kill you," he continued. "If you need me, I'll be back in the car."

Beast spotted Barry from behind his cover and waved. "By the balls," Beast managed before Face slapped him atop the head.

Brain raised a hand to shush his agitated friend. "How many?" he mouthed.

Beast mumbled as Face peeked over the crate. The two stunned men watched dumbfounded as a comely brunette vaulted into view and dashed toward the Spruce Goose.

"Aren't you going to introduce us?" Barry said to his equally agog friends.

There would be no introductions for Doc and Brain were seeing the female for the first time.

The enemy wasted no time, jumping up from various hiding places. They fired at the female, the target managing to stay one step ahead of the whistling lead.

"Serpentine," Beast yelled before a shower of bullets headed his direction.

Tilly Peterson thought she was alone. Luckily for her, the unexpected arrivals had distracted her attackers, and she took full advantage. She reached the metal stairs and scrambled upward, disappearing inside the hull of the Spruce Goose.

There was a brief interruption in gunfire and Barry sprang up from his hiding place and sprinted after her. It was too late for his friends to stop him.

"Typical," Brain commented as he watched his friend ascend the steps.

"Now I suppose we have to go get him," Doc said.

"It never ceases to amaze me how far he will go to meet a woman," Brain countered, both men charging the attraction.

"Wait for me," Beast screamed as he popped up from behind his crate and broke into a simian lope toward the plane.

"There's no back door!" Face yelled, cowering behind the crate. "You'll be trapped!" The handsome blonde actor was weighing the options of dying alone or with his unprepared friends. Both choices seemed equally unappealing. "Wait up," he called out finally, rolling out from under the cover and hopping to his feet.

"Okay, we're here," Face wheezed. "What's the plan?"

No one answered. His five friends were too busy staring at the female. Face found the ensuing silence as uncomfortable as the deadly gunfire he had just witnessed outside the wooden hull.

"Back off," Barry warned. "I saw her first."

"Who the hell are you?" Tilly asked with a cold abruptness that only added to the tension.

"We could ask you the same question," Brain countered.

"Forgive them," Face said. "Unlike myself, my friends lack the most rudimentary of social skills."

"We have no idea what we're doing here," Barry admitted, leaning in slightly to the guest. "You?"

"I was fine until you showed up," Tilly said. "Now we're trapped here."

"Listen to the nice lady," Face said. "She knows how much we're screwed."

Brain pointed to the thick plate of Plexiglass that separated the hull from the cockpit. "Beast," he ordered. "Make a door."

"Knock, knock," Beast exclaimed as he launched his 250-pound frame into the partition. The first impact had little effect, the brutish man ricocheting off the plastic and landing on his ass.

Face, Brain and Doc went to work on the metal stairs that led up into the hull. Lying flat on their backs, they kicked until the metal steps separated from the exhibit.

"What are you doing?" Tilly asked.

"Stalling the inevitable," Brain answered, kicking a final time with the red-faced Doc.

Barry ignored the flurry of action and stole another uncomfortable glance at the brunette. He couldn't help himself. Despite an overwhelming fear for his life, his need for sexual validation from females always came first.

"Ahhh," Beast screamed, the full force of his body colliding with the barricade. The last impact proved to be enough, ripping the rivets from the hull and the human battering ram tumbled into the cockpit.

"Think of Beast as our personal Swiss Army Knife," Barry explained. "Name's Barry."

"Here they come," Doc warned, rolling backwards and hopping to his feet with the agility of a man half his weight. The three were up and scrambled into the cockpit.

Beast had taken the copilots seat. Barry was inside second and plopped himself down beside the big man. The others joined them forward. Barry looked over the series of metal toggles, gauges, throttle, and steering yoke. His feet located the rudders and pushed.

"Okay, geniuses," Tilly blurted. "Now what?"

Brain and Doc said nothing. Beast was too occupied to answer, making slobbering motor sounds as he cranked the yoke.

"Yeah," Barry said. "Now what?"

The attention was suddenly and quite unexpectedly on Barry. What little bravado he had remaining, vanished. He felt the weight of their stares. He heard the muffled exclamations of the assassins just outside the plane. Each of his friend's faces betrayed a total lack of any viable escape plan. He knew them all far too long. They were doomed and there was nothing any of them could do about it.

"Well, we certainly can't fly it out," Barry muttered finally.

"Duck and cover," Doc shouted as two bullets pierced the wooden hull and whistled over his head.

Face hit the floor first in a coward's version of downward facing dog. His standing friends immediately took advantage, taking cover behind the actor's upraised torso.

"You better not be using my body as a human shield," Face warned. The actor was frozen, his toothless threat aimed at the floor.

Doc and Brain rose and scrambled over to the instrument panel, puzzling over the intricate layout. In a purely desperate move, the two men began flipping switches and toggles.

Face straightened and watched dumbfound. "You've lost your minds," he announced. "It's been fifty years since this thing has had a tank of gas, let alone a regularly scheduled maintenance."

"Always with the negativity," Beast chastised.

"We're screwed," Barry mumbled. He turned to the female. "Any questions?"

"Clap your hands if you believe the Spruce Goose can fly," Beast declared. Several switches, toggles and levers remained in the off position and the big man flipped them with an intensity unrivaled in aeronautic history.

"This is a perfect example of what happens when you submit to peer pressure." Barry said.

Face shrugged. "Just say no."

"Are you all insane?" Tilly shrieked. "Or is it just Torg the caveman and his blonde yoga instructor?"

"That's harsh," Face answered. "One actually practices yoga. I'm an actor and hand model."

They'd be dead soon and there was nothing anyone could do about it. Barry was never going to see his mother again. He wasn't entirely sure why, but he continued to grin at the female, bringing his hands together in a single, methodical clap.

Tilly was enraged and could only express her frustration in a series of grunts and sighs. Doc and Brain joined the clapping. Face was initially reluctant but joined in on the applause a few seconds later. All of the collective male immaturity was focused on the stunned woman.

"You're right," Barry said, addressing the brunette. "We're quite insane. But we have a little something that precious few other lunatics have?"

"What's that?" Tilly managed.

"Moxie," Barry offered. "Some call it grit. Others call it spunk. I call it good old American…"

"Look!"

A green light on the instrument panel flickered. The cockpit filled with amateurs ceased their clapping and stared at the light in disbelief. If they had the time to study the manual in the glovebox, they'd have learned the exact meaning of the blinking light; all systems on the Spruce Goose were now go.

It was the one of a kind oversight that could only have taken place in the small, rural lumber town of Roseburg, Oregon. The deed occurred one year ago to the day and the end result was the single and significant green illumination on the aircraft's instrument panel.

The semi-truck, transporting the main fuselage of the Spruce Goose from Long Beach, had stopped in the small lumber town for refueling. The driver, a skittishly thin man with a red baseball cap, ruddy complexion and dilated pupils the size of ping-pong balls, hopped out of his rig and darted into the adjoining truck-stop to relieve his bladder and invigorate dwindling brain cells with a handful of "diet" pills.

Fueling the rig was the responsibility of gas station attendant Bart Bastion, a twenty-two-year-old redheaded unemployed logger on the first day of a promising new career. Having never fueled a giant semi, Bart neglected to search for a gas tank in any of the obvious places and mistakenly focused his search on the trailer and cargo. He was about out of options when he stumbled onto the wooden fuel hatch.

It was the Goose's first real drink in over fifty years, and it chugged the fuel greedily. Unbeknownst to the trucking company, six thousand dollars were being charged to the driver's Fleet Card. The Spruce Goose was eventually satisfied, and driver and combustible cargo were once again on the road. Twenty miles up Interstate 5, the semi-truck hauling the Spruce Goose ran out of gas.

The furthest starboard propeller on the wing sputtered, belched and ignited in a roaring blur. The clapping ceased as everyone glanced to the right. The accumulated disbelief was not enough to stop the next in a series of propellers from firing.

"It worked," Beast exclaimed. There was the gleam of accomplishment in the big man's eyes. He was quite sure that he had brought this miracle on all by himself with nothing but sheer will and positive attitude. No amount of skepticism from his friends could take away his win.

Barry was frozen. On both sides of him, propellers were a spinning frenzy as the pumps in the giant wings continued to transport the fuel to the engines. "I don't get it," he screamed over the growing noise.

Face was likewise astounded. "What kind of imbecile leaves fuel in the tank?"

"I can't fly this," Barry added. "I'm impaired."

Beast grinned. "Like riding a bike," he answered. "No different than your Atari 2600,"

"Then you do it!"

Beast removed his hands from the switches and raised them over his head. "You called it," he answered.

Barry turned to Doc and Brain who were busy checking the fluctuating gauges and needles.

"I mean how different can it be?" Doc guessed.

"My Atari didn't come with rudders," Barry said.

Lights flickered to Barry's left. More cockpit electronics were coming alive. Brain pointed out each one as he and Doc monitored the growing array of gauges.

"We'll never get this thing off the ground," Face protested.

"There is precedent," Brain said.

"We're inside a museum," Barry shouted over the din of the idling plane. "Where are we supposed to go?"

The last propeller whined, groaning as it initiated the whirring spin.

"Now I lay me down to sleep," Face muttered, swallowing hard. "I pray the Lord, my life to keep."

The combination of roaring propeller blades and sliding crates took the gunmen by surprise. The last propeller surged to life, multiplying the chaos inside the museum. Wind gusts reached epic proportions. Machine guns fired into the air as the attackers turned and fled.

"We're moving," Brain said.

"On what?" Barry screamed over the roaring engines waking from a fifty-year slumber. "Isn't this a sea plane?"

"Sliding," Brain corrected. "If memory serves, this plane is equipped with retractable landing gear. Go!"

Face and Doc dashed back into the hull, searching for the crank and wench that released the wheels.

The Spruce Goose lurched forward; wrenching the wire anchors from the foundations. The plane was free, the hull sliding across the recently waxed floor on a collision course with a looming wall of glass.

From inside the cramped cockpit, the four watched in panic as the giant plane careened toward a vintage, German Messerschmitt Me 262 and Mercury Space Capsule.

"Watch out," Tilly screamed.

"Floor it," Beast roared.

"You want to drive?" Barry answered, jerking the yoke to his right.

Beast grabbed the throttle, thrust it upward and goosed the Goose. The plane lunged right, barely missing the fighter but successfully toppling the capsule. The spacecraft flipped onto its side like an upended children's top and rolled out of control toward the fleeing gunman.

"You got tires," Doc yelled from the back.

A volley of gunfire failed to halt the runaway NASA capsule. A stray bullet ricocheted into the ceiling, razor-sharp shards of green raining down on the displays. The unlucky killer avoided the fatal deluge but not the rampaging capsule. He stumbled, and the spacecraft rolled over him, pulverizing the lower half of his body. Alas, his days as an assassin were over, the killer spending the remainder of his days in an overpriced convalescent home in nearby Newberg.

The Goose crashed through the western wall of the museum none the worse for wear. It rumbled onto the deserted parking lot, spinning slowly in a complete 360. The remaining gunmen panicked. Open-mouthed, they watched as the aircraft rolled away from the museum, executing an ominous turn in their direction.

"I smell gas," Doc said as he and Face joined the others.

"Abandon ship?" Barry offered.

Doc and Brain seemed to be making up their minds between a fiery or bullet-riddled death. Both men decided at the same time and placed a firm hand on Barry's shoulders, pinning him into the pilot's seat.

"Prepare for takeoff," Brain advised.

Brain and Doc thrust the throttles even further forward and the confident thunder of an engine that was decades old answered in kind.

"What?"

Grateful for a chance to clear mechanical throats, the long-silenced engines howled. The Goose picked up speed, on a direct path with the lingering gunmen. Two goons fired at the cockpit before turning abruptly and joining their retreating comrades.

The movie theatre, still under construction, and water park loomed ahead.

"I don't think we have enough room," Barry said, grinding his teeth.

"You'll have to make do," Brain answered.

The pistons were firing with full force, attempting to lift the wooden behemoth off the ground. Barry pulled back on the yoke and it seemed the entire weight of the plane was centered on the stick. The tendons in his arms tightened and knotted. Muscles, hibernating since 7th grade gym class, awakened. Beads of sweat rolled down his forehead and plummeted off his nose. If I can get this thing in the air, he thought, we won't die. The fart, born from physical exertion, caught everyone by surprise. It was his out of shape body's inevitable protest over the strain of the endeavor.

"He farted," Beast howled.

"Now I definitely smell gas," Face added.

The gravity of their plight dissipated as quickly as the odor and a childhood sense of toilet humor had overcome the collective need for survival. It was totally unexplainable and to Tilly, a newcomer to this band, beyond explanation.

"Someone needs to eat more leafy vegetables," Doc diagnosed.

"Hmm," Brain offered.

Tilly pointed. "Look!"

The man with the turret head stepped out of the darkness and directly into the path of the taxiing plane. The new crew of the Spruce Goose watched the tank barrel extend, adjusting and tilting toward the approaching cockpit.

Face couldn't help but notice that their killer's massive frame was draped in an expensive silk Armani suit, black shirt and white tie. "Lethal and dapper," he critiqued jealously.

Barry's unexpected expulsion of gas was forgotten and everyone in the cockpit grabbed onto the yoke and pulled. Mistaking them for brakes, Barry's feet placed equal pressure on both rudders. The random actions were just enough to get the Spruce Goose off the ground.

A flash from the cannon barrel lit up the night. The man with the turret head backed a half step, fighting off the recoil from his metallic proboscis. A shell rocketed out the barrel at a speed of four thousand feet per second and continued on a trajectory that was a split-second away from blasting the entire nose off the Goose.

The Spruce Goose continued upward, the unwieldy aircraft once again finding the will to fly. The craft was currently soaring at an altitude of seventy-one feet, breaking all previous records. The shell passed just under the plywood hull and exploded into the Wild River Ride of the water park, passenger logs launched high into the night sky.

Tanktop made the necessary adjustments in his targeting systems and corrected his stance. His turret shook and clanked as another shell dropped into the chamber. He wasn't sure he'd even need another round for it looked as if the Spruce Goose was about to crash into the movie theatre.

The Goose climbed. Both throttles were fully forward and the theatre dead ahead left little doubt that this hair-raising and historic flight was far from over. Barry cranked the yoke right and the plane banked, the tip of the right wing just missing the upper left corner of the marquee.

"Just like riding a bike," Barry muttered to no one in particular.

The distinct smell of gasoline filled the cockpit as the plane soared over the highway. Barry felt a mechanical jerk as the first of the engines sputtered.

"That's it," Doc announced pointing to the glass dial. "Compression's gone."

Brain leaned over and verified the assessment. "We've got about one minute."

Face pointed to the instrument panel. "But we have plenty of fuel," he protested.

"Let go," Barry shouted, shaking the stick from the other's grasp.

He lowered the nose as the rest of the engines sputtered and flamed out in quick succession. The Goose bounced hard onto its landing gear and rolled into the cornfield on the other side of the highway. Slowing propellers mowed through the corn, shooting shreds of green silk and yellow vegetable in all directions.

"Everyone out," Doc ordered. "Now."

The stench of fuel was toxic, and they had no choice but to hold their breath and find the nearest exit. The plane rolled as Face led them to the hatchway.

"Jump," Beast yelled, shoving the clueless actor out the open hatch. The big brute followed with a reckless bound. Doc and Brain were next, launching themselves out of the plane with the same urgency as their predecessors.

"I was never really fond of corn," Barry shouted, clutching Tilly's arm and escorting her to the hatch.

The couple bailed, landing and rolling clear of the runaway plane. They propelled their bodies until Face, Beast, Doc and Brain scrambled over to intercept them.

"We could have waited until the plane stopped," an agitated Tilly said as she rolled onto her knees.

"I don't think so," Brain said.

The Spruce Goose exploded in a fireball of seventy-year-old wood, the resulting flames lighting up the night sky.

"Whoa," Beast mumbled in awe.

"This is what happens when you don't use the fuel recommended by the manufacturer," Barry wheezed, his hands on his knees and attempting to catch his breath.

"That fire will lead the walking cannon right to us," Doc said.

"I suggest we get moving," Brain offered. He squeezed the handle of his walking stick. Morning was a long way off and he still might need it.

"We could've been killed," Tilly protested.

"Any landing you can walk away from is a good landing" Barry answered.

The stragglers headed south, the opposite direction from where the legendary Spruce Goose crashed and burned. No one was speaking, and all was quiet save for the crackling of flames.

They turned west, maneuvering through the rustling stalks toward the lush forests and hills that blended seamlessly into the Pacific Coast Range. They hiked in silence through the chilly night, their gasping, visible breath a telltale sign of their growing exhaustion. It was unexplainable but the further they moved away from the burning wreckage, the deeper they found themselves in the endless field of corn.

The crackling fire was a beacon for law enforcement and, no doubt, they'd be arriving soon. The authorities would bring with them questions and answering said concerns with any degree of truthfulness would land them all in jail. The only alternative was to keep moving. The farther away from the crash site, the better. With little choice and no conversation, they continued their march, hoping at some point they'd stumble out of this mysterious field of corn and onto a road leading to civilization.

They had followed the six adults for the past hour and had accomplished the task without making a sound. The small, scrawny bodies were caked in years of accumulated dirt and filth, resulting in nature's perfect camouflage. Their unkempt hair was long and tangled with the remnants of dried stalks, highlighting an already aboriginal appearance.

Beast spotted them first. The ambushers were clothed in Super Friend Underoo briefs and armed with pointed wooden spears. This made no difference to the big man. He was ecstatic. "Outta sight," he blurted. "Children of the corn!"

The spears had been fashioned from the fallen branches of fir trees. The tips were sharp and several quick prods to the stomach confirmed it. Doc and Brain, their interest piqued, turned. Two sharpened points were poised mere inches from their exposed necks.

"Indians call it Maize," Beast explained.

"Really?" Face asked, suddenly surrounded. "Are you shitting me?"

The agitated clan grunted excitedly at the sight of the female. The cornstalks rustled once again. more boys appearing and joining the others in a tight circle around the captives.

"They're just children," Tilly cooed, dropping to one knee and extending an open hand.

"Damn straight," Beast reiterated. "Of the corn."

The captors responded immediately to Tilly's maternal instincts. The young males purred like feral cats, gravitating to the woman like a bowl of fresh cream. Two young boys flanked her and grabbed her hands. Grunting curtly, they gestured for her to follow.

"Interesting," Brain observed. "Tribal with definite aboriginal characteristics."

"Watch your hands," Barry warned. "They look like biters." He observed the young boys stroking Tilly's hand and found himself growing increasingly jealous. "I'm giving ten to one, they haven't had their shots."

Several of the boys squawked undecipherable commands and thrust their spears deeper into the cornfield. They clearly knew their way around this Bermuda Triangle of agriculture and wanted the adults to pay attention.

"What do you they want?" Doc asked.

"It appears they'd like us to accompany them." Brain answered.

"To the palace," Beast said. "A palace made of corn."

"Is this a good idea?" Barry asked. He halted unexpectedly, the others continuing to follow on blindly. "We're the adults here. Should we be taking orders from these nose-picking munchkins?"

A sharp prod to the back propelled Barry forward. "Okay," he protested. "I'm sure you're all very exceptional in your own right and your parents are all very proud."

The band of boys led Tilly, Barry and the others deeper into the corn, turning left, shifting right, only to double back in the direction they had just came. It was disorienting and none of the adults could tell where they were. The children had created an endless maze in the vast field, one from which Barry, Tilly and his friends might never return.

"We should come here again," Beast suggested. "When we have more time."

The boys answered with a grunt and thrust their spears at the hulking prisoner.

"Curiouser and curiouser," Brain muttered. His lean fingers fondled the handle of his cane and he contemplated drawing the blade from its sheath. The intellect had never been a big fan of children, untamed or domesticated.

"They're only spears," Doc whispered. "We could run for it."

Brain turned, noting the girth of his companion with an arched eyebrow. "You be sure and let us know how that turns out," he said.

Doc grumbled something incoherent, digging in his pockets for his pack of Camels. He was relieved to find the box crumpled but intact.

"Just my luck," Face complained. "Stuck in one of Stephen King's less enjoyable novellas."

Several small hands shoved the actor and he stumbled forward, falling face first into a huge clearing of trampled yellow husks. Beast assisted Face to his feet as the six adults entered a village constructed entirely of corn. Small huts circled the clearing. A throne, fashioned exclusively from corncobs, was located dead center and appeared to be the seat of power for the pubescent tribe of boys.

Sitting in the chair of authority was a young, male cub eleven years of age. His alert green eyes scrutinized the arrivals closely. He had seen enough adults in his life and was instinctively wary. The hunting party led Tilly to the throne, the adult males stopped short with unwelcome jabs from the wooden spears.

"Hello," The female guest announced. "My name is Tilly."

The leader cocked his head and grinned, displaying clean but jagged teeth. "Wassup biotch?" he managed in a raspy growl.

Tilly's eyes grew wide, stunned at the cultural salutation. She glanced at the equally astounded men. They seemed even more surprised than she was. She smiled. "Fly, little man," she responded confidently. "Representing it old school."

The leader grunted, and the boys released the tips of the spears from the backs of Barry and his associates.

"Hey ya," Barry said, waving his hand in a half-hearted salutation.

The clearing instantly erupted in angry shouts and gestures. Tilly sliced the air with an open palm, gesturing for the fellow adults to remain quiet.

"Dope," Barry muttered.

"They appear to be communicating in hip-hop," Brain whispered to Doc.

"Chickenheads," the leader called out to the tribe. He gestured for Tilly to take her place beside him. "Chill, cave-girl."

Tilly and the leader conversed for over an hour. It was a hushed and at times an animated chat, highlighted by grunts, hoots and an occasional proclamation by the leader of "assed out."

Tilly broke free from her audience with the leader to explain the tribe's strange history. The men listened intently to a tale that was as sad as it was baffling.

The boys were discards of an adult society too self-absorbed to even notice or care. These wild faces, once so innocent, had never been fortunate enough to grace the back of a milk carton or to have their stories featured on a special "CBS 48 Hour Mystery." The boys were human refuse, discarded by the ones charged above all else to love, care and protect them.

There was no stopping the adults once word spread of the supernatural dumping ground. Every October, parents lured innocent faces with a promise of tractor rides, pumpkin patches and caramel apples, discarding their unwanted male offspring into the inexplicable confines of the corn maze. Adults traveled from as far away as Spokane on the slight chance the mysterious maze might swallow up their uncontrollable progeny.

It was not a perfect metaphysical science and simply entering the maze was no guarantee of a childless life. Girls were never taken, and some parents had been known to make the trip repeatedly to test their luck. Some journeyed back time and time again in hopes of embracing a childless life. Meanwhile, their unsuspecting children sat in their expensive child seats, unaware of a fate that could have very well swallowed them whole. The authorities suspected nothing. Occasionally, a family member might question the sudden and unexpected disappearance of a child and an official investigation was launched. Nothing ever came of any of these official probes, the evidence having vanished into thin air.

The tribe's diet subsisted mostly of corn, the wild boys stripping off the golden kernels and storing it for the winter in tiny holes they had dug in the virgin forests that surrounded their home. There was also the food stolen from the museum across the highway. The snack bar was replenished regularly, their repeated raids rewarded with cases of Skittles and frozen corn dogs. The boys acquired a taste for both the colorful candy and the frozen product they had christened stick meat. It was quite a life the lost boys of Yamhill Country had forged for themselves. Left to their own childhood devices, they survived and even prospered.

Tilly took her place at the young leader's right. "Cock Diesel's attempting to put a cap in the ass of my homies," she explained.

Her statement generated an enthusiastic response. Boys hooted, thrusting their spears high over their heads. It took the leader rising off his throne to quiet the noisy mob.

"Cha!" the leader shrieked, the rest of the community joining in with the nonsensical chant.

"Cha! Cha! Cha!" the tribe echoed.

"Got to love a good cha-cha," Barry offered quietly.

Beast was spinning, a whirling dervish of dancing frenzy. "Pop, pop. Pop! Watch the mother fuckers drop," he chanted.

"Someone's forgotten to take their Ritalin," Face observed.

Doc and Brain studied the boys with the scientific detachment of anthropologists.

"Should we be worried?" Barry asked.

It was Tilly who answered. "They're working themselves up toward a confrontation. Gangland style."

"And this helps us how?" Barry asked.

"I guess that depends on whose side you're on," Tilly answered.

"Kids," Barry mumbled. "What can you do?"

Face bounced up and down wearily. "When in Rome," he said. "It's been years since anyone's taken me dancing."

The site of the actor pogo-sticking only added to the frenzied proceedings. Their hosts, born mimics, followed the actor's lead with wild abandon. Even Doc and Brain were bobbing their heads in time to the feverish chants.

The shell whistled overhead and scored a direct hit on the corncob throne. The resulting concussion threw anyone within a five feet radius to the ground. The leader avoided catastrophe, pin-wheeling out of harm's way in a series of perfect cartwheels. Dry husks ignited as scorching flames spread rapidly throughout the village. A crackling roar of destruction accompanied the deadly inferno.

"We've got to get these kids out of here," Tilly screamed.

Before any of the other adults could respond, the boys had taken matters into their own hands. They counterattacked, charging the arrival with nothing but wooden spears, jagged teeth and unsuppressed fury.

Tanktop stepped into the clearing, his gun barrel smoldering from the expelled shell. The eyeless turret swiveled back and forth, taking in the destruction that surrounded him.

"Stop them," Tilly shouted to the idle men. "They'll be killed!"

Her protest was in vain. The children attacked the steel-plated villain like a swarm of angry bees. They covered the metal henchman, poking and stabbing him in the feet and legs with their sharpened sticks. The few boys the giant did throw off were instantly replaced by more members of the kicking, biting tribe. Tanktop stumbled back into a row of corn as more of the boys piled on. Soon all the combatants had vanished into the bordering cornstalks.

Tilly was paralyzed, the giant flames cutting her off from the battle. She was grateful that Brain and Doc possessed the foresight to grab her by the elbows and hurry her away from the chaos.

"We leave now or we're dead," Doc ordered. "This way!" The portly chemist had clearly taken charge.

More of the boys had engaged the enemy. It was an uncontrollable force only witnessed by popular uncles and harried daycare workers. They leapt onto Tanktop from every direction. They bit the villain with jagged teeth and pounded on his huge frame with tiny balled up fists. The metallic giant was unprepared for such a battle. The boys were dangerous. He fell backwards and was now flat on his back, ears of dry corn and frozen meat products rammed into the cannon barrel.

Flames consumed the corn with a vengeful thirst that'd soon swallow both villain and attackers. There was little hope of survival and yet the boy warriors showed no sign of giving up. Tanktop struggled, his weapon useless under the assault of dirt, corn and meat. The metallic henchman's last desperate move was instinctive and irreversible. The children heard the menacing clang and instantly backed off the hulking body. They only had a few seconds and the boys took full advantage, exiting through a parting in the scorching flames.

Tanktop's instrument panel blinked an increasing number of error messages. The harbinger of his own doom was the ominous electronic beep that signaled there was no way to stop his cannon from firing.

The force of the explosion knocked Barry and Tilly off their feet, and both tumbled onto a batch of dry dirt. Unaware of their prone comrades, Brain, Doc, Beast and Face stumbled over the two, the six adults reduced to a protesting pile of human flesh.

They scrambled to their feet, spotting the second growing inferno.

"They were just kids," Tilly offered after a dismayed pause. "They died trying to save us."

As if to answer her concern, an unmistakable series of youthful hoots and shouts called out in the night. The tribe of parentless, corn-fed boys had survived and would live to fight another day.

It was a small overpriced motor court located on a grassy bluff overlooking Haystack Rock. They were lucky; it was off season and the credit card machine in the small lobby office was out of order. One cancelled credit card imprint later, the five men and one woman were sheltered in the small, quaint cottage #7 with the door locked and the drapes pulled.

Two hundred and thirty-five feet of sea stack rose out of the gray Pacific Ocean like an angry oversized fist. Advertised as ocean view, the unique formation of giant rock and surrounding Pacific were only visible by craning your neck through the cottage's small kitchenette window. The scenery hardly mattered. The adults were now on the run and only intended to stay long enough to catch their breath. They had broken into a museum, taken a priceless footnote of aviation history out for a joyride, setting fire to it and thousands of acres of cornfield. They had no choice but to run. They were six outlaws ensconced in a tiny, romantic cottage intended for two.

The two-cup coffee pot had been brewing non-stop since six in the morning. Face had returned to the office on three separate occasions to pick up additional packets to keep everyone caffeinated. The sleepy person at the front desk seemed oblivious to the mass consumption of coffee by the same sex couple registered to the unit. The elderly innkeeper would be relieved of duty soon and the business of the two strange men inside the cottage and the dwindling coffee packets would the responsibility of the next shift.

The consumed java added a collective jitteriness to their plight. A new day was just getting started and already the options of those hiding out in the cramped quarters seemed unquestioningly slim. Tilly was asleep in the only bedroom, separated from the muffled chatter by a hallway and a closed door. Brain and Doc lounged on the loveseat while Face and Barry sat across from each other at the small dinette table. An agitated Beast paced between the tiny kitchen and living space, muttering to himself incoherently.

After several seconds of intense soul-searching, Face raised a hand. "Okay," he said. "Who's for turning themselves in?"

"Pussy," Beast snarled.

"It's required that you be judged mentally competent to get a vote." Face fired back.

Barry remained silent. He agreed with his friend's assessment. It was abundantly clear that jail time was now a part of his future and he secretly wondered how he'd fare in prison. Still, on the positive side, it was free room and board and he was currently looking for a place to stay.

"We'll throw ourselves on the mercy of the court," Face pleaded. He pointed at Beast. "We'll say our special needs friend got locked in the museum after closing."

"And borrowing and crashing a piece of American history?" Doc said. "How do we explain that?"

The question sent Face into a grumpy submission. "The keys were left in the ignition?" the actor guessed.

Tilly's purse sat on a small end table in the hallway. Barry noticed that Brain and Doc couldn't take their eyes off of it. Did his friends believe it contained important clues?

"Oh no you don't," Barry cautioned.

The warning had the opposite effect. Beast had now focused his limited attention on the accessory. Brain glanced at the bedroom door and nodded. Beast's hand shot out, snagged the purse off the table and transported it to the loveseat. Barry was up in a flash and snatched the handle before the purse landed in Brain's lap. The purse was upended, spilling female specific contents onto the cushion and floor.

"You can't go through people's things," Barry protested. "It's not ethical." The two men ignored him, picking up the items from the floor. "Any weed in there?"

59

Doc and Brain were already at work, sifting through the personal inventory. Beast remained standing, hovering excitedly over his two associates. He reached down, grabbed a paper tube and hurled it at Face.

"What the hell?" Face blurted, deflecting the object.

"Tampons for a pussy."

"That's it!" Face exclaimed. The actor stood defiantly. "Screw the lot of you. It ends here. I'm done. I'm out!"

Face marched to the front door. He grabbed the handle, facing them defiantly. "I've had it up to here with all of you. I've wasted enough of my time, sacrificed my career, and for what? Rummaging through a woman's purse? I'm sorry but I can't hang out with you guys any more. And don't you dare try and stop me. There's nothing any of you can do." Face focused his attention on his only ally. "You coming, Barry?"

Barry released the purse and joined him at the door. "Face's right," he said addressing his preoccupied friends. "I let you drag me along because I've got nothing going on in my life. That's no excuse. I'm going to move out of my mother's basement into a cozy 6 by 8 feet jail cell."

Brain studied the handwriting on the business card. "Fascinating" he muttered.

Doc snatched the card and read.

Even Face was curious. "What?" he asked.

"Portland Police." Doc answered. "Narcotics."

"She's a cop?" Barry asked, forgetting what he just said and hurrying back to the loveseat.

"No name here," Doc offered. "There's a date and time written on the back. Must be an appointment."

"This is big," Barry mumbled. "I've never dated a cop."

"Terrific," Face mumbled, releasing the handle and stepping away from the door. His closest friend had the attention span and hormones of a thirteen-year old boy.

"Maybe she's a dealer," Barry mused. "I don't know if I could date a drug trafficker. Doesn't seem ethical."

Doc removed his portable magnifying glass from his jacket and conducted a quick scan of the purse. "No sign of narcotic residue."

"Which is it?" Barry asked. "Cop or pusher? I have an important decision to make here."

"I'd need a microscope to be sure," Doc said, ignoring his friend.

Beast unfolded a typed document. "Worthless," Beast growled. "Nothing but symbols and numbers," He was about to wad it up when Brain liberated the sheet of paper and handed it over to Doc.

"It's a lab report," Doc confirmed. His pudgy finger pointed to a series of symbols and numbers. "Synthetic," he added. "An expectorant."

"Cough syrup? Barry asked.

"It's a fuel additive," Brain offered. "For rockets."

"It must have found its way on the street where someone discovered another purpose." Doc said, not truly believing the validity of his own theory. He shrugged. "It's a good guess."

Beast slapped Face on the back. "No shit!"

Face braced himself. Another impact and he'd end up on the floor.

"I still don't understand," Barry said.

Doc lit a cigarette. "People huff gas," he explained. "The oxygen in the blood replaced by the harmful chemical vapors and fumes."

"That shit will kill you," Beast said with the dire earnestness of someone who might have indulged.

"Are you sure?" Barry asked, turning his attention to the sheet of paper.

"It could very well release the same endorphins as amphetamine or cocaine."

"One way to find out," Beast said. "You'll need a Guinea pig. Cook me up a batch."

It seemed to Barry that chemist was actually considering the idea.

"We don't have the materials," Brain answered. "And no idea of where to find them."

Barry glanced at the closed door to the bedroom. "I'm so conflicted," he announced.

"I'm open to other theories," Doc said, inhaling from the cigarette.

"She's right," Barry said, taking the folded piece of paper and placing it back into the purse. He was once again considering the invasion of privacy. "You're all crazy."

"She narced out her own mother," Beast bellowed. "That's just sad."

"Is this how desperate you've become?" Barry said, scooping up the remaining contents off Brain and Doc's lap. He held the items in one hand. "You're making this shit up as you go along. News flash! You're guessing. None of you know what you're talking about!"

"You could have at least asked me," Tilly announced softly. She was standing in the open doorway and her arrival had clearly caught everyone off guard. "I'd have said no, but you could have at least asked."

"It was them," Barry sputtered, pointing to his friends. "I told them to put it back."

Tilly noted the evidence in Barry's hands. The others looked away as if further eye contact with the woman carried a degree of guilt.

"None of you have the right."

Barry walked to Tilly. Tears welled up in her eyes. He placed the contents in her bag. "You're right." Barry said. "We are morons."

Tilly slapped Barry hard across the face. The sound echoed through the small room sending a collective chill through the rest of the men.

"He certainly had that coming," Beast announced.

Face retrieved the Tampon off the floor and walked it to the owner. "Sorry," he mumbled.

Barry's face was throbbing. He massaged the flushed skin of his face with an open hand, feeling the heat radiating from the blow. Once again, he had been humiliated and held his friends directly responsible. It was just another in a growing list of arguments to jettison this whole adventuring idea and return home to face the consequences.

Tilly, having all she was going to take, exited through front door.

"It's not safe out there," Barry called. A slamming door was his answer. He held out the compromised bag. "Your purse?" He turned to Doc. "Nice work. Now she'll never go out with me."

"Yeah," Face agreed. "Was the slap your first clue?"

"Talk to her," Brain suggested. "Apologize for your egregious behavior."

"My behavior?"

"You're an animal," Beast reiterated.

"She's upset," Doc said. "She could use a friend."

"I'm the last person she wants to see," Barry argued. "Thanks to all you."

"There was a real chemistry between you two," Brain noted. "What do you think, Doc?"

Doc nodded. "Eh, sure. I guess"

The four friends possessed special powers when it came to manipulating their friend. Barry had always been a follower and was easily swayed. Countless times in the past 24 hours, they had talked him into doing things that any ordinary human being would refuse.

"She slapped my face," Barry argued.

"Deserved" Beast said.

Face walked into the hallway. "I'm taking a nap," he said. "Be sure and wake me when the SWAT team arrives."

A reluctant Barry found Tilly standing at the juncture of incoming tide and dry sand. Haystack Rock was on their left and a flock of seabirds squawked as they hovered above the giant sea stack. The beach was deserted, the gathering dark clouds and earliness of the hour ensuring the two's privacy. A drizzling rain warned of wetter weather to come.

Tilly stared into the churning gray surf, watching as the waves pounded the shore. The dreary gray morning matched her mood of anger, fear and growing anxiety.

Barry studied her from a few steps behind, summoning the courage needed to go another round with the volatile female. "That's quite a slap," he said finally, attempting to be heard over the thundering Pacific. "My ears are still ringing."

"I'm just getting warmed up," Tilly answered without turning.

"Pardon?" Barry countered, using the overpowering sound of the surf as an excuse to approach.

"I said, how'd you feel..." She stopped herself. "Never mind. It's not worth the effort."

"Look," Barry explained. "I had nothing to do with that purse business. My friends obviously lack sufficient social skills to interact in a civilized society." He took a deep breath and continued. "They had this crazy idea that if I came out and apologized, you'd explain what's going on. I told them it was none of their damn business."

His non-apology resulted in a no reaction whatsoever and the two continued to stare at the gray horizon.

"Mine either," Barry added.

It was an awkward moment. Tilly's eyes once again filled with tears. "I may have had problems in the past, but I'm no drug dealer. My mother had nothing to do with this. It's..." She paused. "It's my fault."

"Okay."

"I was only hiding it in her house until I could figure out what to do with it. I had to stop it. It was killing people."

Emotions are uncomfortable things. Barry had managed to suppress his for an entire life. He had no clue as to how to proceed.

"Why'd they want to kill your mother?"

"She found it before I could get it back."

"Where did you get it?"

Tilly drew a deep breath, letting the brisk ocean air steady her nerves. She glanced at Barry. He's such an ass, she thought, sniffling and wiping her nose with a sleeve. Still there's something about him. She jettisoned the last thought before it had any real chance to gather emotional weight.

"I stole it," she said, avoiding eye contact.

"From who?"

She trembled, and Barry wasn't sure if it was emotion or the temperature. He had never been the greatest judge of a woman's needs. He placed an arm over her shoulder, and it was immediately shaken free. "Sorry," he mumbled.

"You really want to hear this?" she asked.

Barry nodded, unsure of what to say next. He shuffled nervously, cursing his friends for sending him on this fool's errand. Still, she was attractive, and she seemed to be warming to him. It was precisely this type of ignorance responsible for his chronic failure in maintaining intimacy or sustaining a relationship.

"Okay," Tilly said, "but this may take a while."

"This is my fault," Tilly repeated, her voice betraying the unmistakable tremor of someone under extreme pressure. "I'd been clean and sober for over a year…"

The squat unpleasant messenger wore a navy-blue pea coat, matching beret and possessed a jagged facial scar that ran from his left eyebrow, across the bridge of his nose to the bottom of his double chin. He had separated Tilly from her friends as they exited the Eastgate movie theatre during a late afternoon matinee. It was a rare day of sunshine in Portland and the heavy traffic on nearby 82nd Avenue reflected a populace eager to take advantage.

"Ain't no place you can hide," Beret declared in a menacing whisper. "Best say goodbye to your friends."

Tilly answered her companion's concern with a reassuring smile. "It's okay," she said. "I know him. I'll catch up with you later."

The friends, unaware of Tilly's past, retreated guilt-free, abandoning their friend with the beret-sporting messenger.

"What does Todd want?" Tilly asked impatiently. She attempted to stay calm, her shaky tone betraying she wasn't quite pulling it off.

"He's missed you," Beret explained. "And the money you owe him. He misses the money most of all."

Dealing was unpleasant business and partnering it with a year of sobriety was impossible. Portland was a small town and there was always a chance you would bump into someone who might challenge any sort of self-restraint.

66

"Chill out. He just wants to see you."

"I'm not using any more."

"Using don't concern him."

Beret marched Tilly to the curb as a familiar gold Pontiac Firebird pulled up. The passenger door swung open and Tilly slid into the backseat, concealing a growing fear that she'd never see her mother or friends again.

Cocaine had been added to Tilly's college curriculum the first semester of her second year. Her student advisor was a bass guitar player of Slavic descent and class orientation took place in one of the many second floor practice rooms. The muffled jazz that escaped into the hallway only added to a buzzy sense of self-brilliance and nervous euphoria.

Tilly indulged in the new hobby at every opportunity and soon after became a recruiter. She had taken a sizable part of her father's life insurance money and became the owner of a slightly-used Dodge van. It had become a drug-influenced dream to crisscross the country, searching for new recruits to join in her new, favorite pastime. The easy transformation to dealer made perfect sense; any transactional profit would naturally be transformed into her own supply. It was simple economics, and the theory worked for exactly six days.

Three months and several pissed off suppliers later, Tilly was back in her childhood home and taking the first important step in her recovery; admitting to herself that she was powerless to her addiction of the snow-white happy dust. Several dealers, including the Slavic recruiter, were soon behind bars and Tilly had embraced a life of sobriety. During the tumultuous period of parental fretting, her mother gained several pounds and had enrolled in Weight Watchers. The guilty daughter dropped out of college to take care of her, pursuing healthier interests, including rock climbing, wind surfing and any other sport that offered a more natural fix of adrenaline.

The driver of the gold Firebird was Todd Tetris, a big-neck jock Tilly had met while skiing Mt. Hood Meadows. Their encounter had escalated into a brief, sexual, cocaine-fueled fling, a decision she regretted at once. It turned out that Todd was as dangerous as he was handsome, and she had wisely broken it off. Despite the satisfying physicality of their affair, she did not regret her decision. The aroma of violence was palatable around the man and she did not want to wait around long enough to experience it first-hand.

On the first day of her recovery, Tilly left a voicemail for Todd relating her new lifestyle, including a brief mention of the substantial amount of money she owed him. She promised to pay it back, with interest, as soon as possible. The message was now over a year old, and she hadn't repaid a cent. She hadn't heard a word from him and mistakenly believed she was off the hook. Now, she clearly saw how wrong she was. Todd Tetrus was back in her life and expecting payment with interest.

The automatic gates clanked open with the welcome of a minimum-security prison. To Tilly, the sight was a depressing reminder that these sorts of storage units were a drug addict's last attempt to stay one step ahead of homelessness. Security at the complex appeared lax. After parking the Firebird, the three took a short stroll to the first building. Tilly glanced around the area for the best place to hide if she was offered the slightest chance of escape and found none.

"How many units do you rent?" Tilly asked. It was a feeble attempt at small talk to prolong her life.

Beret approached the sliding metal door as Todd unlocked the latch and grabbed the handle. Both quickly checked their surroundings before rolling the noisy door upward.

"Watch your step," Beret warned. "Wouldn't want you to hurt yourself."

Daylight flooded the open storage unit and exposed rows of bright yellow barrels stacked three high. A red hazard symbol on the barrels was Tilly's first clue the drug dealers were up to no good. The writing was Spanish, but she was confident enough in her translation. "Propulsor," she said. "Propellant."

"The secret ingredient," Todd said. "We add a couple tablespoons per ounce to inferior street product to give it a little kick. We call it Dragon Dream. We have tons of it."

"Where did you get it?" Tilly attempted in her most casual voice.

"Don't concern yourself with the particulars," Todd answered. "You just worry about selling it."

"I'm no scientist and took only one year of Spanish," Tilly offered, "but that's rocket fuel."

The slap sent her reeling into the first row of barrels. She placed a hand to her face and recovered her footing. Beret tossed a baggie filled with a mix of white powder and green crystals, hitting her in the chest. Tilly snagged the bag before it hit the ground.

"Dragon Dream," Tilly muttered to herself. She studied the bag's contents with an abuser's curiosity. There was still a tiny part of her that hungered to try it, but she quickly rebuffed the temptation. "I don't care what you call it. It's still poison."

"But what a ride," Beret snarled.

"You think I'd put a product on the street that wasn't tested?" Todd offered. He pointed to the baggie. "Pass it out to your friends at parties. Just a taste and see what happens. In a week, they'll be dying to get more of it."

"I won't." Tilly answered. "I'll pay you back. But there's no way I'm doing this."

Todd nodded to Beret. The thug grabbed a reluctant Tilly by the arm and moved her outside, dragging her toward the next unit. Todd was one step ahead and had a hand on the rolling door. He slid it up and the clacking metal revealed way more than Tilly ever wanted to see.

They huddled in the back, cowering at the invasion of sunlight. They were a mixed threesome, comprised of two emaciated males and one female. It was difficult to figure an exact age as they were so broken. They squinted at the arrivals and cowered. The male reached out a trembling hand. Was the pathetic soul asking for help or more of the drug she had clutched in her hand?

"Say hello to my focus group," Todd said. "Maybe you'd like to join them. We can always use more product testers."

Tilly glowered at Beret and Todd and took a step deeper into the second locker. "Those crystals are rotting them from the inside," she said. The baggie remained clutched in the hand behind her back. Even in the shadows, the human zombies could see her shaking the enticing green and white substance. The drug was too much to pass up. The three groaned and reached out with filthy, gnarled fingers.

"I've made mistakes," Tilly said. "But this is not going to be one of them."

The three derelicts were standing, and Beret was nervous. "Get back," he snarled.

Tilly continued to taunt the addicts with the baggy.

"Stop them," Todd ordered.

He was too late. They were too near the baggy. As the drug zombies reached out, Tilly sidestepped and moved forward, Todd and Beret passing her. Tilly reached daylight and jumped, snagging the unit's handle. With one yank the metal door crashed to the cement, and she threw the latch locking all inside.

The haunted faces were a grisly reminder of the lethal danger she held in her pocket. Tilly stopped at the nearest police precinct long enough to pick up a business card. Her nerves got the better of her and she left without reporting the drug or her abduction. It was her past that made her rethink the visit. She decided instead on an old friend who was a chemistry major at the college. Her friend agreed to her request, taking a small sample and promising to have the results for her later that night.

She was grateful her mother wasn't home. There were still questions that Tilly couldn't answer. If she stayed, she'd place her mother in danger and she couldn't let that happen. The house was quiet. The only sign of her mother was the handwritten recipe book and an unopened container of granulated sugar. Tilly glanced at the near perfect handwriting that was so much her mother. The recipe called the treat Heart Smart Sugar Cookies and the baker must have been at the store for more ingredients.

Tilly glanced out the window and watched as the familiar Firebird pull up front.

The contents of the bag were hastily emptied into the candied sugar jar as Todd and Beret marched up the walkway. She sealed the container and placed it far in the back of the highest kitchen shelf, praying her mother would never find it. Tilly planned to return for it later. She'd get the report on the new drug soon and the container contents would be all the evidence she'd need to get Todd and Beret thrown in jail for a very long time. The unfriendly knock came as Tilly shut the cabinet. She moved to the back of house, slipping out the sliding door of the kitchen and onto a redwood patio. She dashed through the backyard, vaulting over a small fence and into the yard of the unsuspecting Gassaways.

That was just one month ago. The sudden and unexpected death of the chemist friend had convinced her to stay as far away from her mother as possible. Retrieving the deadly substance had been postponed. While she waited, her mother had been murdered.

Tilly's story was complete and even the narcissistic Barry could see that the telling had taken a toll.

Recovery counselors had cautioned her that without truth there was no healing. She had just shared intimate details of her life with a man she barely knew. Countless recovery slogans ricocheted in her head, matching the rhythm of the pounding surf. When it came down to it, she suspected the platitudes were all bullshit. Right now, she was beyond caring about being judged. She wanted her story told. Now that it was, she'd deal with the consequences.

The gray sky was chilled by the arrival of a drizzling mist and it was Tilly's first still moment in days. Barry clasped Tilly by the upper arms. He turned her gently and pulled her close. He looked into her wide brown eyes and leaned into her.

"What the fuck do you think you're doing?" Tilly shrieked.

"I thought," Barry stammered, unable to complete the flimsy excuse.

"Well, you thought wrong!" she blurted, breaking off the embrace and turning her back on both Barry and the Pacific.

"I thought we were sharing a moment," Barry mumbled.

Tilly threw her arms up in the air, more a signal of frustration than capitulation. "Jesus Christ. You're the worst of them," she said, pointing an accusing finger toward the motel. "I don't need your adolescent shit in my life right now!"

She made her way to the sandy slope that that led to the parking lot and cottages. Barry hurried past the wisps of tall grass, struggling to catch her.

"Me?" Barry shouted. "You're the one with intimacy issues."

"Oh, keep talking," Tilly answered. "You're making it all of so much better."

"Really?" Barry said. "It's not usually this easy."

"Are you insane?" Tilly said. She stopped and glared at him, daring him to answer.

"Guilty," Barry offered in an unexpected burst of honesty. He stopped a short distance away to give her some much needed space. "I know a couple of women who might agree with you. Three if you count my mother."

It was the first sign of a thaw between the two and Barry stepped closer.

"I'm sorry," he said. "I'm an idiot. I haven't slept in days and I've always had a hard time communicating with people who are smarter than me."

Somehow, he had finally managed to say the right thing. Her eyes brightened, the faintest smile forming over her lips. He was a moron and there was nothing she could do about that. But he had listened and followed it by apologizing for his insensitivity. Perhaps there was a bit more to this man.

The whir of the droning motors was no longer drown out by the changing tide. "Wait," Tilly said. "You hear that?"

The two turned, watching as three, small aircraft soared over the southernmost tip of Haystack Rock. The silk sails were pitch-black in color and the whirring vehicles dangling below resembled go-carts powered by oversized fans. The pilots of the ominous craft were attired in black, rain-slicked leather, their entire heads covered by matching hoods. The eyes of the airborne Ninjas were obscured by shaded goggles.

Not caring to wait to find out their intentions, Tilly and Barry scrambled up the dune in a mad dash for safety. The distinctive growing noise of the aircraft signaled the vehicles were closing in.

Barry watched as Tilly arrived at the top of the dune. She was now in a perfect position to be snatched. "Get down," Barry screamed.

He was too late. Two paramotors swooped down on either side of her as gloved hands left their respective controls. It was easy as that. Tilly struggled, but it was no use. The pilots lifted her effortlessly, banked over the dunes, and carried the unwilling passenger over the crashing surf. Tilly's panicked protests were soon lost over the thundering waves of an angry sea.

It was the job of the third aircraft to deal with Barry. The paramotor executed a wide circle above the gravel parking lot. Barry faced the ocean as the front end of the metal craft slammed into his back, the blow sending him tumbling back down the dune. He reached the bottom and hopped to his feet. He searched for Tilly, glimpsing the retreating paramotors soaring over the southern side of the giant rock.

The aircraft executed a final turn to finish him. Barry raced back up the dune. He felt the vibration of the motor and a rush of air at his back. He reached the summit of sand just before enviable contact and, in a move that surprised even himself, he spun and jumped, launching himself into onto the metal nose of paramotor.

It was a desperate move, and he was not sure why he made it. The shocked pilot pulled up, taking both himself and the unwanted hitchhiker higher into the gray sky. Barry's upper body lay draped over the front of the craft, his flailing legs dangling over the side. He secured his precarious position by wrapping an arm around a series of aluminum pipes. With a free hand, he reached out and grabbed the pilot by the throat. There wasn't enough time in the world to explain his actions. It was as if he were suspended above the craft, observing his perilous struggle for life or death below. The uncharacteristic act of bravery had come from deep inside himself and from a place he never knew existed.

An hour had passed since Barry and the mysterious woman had left the cottage. Doc had stepped into the parking lot for another cigarette, Brain and Beast tagging along. A groggy and cranky Face, unable to sleep, left the comfort of the bed and straggled out a few moments after. The four men stood on the uneven gravel, surrounded by a sheet of cold drizzle.

"Is that?" the actor muttered, his sleepy eyes wide and pointing at the paramotor swinging high over the Pacific. "It can't be."

"It sure as hell is," Beast bellowed excitedly as he raced down the dune.

The others chased after the big man, attempting to keep up.

The pilot had neglected the stick, attempting to beat off the unwanted passenger with both hands. It was the wrong choice. The flimsy craft now swayed precariously under the sail. Barry secured his remaining leg onto the frame of the cockpit, his left arm locked on the roll bar. The pilot dislodged Barry's hand from his throat but lost control. The paramotor plummeted, the pilot making a desperate grab for the stick. Barry's free hand shot out in a flash, grabbed a handful of fabric and yanked, slamming the pilot's head into the instrument panel. The second part of the maneuver proved more complicated. Barry released his other hand, only his legs preventing him from a forty-foot plummet into the unforgiving sea. He unbuckled the pilot's seatbelt with one hand, while the other latched onto the pilot's shoulder. As the craft made another swing, Barry used the momentum to separate the pilot once and for all from the paramotor.

Barry clambered over the top, finding his way to the vacated pilot's seat. As he struggled for control, he glanced below, watching the pilot splash into the violent surf. He focused his attention forward, the formidable Haystack Rock looming on the horizon. One second of indecision and he'd crash, nesting with the squawking seabirds for the rest of eternity. He steadied the aircraft just in time and executed a sloping pass around the rock. As quickly as the cowardice vanished, it returned, leaving Barry with no idea of how to get the aircraft back on solid ground.

He climbed higher, surveying Haystack Rock from all sides. The two enemy paramotors had vanished along with their captive. Barry swung his aircraft around and headed east, toward the four anxious men waiting for him on the beach. He took a deep breath and pushed the stick forward, the nose aiming for the sand. Several feet off the ground, he cut the throttle, landing with a series of hard bumps. It was anything but a perfect landing.

His friends raced toward him, and he saw firsthand all the unanswered questions on their faces. They appeared as taken aback by his newly discovered heroism as he was. Barry was in no condition to care what they thought. He climbed out of the seat, his heartbeat racing. He couldn't draw a decent breath, felt light-headed and both legs had the consistency of warm Jell-O. Before they reached him, Barry fainted, dropping unconscious into the sand.

Beast sat in the pilot's seat, his mouth puttering in an attempt to recreate the sound of a paramotor in flight.

"I told you," Barry explained. "She disappeared." He sat in the sand with his back against the craft. His face remained flushed, his breathing and heart rate slowly returning to normal. "I tried but I couldn't find her."

"I'll take her up," Beast offered. "I'll find her."

The others ignored him, the big man returning to his passionate sound effects.

"They're not built for distance," Doc said. "They couldn't have gotten far."

Brain's lean fingers caressed the handle of his cane. "I wonder."

"Tide's not in yet," Doc said, sensing his friends hunch and lighting his 16th Camel of the morning.

"I'll go," Beast blurted. "Help me get this thing started,"

"When the tide comes in, you'll get stuck," Face warned. "Then you'll need someone back in the dry, warm room to call the Coast Guard."

Brain marched toward the formations of craggy rock and tide pools that were submerging the trail to Haystack Rock. "I don't think so," he called out.

"You go on," Beast said, perplexed at the complexity of the instrument panel. "I need to find the owner's manual."

Doc followed Brain across the rocks and Barry straggled behind.

"Wait," Face shouted. "Haystack Rock is a Federal Bird Refuge. You'll be breaking the law! There will be serious consequences. There's a dry copy of the Yellow Pages in the room. I'll call and consult an attorney."

Face's objections were ignored, and the actor jogged to catch up. Barry and his friend now straggled behind their two colleagues. "A legal opinion never hurts," Face added breathlessly.

"I'm sure Doc and Brain appreciate your concern," Barry answered.

"Fancy flying up there," Face continued. "Required a degree of bravery amongst over things. No offense but bravery has never been part of your rather complicated personality."

"None taken," Barry answered. He had gone over the same question in his mind repeatedly. Something had managed to reach through all his panic and cowardice and had taken control. It almost felt instinctive and was very disconcerting. No doubt about it, he was losing his mind.

Face sensed his friend's discomfort and placed a hand on his shoulder. "Heroics are overrated," he declared. He turned back, glimpsing Beast in the cockpit of the paramotor. "Don't touch a thing until we get back." he called out.

"You think we'll find her?" Doc asked his lean colleague.

"When you've eliminated the impossible, whatever remains, however improbable, must be the truth," Brain answered, waving the tip of his cane at the giant sea stack.

Doc snubbed the cigarette butt against a rocky outcropping, placing the dead cylinder into the coin pocket of his jeans. "No shit, Sherlock."

"Where's the glove compartment?" Beast called out from inside the cockpit of his new toy.

It was high tide and the four adventurers found themselves stranded on the rocky monolith, surrounded on all sides by a violent green ocean. The once harmless drizzle had turned to a pelting rain, the endless particles of water biting at their exposed skin. A howling wind accompanied the rain as immense waves crashed against the rock, making their ascent all the more perilous.

Brain led the way, maneuvering across the narrow trail along the edge of the jagged sea stack. He waved his cane at a belligerent seabird and it took flight, assaulting the human invaders with an onslaught of squawking profanities.

"Can we rest five minutes?" Face called out from the back. His legs ached, and his hands were raw from the cold and wet.

No one answered. The others were too busy fighting off their own physical limitations to respond.

"You need special equipment to be a rock climber," the actor continued. "It takes shoes, pitons, hammers and rope. I'll go back to the room and phone around. We can try again when we're better equipped."

The ignored actor watched Doc and Brain climb onto a dangerous ledge that jutted out a third of the way up. Directly below, a wave collided with rock and drenched Face in an explosive shower of icy-cold sea water. "Can't we at least talk about this?" he yelled.

"Damn odd." Doc said, examining a steel ring lodged in the rock. "No rust."

Barry, his entire body clenched against the rock, stepped onto the ledge, peering into the churning sea below. All sign of the bravery displayed earlier had once again abandoned him. His paralyzing fear returned with a vengeance, along with a dizzying anxiety that only heightened his overall sense of dread. He reached the two men studying the steel ring. "What?" Barry managed, after catching his breath. "Why have we stopped?"

"These rings were placed here recently," Brain explained. "They follow this ledge to the far side."

"Are we there yet?" Face asked as he joined the others.

"Not quite," Barry answered. "It looks like we're going to have to keep going."

"I've have an idea," Face called out. "Barry and I will wait for you here." The actor watched another wave collide with the rock, cutting off their escape route with several inches of water.

"Your call," Brain answered.

"Can I take a minute to think about it?" Face asked.

Barry took a deep breath and followed the others. Despite his fear, something deep inside urged him to keep going. The actor struggled to keep up.

"Everybody watch your step," Doc warned.

"And stay ahead of Face," Brain added. "You don't want him dragging you down when he falls."

"Sarcasm is not an attractive trait in a man," Face managed, spitting out a mouth full of salt water.

The footing was slick from the constant onslaught of ocean, rain, and bird excrement. Barry and Face clutched onto the rings fearfully as Doc and Brain maneuvered a corner and disappeared.

"It's happening again," Barry muttered to himself. An unexplainable rush of calm was returning. The wave of fearlessness started in the pit of his stomach and radiated throughout his body. The effects were faster than any drug, his newly discovered awareness seemed to be reacting to the mix of elements and unknown danger.

"I'm afraid of everything," Barry muttered. "What the hell is going on?"

"Shut up," Face said. His foot slipped, leaving his body dangling over the angry sea. "I'm not talking to you right now."

Barry extended a hand and effortlessly assisted his friend back onto the ledge.

"You just saved my life," Face exclaimed breathlessly.

"That's exactly what I've been talking about," Barry screamed. "This is not like me."

After twenty seconds of Face's spirited commentary, the two continued onward. They made their way to the ocean side of the rock and rejoined Brain and Doc. The two men were hanging one-handed by the rings and peering straight down into the face of an Olympic-sized tide pool forty feet below. Each of the men clutched a large rock.

"Wait," Doc cautioned. "Not yet."

Barry and Face watched as the frothing wave subsided and exposed the shallow pool.

"Now," Doc instructed and Brain released his rock.

Face and Barry exchanged a clueless glance. The answer didn't take long. A resounding bang echoed upward as the rock hit the surface of the tide pool and bounced.

"Plexiglass?" Brain guessed as Doc dropped his rock.

There was another sharp clatter as the second rock met the camouflaged surface. A second later, the next wave rolled in and obscured the pool.

"I guess metallic," Doc answered.

"I don't get it," Barry said. "You think the paramotors were launched beneath that?"

"It's not without precedent," Brain said.

"'You Only Live Twice. ' Sean Connery's last real Bond." Doc added.

"Lewis Gilbert. 1967." Brain noted. "Not the best in the franchise but, like the rest of the Connery's, worth a repeated view. Further investigation is warranted."

"What the hell are they talking about?" Face screamed.

"They're debating entries in the Bond franchise," Barry answered as he made his way downward. "Doc is obviously a Connery fan while Brain clearly prefers the rapier wit of Roger Moore."

"Oh," Face muttered, following Barry, Brain and Doc into the heart of the rock. "Important stuff."

"Yeah," Barry answered. "Don't dawdle."

The assault of rain and waves did nothing to deter two of the four men. The mystery below had ignited a curiosity more powerful than the elements. Each subsequent attack of the tide was met with an enthusiastic shout, the men hunkering into the rock and clutching onto the steel grips for dear life.

It was an hour before the four found themselves on the edge of the mysterious tide pool. An overhanging outcrop of dark rock bordered the pool and protected the four from the worst of the waves and weather. They huddled in the wet darkness, looking out over the rocky basin filling and emptying of seawater.

"Ingenious." Brain muttered. "A base of operations hidden by tons of solid rock."

"Now all we have to do is wait for them to open it," Doc added.

Both men appeared more than satisfied with their deductive skill.

"So that's it?" Face complained. "We wait here until it opens. What if you're wrong? We could freeze to death before that happens."

The two men appeared stunned by the actor's burst of negativity. There simply was no other way to get inside. Clearly flummoxed, the two thinkers stood in the pouring rain and stared at the wet puzzle before them.

"Great job," Face summarized. "I'm glad I left the comfort of a dry motel room to go explore some secret lair."

Clang. The metallic bang sounded from behind and caught the three men off-guard. They turned and found Barry standing next to a steel door hidden behind an outcropping of rock.

"Or we could just open this hatch and see what's inside," Barry suggested. His hands were clutching the slick wheel. "A little help would be nice."

"It could be a trap," Doc cautioned.

"Seriously?" Face blurted as Barry focused his entire strength on the wheel. "Let's just think about this. We don't know what's waiting beyond this door. Our next decision could very well define the rest of our lives."

"When you put it that way," Brain mocked.

"I hope he acts better than he writes," Doc critiqued, assisting Barry with the groaning hatch.

"It's called improvising," Face answered. "And I'd like to see you do better."

"Your performance was inspiring," Barry joked, ushering Face inside. "Let's go define our lives."

"Very funny."

"Sorry."

The steel door opened onto a slick metal grating and a series of winding stairs. The construction was bolted directly into the rock and led downward into what appeared to be a grotto. The destination was difficult to make out with only the sliver of gray daylight spilling in through the open hatch. A sloshing tide churned in the darkness and was accompanied by the intermittent bark of a sea lion. The distinct sea smell was pungent and complimented the non-mistakable aroma of deceased sea-life. With little choice, the four men began their descent.

"I don't get it," Doc said, his voice raised to be heard over the churning tide. "Portland, McMinnville to Cannon Beach. What's the connection?"

"The girl," Brain answered. "She's the key."

"Well it's not me," Barry reported to no one in particular. "You can't blame me for any of this."

Doc and Brain remained suspiciously silent, gawking at their friend. Their stunned faces betrayed a secret that was growing more apparent with each passing second.

"What?" Barry asked.

For the time being, Barry, Face and Beast were better left in the dark. Without saying a word, Doc and Brain turned back and resumed the journey downward. The steps ended, the two men finding themselves back on a ledge of slippery rock that led down to the punchbowl.

Doc fired up another Camel. "The whole set-up must be a hub for a distribution center," he explained.

"Drugs?" Face guessed.

"That's what I thought," Brain said. "But there's something bigger that we're missing."

"Maybe we just admit we're in over our heads," Face muttered, "and call Scooby Doo."

"Tilly was onto something," Barry offered. "This all has something to do with rocket fuel."

"Not bad," Doc said. He inhaled deeply from his cigarette and marveled at this friend's lucidity.

"Hmm," Brain added.

"Beast will be sorry he missed this," Face moaned. "He loves The Goonies." The actor stopped. Something had reached out of the wet darkness to grab hold of his foot. "Damn," he said.

"What is it?" Doc asked.

"I stepped in something," Face said. "It's wet and squishy and it's wrapping around my leg."

"Step out of it," Brain suggested calmly. He turned to the two men in back.

"I can't," Face said, a tremor of fear registering in his classically trained voice. "It's not letting go!"

"It's stinging me," Face screamed.

The giant sea anemone had anchored itself on a small rocky outcropping just off the trail and had waited patiently. It had called the soggy location home for three months and the deadly, orange blossom had done extremely well, feasting on the abundant sea-life that meandered past its colorful tendrils. The human foot inside the size ten shoe promised to be the biggest meal of its life. Along with a successful digestion came extreme bragging rights amongst all phylum <u>Cnidaria</u>, class, <u>Anthozoa</u>, subclass <u>Hexacorallia</u>. The orifice of the giant creature was three feet in diameter and the fleshy orange mouth closed easily around Face's leg, attaching itself to the human mid-calf where the second phase of food preparation was well under way.

"I can't feel my foot," Face wailed. The outburst was not a total truth. He could still feel the hundreds of tiny pinpricks biting into his ankle as the attacker anesthetized the oversized victim.

"The nematocysts are already at work," Doc explained. The chemist knelt and studied the giant anemone. "If we don't do something, he'll lose that leg."

"Not the leg," Face whimpered, wincing as the creature's grip tightened. He was now experiencing a total loss of feeling below the knee. "Legs are an actor's most important tool."

"I always assumed the voice was the actor's most important tool," Brain offered in his customary unperturbed monotone.

"This is hardly the time to discuss the particulars of my craft," Face bellowed. "Get me out of here!"

Brain unsheathed the sword cane. This was the precise moment he had been waiting for. At long last, he'd make use of his weapon, baptizing the blade into a life of adventuring. He handed the ornate wooden sheath to Doc. The razor-sharp rapier had been designed to his exact specifications and was illegal in 48 of the 50 states. He ran a lean finger along the tip of the weapon. "This should do," he muttered. "Stand back."

"What the hell are you doing?" Face bellowed.

Doc took a long draw from his cigarette. "This might be a good time for you to consider voiceover work?"

"Oh my god," Face stammered. "You're actually going to do it. You're cutting off my leg."

Face watched Doc and Barry back away. Brain held the handle of the weapon in both hands at eye-level. Grimacing, he forced the tip of blade into fleshy orange. A solid stream of excrement was the creature's defense, and it carried enough force to score a direct hit in the pale thinker's startled face.

"Stand back," Barry warned. "Looks like we got ourselves a squirter."

Brain was clearly humiliated, the defensive spray continuing to douse him with liquid indignity. He removed the tip of the blade from the fleshy creature, turned to the portly chemist and shrugged.

"I guess we'll just have to leave him," Doc said, handing the sheath back to his friend.

Brain rubbed his face clean with the sleeve of his jacket. He lifted the black denim to his nose and sniffed. He recognized the distinct odor immediately and realized he didn't have much time.

Face looked desperately to the two men and their combined inaction did nothing to ease his growing fears. Doc smoked calmly while Brain seemed to be considering where he had gone wrong.

Only Barry was calm, rummaging through the pockets of his jeans. "Anyone got any change?"

"What are you talking about?" Face wailed. The actor's voice was cracking under the strain. "You need to feed a parking meter?"

Doc and Brain remained unclear of the plan but checked their pockets anyway.

"I need pennies."

Both men now understood what their friend had in mind and doubled their efforts.

"Three cents here."

"Seven."

"It will have to be enough."

"Wait," Doc said. "I have a 1924 Wheat Penny. What's that worth?"

"Really?" Face shrieked.

"Kidding. It's worth $450. I don't really have one. I wish I did."

Barry kneeled next to the anemone that had trapped Face's leg. "Now for the next step."

"What are you doing?" Face said. He turned to Doc, his concerned expression pleading for a comforting answer. "Will it work?"

"If he has the time," Doc offered. "If he has the time."

"Odd," Brain interjected with a scientific detachment. "My face is numb."

The colorful tendrils tightened around Face's leg.

"Zippo." Barry said, extending his open hand to Doc.

Doc handed his prized possession over. "Careful. That lighter was a gift."

The lighter was a present from the R.J. Reynolds Tobacco Company, a reward for Doc's lifelong patronage of the industry. Doc considered the lighter, matching baseball cap, jacket and duffel bag prized possessions.

Barry flipped open the Zippo and struck the flint with his thumb. The flame ignited, and he held the yellow and blue heat against the flesh of the polyp. The orifice shuddered, opened slightly and he slipped the pennies inside. The copper-plated seasoning resulted in a volcanic regurgitation. The creature bloomed, followed by a violent expulsion of the actor's leg. The pennies were refunded in one climactic belch.

"Grab him." Barry ordered.

Brain and Doc complied, hoisting Face by the elbows and moving him away from the hungry anemone.

"You're very lucky," Doc said to the recovering actor. "Most sea creatures that acquire a taste for ham don't give up so easily."

"Hilarious."

"Well done," Doc offered as Barry handed him back the lighter.

"I kampt pheel mive thace," Brain mumbled.

A hidden sea lion barked, calling out from the darkness. It was a lonely commentary on their journey to the center of the hollow rock.

"Something I learned as a kid," Barry answered. "How's the leg?"

Face grimaced. "The sooner we find your new girlfriend, the better I'll feel."

"You really think I have a shot?" Barry asked.

"Get your hands off me!" Tilly's desperate scream came at the precise moment powerful work lights switched on and flooded the inside.

A yellow sub bobbed atop the foamy green punchbowl. The vessel was moored to a dock of metal grating that kept it from floating away and crashing against the rocks. It seemed that no expense had been spared in turning the interior of the sea stack into a submarine pen for small and mid-sized submersibles. The paramotors were stored in nearby racks for easy access, the sails folded up in a neat stack. Nearby, a generator thrummed, supplying the lights and adding a smell of diesel to the assortment of other odors.

The two paramotor pilots had removed their hoods. Both men were muscular blondes with a distinct Nordic heritage. Their hair was cropped short and both possessed blue eyes and square jaws. The men carried machine guns and flanked the female prisoner.

Tilly peered up, scanning the faces of the men she had met less than twenty-four hours earlier. She considered her odds of being rescued decidedly mixed.

"What now?" Face whispered, forgetting his leg and distressing over the sight of the gun barrels raising in their direction.

"Can you believe it?" Barry called out. "We're lost. We were trying to find the Seaside boardwalk. We heard they have bumper cars."

Tilly took full advantage of the distraction, elbowing the man on her right. Her captor stumbled off the grate and splashed headfirst into the ice-cold water. The blonde to her left leaned in to correct the prisoner's behavior, Tilly rewarding his effort by using his own momentum to hurl him into the sea.

Both henchmen sputtered and floundered, splashing away in the choppy water. Their shouts were in German and no aid from anywhere was forthcoming. The open hatch atop the submarine closed with a clang and the vessel submerged, seawater enveloping the bright yellow conning tower as it sank below the surface.

Tilly leaped from the metal dock, landing on the slippery rock. A brief sprint later, she had reunited with her new friends. Brain, Doc and Face pulled the floundering men from the water and relieved them of their weapons.

"We have to leave," Tilly urged. She grabbed onto Barry and pushed him in the direction in which they came.

"Wait," Barry said. "Are you okay?"

A curt nod was his only answer as the freed captive turned and pointed in the opposite direction. The whir of gyros captured the rescuer's attention and filled them with a familiar dread. It was a recognizable sound that accompanied a distinct profile. Tanktop stepped out of the darkness, his long barrel pointing directly at the six. He said nothing, a large hand gesturing for the two drenched Germans to recover their machine guns.

"He's starting to get on my nerves," Barry's comment had exited his mouth before his brain had time to stop it.

The humiliated Germans reclaimed their weapons and joined their metal-headed superior.

"Leaving without so much as a goodbye," Another figure stepped out from behind the cover of a high rock. "I'm beginning to think you don't like me anymore," he said.

"Todd Tetrus," Tilly snarled. "I should have known you'd be skulking about."

"Wait," Barry interrupted. "You two know each other?" The question resulted in an uncomfortable silence between the two ex-lovers.

Todd made a slow circle around the captives before halting at Tilly. "You did a magnificent job of tying up the loose ends," he said, leaning in and kissing the startled Tilly on the cheek. "Thank you."

Todd addressed Tanktop: "Now we both have what we want," he said. "I've got the girl and you have the fuel and this little merry band of nobodies."

Tilly swiped a hand over her cheek to wipe off the unwelcome intimacy. "Fuck off," she barked.

Barry grinned and extended a hand. "Name's Barry," he said, looking Todd straight in the eye. "So, how long have you two been dating?"

Todd said nothing, the two men continuing the stare-down. It was Todd who blinked first, chuckling before finally looking away.

Seawater foamed and bubbled around the surfacing yellow tower as the sub resurfaced.

"She's moved on," Barry explained. "It's all so exciting and we're both positively giddy from the newness of it all. But I don't want you to miss your ride. Maybe we can catch up later."

"I doubt we'll get the chance," Todd answered as he accepted Barry's hand.

Todd squeezed. The pain was excruciating and was close to breaking all the bones in Barry's hand. The ex-boyfriend leaned in as his grip tightened. "Have you fucked her yet?" he asked quietly.

"He's charming," Face noted, turning to Tilly. "I don't know why you ever left him."

Barry said nothing. He didn't need to. Tilly charged her ex-lover with the force of a small hurricane. Barry slipped his hand free as Todd stumbled backward from the unexpected blow. The two uniformed henchmen intervened, pulling the kicking Tilly away.

"You see?" Todd said. "A real fighter. Don't you worry. I won't let all that passion go to waste."

"I'm not sure I like you," Barry explained. "And I don't think my friends like you either."

"No argument here," Doc said.

"Agreed," Brain offered.

"Sticks and stones," Todd said, nodding at Tanktop.

"You see, we never cared much for bullies," Barry gestured to his friends. "We're proud alumni of our high school audio-visual team."

"We're done here," Todd announced.

Tanktop nodded at Todd and pointed to the open hatch of the submersible.

"San Francisco wasn't part of the deal." Todd said. The so-called tough guy was clearly nervous and taken back by the sudden change of plans.

The bully was now visibly agitated. The promise of an unexpected trip to San Francisco had changed his whole demeanor. The attitude ceased when he heard another shell clank into Tanktop's turret chamber.

"That's a shame," Barry said. "You seem like such a nice guy."

"They call him Tanktop," Todd explained. "He kills people."

"And people complain that Detroit will never make a comeback," Face muttered to no one in particular.

Tanktop nodded to the blonde accomplices, and they stepped behind the two, escorting the apprehensive Todd and Tilly toward the submarine.

"You're lucky you'll die first" Todd offered nervously. "This whole thing is so much bigger than I ever imagined."

Barry shared one last look with the combative Tilly as the two men lowered her into the hatch. The fear of the unknown was clear but there was something more he was witnessing. She'd remain defiant to the last.

Before her escort disappeared below, Todd nodded, pointing an accusing finger at Barry "Trust me, you'll regret ever knowing her," he announced sharply. "She's nothing but trouble."

The two Nordic henchmen followed close behind and the hatch clanged shut. The frothing bubbles returned, and the sub vanished under the surface of the green water, taking Todd Tetris and Tilly on a voyage to the bottom of the sea.

"San Francisco is a great theatre town," Face sighed. "I saw Chorus Line with the great Donna McKechnie in the summer of 77."

Tanktop remained still during the farewells. His barrel zeroed in on the four interlopers, their fate once again in the hands of the metal giant. The hidden sea lion echoed their death sentence with a series of hungry barks, emanating from the darkness above them.

"Wet down here," Barry said, pointing to the turret. "I hope you paid extra for the under-coating."

The sea lion announced his unexpected arrival with another bark. It had remained hidden in the dark recess of rock directly above the metal executioner. The mass of brown blubber was clearly annoyed, moving, growling, honking and slapping his fins against the wet, rocky perch.

Tanktop's targeting mechanism was already at work analyzing the threat. Before he could stop it, computers had cranked his barrel upward and the cannon fired.

The unexpected explosion sent Tanktop stumbling backwards. The startled sea lion retreated into the darkness as the ledge collapsed in an avalanche of smoke and rock.

"Jump."

The four men leapt into the icy water as a wall of crumbling rock tumbled down on the villain. They were all good swimmers but quickly fell victim to the unforgiving tide, the surging waves bouncing them off course and hurling them into the jagged rocks.

The dust settled, and they saw Tanktop on his back, buried under a pile of volcanic rubble. His smoking barrel remained visible, protruding from the prison of rock.

The four swam through the small cave, emerging into the gray, drizzly daylight. Exhausted and freezing, they slowly paddled their way around the side of the giant sea stack toward the shore.

"I don't think I can make it," Face sputtered. His teeth chattered, and he had just swallowed a lungful of Pacific Ocean. "My whole body is numb."

"Drowning is the least of your worries," Doc said as he swam to the actor.

Tanktop emerged from inside the monolith. He had somehow dug his huge frame out of the rubble and, despite his size, maneuvered confidently along the ledge. The villain halted to check the escapees' progress.

"How can he still be alive?" Barry managed.

The freezing water temperature was taking a toll on all of them. The shore seemed an eternity away and climbing back onto the rock posed its own risks. They watched the barrel extend. His weapon appeared to be functional and at this range he surely couldn't miss.

They heard the sound of a familiar motor and focused their attention skyward. A black sail appeared, rising over the rock behind the unsuspecting metal man. The chassis swung into view, exposing an exuberant Beast in the pilot's seat.

"Coming through," Beast bellowed as he aimed the front of the craft into the back of the steel-plated henchman.

The small aircraft met villain soundly, knocking him off the rock and sending him turret first into the ocean. There wasn't much of a splash. the weighty headgear sending the assassin straight to the ocean bottom.

Doc led the group in a resounding cheer. Their bodies were turning a collective blue, but they still possessed enough energy to celebrate the victory. Beast concluded the heroics by circling Haystack Rock in a victory lap. When he returned, he transported each man to the sandy shore.

"I don't care what you say," he repeated to each of the passengers on their individual rides. "I'm keeping it."

"Your mother and father are dead, son," the red-nosed Priest explained in a thick, whiskey-soaked brogue. "Your thieving soul belongs to the church now."

Despite all the horrifying news, Alphonso refused to cry. His once exuberant and youthful face was now a fleshy mass of painful pink and red scars and excruciating pain accompanied his every facial gesture. Despite the unfairness dealt to his childhood and the smoldering hatred he held locked in his heart, the boy was finished with tears. He preferred to focus his attention on what mattered most to him; revenge.

Tankop plummeted to the ocean floor head first, his muscular body trailing helplessly behind the weighty turret. Seawater rushed into the headgear, short-circuiting sophisticated technology with a series of electric pops, sparks and sizzles. The villain was not optimistic about his chances. The gunpowder was drenched, rendering any remaining shells useless. If he did not manage to reach the turret release, he would drown at the bottom of the ocean.

The escape feature on the weapon had been designed with just such a scenario in mind. If he could manage to free an arm and locate the escape latch, he'd eject from the steel headgear and bob back to the surface like a muscle-bound cork. The release was located just inside the left shoulder plate and was easy enough to find on dry land. With the rapid descent, it was near impossible. Speed and water pressure had combined, pinning his arms to sides, leaving him only one slight chance. An air pocket had formed inside the turret. When he reached the bottom, he may have just enough time to free himself from his metal prison.

His parents had never been churchgoers. Save for holidays, they were seldom seen at the small, neighborhood parish in rural North Dakota. The first time the boy laid eyes on the old Priest with the wavy white hair and bulbous red nose was from the hospital bed.

"I don't want to belong to the church," Alphonso declared defiantly. "I want to see my mom and dad."

The Priest glared at the boy with tired, bloodshot eyes. The rebellious pup deserved the back of his hand but there were too many witnesses loitering in the hallway. "The only way you'll see your mother and father again," the Priest answered, "is if you follow them on the very same path to hell and damnation."

Alphonso Patricio Descarte, was the only child of an Italian immigrant and his seventeen-year-old American bride. The couple met in a New Jersey movie theatre and, halfway through a Bowery Boys film, "Spook Chasers," the couple had fallen helplessly in love. The dayworker and his date shared two fundamental passions in life; a love for bug-eyed comedian Huntz Hall and the promise of the American dream.

Alphonso was born after a rushed courtship and the new family soon moved to the northern Midwest, the parents believing the prairie state to be as full of promise as it was tornadoes and sub-zero temperatures. The parents found work quickly. Geneseo secured work as a civilian day laborer at the nearby air base. Bethany, the young bride, as plump as she was vivacious, became a popular waitress at the neighborhood Dairy Queen. There wasn't much money starting out, but somehow the two managed.

Young Alphonso grew up in a house that provided healthy Midwest portions of food and adoration. He was a studious child who spent as much time pouring over technical magazines as strengthening the muscles in a growing, slightly overweight body. At four, he had already lost the baby fat and was lifting weights fashioned from soup cans and wooden rulers. That, along with a high carb diet, favored among Dakotans, was responsible for his abnormal growth. By eight, he was spending the entirety of his frugal allowance on home electronic kits. At nine, he had surpassed these kits and his parents, with limited financial resources, were forced to become creative.

Geneseo and his exceptional son began visiting the Minot Municipal Dump on weekends, rummaging through the smelly heaps for abandoned televisions, discarded stereos, radios and broken appliances. Every mechanical device in their modest home was now working beyond expectations and the boy was desperately in need of new challenges. Word spread, the neighbors soon taking advantage of the nine-year-old whiz kid. He was a true marvel and Geneseo and Beth realized that the only limit to their son's talents was a lack of repairable junk.

It was not the best plan. The equipment, lying around deserted hangers and abandoned barracks, was serving no purpose that Geneseo could see. It had been scrapped by an Air Force rapidly outgrowing post war technology. If the desperate father had put more thought into the matter, he might have reconsidered. But the immigrant was at his wit's end and that, mixed with a lack of common sense, proved to be his undoing.

Geneseo's traitorous career turn began when he found a discarded hydrogen tank and welder's helmet in an abandoned locker and took both items home. The naïve immigrant believed that his rich and benevolent Uncle Sam would never miss the items and, in fact, might even consider their removal a favor. Unbeknownst to him, the United States Air Force maintained a strict inventory that accounted for every screw, empty hydrogen tank and discarded welder's helmet.

The father achieved infamy sometime between the disappearing mess tray and the theft of a non-functioning radar array. Geneseo was now on the command watch list, the full attention of the military police focused exclusively on the immigrant. He was a foreigner, and this made him the ideal candidate for treasonous espionage. The suspect was a communist, no doubt using the missing cafeteria tray and welder's helmet in an attempt to overthrow the United States government. The base was placed on top secret, high alert and waited patiently for the next act from the foreign saboteur.

"You'll live in an orphanage with other boys," the Priest explained, drawing deep from his unfiltered cigarette. "Other bastards just like you who pay for their parent's sins by serving the greater good of the church." And, if you're very good, I might even teach to box."

"I don't want to learn to box."

The boy's insolence was met with a stinging blow to his raw face.

"Here endeth the first lesson."

In the comfort and security of his own home, hidden away in the small garage, eleven-year-old Alphonso remained hard at work. He converted the small garage into his personal work space and was building a suit of iron like the one he read about in his favorite comic book. It was crude, and definitely in the early stages but, once completed, would be the envy of the entire neighborhood.

He took a short break to admire his handiwork. Satisfied, with his results, he continued to bang away at the metal, forging a heroic new identity and vowing to make the world a better place for everyone, especially his loving and overworked parents.

It's a rookie mistake and, even at eleven, he should have known better. One ill-timed bang was all it took. An errant spark set off residual gas in a nearby hydrogen tank, the resulting explosion blasting away the entire wall of the garage. He was surrounded by flames and Alphonso had no chance of escape, his flawless olive skin already blistering from the heat of the angry heat.

It was only through the decisive actions of the mother that the boy survived. She had seen her fair share of grease fires at the DQ and was respectful of both their power and destruction. She was kneading hamburger when she heard the explosion. Acting without a thought to her own safety, she threw open the kitchen door and braved the maelstrom. In one daring maternal swoop, she rescued her only child from certain death.

The husband was not informed of the son's injuries or his wife's bravery. He sat alone in a dark room surrounded by armed military police and a small group of civilians in dark suits and sunglasses. He had been placed under arrest without the right to even a phone call. He had surrendered without incident, believing this to be all one giant misunderstanding. Never in his wildest dreams did he imagine that his crime would result in never seeing his family again.

Alphonso lay in a hospital bed in critical condition, severe burns covering over 90 percent of his body. The frightened child was alone and in the process of being prepped for hours of painful surgery. He was fighting for his life, totally unaware of what the unforgiving world had in store.

He spent his first days in the hospital bed frightened and alone, wondering what happened to the mother that had saved him and the father who indulged his every whim. Layers of bandages covered a scarred face and hid a multitude of spilled tears. Days passed into weeks and a child's undying optimism slowly faded as he realized his parents were never coming through the door to rescue him.

In the following three months, Alphonso did not have a single visitor. There was a brief visit by the nervous family priest who was instructed by the authorities not to utter a word regarding the absence of the boy's parents. The young patient was well cared for by staff but there was an underlying level of disdain for the boy; the sins of the treacherous parents inherited by their offspring.

Alphonso eventually discovered his mother and father's fate on the front page of a discarded newspaper. A cruel pediatric nurse had left the daily on a nearby visitor's chair, the bold letters of the front-page headline large enough for the boy not to miss. The title, "Traitorous Immigrants Sentenced to Electric Chair," seared into his mind and proved just as powerful and damaging as the flames that had disfigured him for life. The rage over his parent's fate burned deep, branding him with a hatred that grew every day.

"I don't want to go," Alphonso shouted at the Priest. "You can't make me."

"No good will ever come from a disobedient orphan," the Priest declared. "Did I happen to mention that Saint Hillary's is the only orphanage in the United States to have their very own cannon?"

The comment stalled the rebellious boy.

"Hasn't worked in years," the Priest continued. "But it's there all the same. I like to think it's much like the precious virgin mother, standing watch over all of us."

The boy was fascinated. Firearms had become a special interest to him of late and he had never seen such a powerful weapon up close.

The other boys shunned him. He was a monster, forged in fire's own image. The only solace Alphonso found was in weightlifting and keeping track of a technology that was changing weekly. Sometimes he combined disciplines, reading the latest technical journal while bench-pressing three times his growing body weight. But always in the back of his mind, he seethed over the unjust execution of his parents and plotted revenge.

"You have no choice in the matter, son," the Priest explained as the two exited the hospital's main entrance and climbed into the awaiting taxi. "Your entire life will be repayment for your parent's sins. May God have mercy on their unrepentant souls."

"When do I get to see the cannon?" the boy asked.

The beep in the telephone earpiece was as jarring as the message that followed.

"Hello Mr. Levitt. According to our records, the outstanding balance of $3,301.88, including a late payment fee of $162.00, on your account with Orchard Bank has not been settled. Failure to settle the account within two days will result in legal proceedings to retrieve the debt. Thank you and have a wonderful day and thank you for calling Orchard Bank."

Barry hung up the phone and studied the anxious faces in the small room. He knew the phone call was a fool's errand. Attempting to increase his credit limit was like trying to win an argument with his mother; a complete waste of time

"So?" Beast asked.

"Anybody else need to make a call?" Barry answered.

Beast plopped onto the sofa. "I recognize the foul stench of bad credit anywhere," the big man growled.

"What?" Barry barked defensively. "I'm a little late. They'll get their money."

"How bad is it?" Face inquired. "Mickey Rooney or Mick Fleetwood, we have to tour again, bad?"

Barry shrugged. "I'm no worse off than any of you."

The statement was true. Each of the five had their own credit issues. Doc was neck deep in student loans and was attempting to pay them off by selling recycled bundles of newspapers to a roofing company. Over the last two years, Brain, an amateur audiophile, had financed a small fortune worth of stereo equipment and had no visible means for ever paying it back. Face, on a never-ending quest to hone his craft, had squandered

100

his small inheritance on a mail order mime course. Beast lost what little money he had, becoming a licensed breeder of Sea Monkeys. They were all penniless and the cost of fighting injustice was climbing.

"Maybe we should just table the credit card option," Barry said. "There's got to be another way to get to San Francisco."

From their expressions, he could tell that his friends had arrived at the same conclusion. It was desperate move to be sure, but all felt it worth the risk. It was time to crack open the bank of Barry's mother and see what loose change rattled out. It had been less than 48 hours since Barry had been evicted from the basement. A lot could have changed since then.

"The answer is no."

The response had required no time and the conclusion was not open for debate. Barry could hear the television blaring in the background. The cost to his self-esteem was high but his friends were counting on him.

"My car broke down and I'm stuck in Cannon Beach," Barry whined.

"You don't own a car," his mother fired back. "Your car was repossessed. And what are you doing in Cannon Beach?" The tone of her interrogation was hurting his head. "You promised to drive me to my doctor's appointment."

"I'm looking for a job."

"A job? At the beach?"

Barry had managed to get her attention. Now he had to attempt to keep it. "Yeah," he continued. "I applied for the position of..." He stalled, closed his eyes and concentrated. "Lifeguard."

"It's October."

"They hire early, and it pays to beat the rush. I think the first interview went extremely well." Barry took a deep breath. "Plenty of training involved."

"Do they offer benefits?"

"Health. No Dental or vision," the son explained. "But they do match up to three percent of your contribution to the 401k?"

This tidbit of information stalled his mother. Her interest had been piqued.

The others in the room were astounded at the ease by which the untruths flowed from the son's lips. Even Face, a trained professional, had to admit the performance was damn near flawless.

"How much do you need?"

"Six hundred dollars."

"Why in heaven's name do you need four hundred dollars?"

Already she had managed to negotiate the price down by a third. She was shrewd but there was a slight interest here and Barry intended to capitalize. "A swimsuit," he continued.

"Four hundred dollars for a swimsuit?"

"And I need one of those red plastic things the lifeguard's use when they run down the beach."

"It's called a rescue float," Brain whispered.

"It's called a rescue float and you have to supply your own. It's just like the one you see on that show you like," Barry continued.

"The Equalizer?" his mother answered.

"Baywatch." Barry corrected.

There was a pause as the force that was his mother processed the credit application. "I am so disappointed in you, Barry," she began. "What have you done with your life? Nothing." In most of these discussions she tended to answer her own questions. "Your Uncle Jim tried to get you a job at the Post Office. Too much walking you said. I called your cousin at the cable company. That was a great job. You said cable was the death knell of the entertainment industry. What are you waiting for? The heavens to open and drop a career and decent living into your lap? Your late father. God rest his soul, and I have always been very supportive. You're thirty years old, Barry. That's too old to be doing nothing. The answer is no."

It was amazing after such a tongue lashing that her voice could register affection. "Love you, dear," she said cheerily. "Oh, I almost forget. The police called. They want to talk to you."

"What did you tell them?" Barry asked, mouthing the word police to his colleagues.

"I'm your mother, Barry, what do you think I told them?"

"Love you too," he said, suddenly in a hurry. "Gotta go." Barry placed the receiver into the cradle and addressed his dispirited colleagues. "We haven't much time."

It took an additional three cups of coffee for the five minds to rally their collective concentration and solve one very significant problem.

"Car Title loan," Doc suggested.

The others were pleased with the resolution, collectively grinning over the genius of their problem-solving skills.

It was Face that put an abrupt end to the revelry, drawing the others back to the realm of reality. "Hold up," he said. "We left the car in McMinnville where it's now most likely Exhibit A."

Beast watched as all eyes settled on him. "Not the flying go-cart?" Beast protested.

"We'll need a vehicle title," Doc said.

Brain removed the motel stationary from a drawer and was gently tearing the motel logo off the letterhead. With the right pen, a bright light and candle wax he was sure he could fool any employee of such an establishment.

Tilly Peterson was on the final leg of her journey. One Triton mini sub, a Panamanian fishing trawler, and a cramped car trunk had all been utilized in transporting the prisoner to the secret destination. Blindfolded, she bounced around in the dark space with only a scratchy wool blanket to protect her head. She was tired, angry, and planned to let someone know how she felt as soon as she was released from the confines of sedan's luggage compartment.

The prisoner was unloaded onto a street filled with the noise and bustle of an overpopulated city. There was an overwhelming scent, a mixture of sweet-smelling garbage and spoiled seafood that was unique to one of the great American neighborhoods. When she was finally out in the open, the distinct foreign chatter confirmed her suspicion. Even blindfolded, Tilly Peterson could tell she was in San Francisco's Chinatown.

Days of confinement made her appreciate the warmth of the mid-afternoon sun on her face. Save for a bouncy ride in the trunk, she had been treated well but sensed somehow that was all about to change. Her captivity and transport had been an afterthought, a last-minute decision to accommodate a special request.

"So, this is the bird?" The speaker's nationality was evident in each slurred syllable.

The blindfold was removed, and Tilly found herself in a large, dark hall. Her eyes took their time to focus on the surroundings and when her vision cleared, she found herself staring directly into the blood-shot eyes of a very familiar redheaded Irish singer.

"Shamus O' Holligan," she stuttered. "From the Posers?"

"In the flesh, bird." The lead singer smiled, revealing a mouth devoid of teeth. He sat on top of a wooden stool, bending over to sip through a child's curly straw that had been inserted into his bottle of Jameson's.

A stale odor of spilled beer and cigarettes permeated the mid-sized concert hall, the type favored by musical careers either on their way up or down. Counting both the balcony and floor, Tilly guessed the capacity to be around a thousand.

A shaken Todd stood behind her. She had not laid eyes on him the entire trip and glanced over her shoulder, noticing that he was peering nervously into the darkness. He placed his hands on Tilly's shoulders and she shook herself clear.

"Easy," Todd whispered. "If you'd have kept your mouth shut and done what I asked, we wouldn't be here."

"Fuck you," Tilly blurted.

"I did. That was my first mistake."

The work lights clicked on and flooded the hall with a harsh glare. The abrupt change in ambiance nearly toppled the lead singer and he grabbed onto the microphone stand to steady himself. "Here comes the thunder," Shamus stammered as he fumbled with the bottle. "And it ain't all right."

The voice broadcast through the venue's speakers, resonating with a sinister lack of emotion. "I am so disappointed," it began.

Tilly shielded her eyes. "Who are you and what do you want?"

There was a noticeable change in Todd's demeanor. He fidgeted, shifting his weight from foot to foot. Again, his hands squeezed Tilly's shoulder blades. "For god's sake just shut up," he urged in a harsh whisper. "How was I to know it was yours?" I got almost all of it back." There was another uncomfortable pause. "I did what you wanted."

"He was selling it," Shamus countered. "Ripping you off and selling it as a drug."

Tilly drew a sharp breath. The tension on the dance floor was palpable.

"And the others?" the disembodied voice asked.

"What others?" Todd queried nervously.

"The five gentlemen from the air museum. The ones following you."

"Wait," Shamus added "You were followed?"

"They're nobodies," Todd countered, his level of panic rising. "I don't even think they own a car."

"You're a bloody arse," Shamus blurted. "That's what you are."

"And the tank?" the voice inquired.

"How the hell should I know?" Todd answered. "He was with them when I left."

"Rat bastard," Shamus screamed, hopping off the stool and lunging for Todd.

Tilly slipped aside, narrowly missing a collision between the two men. The attack caught her ex by surprise. Despite his drunkenness, the singer's grip was athletic and unforgiving. Todd gasped for air and clawed at his throat.

"Get him off," he gurgled.

Tilly stumbled backwards, watching as Todd's face turned a ghastly shade of gray. Todd, the abuser, had been reduced to a petrified child. He crumpled to the wooden floor, Shamus following his victim all the way. His death-grip never wavered until he was sure his victim had lost consciousness or was dead. Unfortunately for Todd, it was the latter.

Shamus wheezed, released his victim and staggered to his feet. The perpetual drunkenness had returned with the dispatching of Tilly's ex. "No bloody use to anyone, if you ask me," he muttered.

"Did you have to kill him?" Tilly protested. She had seen enough killing to last a lifetime.

"He's a thief and a liar," Shamus answered as he climbed back onto his wooden perch. The singer's bottle of Jameson's was not where he left it. He looked around, locating the spilled bottle under the stool.

"We're not done."

The comment caught the drunken singer off guard. Shamus peered up at the speakers.

"Your constant bungling has thrown off my timetable."

"Are you shitting me?" Shamus slurred. "It's only been two weeks."

"And the interlopers?"

"How was I to know they were important?"

"It's a little late to be asking."

"You can't kill me," Shamus stammered. "The band's playing the House of Blues on Sunday" When there was no reaction a sudden seriousness overtook him. "My mates are depending on me."

"They'll get over it. They may even thank me. You do have a habit of disappearing upon occasion."

"Yeah," Shamus argued. "But that's because I'm a drunk."

Tilly listened, searching for a way to escape. The nearest exit seemed an eternity away.

"You're an alcoholic lout who can't seem to follow the simplest of instructions."

"Well that ain't exactly nice, is it?"

The hairs rose off Tilly's arm and a slight tingling sensation danced over her exposed skin. She stepped back as the very air surrounding the singer grew thick with the sweet smell of ozone.

Shamus remained motionless as lethal snakes of electricity appeared out of nowhere and illuminated the singer's head in a halo of death. His bloodshot eyes darted around blackened sockets in panic over an uncertain fate. His unruly red hair stood on end as the sound of droning bees filled the hall.

"I don't want to die," Shamus whimpered.

"Nobody ever does," the voice cooed.

A horrified Tilly watched the singer's head swell. The skin on his face pulsated, the singer's face resembling a stretched balloon fluctuating between amounts of pressure.

"Please stop," Tilly pleaded, her back pressed against the far wall.

"May flights of angels sing thee to thy rest," the ominous voice eulogized.

The singer's neck billowed out like a bullfrog. This time the pressure proved too much, Shamus's head exploding with a sharp crack. Brain matter, bone and blood burst out of the exposed cavity as the decapitated torso plummeted off the stool and landed on its own bloody insides.

"How rude of me," the voice offered, the scent of ozone fading from the crime scene. "Welcome to San Francisco, Tilly Peterson."

Tilly ran. She left behind two dead bodies, victims of the omniscient voice. She did not intend to be the third.

The front doors to the nightclub remained unlocked and Tilly threw them open with a bang, fleeing into the late morning bustle. She never once looked back and did not stop to catch her breath until she arrived at San Francisco Bay and the historic Ferry building.

Barry had lost track of his immediate surroundings and circumstances. Unconscious, he was in a semi-dream state and it was here, in the deep recesses of his mind's eye, that he first witnessed the arrival of the mysterious stranger. The dream guide was an imposing figure, over six feet with a well-cut, he-man, physique. He appeared to be the same age as Barry but that's where any similarity ended. From the top of his jet-black buzz-cut to the heel of his leather jackboots, the male was the perfect human specimen. A slight smile on the handsome, tanned face noted a familiarity that was not lost on the dreamer.

"What do you want?" Barry mumbled.

The man's only response was an unsettling bodily vibration that seemed to be an intense but slight tremor. The stranger turned, striding confidently back into the void. Barry hurried to catch up, but it was useless. The faster he moved, the further away the stranger appeared.

"Hold up," Barry mumbled. "I think you need to tell me something."

The fare for a single passenger was 69 dollars, the trip from Eugene to San Francisco scheduled to take just over 24 hours. There was a two-hour stop for dinner in the Rogue River Valley, travelers enjoying a romp in a hot spring before sitting down to a vegetarian banquet prepared by their extremely likable, unhygienic driver. The bus was chronically behind schedule; a setback expected by anyone who chose The Green Tortoise as their mode of transportation.

A bright sun rose above the eastern mountains, bathing the high desert in the soft pink of a new day. The bus had just completed the arduous climb up the Siskiyou Mountains and was barreling down Interstate 5, maneuvering through a curvy descent that emptied into the State of California.

Face squatted on what he was sure was a louse-ridden futon, complaining to anyone who'd listen about the travel accommodations. Brain and Doc sat nearby on a pair of wooden benches that faced each other. The two men were engaged in a hushed discussion. Barry, in the throes of a fitful sleep, was next to Doc, his head resting against the window.

The unmistakable aroma of smoldering marijuana overpowered the entire vehicle and not a single passenger seemed to mind. Those not indulging in the type C felony were asleep, the diverse collection of snores originating from the many bunks, futons and seats scattered throughout the bus. This distinct 1960's ambiance came free with every ticket on the G.T.

Beast concluded a one-sided conversation with the bus driver and made his way through the narrow aisle. Those nearby and awake had been treated to a three-hour lecture on such diverse topics as the Illuminati, the Queen of England and a gentleman by the name of Lyndon LaRouche. "Follow the money," Beast lectured. "The Rothschilds, Rockefellers and Osmond Family Singers are all in on this together."

The driver, grateful for the pause in his education, leaned over the steering wheel and peered through the bug-splattered windshield. "Put the weed away," he called out. "Next stop's the California Fruit Inspection Station."

Believing his entire body infested with lice, Face climbed off the futon and joined Doc and Brain. His attempt at any kind of rest had been unsuccessful. "Who's in charge of the delouser for this expedition?" he said, furiously scratching under his left armpit. "I'm being eaten alive."

"I can't," Barry mumbled, his eyes fluttering beneath the lids. "I don't know what the hell I'm doing." He startled

110

himself awake, his eyes focusing on his four closest friends staring back at him. "Having fun?" he said.

"You really think we can find her?" Face asked with his usual pessimism. "San Francisco's a big city."

"Not so big," Brain corrected. "Bay to breakers is less than seven miles."

"But you don't know where she is," the actor protested. "Just a small detail."

Doc cleared his throat of accumulated tobacco. "Maybe it's just a matter of letting them find us," he said.

"That doesn't sound dangerous," Face grumbled.

"Was I talking in my sleep?" Barry asked.

Face nodded, deciding to change tactics on his war with the imaginary lice. He ran his hands through his blonde hair furiously, checking his palms quickly for hitchhiking parasites.

"Relax," Doc said. "There's not been nearly enough time for an infestation of your pubis follicles."

"Gee, when you put it that way" Face muttered. "I feel much better."

"I was dreaming of a man," Barry said. "A stranger. I think he was trying to tell me something." Face ignored him. Only Brain and Doc showed any interest in the mention of a dream stranger

"A man?" Brain commented, shifting in his seat.

"I can't explain it," Barry admitted. "It almost felt like I was supposed to know him."

Beast returned, slapping the ever-annoyed Face on the back. "Sweet ride, don't you think?"

"First class all the way," Face moaned, struck by the sudden urge to scratch his groin. "The smell of pot mixes ever so subtly with all the unwashed body odor."

"Why me?" Barry asked himself. "What would he want with me?" Barry's inner dialogue had spilled out into the conversation.

Doc and Brain turned away. Both knew they could not keep the secret much longer.

As the bus readied its final approach to the inspection station, the groggy passengers peered out their individual windows. A sooty black smoke scarred the blue mountain sky. The long line of vehicles had been abandoned, panicking motorists fleeing on foot across the harsh landscape. The fruit inspection station was under attack.

A lone Highway Patrolman, gun drawn, fired indiscriminate shots at the station. Mirrored sunglasses, too big for his face, highlighted the young and determined face. With each blast of the automatic, the officer signaled he was not about to surrender the station to the unseen enemy.

The flames, desperate screams, and collective panic all signaled an escalating chaos, the perpetrators hidden from all of the gawking passengers.

"Holy shit!" the bus driver shrieked as he slammed on the brakes.

The bus reacted to the driver's impetuous decision with a shuttering lurch. Dozing passengers tumbled into the aisle and fell onto those asleep on the floor.

Barry clutched the back of the bench as the bus careened into a screeching, teetering sideways slide. "Hold on!" he shouted.

The bus toppled on its side and slid with a screech of grinding metal. The screams of terrified passengers were muted in the ensuing chaos.

"Women and children first," Doc shouted as the bus came to a stop.

Beast was up in a flash. The big man utilized the seat backs, swinging over the prone bodies toward the emergency door at the back of the bus. Brain and Doc had kicked open their window and Face was hard at work behind them, forcing his window open with pounding fists.

It had taken fifteen seconds to open the three emergency exits and an additional four minutes to get everyone out. Barry stood on the top of the upturned bus and assisted the last of the stunned passengers out of the wreckage. In one instinctive move, he hoisted a shocked teen out and over to the edge where Beast waited to lower her to the pavement.

"Well done," Beast said. The big man was clearly delighted by Barry's return to a heroic state of mind.

"I know," Barry answered as he jumped off the side of the bus. "This is so not me."

They had been lucky. Everyone was out. There were no fatalities and only a few cases of various sprains, cuts or bruises. The five gathered near the bus wreckage, gesturing for the remaining passengers to hobble off toward the other escaping drivers and passengers.

"Anybody see anything?" Barry asked.

Preferring to get his information first hand, Beast sprinted off toward the Highway Patrolman.

"We're about to find out," Face answered, pointing at the rampaging Beast.

Barry's sense of personal preservation was receding once again. The events of the past two days had awoken something deep inside; an unexplainable need to protect his friends and an unsuspecting general public.

"Brain and Doc, stay here," Barry blurted. "Face, with me."

The chemist and his friend watched in bewilderment as Barry and the reluctant actor sprinted toward the burning building. Doc lit a cigarette.

Brain responded to the habit with a bemused smirk. "Really?" he asked.

Doc shrugged. "Calms the nerves," he answered.

"What do you make of our friend's unexplainable change in behavior?" Brain asked.

Doc shrugged. "Must have something to do with the letter," the chemist answered, inhaling the smoke deep into his lungs. "I think he knows."

Doc removed the folded paper from his back pocket and read the message again. The two had examined the correspondence over a hundred times and still puzzled over the exact meaning.

"Son,

Do right. Love, Dad."

The message was typed in a simple Courier font. A small handwritten message in neat cursive was below.

"To his Friends,
Forces are at work that will change his life forever. Keep him safe."

"He's not the same," Doc observed, returning the cryptic message to his back pocket. "We show him this, he'll crack up for sure."

"Perhaps," Brain added thoughtfully. "But for now, we continue to follow the instructions."

"Keeping him safe is proving more and more difficult," Doc said, glancing in the direction where he had last seen Barry and Face.

"So, it would seem."

"We could always lend a hand," Doc suggested.

"We're men of science," Brain chastised. "Our job is to observe and document. To provide unbiased direction and feedback."

"Then why do you carry that sword cane?" Doc asked slyly. "For observing and documenting?"

Brain's long pale face turned red under his friend's interrogation. "Better to have it and not need it than to need it and not have it."

"Flawless logic."

"Thank you."

"I was being sarcastic."

Beast loped onto the scene and his unexpected arrival had changed nothing in the patrolman's behavior. The officer lowered his weapon, determining at the very last second that despite any similarity, the visitor was not the enemy. He peered over his sunglasses. "Sorry," the patrolman offered, his voice hoarse from the escalating chaos. "I thought you were one of them."

"One of what?" Beast asked as he doubled over to catch his breath.

The patrolman pointed his automatic at the far side of the building. It was a distinctly different view from that of the smoldering bus. "There," he answered. "They're everywhere!"

As of the last fiscal year, removal of seized fruit from the California Inspection Station had been cutback to once a week. This cost-cutting measure resulted in a lingering infestation of fruit flies and a distinct smell of decomposing sucrose that carried all the way to the snow-capped Siskiyou mountains. The confiscated contraband was stored in metal bins and located in back of the building, secured by a series of sophisticated locks. While such precautions were adequate in warding off curious bears and gypsy moths, they were no match for the distinct and nauseating smell. Removing the fruit once a week was simply not enough, the current attack on the California Fruit Inspection Station a direct result of the bureaucratic oversight.

"Bigfeet," Beast shouted, capturing his first look at the rampaging giants.

The mythical creatures had stepped directly out of the scientifically questionable Roger Patterson film and into the reality of the burning outpost. The humanoids were well over 12 feet tall and covered head to toe in a mangy brown fur. The beast's long faces resembled that of the Orangutan, the distant simian cousins sharing the same deep-set eyes and expressive, oversized mouths. Four of the creatures had gathered at the farthest side of the building and were concentrating their entire effort on attempting to open the locked bins. Beast watched in delighted amazement as the giant mammals attacked and withdrew, puzzling over the best way to get to the fruity treasure inside.

"Hmm," Brain muttered. "Our enthusiastic colleague has just referenced a creature unique to North American mythology."

Brain and Doc monitored the chaotic proceedings from the relative safety of the wrecked bus. Despite the excited calls by their friend, they had yet to see anything out of the ordinary.

"Drugs?" Doc commented, referring to Beast's unexpected reference.

"Perhaps," Brain countered, massaging his prominent chin with lean fingers. "One could also attribute the illusion to the high desert sun mixed with the lack of a suitable hat. I remain unconvinced."

Face and Barry came to a halt near the front entrance of the station. The intense heat kept everyone at a safe distance. Barry took a step toward the flames, raising an arm to shield his face. The heat was intense, and he knew instantly there was no way they were getting any closer.

"What's the next move?" Face said, gripping his friend by the shoulder. "We wait for the fire department, right?"

"I've got to find a way inside" Waiting had not occurred to Barry. His new and unexplainable instincts overshadowed any sense of self-preservation. He was more surprised by these startling new impulses than his friends.

"No way in," Barry answered. "Let's try another way."

The two doubled back, detouring around the far side of the building. Whoever remained trapped inside, had little time. Barry's new awareness reminded him of this with every step. Lives were at stake. And, as much as he wanted someone else to deal with the catastrophe, it was up to him.

Fire had consumed a third of the building. One unobstructed window remained on the northwestern side. Barry took the lead, the two men racing to the only possible way inside.

"Stand back," Barry ordered, his elbow meeting the window, the glass shattering on impact. "Anyone here?"

The two friends paused for a moment, Face turning from the window and studying his friend. "I'll go," the actor said finally.

"What?" Barry blurted. "You?"

"That's rude." Face exclaimed. "Give me one good reason why I can't."

Barry grimaced. "Look, I can't explain it," he answered. "It's just something I have to do."

Face considered the last statement, weighing the argument carefully. "You may be right," he insisted. "Grab that crate over there. You can use it to climb inside."

Barry moved away from the window, hurrying towards the empty container.

Face cleared the remaining shards of glass with the aid of his balled-up jacket. "If anyone asks, I'm doing this strictly for the reward," he said. "I'm thinking of getting veneers."

Barry turned back to the window in time to see Face leap up and slide through. "Wait!"

"I'll be back," the actor called out from inside the smoky room. "I got this."

"No messing around in there," Barry ordered. "Two minutes and I'm coming in after you."

"I'll never get this smell out of my clothes," Face complained, his voice trailing off into the crackle of smoke and heat.

A roar of frustration accompanied the crash of hard metal. Barry spun, watching as a hairy giant bounded onto the storage bin. He watched in awe as oversized, hairy fists pummeled the metal lid in frenzied frustration.

He was down to his last bullet, the highway patrolman wasting his entire allotment of ammunition firing at the wind, the sky and burning building. He took a deep breath and aimed his Smith & Wesson 4006 TSW at the tormented American Yeti pounding helplessly against the southern wall. Having wasted all his bullets on warning shots, the officer dropped into a stance suitable for dropping a rampaging Bigfoot and steadied his aim. He drew a deep breath and held it, his finger curling around the trigger. There was no way he could miss. Not from this distance. He would send that hairy son of bitch straight to hell.

"No!" Beast's fist struck the patrolman's forearm. The gun barrel dropped, the weapon discharging with a sharp crack into the pavement.

The enraged patrolman pivoted to the interloper. Beast was ready, his burly fist meeting the officer's chin. The cop's entire body crumpled on impact and Beast planted a heavy boot into his chest, pinning him to the concrete.

"My hand slipped," Beast offered sheepishly. "Sorry."

"Anyone here?" Face called out. He was making his way from bureaucratic room to room, into the very heart of the flames. "I'm here to rescue you."

The air was thick with smoke and the actor's eyes burned. Each empty room brought with it another wave of oxygen depraved annoyance. He was having second thoughts about the whole hero thing as it became more and more obvious that everyone had made it out of the inferno alive. Lungs, legs and his failing resolve couldn't hold out much longer and he was clearly past the two-minute limit set by Barry. One more room, he convinced himself. A quick check in and I'll get the hell out of here.

Face threw open the final door and a blast of scorching heat seared his entire body. The source of the blistering hellfire was close. Through the smoke, an ominous orange radiated through the walls.

"Anyone..."

It was an obvious cry for help that originated from somewhere just beyond the dense smoke. The ensuing whimper was an infant or a toddler, an unlucky offspring suckered into take your child to work day. Face acted uncharacteristically decisive, dashing further into the smoke toward the source of the helpless cry.

It leapt onto him from a file cabinet, wrapping grateful arms around his neck. Face staggered, his own hands reaching to pull the desperate appendages from his windpipe. Soft, downy Cashmere was the first thought coming to his asphyxiated mind. This panicked kid came from money. Maybe he was right all along and there was a reward.

"It's alright," Face sputtered. "You'll be okay."

The arms relaxed at the sound of the classically trained voice. Face positioned the cashmere-covered arms over his shoulders. "Let's get you out of here," he said. "And you be sure and tell your Mommy and Daddy that it was me who rescued you."

"Jaws of Life!" Barry shouted. He reached the side of the building and spotted Brain and Doc observing the escalating pandemonium with a detached interest.

Spurred on by the sudden authority in Barry's voice, Doc flicked away his cigarette and joined Brain in a dash to the black and white patrol vehicle.

Brain glanced over his shoulder and noticed that Barry was no longer there. "Interesting choice of weapons," Brain managed between gasps.

Doc was at the driver's side of the cruiser. He reached in to pop the trunk, Brain meeting him at the back of the vehicle.

"What the hell do you think you're doing?"

Doc turned, facing off with the crazed highway patrolman. Out of bullets, the frantic officer had decided the best course of action was to get to the patrol car and call for backup. "This is an official vehicle of the California Highway Patrol," he warned. "And you two are breaking and entering"

"Not looking for a weapon," Doc explained. "Jaws of Life."

Doc backed out of the trunk and into the patrolman. As the two collided, a gleaming steel blade came into view and pressed against the officer's throat. Doc stepped away, pulling the bulky life-saving apparatus out of the trunk.

119

"Your hippy friends won't get away with this," the patrolman promised, his wide eyes focusing on the steel biting into his flesh.

Doc hoisted the contraption onto his shoulder. "Never piss off men of science," he warned. "We're the underpaid, unappreciated saviors of the world."

"You may leave," Brain added.

The patrolman turned and sprinted off toward the upturned bus.

"You realize, of course, that's assaulting an officer," Doc observed. "We could pay for that remark."

"I found his behavior churlish," Brain explained.

"You make sure to explain it that way to the judge."

Brain sheathed the sword cane, the two transporting the life-saving device to Barry's last known location.

A powerless Beast watched the hairy Sasquatch pound the wall of a building consumed by flames. The creature's helpless call was part howl, part screech, and all panic. The giant seemed desperate to get inside. Deep set eyes pleaded to Beast for help, comfort or both. Another wail accompanied the despondent look and Beast knew he had to act. He wasn't sure how he could help but was not about to let this fellow humanoid suffer. He howled. It was a mournful bellow that rivaled that of the legendary missing link. Both beasts pounded against the wall in frustration.

"A little help, please." The familiar voice came from the side of the building and Beast recognized it immediately.

"Face!"

Beast arrived to find Face leaning out the broken window. The young Bigfoot whimpered, its long furry arms draped around the actor's shoulders. The oblong face was buried into the actor's chest.

The adult Bigfoot rushed to her offspring and, with one swing of a massive arm, knocked Beast on his ass.

The young mammal released Face's neck, using the actor's back as a launching pad. The actor staggered back into the wall as one hundred and ninety-five pounds of infant Bigfoot launched itself, landing gracefully into the mother's arms.

Beast climbed to his feet and assisted Face out the window. "Nice!"

"Kid's got quite a grip," the actor mumbled, dizzy from the effects of both smoke and effort.

Both men turn in time to catch the metal fruit bin crash to the ground. Three of the Bigfoot clan stood on top of the metal bin, stomping in a crazed frustration. Despite the ferocity of their attack, the treasure remained locked inside and out of reach.

Doc and Brain, lugging the jaws-of-life, rounded the corner and entered the turmoil. Realizing it was never a good idea to get between a Bigfoot and a fruit dumpster, the two halted. The scientists powered the hydraulics while handing the end of the contraption to Barry.

"What's the plan?" Brain asked.

"Let's give them what they came for," Barry said.

A hiss of compressed air followed a loud clacking as the jaws powered up. The pinchers met grinding metal and the timid giants scattered. Frustrated yelps surrounded him as Barry pinched the final lock. With one pull of the trigger, the lock shattered, the lid flipped open and a week's worth of rotten fruit spilled onto the pavement. The humans backed away as the entire clan of the creatures rushed in and surrounded the sweet bounty.

Face and Beast joined the others, all watching as the giant beings gathered up the moldy fruit. Within minutes each creature had more than enough to carry back to their alpine lairs. The majestic animals then turned their attention northward, loping back over the dry valley landscape on the return trip to the mountains.

"Weekly World News was right," Beast proclaimed. The big man was clearly in awe.

"Goodbye, little guy," Face muttered, the resulting tear already halfway down the actor's cheek.

"You're blowing my mind, Face," Beast proclaimed, slapping his friend hard on the back.

"Stop that," the actor grumbled, returning the violent sign of affection with a wary smile. "Besides, how could I ever refuse one of your relatives?"

Sirens wailed in the distance, drawing the curtain on one adventure and heralding the next.

The occupants of the Redding CHP drunk-tank had been transferred to make room for the domestic terrorists. Law enforcement, from Yreka to Corning, had been appraised of the situation and remained on the highest alert. The appropriate Federal Agencies had been notified of the threat and were monitoring events in Northern California closely. The highest priority was getting these violent anarchists before a judge, sentenced, and transported to the nearest federal penitentiary before they could do further harm.

"Guarding these butt-wipes is the biggest thing to happen to our troop since Scoutmaster Scott was arrested in the Better Buy Parking lot for indecent exposure."

It was an era of belt tightening, and everyone with the remotest of ties to law enforcement had been asked to pull their weight. This included the Boy Scouts of America, local troop 32. The two seventeen-year old Explorer Scouts, currently guarding the prisoners, performed their assignment zealously, peering through the small drunk tank window while hurling colorful obscenities at the five captives.

"They don't look so tough," Matt, the heavier of the two scouts, observed. He swept the greasy black hair out of his eyes and shoved his colleague away from the door.

"What are they doing now?" Jim, the pimple-faced, skinnier teen asked as he regained his balance. "They say the Fruit Inspection Station was only the first target and that all the rest areas along Interstate 5 are at risk."

"Ass-clowns," Matt growled. "Hitting us where it hurts the most; the shitter." The observation was followed by a hearty guffaw that morphed into a resonating belch. "Someone should teach these terrorists a lesson."

"We'd keep them handcuffed, right?"

"Yeah," Matt assured the colleague. "We'll go strictly by the book."

"I say we run for it."

It was better to say nothing. Commenting on any of Beast's ill-advised plans only seemed to complicate matters. Face shook his head in defeat. "The door's locked, and we're handcuffed to a rail."

The five men sat on a hard, wooden bench. The handcuffs and chain connected them by the wrists and wrapped around the metal bar, securing the prisoners and keeping them from moving more than a couple of feet in any direction.

"You're such a downer," Beast said, rattling his length of chain for emphasis.

Barry overheard bits of a hushed conversation between Doc and Brain. He understood little but knew the men well enough to be uncomfortable with the plotting. "We're not escaping," Barry declared. "Are we?"

"If we have enough chain, it may just work," Brain muttered.

"That's a lot of amps," Doc answered. The portly chemist was staring up at the lone light bulb in the center of the ceiling.

"I say we do it," Beast said, leaning as close as he could manage. The big man had no idea of what his colleagues were planning but that never stopped him before.

"You stay out of this," Face said. "You'll only get us shot in the back."

"You're a glass half full kind of guy, Face." Beast growled, shaking his head with displeasure. "Every dark cloud has a silver lining."

"Also deafening thunder, electrifying lightning and a drenching rain shower," Face concluded.

"Hold up." Matt said, his face pressed against the thick pane of safety glass, his hands framing his oversized head. "They're talking about you."

"I don't," Jim stammered. "Wait. What?"

"I read lips. Self-taught. If they get free, they're going to do something terrible to you."

"Me?" Jim stammered. "What did I do?"

"Do terrorists need a reason to do anything?"

Jim attempted to push his colleague away, but Matt's girth proved too much. "Let them try," Jim blustered. "I'll kick their ass!"

Matt had played his impetuous friend perfectly. The provoked Jim would now do something completely stupid and Matt was right where he wanted to be. The heavy scout reached down and felt the sleek, smooth comfort of his club. With any luck, he may get a chance to use it.

The five men had spread themselves across the bench. The ugly, hairiest, of the five prisoners was standing, reaching up with his free arm toward the overhead light. The lanky curly haired prisoner, closest to the small window, was grinning at the Explorer Scouts and waving his free hand.

"What are they doing?" Jim asked, eager for his turn at the small window.

"He's flipping you off," Matt answered. "He wants to make you his bitch."

"Bitch?" Jim protested. "Why? I don't even know this guy."

The light flickered inside the drunk-tank.

"What was that?"

"They broke the light!"

"I'm nobody's bitch." Jim managed, shoving his friend away from the door. He inserted his key into the lock. "Get out of my way!"

"Shouldn't we call someone?" Matt asked innocently.

"Move away from the door!" Jim ordered, turning the key and gripping the door handle.

"Now," Doc shouted as Beast inserted his finger into the broken light socket.

The door swung open as 120 volts raced through the five men. Barry, closest to the door, completed the chain by latching onto the Explorer and displacing the charge through the teen's thin frame.

"Ah-ah-ah-ah-ah-ah," Jim stammered.

The jolt slammed Jim's quaking body into Matt. Taking the full brunt of the charge, the two quaking scouts collapsed onto the floor.

Beast was thrown clear of the socket and dropped hard onto the bench.

Barry and Face dragged both Explorers inside the tank.

"Please don't rape us," Jim wailed.

"Now you know why I never joined the Boy Scouts," Face explained.

Beast's smoldering hair gave off the rancid odor of overcooked keratin. Dazed, the big man slid up beside the chagrinned Face.

"You need a comb," Face commented.

Barry kept his arm around the thin Explorer's neck, applying enough pressure for the teen to fear for his life. He whispered in his ear. "We'll need to borrow your keys."

Jim made a trembling gesture to his right front pocket. Barry confiscated the keys and unlocked his handcuffs, passing them to the next in line.

"He said you flipped me off," Jim confessed, his voice trembling. "He said you wanted to make me your bitch."

"I'd say your friend just earned a merit badge for being an asshole," Barry said. He turned to the bigger of the two. "Tell your friend you're sorry or I kill him."

Matt whimpered. "I'm sorry," he stammered.

"I'm kidding," Barry explained. "I would never kill anyone. But now you've seen first-hand how words can hurt."

"What now?" Face asked. "A whole building of cops will be here any minute."

The explosion rocked the foundation of the building. Anxious shouts of the duty officers called out from the smoky darkness. Panicked footfalls raced to the source of the chaos.

"Now look what you did," Face said.

"Me?" Beast countered. "What did I do?"

The five removed the cuffs and chains and lay face down on the tile floor.

"What the hell was that?" Matt wailed from his prone position. The scout's pudgy hands were clamped tightly over his ears.

"155?" Doc muttered to Brain.

"Affirmative," Brain answered, his keen eyes peering through the dusty lenses of his glasses.

"Tanktop!" The two men said in unison.

The human artillery had defied the odds again, surviving the ocean plummet and resuming the chase in an entirely different state. To this cold-blooded, steel-plated predator, the hunt was as important as the kill.

"How does he keep finding us?" Barry asked to no one in particular.

"Persistence and a very detailed Thomas Guide," Face quipped.

"We going to lie around all day or do something?" Beast roared. "No prisoners!" The rampaging Beast roused the remaining four to their feet, following the big man's charge out of the room.

"Hello?" Face called out. "A plan would be nice."

Tanktop had survived. For a second time in thirty-six hours he had defied the odds. As his body plummeted to the ocean floor, he had managed to activate the escape latch. Free of the anchoring headgear, his steroid-enhanced body bobbed effortlessly back to the ocean's surface. Despite an angry surf, he found his way to shore. The beach was deserted, and he waited through the stormy weather until darkness obscured the stormy coastline.

Night eventually fell and Tanktop hiked the 22 miles to an abandoned aquarium in the neighboring town of Seaside. The dilapidated building was the perfect villain's hideout. Here, amongst an aroma of dead fish, salt-water taffy and human vomit, the villain stored the extra suit of clothes along with an emergency turret and shells.

No one could ever understand the personal sacrifices he had made to ensure his technology was maintained and he intended to keep it that way. It was what made him unique amongst a crowded field of assassins.

There was one small issue. His employer had issued a change in plans. The cryptic voice message was replayed as he placed the replacement turret over his head and activated the heavy helmet's built-in voicemail. The directive concerned the same five puny humans who had bested him on the jagged rock. He listened stoically, a rage of hate swelling up from deep inside.

The metal villain had been humiliated. The urge for revenge on these five amateurs consumed him. The cold-blooded, half machine found himself reverting back to the maligned little boy who had been teased, bullied and beaten at the midwestern orphanage. This new enemy had aroused a fury that demanded payment with nothing short of their lives. His employer knew nothing of either his history or this childhood rage. And, rightfully so. He was killer for hire and paid to do a job. For now, he'd do as he was ordered. But, he vowed, the five would pay. And if anyone dared interfere, employer or not, they'd experience his unique brand of vengeance.

For the patrolmen on duty, things had suddenly gone bat-shit crazy. The already memorable events of the day had taken yet another unexpected, hair-pin turn. A suspect, with a cannon for a head, was blasting his way through the front doors and blowing their beloved station to smithereens. In the history of law enforcement, there was no precedent.

The officers concentrated their small arms fire at the intruder's torso. Several officers couldn't resist firing a round or two at the steel-plated head only to hear the pleasing but worthless ricocheting ping resulting from their folly. Shots to the body, however, proved just as useless. The fashionable tailored Italian silk suit appeared to be made of Kevlar.

Even the occasional shotgun blast didn't slow the villain, the human tank only taking a slight faltering back-step. He was a human blitzkrieg, advancing while bombarding the front desk, the office and vending machines in the small but popular break room.

Barry, Beast, Doc and Brain hunkered behind a series of overturned evidence lockers and waited for the fight to come to them. Overhead sprinklers drenched them with lukewarm water while a thick, black smoke billowed in from a nearby hallway. The noise from the one-sided battle escalated, and they would not have a long wait.

"No way out the back," Face announced, crouching down and joining them.

"I'm open to suggestions?" Doc said.

"My walking stick," The preoccupied Brain muttered. The lean man crouched over a pile of evidence boxes and rummaged through them furiously. "This catalogue system is appalling." He located his weapon next to a several stacks of crisp thousand-dollar bills and a pound of cocaine. Ignoring the money and drugs, he grabbed the cane and unsheathed it. "I'm good."

Barry grew more panicked with each explosion. He now felt the weight and responsibility of everyone in the building and was no longer able to cope. Who was he fooling? He was no leader, self-appointed or otherwise. One second, he's in control, the next his confidence is replaced by a paralyzing self-doubt that bordered on dread. His earlier heroic interventions were nothing more than psychological anomalies, explained away by an ongoing psychological disorder.

His friends stared at him as if their survival depended on it. There was no mistaking this need. Barry's face was flushed and no matter how deep a breath he took, no oxygen made it to his lungs. He did manage to swallow, and it felt like a large, dry rock had been jammed midway down his throat. "Okay," he started but nothing followed. His ears were ringing, and his heart raced. Each beat of the organ was a resounding thump that reverberated throughout his entire body.

"Are you feeling alright?" Doc asked.

"He's cool," Beast fired back. "He's just thinking. Right, Barry?"

Barry watched his friend's lips move but had not heard a word. Chaos, smoke and fire surrounded them, and he could no longer summon the will to speak. The war in his own mind was far more paralyzing than the battle rapidly approaching. He felt a curtain dramatically coming down on his old, once comfortable life and things would never return to the way they were.

"Talk to us." Face coaxed.

"Fix him," Beast pleaded.

"I got nothing," Doc answered, turning to Brain. "What do you think?"

Their friend had checked out. The explosions and helpless screams were now only faint echoes, muted in his mind. The paralysis had taken control, and he'd never come back. The vortex of fear was collapsing onto itself, shutting him off from them forever.

The far wall crumbled, plaster, wood, and metal dropping from above. Beast threw a protective arm over Barry's head to deflect the debris, his friend's failing to recognize the danger or the heroic gesture.

Tanktop stepped through the rubble. Hidden hydraulics hissed as the giant weapon rotated, his turret surveying the smoldering carnage. The five were hiding somewhere close and he knew it. One more shell would make short work of them all. Recent orders be damned, Tanktop was going in for the kill.

Barry sensed the villain was searching for him alone. His tunnel vision had transformed into a dizzying kaleidoscope of terror. In this chaos, the man with the crew-cut had returned to his mind's eye. The stranger stood in the distance, oozing the self-same confidence and exhibiting his signature and assuring half smile. He was clearer than in his last manifestation and his unexpected arrival was strangely reassuring.

"I don't know what you want me to do," Barry moaned.

"The Sea Questor," the stranger answered calmly. "Get to the ship."

The battle cry caught everyone off guard. It was youthful, exuberant and had not come from any his friends.

"Whoa," Beast bellowed. The big man was clearly impressed. "Check it out!"

Barry was startled back to consciousness by the impetuous actions of the two Explorer Scouts. It was almost surreal, the two teens racing past the five gawking onlookers on a collision course with the 500-pound steel-plated giant. Leading the charge, the much-maligned Jim.

It was not the enemy Tanktop expected, but he was ready just the same. With an audible clank, another shell dropped into the chamber.

"I'm nobody's bitch," Jim shrieked.

The barrel extended in the teen's direction, the unseen sights and gyros locking onto the oncoming target.

The crippling fear left him as quickly as it arrived. The man vanished from Barry's consciousness and before he knew it, he was up and sprinting after the two Explorers.

This sudden act of bravery caught three of the remaining four off guard. Not Beast. The rampaging man-child was on his feet and dashing after his friend.

Barry launched himself off the floor, striking the heavier of the two explorers. Beast followed Barry's lead and all four hit the floor as the retort of the cannon barrel rocked the hallway. The shell whistled overhead and exploded into the far wall. Structural load was at critical mass and the ceiling gave way with a resounding crash, a deluge of concrete and plaster dropping on top of Barry, Beast and the two teens.

An unexpected rage overtook Face. He was up and sprinting atop the rubble that had buried his friends. The actor hurled himself into the air, his arms extending out toward Tanktop's legs. It was a clean tackle. The villain was unprepared and stumbled, falling backward through the entrance he had just created.

The rest of the survivors were up now and supporting Face. Two brothers had fallen. They were not about to give up another. They swarmed the metal giant, each doing their part to keep the enemy off his feet. Doc, the heaviest, lay across the villain's massive chest. Face was sprawled across legs the size of small tree trunks. Brain, taking a clue from the children of the corn, rammed plaster, cement and rubble into the cannon barrel. All knew full well that they could not afford to let the human tank fire off another round.

Three black helicopters hovered over the rubble, mechanical vultures approaching a smoldering carcass. As they lowered to the charred earth, Commandos, armed with lethal Sig Sauger 551s leapt from the craft and secured the perimeter. The forces were split, the second half of the team charging the remains of the station to apprehend the high-tech villain. It had required no law enforcement skill to determine the five suspects were, in fact, the true heroes of the day. Shell-shocked witnesses were plentiful. Stumbling amongst the ruins, officers and civilians all testified to the heroism of the three surviving prisoners. Four of their number had died, making the ultimate sacrifice and giving up their lives to save every other person in the station.

Brain, Doc, and Face wandered aimlessly through the adjoining parking lot. Their closest friends were missing, presumed dead, and a resulting sadness had given way to despair. The interviews with the Feds turned out to be nothing more than quick tailgate debriefs, the shell-shocked survivors relating what little they knew. It soon became painfully obvious that the three remaining heroes were nothing more than lucky amateurs in way over their heads.

The survivors cooperated fully, testifying truthfully about the drugs, rocket fuel, the last flight of the Spruce Goose, German paramotor pilots and the missing woman. The Feds offered a full pass, listening patiently for a while and but more interested in the giant man with the metal chapeau. The one who had caused all this destruction seemed to be their number one priority.

The sun was settling over the mountains that surrounded Whiskeytown Lake when the survival dogs arrived. The rescue team was dispatched promptly, Doc, Brain and Face watching anxiously as the trainers lead the eager canines into the rubble. There was nothing left for them to do but mourn the loss of their friends.

Losing both Barry and Beast had blindsided Face and the actor was devastated. A detached numbness had settled on Brain and Doc as all three stood silently in the parking lot, watching the rescue dogs bark and sniff, hell-bent on finding something to please their grim masters.

Doc had seen enough and wandered across the road to a convenience store for a pack of cigarettes. The brooding Brain followed, the tapping of his cane echoing off the pavement. Face, alone with his grief, attempted to make sense of it all.

"We'll keep looking, right?" Face blurted upon the two men's return. "Even if they don't find them, we'll continue to look." He was anxious to shake the two men out of their depressed complacency.

"Barry's dead," muttered Brain. "So is Beast. I'm sorry Doc and I dragged you into this. We never thought it would cost anyone their life."

"I wish I'd never seen that damn letter," Doc mumbled as he lit another cigarette.

"Wait," Face interrupted. "What letter? What are you talking about?"

"Never mind," Brain answered. "It's not important." The statement was made in his customary monotone. The finality of his words was as jarring as if they'd been shouted.

"We were wrong," Doc mumbled, shrugging. "We certainly didn't want anyone hurt."

Face fumed. He, more than any of them, had been skeptical of this whole half-assed adventure thing. Now he had discovered a reason for this tragedy and hell or high water, he'd get to the bottom of it. "What letter?" he repeated.

The two colleagues, shuffled nervously and stared at each other, silently debating how best to start. After an uncomfortable pause, they took turns, explaining. They finished by sharing a brief glimpse of the secret correspondence they had been hiding for over a week.

"And all this time, Barry didn't know?" Face confirmed. "Well now, sure as shit, you're both staying here to help me find them. Dead or alive, you owe them that much." The actor alone supplied the much-needed voice of reason. His closest friends had paid the ultimate price for this secrecy. Face swallowed past the overwhelming lump in his throat. "We're not going to let it end this way."

"Maybe Face is right," Doc said.

The retreating Brain halted. "We make our decisions based on facts not hope," he stated coldly, his back turned on his remaining friends.

"Eidetic memory does not make you an expert in the scientific process," Doc argued. "It only makes you a winner in Trivial Pursuit."

Brain turned, his pale face red with emotion. He tapped the tip of the cane on the concrete several times. "Such glaring generalizations are beneath you," he accused.

"I apologize," Doc said.

"Accepted under extreme duress," Brain countered.

Face and Doc stared at Brain, concentrating their collective will on the dissenting friend. Remaining was the right thing to do.

"I'll stay," Brain muttered. "But I'm not calling his mother."

With consciousness came an unwelcome void of darkness, excruciating pain and a sharp ringing in their collective ears. Barry had only one priority, making sure the impulsive Beast and the two scouts had survived the fall.

"Shut up." It was the distinct growl of his friend. "How can I hear the ringing in my ears with all your caterwauling?"

The heavier of the Explorers had somehow aroused Beast's wrath. Barry could hear him weeping while the skinnier of the two whispered for help. Beast and Barry rolled off the teens and stood.

"All good?" Barry asked, grabbing the skinnier one by the elbow and assisting him to his feet. The heavier scout refused to move and remained curled up in the fetal position.

There was no sign of the paralysis that had gripped Barry so severely only minutes before. The pendulum swinging between fear and heroics was once again in a positive direction. He made a mental note to question his sanity when he had a moment to spare.

"Suit yourself," Beast growled.

"We need to find a way out," Barry suggested. "You two Boy Scouts up for a hike?"

"No," Matt blurted. "And as soon as you get me out of here, I'm quitting."

"That's the spirit," Beast mumbled.

"I'll keep an eye on him," Jim offered. "And I'm sorry. We both are."

"Law enforcement may not be a good fit for you," Barry directed the statement at the heavier of the two. "You might want to change guidance counselors. Sit tight and we'll send someone back for you."

"Don't leave us!" Matt exclaimed. "We'll die."

The remains of the building moaned a brief warning before the basement floor collapsed again, dropping everyone deeper into a black and dusty void. The second landing was even harder than the first, dirt and rock replacing bureaucratic linoleum. Barry and Beast hit and rolled, grabbing the two scouts and yanking them out of way before two floors of accumulated debris buried them.

Barry performed another quick physical inventory. There were scrapes, cuts and bruises but that was the extent of his injuries. The ringing in his ears had subsided, and no bones were broken. "Everyone okay?" he asked for the second time.

Beast threw off a large piece of plasterboard. "Whoa," he offered, rising to his knees.

Barry turned to the two scouts. "The good news is I think that's the last of the falls," he announced. He reached out, his hand settling on a dirt wall. There was none of the dankness associated with being deep underground. A slight wisp of air-conditioned breeze originated from somewhere ahead.

"Stay put," Barry ordered.

"We'll be right here," Jim reminded them. "Waiting."

"What about the spiders?" Matt asked.

"Remember, Black Widows prefer cool darkness," Beast explained.

"We're surrounded by cool darkness," Matt screamed.

"A tunnel from Mexico to Chicago," Beast commented five minutes into their journey. "Could this be it?"

"Let's just concentrate on finding a way out," Barry answered.

They continued through the underground passage, groping their way along the dirt wall. As Barry and Beast stumbled around a corner, the pungent odor of a distinctly illegal vegetation greeted them.

"I'd know that intoxicating bouquet anywhere! Beast exclaimed as he quickened his pace.

Barry recognized the scent as well. His newly found courage had not affected his sense of smell. The distinct aroma was a mixture of freshly cut lawn, rain forest with just a hint of vanilla bean. He spotted the glimmer of artificial light reflecting off the sheer rock and followed his friend toward the brightness.

Beast halted. "Heaven" he muttered. "We've died and gone to heaven."

Barry joined him inside the colossal cavern carved out of solid rock. It was the most massive grow operation he had ever laid eyes on; an agricultural cathedral hollowed out of sold bedrock. It was at least the size of a football field and both men remained stalled at the entrance, gazing out over the spectacle. Thousands of grow lights hung above the tall, leafy marijuana plants, the cumulative brightness from the mini artificial suns intense.

"Dibs!" Beast called out. The big man's enthusiasm unchecked. "Finders keepers."

The sticky, sweet smell alone was enough to elicit a contact high. Before Barry could stop him, Beast was running as fast as his powerful legs could take him toward the first row of plants. Surprise overtook delight and the big man stumbled, tumbling face down into a leafy row. He had tripped a hidden wire and the blast of a klaxon sounded immediately.

The alarm reverberated through the cavern, bouncing off the rock like a berserk handball of sound. Barry spun in a quick 360, searching for first responders. Such an enterprise was bound to be protected and it was only a matter of time before armed security arrived.

"Whoops." Beast offered sheepishly as he climbed back to his feet. "Sorry."

"Can't un-ring the bell," Barry muttered, backing away. "Let's just find another way out."

The alarm ceased as Barry joined his clumsy friend. A quick examination of the trip wire revealed an elaborate system that seemed to run through every row of the illegal crop.

"Odd," Barry muttered. "Why go to all the trouble of an alarm if nobody is going to answer it?"

"Maybe nobody's home" Beast offered optimistically.

"Or maybe they don't need to answer," Barry replied. An unfamiliar tremor raced through his body. His senses had become alert, sensing an unseen danger. The sooner they left this place, the better he'd feel.

It was hard to tell from which direction they came. The noise was distinctly agricultural, half slicing, half clacking, and grew steadily. Neither man had ever set foot on a farm and it took several seconds to recognize the contraptions rolling their way.

"There!"

Both men refused to move until they were sure their eyes weren't deceiving them. The three machines appeared to be a lethal combination of harvesting combine and robot. Thin metallic appendages hung off barrel-shaped torsos. At the end of the metal arms, razor-sharp, stainless-steel scissors gleamed in the harsh light. Each unit was under four feet tall and propelled itself along the dirt with the aid of a whirling wheel of blades slicing through the aisles of marijuana on a direct path toward the uninvited guests.

"They could be friendly," Beast offered.

"I'm going to have to disagree," Barry answered. He placed a firm hand on Beast's shoulder, turned and directed his friend toward the darkness of the tunnel.

The gate dropped and blocked their escape. The security grill hit the dirt with a finality that signaled closing time at the mall. Barry rattled the barrier for any sign of structural weakness and found none. He turned to check the progress of the robotic combines. Whirring blades threatened as the robot harvesters closed in. Scissors snipped and snapped, the deadly blade's rising in anticipation of the human harvest.

Beast pulled several confiscated buds out of his pocket. "Maybe I should put these back," he offered.

The robots, incapable of negotiation, had cut the distance to the two men in half.

"They don't have to be such dicks about it," Beast said.

"We'll split them up," Barry suggested. "Maybe that will slow them down until we can think of something."

"Right."

"When I give the word."

Beast didn't wait for any word. He was off. Two robotic combines emerged from the rows, executed abrupt left turns and followed the big man. Metal appendages threatened, slicing the air with metallic clips of doom.

Barry sprinted off in the opposite direction. He hopped several full-grown plants and doubled back toward the metal grate that blocked the tunnel. He glanced over his shoulder and saw that only one robot followed. The small number of

140

pursuers offered no relief. One of these death machines was more than capable of getting the job done. The robot shredded effortlessly through the plants, rolling blades kicking up clouds of red volcanic dust off the cavern floor.

Barry concentrated on any way of getting out. It was no use. No matter how hard he tried, no lifesaving plan manifested itself. Intelligence, it appeared, was not a part of his newly inherited fearlessness. The robot closed in, leaving a trail of sticky green Sativa in its wake. Barry was about to suffer the same fate as the vegetation on the ground. Perhaps his friend was faring better.

Beast's mortality hung in the balance and he couldn't have cared less. Two robots were hot on his trail, pursuing him at breakneck speed and, so far, the hairy hulk of a man had eluded them. Leaping over the plants with an almost primitive grace, he hooted and even reached out to snatch an occasional bud. He was preparing for another jump when his foot snagged another unseen obstruction and he tripped, once again vanishing behind a row of leafy plants.

"Shit," Beast blurted on his way down. "All good."

Barry was pinned against the metal barrier, following the frantic footwork of his friend. "Beast," he yelled.

Beast was pushing himself off when he grabbed onto the root cause of his ill-timed fall. In one pull, he had yanked the thin, black irrigation hose out of the ground. The sudden change in pressure resulted in a steady stream of water and the big man took advantage. He rolled onto his back and raised the arc of water toward the metallic attackers. He squeezed the hose with both fists, aiming the stream at the exposed mechanics of the robotic enemy. Water met internal circuitry and the effect was instantaneous. Motherboards sizzled, crackling sparks rocketing out the barrel-shaped torsos. A series of internal explosions followed as the two machines were reduced to smoldering rolling piles of clanking metal. Each trembled and rattled, emitting an electronic squawk before finally halting dead in their tracks.

Barry remained pinned against the barrier, staring into the blinking lights of the faceless robotic harvester. In one last desperate attempt to save his own life, he summoned a mouthful of saliva and readied to launch the biggest, wettest loogie of his life. He had one shot and dug deep, launching the foamy concoction at a servo gear between the bucket head and shoulders.

It was a direct hit, and the robot stalled for a brief second as if only suffering a slight affront. The ball of spit had been as effective as a rubber band against an aircraft carrier and, after a split-second stall, the robot continued forward. Snapping blades rose up toward Barry's throat. Water was the answer, but Barry clearly didn't have enough to do the job. An idea came to mind, but he had to act fast. He only had seconds. Barry dropped trou and grabbed onto his body's natural hose. Never good under pressure, he summoned up whatever ammunition remained sloshing around in his small bladder. He fired at will and began the ultimate humiliation for both man or robot.

The robot stalled as Barry fired the golden stream at every exposed vulnerability. The effects of the highly acidic concoction were instantaneous, wreaking havoc on the circuits hidden inside the metal shell. The unorthodox move proved to be just in time, the left scissor blade stalling an inch from Barry's throat. The frantic human now found himself out of ammo and shook furiously.

A bright flash accompanied the explosion. A blade rocketed off the left appendage, lodging in the metal grate inches from his face. Barry took a deep breath and holstered his weapon as an ecstatic Beast joined him.

"Awesome," the big man exclaimed, his voice echoing off the underground cavern walls. "Nice shooting."

Barry fastened the last button to his fly and smirked. "No matter how much you shake and dance, the last few drops…"

"Kick their ass," Beast concluded.

Beast studied the metallic remains lying in the dirt. Ignoring the recent coat of urine, he lifted the torso and examined the stenciled black printing on the back. "Thunder Telecommunications. Hecho en Panama," he read out in very slow and pedestrian Spanish. "What does it mean?"

"We've seen those words before," Barry said. "Inside Haystack Rock. I think it means, made in Panama,"

The two men looked out over a green sea of illegal plants. To the connoisseur, it was a picture postcard site but both men now realized there was more here than meets the eye.

"Smoke 'em if you got 'em," Beast declared, the big man rummaging through his pockets. "Hand me the robot's head and I'll make us a bong."

Barry glanced at the short-circuited robot. "No time," he answered, not believing his own abstention. He pointed in the direction where the robots arrived. "Let's find out where they came from. It may lead to a way out."

The two men maneuvered through an aisle of leafy, adult plants. "Shame to let this all go to waste," Beast muttered.

They exited at the opposite end, resuming their journey through a smaller connecting tunnel. After several turns, the two found themselves back in a familiar pitch-black darkness.

"How long have we been down here?" Beast asked.

"Long enough for me to have to pee again." Barry answered.

At long last, a sliver of light appeared ahead and eased the two men's concern. It was a natural source, dusty rays of sunlight streaming in from an unknown location. As they drew closer, they recognized the open hatch in the roof of the cave. A wooden ladder climbed up to the hatch.

"After you," Beast offered upon arrival.

"Don't mind if I do," Barry answered, grabbing onto a rung. The ladder was only seven feet high and in no time his head had popped into the bright daylight. He glanced down at his friend. "Hold onto yourself, Bartlett. You're twenty feet short."

"Shut up," Beast chuckled, recognizing the reference to "The Great Escape" instantly.

"Climb on out of there," someone unexpectedly ordered. "Nice and easy." The voice was young, unpleasant and distinctly female.

Beast remained silent, his brown eyes blazing at the prospect of another foe. He latched onto the ladder with his huge hands. "One thing you should know about us," he snarled, wrenching the ladder from the hatch above. "We never go nice and easy."

The ladder snapped free. Barry released the ladder, letting gravity do the rest. He had made several falls already today, and this one proved to be a piece of cake. Beast righted his friend midway through the descent and Barry landed feet first as the first gunshot ricocheted behind him.

"That's just rude" Beast commented as the two backed into the darkness.

"It's an abandoned ice house," Barry explained. "And something tells me these guys aren't selling ice."

Beast padded his bulging pockets. "No way I'm giving this back."

Another pistol shot zinged off an unseen rock.

"I wouldn't worry," Barry said. "I think they have other things on their minds."

"They've got to find us to shoot us," Beast said in a loud whisper. "We're safe in the dark."

An electronic hum heralded a long line of overhead fluorescent tubes flickering and igniting, flooding the once dark tunnel in a bright, white light.

"I count two," Face reported. "And they're armed."

Face joined Doc and Brain, crouching behind an oversized boulder. All three men were now in a perfect position to monitor any suspicious movement between the yellow house and the abandoned ice factory. It was the sharp retort of a single gunshot that roused the three from their melancholy and caused them to focus their attention on the fabricated metal building across the highway. The fact that someone was shooting so close to the previous battle zone was suspicious and each man clung desperately to the hope that the intended target, or targets, might be one or both of their missing friends.

A male wearing a red bandana over stringy blonde hair exited the yellow house and sprinted to the ice factory. An automatic pistol was held discretely at his side and he glanced toward the rubble that once was the highway patrol headquarters several times. A tall bearded gentleman, wearing cut-offs and a tie-dyed tee shirt knotted off above his swollen midriff, followed. The second gentleman's unique ensemble was topped off by a British Deerstalker cap and an ornate tobacco pipe that resembled a smoldering clarinet.

The abandoned icehouse was the only way in or out of the underground operation and the structure had been strategically located so the investors could keep an eye on the lucrative enterprise. The mysterious, unseen employer had insisted the entire operation be underground, well removed from the prying eyes of competitors and the heat-seeking cameras of the D.E.A. Despite the enormous expense, the underground construction had been completed and the clandestine grow operation was officially in its first year of business. One third of the C.H.P. officers across the road were active partners in the illegal operation and this made for near perfect security.

The voluptuous redhead wore cut-offs and a flowered halter that barely contained her fleshy assets. She jiggled inappropriately with every move which did not go unnoticed to the men watching her. She stood outside the ice house, waving another lethal-looking automatic. Meeting bandanna and midriff, she pointed inside.

"She's cute," Face whispered. "In a harsh drug dealing kind of way."

The three dealers argued, the redhead becoming even more agitated. Her freckled torso shimmied with every angry gesture and all the waggling flesh did not go unnoticed by Face. The actor clearly was spellbound by her performance. "Barry and Beast are there," he said. "I'd bet my entire artistic career on it."

Many verbal comebacks came immediately to mind, but Doc and Brain held back. There wasn't the time.

"That redhead is interesting," Face continued. "She's the key to this entire thing." Face was standing, straightening his clothes and dusting off the accumulated dust from the earlier battle. "I need to interrogate her," he decided out loud.

Face made a beeline toward the ginger haired siren. It was well worth the gamble. If his friends weren't inside, he could at least introduce himself.

The actor was tackled from behind and hit the ground hard. "Son of a bitch," Face managed before a hand clamped over his mouth. He struggled, opening his eyes to the familiar faces.

"They're armed," Doc cautioned. "Yellow house is empty. We'll start there."

Doc and Brain crept toward the house. The exasperated Face following a few steps behind.

The front door was unlocked and the three slipped in unnoticed. The living room and kitchen were empty and free of furniture or appliances. Sleeping bags were scattered on the worn carpet and were the only proof the house wasn't vacant. The three split-up and began a search.

"Hair, Hot L Baltimore and Man of La Mancha, Face read from a pamphlet he had found on the kitchen counter. "Shasta Arts Festival. This is an ambitious season."

Before he could fully critique the repertory of plays, Doc called out from another room. "In here."

"Propiedad del Ejército de Panamá" was stenciled in bold, black letters on each crate. Face and Brain joined their colleague at the doorway, clearly puzzled by the familiar branding.

"Same labels as Cannon Beach," Doc observed, lifting the lid and peering inside.

"Theatre people," Brain mumbled. "They're the same all over."

"I'm sure there's a logical explanation," Face explained, peering over his friend's shoulders. "Maybe they're considering "Evita" for their fall season."

"I don't think so." Doc muttered. He craved a cigarette but was surrounded by a room full of munitions. Best wait.

"Compliments of the Army of Panama?" Brain said as he removed a rifle from the packing foam.

Each crate contained a lethal assortment of death. Automatic rifles, handguns and grenades were all nestled snugly inside the packing material. There were enough munitions in the bedroom to arm a battalion.

"Don't kid yourselves," Face continued. "Evita is powerful theatre. It embodies all the magic and pageantry of a third world dictatorship."

Doc lifted a dusty burlap bag off the floor. It had been resting against the crates and had yet been unnoticed. The chemist reached in, pulling out a small green bulb caked in dirt. "What have we here?" he asked.

"Organic Brussels sprouts," Face answered. The actor thrust in a hand and pulled out several. "I'm starving. I haven't eaten in days."

Doc stopped Face a split-second before the actor could dart off in search of a sink.

"It's peyote," Doc warned.

"How would you know?" Brain asked, slapping an ammo clip into his weapon. The pale, lean thinker disapproved of drug use, limiting his own chemical relaxation to an occasional glass of Bailey's Irish Cream.

"I may have devoted some time to the studies of Carlos Castanedes and the teachings of Don Juan," Doc confessed.

"What?" Brain managed. "When was this?"

"I'm not always with you," Doc argued.

"Maybe you should be."

"I miss the gypsy life of the theatre," Face continued. "It seems like ages ago. I was such an innocent."

Ignoring this bit of theatrical history, the heavily armed Brain and Doc headed back to the front door.

"What about me?" Face asked. "Maybe I should take a gun."

"Innocents shouldn't play with guns." Doc explained, switching off the safety on his weapon. "Take the flyer."

"It's loaded with entertainment," Brain added.

"It was two months of my life," Face reminisced with a forlorn look. "One night I was the dancing my heart away in 42nd Street; the next I'm the Duke of Burgundy in King Lear. You're totally underestimating the enchantment of summer theatre."

The three exited the abode and crept toward the icehouse. They were unsure of their next step but, by now, that was standard operating procedure. They sought cover behind a large trash bin, peering through the building's open doors. They spotted the open hatch in the middle of the warehouse cement floor. The thespian drug-runners were standing above the hatch, gazing downward like highway workers considering a pothole.

"I'm not going down there," bandanna protested. "I'm not screwing with those robots. Remember Crazy Henry? One of those metal bastards cut off the tip of his finger."

"Well I can't go," the pipe smoker explained. "I have rehearsal in twenty minutes and I still haven't rinsed out my dance belt."

"Oh, for the love of Christ," the redhead blurted. "You're both pussies. I'll go."

"No one's going anywhere."

Doc and Brain strolled through the open double doors, their carbines aimed at the three hippies gathered at the hatch. Face brought up the rear, the theatre pamphlet rolled tightly in his clenched fist.

"Who the hell are you?" bandanna asked.

"Throw down your weapons and back away from the hatch," Brain ordered.

"We're actors," the pipe smoker stammered. "At the college."

"Shut your mouth. You want to get us killed?" bandana blurted. He turned to the intruders and smiled. "What's up?"

"I'll be the judge of who is and isn't an actor," Face declared, stepping forward with an attitude signaling he had it all under control. "What is Willy Loman's primary motivation in the first act of Death of a Salesman?"

Brain handed Face his weapon as Doc backed the stymied actors away from the hatch. "What's down there?" he interrupted.

"None of your business," the redhead answered.

"Cultivating robots," the bandanna explained. "Don't fuck with them. They'll cut your balls off."

"Fascinating," Brain commented. "Automatons, with such a specialized skill set, must be verified."

Doc handed his rifle to the unprepared Face. The actor was busy scrutinizing the redhead and fumbled what should have been an easy pass-off.

"Watch where you are aiming that, numb-nuts?" the redhead cautioned.

149

"What, with my tongue in your tail?" Face quoted, recovering a more suitable handling of the weapon.

"In your dreams," she fired back.

"Saucy Kate," Face answered. "That was a quote from "Taming of the Shrew," Act Two, Scene One. We should do a read-thru sometime."

"No ladder," Doc observed.

Doc lowered himself through the hatch and dropped into the darkness. Brain slung a rifle over his back and followed the chemist into the hole, leaving Face alone with the confused prisoners.

"Don't say I didn't warn you about the robots," bandanna called after.

A smug Face held a rifle with one hand as he browsed through the pamphlet.

"Will this take long?" the pipe smoker asked anxiously.

"Never mind that," Face answered. "You never answered my question."

"How would I know what Willy Loman's motivation is? I'm a dancer." To prove the point, pipe smoker executed a flawless pirouette.

"Nice," Face commented. "But you're more than just a dancer. Your body tells a story with each choreographed move."

"Jesus," the redhead said. "Kill me now."

"Shut up," the pipe smoker interjected. "That's what I tell my parents."

"It's called teaching out," Face lectured, brandishing the weapon while directing his comments to the redhead. "It's what true artists are tasked to do." He unfolded the pamphlet and held it open. "Which play?" he asked.

"Hair," the pipe smoker offered.

"I don't consider Hair real theatre," Face critiqued. "More of a happening. I'm speaking from experience. American Academy of Dramatic Arts. Class of 1979."

"New York or Pasadena?" the annoyed redhead asked. She was clearly challenging him.

150

"Does it matter which coast?" Face answered. "The fundamentals of our craft remain the same."

"It matters, douche-bag," she fired back. "The New York school is established and has a proven track record of graduates. West Coast just opened, and I've never heard of any of the people teaching there."

"Pasadena has great teachers," Face countered defensively. "This is clearly a case of west coast theatrical prejudice."

"Guess that makes me a snob," the redhead answered, revealing a black Glock she had stashed in the back waistband of her shorts. "Lecture's over."

"Learning your craft is never over," Face corrected, dropping his rifle, the heavy weapon clattering on the concrete. The actor was clearly flustered over his lack of prisoner control and raised his arms over his head. "And you, young lady, will never get far in the theatre until you learn respect and gratitude."

"Do you believe the robot story?" Brain asked.

"May just be an attempt to scare us."

They had taken only a few steps when the familiar voice called out. "Doc! Brain!"

Beast crept up from behind, sweeping both men in his arms and lifting them off their feet. The unexpected exchange caused Brain to drop his weapon.

"What kept you?"

"Barry?" Doc asked hopefully.

Barry stepped out of the darkness and picked up the rifle. "You dropped something," he said, offering back the weapon with a sly grin. "And there are robots."

"Where?"

"Too late. Barry pissed all over them," Beast explained gleefully.

"Likely story," Brain said. He was not amused and never joked when robots were involved.

"Let's go," Barry suggested.

"There's no easy way to tell you this," Brain explained. "But some people may be under the impression that you're dead."

"My mother?" Barry asked.

Doc was nervous. "The Feds may have already talked to her," the chemist admitted.

"We felt it was a job best left for the professionals," Brain added.

"I'll call later," Barry said.

"A card's always nice," Beast suggested.

The thespians had escaped but not before turning the tables on their fellow actor. The humiliated Face was found naked, bound at the wrists, feet and was left squatting in the filthiest corner of the abandoned ice house. One of his own dirty sweat-socks had been removed and stuffed in his mouth. It was shameful treatment and not befitting an esteemed graduate of the west coast chapter of the A.C.D.A. All of his talents had been laid bare from his artistic toolbox and the hapless victim could only grunt upon seeing his friends.

Beast, recovering from a fit of boisterous laughter, lumbered over and removed the sock. Wrinkles of amusement highlighted his brown eyes and the infectious grin covered a third of the big man's face. "Naked is not a good look for you," he said.

"And to think I actually missed you," Face managed, still gagging over the taste of his own foot.

The bonds were cut with the aid of Brain's sword cane and Face was assisted to his feet, rubbing the circulation back into his wrists and hands.

"We need to find you some clothes," Barry promised. "That physique might cause undue attention."

"I'm not ashamed of this body," Face protested. "It's the tool I use to communicate with my audience."

"Small tool," Beast quipped.

"It's cold and frightened," Face exclaimed. "I'd like to see you under the same circumstances."

"What happened to the others?" Doc asked, hoping to bring propriety back to the conversation.

"They raced out of here," Face answered. "Something sure spooked them."

"Are you sure it wasn't the sight of you naked?" Beast suggested.

"Can we just leave?"

"I saw some clothes at the yellow house," Doc suggested.

"Why?" Beast asked. "He's not ashamed."

The actor's new wardrobe consisted of flared corduroy bellbottoms, a silk pirate shirt with puffy sleeves, leather frilled boots and a recently-rinsed dance belt. Face found a bonus in the right front pocket: keys to a 67 gold Pontiac LeMans parked discretely behind the yellow house. The car had been stashed nearby for fast getaways, early rehearsals and had been left in the hasty retreat.

The five piled into the car, Face taking the wheel. "Next stop, the city by the bay," the actor declared.

"San Francisco," Barry clarified. "Let's go find that girl."

"Nice ride," Beast critiqued, sandwiched between Doc and Brain in the back.

Five miles outside the city limits, they learned the real reason the thespian drug-runners had not bothered to take the car. The gas tank was bone dry.

They managed to push the heap to the side of the freeway, arguing over next steps when the pink Mary Kay Cadillac appeared out of the harsh, shimmering daylight, slowing to a stop in the emergency lane. The oversized sedan was several years old but well maintained. Doc, Brain, Face and Beast jogged toward it, giving little thought to who might be waiting for them inside.

The good Samaritan had obviously gotten far in the cosmetic game. Pink Cadillacs were the reward for closers. Barry quickened his pace and pulled ahead of the others. The passenger door swung open and he leaned down to catch a glimpse of the driver. There still remained plenty enough reasons to be cautious.

One look and it became obvious that the driver had not made his living selling make-up. The elderly gentleman was tall, the oversized Cadillac perfect for his stature. He appeared to be in his seventies but there was a strange timelessness about him that made pinning an exact age difficult. He leaned out over the bench seat with a warm smile. His hair was white and slicked back with a scented hair product that was popular decades ago. His green eyes were keen with an alertness that one did not always associate with the elderly. The driver's humongous hands rested on the fuzzy pink steering wheel cover. His face brightened at the sight of Barry.

"You boys need a lift?" the old gent asked.

The men nodded without hesitation. Caution had been left with the discarded car on the shoulder of the freeway

"Hop in."

The Caddy, built in the mid-seventies, provided enough red leather seating for all. Barry slid into the front seat, the four others opening the back-passenger door. If it was a trap it was too late. Somehow, Barry didn't think so. There was something familiar and comforting about this stranger.

"Heading south?" the man asked as he merged the great pink machine back onto the freeway.

"Bay area," Barry answered. It was best to play his cards close to the chest. "We have family there."

"Holy cats," the man exclaimed. "It just so happens that I'm heading to the city. Friends call me Reese."

Introductions took several minutes with each of the hitchhikers taking special care not to reveal anything about themselves or their adventures. Beast remained too preoccupied for intros, quietly ribbing Face on his apparel.

"What do you do?" Barry asked after ten minutes of silence. He glanced in the rear view and saw that Brain, Face and Doc were already snoozing in the back.

"Architect. Strictly part-time. Retired," Reese answered. "Excuse me for saying this, but it looks like you boys have been through the ringer."

155

The old man gave Barry a thorough inspection as he drove. It was not obtrusive or entirely unwelcome and was as if the older man was sizing up a long, lost relative.

It was Beast who saved the day when the ongoing silence became too uncomfortable. The big man leaned up and over the front seat. "You happen to have any rolling papers?" he asked.

Barry turned to the back seat, signaled with a glance it might not be the right question for a perfect stranger. Beast was undeterred.

"Do I have rolling papers? Holy cats!" The old man popped opened the dash with a bang from his giant fist, the lid dropping into Barry's lap. "I also have tobacco."

"No thanks," Barry answered. "I think he's good." He handed the rolling papers to his friend.

While Beast concentrated on the task at hand, Barry closed the glove box. "Nice car," he said.

"Oh, yeah," Reese answered. "A peach. It's the wife's. She'll be plenty steamed when she finds out I've taken it without permission. You married?"

"No."

"Girlfriend?"

"That's complicated," Barry answered.

"No girlfriend," Beast concluded with a finality that made sense under the circumstances.

"Not unlike a certain fellow I used to know," Reese answered. The old man grinned. "Wasn't into dames for the longest time."

"Oh, I'm not..." Barry began, suddenly uncomfortable with the way the conversation was heading. It was none of his business and he never completed his thought.

"Neither was he," Reese answered. "Shame you two never met." The old man's attention was focused on the cement ribbon of freeway ahead. "Passed on years ago."

"Bummer," Beast offered. The big man was distracted, putting the finishing touches on a hastily rolled joint. "Canoed it."

156

It was quiet for several seconds before the man who called himself Reese continued. "He was your father," he announced with all the coolness of light, unimportant banter.

It suddenly made sense why the old man couldn't keep his eyes off him. He had obviously mistaken his younger passenger for someone else. "You're mistaken," Barry said finally. "My father was an accountant."

"That was your adopted father," Reese corrected. "I'm talking about your birth father."

The long, drawn-out whistle originated from the back. It was Beast's only commentary on the driver's startling revelation.

Reese glanced into the rearview. "Five," he muttered to himself.

"I beg your pardon," Barry said.

"I'm sorry." Reese said, slapping the furry wheel with an oversized palm. "There were five of us who worked with your father. The greatest collection of friends a man ever had. All remarkable fellows. And now there's five of you." The old man savored the similarity. "Holy cats."

"I'm still not following you," Barry whispered. "You knew my real father?"

Reese paused, and his thick brow furrowed. There was history in the old man's thoughts. It was a weight the tall man had been carrying for over thirty years. "His name was Rock Ravage," he announced. "Those who feared him, called him the Ravager."

"Sounds like the title to a cheap paperback."

"Yeah, we heard that a lot. Never-the-less, he was the greatest man who ever lived."

157

Tilly should've pulled over the first cop she saw. Not that the authorities would ever believe her frantic tale of drug dealing boyfriends, washed up Irish punk singers, half-human tanks and exploding brains. They'd have no choice but to lock her up and a three-day evaluative stint in a nearby mental hospital was not her ideal way of getting away from it all. Right now, she trusted no one with her story and intended to keep a wary eye on anyone who came close.

Was it her imagination or did everyone on the busy street and sidewalks seem to be watching her? It was crazy but try as she might, she couldn't shake an overwhelming sense of paranoia. Given the current state of affairs, she didn't see her volatile mental state changing anytime soon.

She wandered between Fisherman's Wharf and Pier 39 attempting to blend in with the mix of tourists, colorful street performers and a growing homeless population. Her anxiety grew with each step and she couldn't shake the feeling that she might have done exactly what her captors had expected; that it was only a matter of time before someone snatched her, dragging her kicking and screaming back to the deserted nightclub and that horrific, disembodied voice.

There was only one place in the city that she'd feel safe and she came upon the idea while pacing nervously between tourist locations. She had decided to hide out on the rock, the formidable federal fortress jutting out of the middle of San Francisco Bay. Once there, she'd disappear in one of the hundreds of cellblocks and only come out when she was positively sure it was good and safe. Getting there without the benefit of money posed a problem. She positioned herself on a nearby bench, watching the men, women and children board the tourist boat for the next scheduled excursion. It was an outlandish plan, but an increasingly desperate Tilly saw it as her only option.

She zeroed in on an elderly woman speaking German. The old woman looked vulnerable and wealthy. Tilly stood, took a deep breath and approached. "Excuse me," Tilly said, interrupted mid-sentence by a firm tap on her shoulder.

"Have you ever taken the Singularity Test?"

Tilly turned, swinging a clenched fist toward the source. She managed to pull her punch just in time. The teen girl, dressed in white blouse, short-shorts and tennis shoes, held up a thick paperback copy of "Diatribe" to ward off the blow.

"Whoa," the girl said, ducking and smiling at the same time. "Easy. We're good. It's good."

The German woman brushed off the intrusion as a prime example of another rude American and hurried past the wooden barrier and gangplank.

"No," Tilly said, retrieving her errant fist while proceeding to take a deep breath. She searched for the woman and found that she had disappeared. "Shit."

"No problem," the girl said. "You're too old to be a stowaway."

The girl possessed sun-bleached blonde hair, freckles and looked as fresh and wholesome as a girl in her late teens should. Her alert green eyes instantly put Tilly at ease. At this point in her life, it was something she hardly thought possible.

"How did you know?" Tilly asked, the thumping in her chest returning to a more comfortable rhythm.

"Abusive boyfriend." The girl's last statement was not a stretch. "It's all over your face. All of us are running from something. Have you read it? Diatribe?"

"Now's not a good time."

"That's funny because you look like you could use it," the girl said. "My name is Denice. No s," she added. "Spelled with a cee. You should take the test."

"This test," Tilly asked, watching as the tour boat and any chance of safe sanctuary pulled away from the dock. "Do you take it here or do you go somewhere?"

"God no," Denice explained. "Too noisy here. It's not far. I can take you if you want."

Tilly looked over at the island landmark in the middle of the bay. She was out of other options. "Where?" she asked. "I've got to warn you, I have no money."

Denice grabbed Tilly's hand and assured her with a nervous smile. "You won't need any money," she said. "Not where we're going. You never told me your name."

"Tilly. Tilly Peterson."

The two women walked the short distance to the Embarcadero and waited a few minutes for the arrival of the bus. Tilly later learned that the vehicle had deposited the young fishers of souls earlier in the day and offered hourly departures to transport the catch back across the bay. Tilly didn't care. The further away she got from the city, the better she felt. The sense that everyone was watching her faded with each mile and she was already planning a way to ditch the blonde when they arrived at their destination.

The bus unloaded in a seedier part of downtown Oakland that was highlighted by two golden age movie palaces on either side of the block. Tilly and the blonde recruiter stood in front of a building that declared itself the Luminary Centre, watching the other zealots and their guests file inside. The two women entered unmolested, passing a pleasant male receptionist and climbed the wooden stairs to the second floor.

Tilly was led into a small, windowless room containing a rickety wooden desk and a chair. Atop the desk was a neat stack of paper and a sharpened number 2 pencil.

"This is it," Denice reported. The teen was suddenly uncomfortable as if being in these familiar surroundings brought back unpleasant memories. "You get started and I'll bring you something to drink. What'd you like?"

"Water will be fine."

"You sure? We have everything."

160

Tilly was hungry and thirsty. Something that provided a quick energy boost might prove useful. "Orange juice," she answered. "That'd be great."

"Coming right up. You get started," Denice urged. "I'll bring it to you."

Tilly sat in the chair and broke the seal on the test. She opened the booklet and read the first question.

"Do you make careless statements or untruths which you later regret?"

It was an easy yes or no question and Tilly was considering her answer when the door opened, Denice reappearing with her drink.

"Remember," Denice cautioned, "it's a test of your spiritual temperament. There are no right or wrong answers."

Denice set the bottle of juice on the table, looking over Tilly's shoulder as the pencil hovered above the "yes." She whistled, a not-so-subtle hint that the answer was wrong. Tilly glanced up at her spiritual advisor and she shook her head.

"No?" Tilly asked.

Denice said nothing, backing to the door. The teen was even more anxious now, her eyes darting around the small room. It was as if she already knew the test results and the final grade was not good.

"No right or wrong answers," Tilly echoed.

"That's right," the wide-eyed Denice offered, closing the door behind her.

Tilly moved onto the second question, hoping the intent was clearer.

"When others are getting aroused, do you remain fairly composed?"

What sort of quiz is this? Her anger grew in direct relation to the stupidity of the question. She shoved the chair away and threw the pencil on the desk. She was aroused, deciding then and there to get the hell out. She uncapped the orange juice and drank. She never realized how thirsty she was. The beverage was ice cold, and the sweet liquid felt good on her parched throat. Another beverage and she might be able to endure a couple more questions. Tilly decided she'd test her luck and called out to Denice for another refreshment.

There was no answer and Tilly rattled the handle, her anger growing with each futile turn of the knob. She had been tricked, locked in from the outside. The queasiness in her stomach came on unexpectedly. If she didn't sit fast, she'd throw up. She spun her head, looking for a garbage can. The movement was too quick, and she stumbled.

"Help," she managed as she backed away from the door and dropped back into the chair. Her vision was blurry, and she cupped her throbbing head in her hands. Her eyes somehow focused on the next question on the test. The words were blurry, but she concentrated hard and they slowly took shape: "Do you browse through railway timetables, directories, or dictionaries just for pleasure?"

Tilly awoke on a deck chair aboard a large vessel that smelled of fresh paint and diesel. Her head was pounding, and the overpowering smell was churning an already queasy stomach. She made her way to the rail and took a series of deep breaths. She watched as young deckhands ran fore and aft, fulfilling various tasks and duties. The attractive crew was dressed in uniforms of white shorts and Polos. All of them appeared to be Tilly's age or younger, were attractive, and shouting in an Americanized English that did not hide European accents.

She glanced behind her and noted the life preserver mounted to the steel hull. The name of her floating prison was stenciled on the canvas float in bold, black letters. Tilly Peterson had been shanghaied on a ship calling itself "The Argo 2."

The rocky island of Alcatraz grew smaller in the distance. She glanced up and saw that she was passing directly under the Golden Gate Bridge. She could see the throngs of tourists high above, walking and biking across the orange expanse. They'd never hear a cry for help and the realization brought with it another round of queasiness. She was heading out of San

Francisco Bay and would once again be in International waters. There was no sign of the young woman who called herself Denice. Her kidnapper either remained on land or was conveniently hiding. If, and when, Tilly found her, she would make her pay.

"The Commodore will see you soon," came the directive from the engaging teen who managed to sneak up behind her.

"Does this Commodore realize that kidnapping is a Federal offense?"

"We'll be in open waters soon," the female crew member chirped. It was another natural blonde and Tilly thought this one looked and sounded Scandinavian. "You'll feel better then."

"I doubt it," Tilly mumbled.

"The Commodore is looking forward to meeting you. He's been up the entire night, finishing a very important paper on Zandu."

The Golden Gate Bridge might be the last American thing Tilly ever saw. Her mother was dead, her new friends lost, and she was once again alone and left to her own devices. As the noisy seagulls squawked overhead, she attempted to go over her options. It took no time at all to realize she had none.

Tanktop was out cold, his steroid-enhanced body pumped full of Amobarbital, Methohexital, Thiamylal and Propofol. The powerful sedatives were insurance against any accidental explosions during the sensitive operation, the diverse surgical staff showing the patient the exact same respect they would a tranquilized Rhino.

All the while, the human weapon dozed and dreamt of happier days. Once again, he was the innocent young boy in North Dakota. It was a much happier time, long before the garage fire, the arrest of his parents or the arrival of the red-nosed Priest. The heavy sedation had transported him to a familiar mid-western farm where acres of wheat bent in the summer breeze and a checkerboard collection of fluffy white clouds floated in a crystal blue sky.

The dream changed, his sense of happiness ending abruptly. He watched the approaching thunderhead, a pitch-black gloom swirling together in the sky with unnatural speed. The wind kicked up and the young boy stood silent as the weather mutated into a super storm. The boy realized he was no longer afraid. Death and devastation surrounded him, the entire world would soon bear witness to how cataclysmic this storm would be.

"You knew my father?"

"I was his associate of his for many years," Reese answered. "He was also my closest friend."

"And my birth mother?"

"Never had the pleasure," the tall man offered apologetically. "She must've been one hell of a remarkable woman."

The hushed conversation continued with several uncomfortable pauses, both men conscious of the four passengers dozing in back. Barry found himself at a loss for adequate words to express himself, his head spinning from the revelations revealed by the driver. He had known he was adopted his entire life, and, up to now, had never given his birth parents much thought. Thinking of them at all was just a lonely boy's fantasy. He knew full well the reality of unexpected births in the fifties. His parents were most likely nothing more than two love-sick teenagers, in way over their heads.

"An exceptional man." Reese continued. He glanced into the rearview mirror and grinned. The sight of Barry's four friends seemed to amuse him.

"What?"

"Nothing," Reese said. "Just takes me back. Never take for granted the true value of friends. They can make the difference between life and death."

Barry's attention focused on the driver's enormous hands on the steering wheel. Balled up into fists, they seemed big enough to smash through doors. "Did my father send you to find me?"

"Hardly. I knew where you were the entire time," Reese answered. He checked the mirror again. "Holy cats! Did your friends show you my letter?"

Barry knew nothing about any letter. How long had his friends kept that bit of information from him? He was angry, and the driver sensed it. If they had just shown him the correspondence, all of this may have been avoided.

"Don't blame them," Reese offered. "It wasn't safe to tell you in the beginning."

Deep down Barry couldn't help but be disappointed. After all the years of friendship, he deserved better. He focused his attention out the passenger window, watching a very dry northern California landscape evolve into a scenic bay and major port. "What happened to my father?"

"Murdered in cold blood. At the hands of a sworn enemy," the old man answered. "He died shortly after meeting your mother."

Barry felt a pang of sympathy for a man and woman he'd never know. "How?" he asked. His head was spinning, and he turned back to the driver.

"At one time there was a man who rivaled your father in almost every way," Reese explained. "As evil as your father was good. Your father bested him on two occasions, but this man refused to accept defeat. These failures festered inside the villain for years and all the while he plotted his revenge. He even went so far as to put a price on your father's head. Word is, he tracked him across an entire continent. He was last seen in the city of your birth."

The family history was chilling. Hatred was a powerful motivator but to go to such lengths to dispatch a fellow human being. Barry found himself overwhelmed. "Why find me now?" he managed. "After all this time."

Reese slowed the pink Caddie to pay the toll. San Francisco Bay and the vast metal expanse that would carry them to the most picturesque city in the world was laid out before them. The old man lowered the window and handed the matronly employee a fiver. "Keep the change," he said. He rolled up the window and turned his attention back to his passenger. "I came to warn you. I forwarded the letter for I believe this man knows about you."

"Why would he even care?"

"Besides the satisfaction he'd get from killing his enemy's only son and heir?" Reese answered. "There's all that gold."

"Wait?" Barry's mind was racing. "Run that last part by me again?"

"You're about to see for yourself," the man offered softly.

There was too much to digest. His father the hero, the unexplained wealth and a man who wanted nothing more than

166

to see him dead. Barry tried to wrap his head around it all, but couldn't, his chaotic thoughts returning to parents he would never know. "And my birth mother?" Barry felt a sorrowful longing that came from confronting the truth. "What happened to her?"

"Passed," Reese answered flatly. "She died protecting you."

They called themselves The Sea Society, their mysterious leader commanding a small navy that crisscrossed the globe in a never-ending quest for power, wealth and spiritual enlightenment. Not only did the world's fastest growing religion have its own Navy, it also possessed an enthusiastic crew of young and attractive recruits to faithfully execute all orders.

The sailors treated Tilly with a cool, polite efficiency, escorting her from the sparse guest quarters to simple meals in the mess. As she ate, she watched the young crew consume vast quantities of coffee and cigarettes, conferring in hushed whispers. It seemed by these intense, muted conversations that the whole organization was built on secrecy.

"The Commodore will see you now," the teenage girl, announced.

Tilly was escorted to the main quarters, located directly under the bridge. Her latest attendant was a pretty redhead who, like all the others, appeared to be in her late teens. The heavy steel hatch to the sanctum swung open, the teen grinning and gesturing formally for the guest to step inside.

"Is there a person on board this ship named Denice?" Tilly asked for what seemed to be the millionth time. "Blonde. Pretty. Spells her name with a cee. I'd like to speak to her."

The teen refused to answer, gesturing again for Tilly to enter. She took a deep breath and complied, passing through as the heavy steel door banged shut. On the far side of the long room, light from the desk lamp reflected off disorganized stacks of yellow and white paper, bouncing back onto the double chin of the man seated behind the oversized, mahogany desk. The remainder of the man's jowly face was masked by shadow.

Tilly marched past a collection of framed magazine covers. The displays were colorful pulp art from a bygone era, authored by names sadly remembered by only a few. "Mad Science," "Amazing Stories," and "Astounding Science Fiction" were the featured titles and each glass encased cover teased a simple but entertaining read. A voluptuous and scantily clad female, cowering in the right-hand corner of each work, had obviously been tossed in as a bonus for the intended young, male audience.

She continued forward until her captor eventually acknowledged her presence, glancing up at her with the small beady eyes of a rodent. He lit a cigarette, continuing the inspection. "Ahoy," he said. "Ever been dead?"

"I beg your pardon?"

The bloodshot eyes followed her, his scrutinizing gaze uncomfortable and dangerous. "The bastards think I'm dead," he announced, drawing deeply from his cigarette. "But I fooled them."

"Good for you," Tilly answered sarcastically. She couldn't help herself. Captivity did not suit her.

"While they fight to control my empire, I'm free to embark on the adventure of a lifetime."

"I see," Tilly said.

The man butted the smoldering remains of his cigarette. He grabbed another from a gold box, lit it with a matching desk lighter and inhaled. "When I was writing for the pulp magazines in New York, I came across certain manuscripts. Most considered these works to be complete fiction. I alone believed these remarkable stories to be true." Two trails of cigarette smoke exited his flared nostrils. "They concerned a man of extraordinary prowess. An adventurer and he-man, much like myself."

"Okay," Tilly said.

"And all these stories share one remarkable thing in common. They refer to a treasure," he explained. "A fortune as incredible as the man himself."

"I wouldn't know anything about any man or treasure," Tilly said. "You may have kidnapped the wrong girl."

"I'll be the judge of that, my dear," her host explained. "Tell me, have you ever been balanced by a professional?"

The Commodore reached over his cluttered desk, handing Tilly two fist-sized rocks. She took them reluctantly as her captor cleared a few papers, revealing a simple wooden box the size of a pencil sharpener. The box featured two black knobs and a glass display with a needle. He answered Tilly's nervousness by turning the controls toward him.

"What's that?"

The redheaded man grinned, his small eyes disappearing into the folds of baggy skin. "Have you ever been under psychiatric care," he asked. He was grimacing now as if the question carried with it a particular disgust.

"I was in rehab. Does that count?" Tilly was not sure why she was being so honest.

"It does," the man answered. "My name is R. Renfield Hammerstein. But you my address me as The Commodore."

"Okay, Commodore," Tilly said, her tone not the least bit respectful. "What's your story?"

"Hold the rocks," the Commodore insisted. "Let's start by knowing yours."

She was instructed to firmly clasp the stones but not to squeeze. Tilly couldn't help herself. As the interrogation progressed, she tightened her grip, feeling with just a bit more incentive she might just crush rocks into a mass of unrecognizable gravel.

Assisted by two nurses on stepladders, the experts painstakingly removed the last remnants of plaster and rubble. The barrel was now clear, and they were about to finally separate the steel-plated turret from the human host.

Reboot commenced when an unobservant nurse inadvertently pressed the hidden button just inside the shoulder plate. A tiny hypodermic needle pierced the skin at the back of the neck, adrenaline surging on a direct path to the heart. The patient was rapidly gaining consciousness with a shell locked, loaded, and ready to fire. There was a clamorous clank as the trigger housing accepted the shell. The operating staff stepped back. Those with a background in munitions recognized the sound immediately. They remained glued to their seats, peering over the rail at the half human tank below. Collectively, they pondered greedily the capabilities of such an exquisite weapon.

The adrenalin found the heart at the same moment the cannon's firing pin struck the shell. The retort resulted in a smoky thunderclap, the round exploding in the hospital ceiling. Chunks of concrete and metal rained down on the retreating onlookers.

The patient, clothed in a blue patterned hospital gown, rose slowly. He threw his massive legs over the operating table and stood. His turret swiveled, examining the unfamiliar surroundings. His oversized head pounded inside its metal casing and even though awake, Tanktop had not acclimated fully. Gyros titled the turret as he glanced up at the amazed faces the survivors in the upper tiers of the operating theatre.

Shouting, pointing and cursing, the experts in their respective fields watched the smoldering weapon inventory the carnage. A few of the gawkers refused to retreat. One did not simply run away from the greatest discovery in munitions history. They hesitated, scribbling hastily written notes to pass along to their research and development teams.

There was no warning, three tiers of the operating theatre collapsing in a thunderous crash that resulted in the deaths of half the CEO's of the Military Industrial Complex. In a matter of seconds, the entire room was reduced to rubble.

Tanktop's killer instinct had returned. He moved through the panic of the hallway like the stainless-steel predator of old. He heard the wail of familiar sirens that always accompanied his particular brand of violence. The sights and sounds of human anguish, his personal calling card, echoed throughout the entire hospital.

"You like Button Fly Jones?"

The question came out of nowhere. Tilly was clutching an entirely new set of volcanic rocks and was unsure of how to respond. "Who doesn't?" Tilly finally lied. "He's a jazz musician, right?"

The Commodore checked the fluctuating needle and leaned over the desk. "That's right," he said. "Jazz." He lit another cigarette and fiddled with the dials on the small box.

"What do you want with me?"

The Commodore glanced up from the display and leered, exposing yellow, tobacco-stained teeth. He inhaled again. The white paper cigarette tube that housed the tobacco collapsed from the intensity of his draw. "To save you from yourself," he drawled in a gravelly Midwestern accent, "while enriching my cause."

"You're wasting both our time," Tilly declared defiantly. "I'm not helping you."

"You've already done your part, young lady," the Commodore answered. "Now it's just a matter of time."

"What are you talking about?"

"I'm referring to your curly-haired friend and his four companions," he answered. "No need to lie. I've been keeping an eye on them for years."

"Barry?" Tilly found herself grateful just saying his name. Was it possible their roles had somehow reversed? Instead of meddling in her life, could she somehow be affecting his? The idea made her head spin. "What does all that have to do with you kidnapping me?"

The Commodore glanced at the pinned needle on the box. "The P Meter never lies," he answered. "You will never get luminous attempting to deceive me."

"I don't want to get luminous!" Tilly exclaimed. "And I'm certainly not joining your seafaring cult."

"You really don't know, do you?" the Commodore wheezed, chuckling. "I have people everywhere. Your friend is headed to San Francisco to look for you. But I found you first." He leaned over the desk. The lamp cast and eerie shadow over his plump, red face. Her host now resembled a fiendish jack-o'-lantern. "I believe Panama holds the key, and that's where we're going."

"Panama?"

"The research backs me up." He pounded the table with a pudgy fist. "It's been there all along. Right under our very noses. Hidden for millennia, long before the age of great flood. In a place called the Valley of the Shadow."

"And what's my part in all of this?"

"You, my dear, are the bait," The Commodore answered.

The man monitoring the needle was a villainous idiot. But there was no mistaking it, he was dangerous. Hundreds of miles out to sea, Tilly was in no position to argue. As fond as she was of the five men, she doubted they'd manage to find her. Still, crazy as it sounded, there was a strange comfort in the fact that they were looking for her. And, for some unexplainable reason, she couldn't stop thinking about the one called Barry. Why couldn't she shake the image of that oversexed slacker out of her head?

They stood on Pier 44, gawking at the schooner moored alongside the dock. It was easily a forty-footer and resembled the luxurious seafaring transportation favored by 30's movie stars on weekend excursions to Catalina.

"She's a beauty alright," Reese proclaimed, a long whistle trailing the statement. "It was your father's. He christened it The Sea Questor."

"It's very nice but what do you expect us to do with it?" Barry asked.

"Holy cats," the man bellowed. "It's yours. She's going to take you to El Dorado."

"El Dorado?"

"Over the Mountains of the Moon," Reese recited, "down the valley of the shadow, ride boldly ride, the shade replied, if you seek for El Dorado."

"I'm not really into poetry."

"Your father discovered it," Reese explained. "The legendary gold mine of a great civilization. He used the riches to fight crime and benefit all mankind. All those other treasure seekers were looking in the wrong place. The mine was in Panama all along," Reese gestured toward the spacious craft. "Your crew is already on board. They're Guna Indians and are the most loyal and trusted friends of the Ravager."

"I'm not going anywhere without my Passport," Brain muttered quietly. The pale thinker had become suddenly nervous, his complexion turning a light crimson.

Beast raced up the gangway. "What are we waiting for?" he yelled to the others.

The rest stalled, exchanging apprehensive glances, their wide-eyed gaze returning to the schooner.

Barry grabbed Reese's elbow and led him a few steps away from the others. "I think you've got the wrong guy. I'm not ready for this," he confessed. "For any of it."

"There is no one else." The old man answered. "When the time comes, you'll know what to do."

"We have no money," Brain called out in an uncustomary agitated voice. It was hard not to notice the change in the lean man's features. He was clearly troubled about something.

"Money has nothing to do with your worries, friend." Reese studied Brain with a penetrating stare. "Is there something you want to say?"

"Money? Did I hear him right?" Doc asked.

"I'll tell you later," Barry answered. "Go ahead. I'll be with you in a minute."

Doc scurried up the gangplank, leaving Brain, Barry and Face with the gentle giant.

"Well?" Doc called to Brain from on board. "You coming?"

"I can't," Brain confessed. "I..." He seemed too embarrassed to answer and focused his attention on the bay.

Face was also reluctant to follow. "We're not prepared for any of this," he complained.

"That's the least of our worries," Barry said. "It's okay. Go ahead."

The reluctant actor joined Doc and Beast.

Brain remained defiant, standing on the dock and refusing to take a step. He fiddled with the head of his cane nervously. "Send me a telegram. I want to know how all this turns out,"

"Holy cats," Reese exclaimed. He tapped Brain on the shoulder and the younger man turned, a giant fist slamming into his jaw. Brain reeled and dropped, Barry managing to catch him before he hit the pavement.

"A little help," Barry called out. "Was that really necessary?"

Face and Beast raced down the gangplank.

"Sorry," Reese offered. "But you've only got a short time and he needed quick persuading."

Barry retrieved the sword cane as the pale thinker was carried onboard. "I guess this is goodbye," Barry said to the trustee of his new life. "Thanks for the ride and the boat. I'm not sure what else to say."

"Nothing," Reese said. "To tell you the truth, I'm jealous. But I've done my job. The torch has been passed."

174

"A torch?" Beast called out. "There's a torch?"

"What am I supposed to do?" Barry asked quietly.

"Most stories start with a good book," Reese answered. The old man winked, conveying some hidden truth.

"Now I'm really lost."

"Check out your cabin," Reese suggested. "Everything you need is there."

The two shook hands and the older man grabbed Barry with those massive hands and pulled him close, squeezing him into his giant frame. It was unexpected and yet strangely comforting. Barry broke off the embrace with a final goodbye and walked slowly up the gangplank.

Guna Indians, dressed in loin cloths and sandals, their faces and mostly naked bodies covered in exotic tattoos, appeared from below and hauled up the anchor in preparation of casting-off. The natives knew their jobs and performed them without saying a word. The four men watched dumbfounded, the schooner eventually pulling away from the dock and heading out into the bay.

Reese stood on the pier and watched. No one saw the tear in the old man's eye. "Sorry for socking your friend," he muttered, turning and marching back to his pink Caddy. The old man longed for the life of adventuring he left so long ago. A melancholy had overtaken him. It was the unique emotion one experiences when hiring your replacement.

They sailed for two days, skirting the scenic California coastline. The Guna crew were exceptional sailors, fulfilling nautical duties with a stoic assuredness that only came with an entire lifetime at sea. Sailing had been a hobby for Doc, and this qualified him as de facto captain of The Sea Questor for the duration of the voyage. The partnership between the chain-smoking chemist and the Guna proved a good one and the vessel made excellent time toward its destination.

Brain spent his first days bent over a rail. When he did manage to feel better, he excused his retching as ongoing experiments in advanced dolphin communication. No one questioned the embarrassed landlubber's explanation for fear of a reprisal from his razor-sharp sword cane. Eventually, what little skin color the lean thinker possessed returned and he carried on as if his violent reticence against coming aboard had never happened.

The four adventurers took full advantage of the leisure time. Comfortable quarters had been provided for all and there was plenty of food and beer in the well-stocked galley. There was no talk of Barry's newfound inheritance as if the conversation might suddenly jeopardize their longstanding friendship. It was decided to best keep quiet and enjoy the benefits of his lineage as they unfolded. There'd be plenty of time to address the promise of untold wealth when their lives were no longer under the dark cloud of constant jeopardy. Beast was the exception, giving no thought whatsoever to any so-called riches. He was having the time of his life. Clad only in his white Fruit of the Loom briefs, the big man ran, loped and leaped from bow to stern, delighted at every experience of his new life at sea.

Face found the new-found energy of his colleague exhausting. The endless exclamations of "Land ho," "ahoy," "bucko" and Face's least favorite, "How much further?" were constant distractions that took him away from his tan time. Several times, the actor threatened to lash the seagoing enthusiast to the forward mast. The idle threat did little to squelch Beast's exuberance. The actor's luck changed unexpectedly when he located the green buds in Beast's discarded jeans. Face had no choice but to hold the pungent herb hostage and Beast finally refrained from pestering the actor.

Brain made use of his leisure time by learning all things sailing, Doc painstakingly teaching out the fundamentals of seafaring navigation. The two men waited anxiously for each day's sunset, conferring quietly while they studied a brilliant night sky and determined their exact position in relation to their Southern course.

After the last few days of non-stop peril, the sailing turned out to be a welcome respite. The friends knew full well the idyllic calm would never last, and it was only a matter of time before fate revealed the next danger.

The only one not taking advantage of the R & R was Barry. He had completely withdrawn, disappearing into the main cabin below when the schooner reached open sea. His excusal was not announced, and he had not showed himself since leaving San Francisco.

"And I'm telling you," Beast repeated. "He only comes out at night when he thinks we're all asleep."

"This is Barry we're talking about," Face commented, "not Captain Ahab. There must be an explanation."

"I've seen it with my own eyes."

"What does he do when he's on deck?" Brain asked, losing patience and eager to resume a discussion of navigation using the sexton Doc had located in one of the small wooden cabinets.

"He speaks to the natives," Beast explained, his eyes growing wide in sincere emphasis. "In their own language."

"Nonsense," Doc said. "Barry can't speak Spanish, let alone some unknown ancient language."

"Don't force me to ration your herb," Face warned.

"This behavior is understandable," Brain explained, mulling the theory with lids at half-mast. "He's been forced to come to terms with a father he will never meet." He waved the tip of his cane for emphasis. "Not to mention inheriting the wealth of a small country. A daunting reality for someone who can't even balance a checkbook."

"Lucky for him, he has us to help out with his finances," Face wisecracked.

It was the middle of the third day and Doc was giving Brain a turn at the ship's wheel. The sails were up and billowing from a brisk wind at their backs, The Sea Questor slicing through a calm, blue water on a simple southerly course. Since the last heading, the schooner had drifted further away from the coastline and was now in International waters.

Beast's shout broke through the peaceful quiet and was heard by everyone on deck. The big man was completely naked, leaning way over the bow and pointing due west. His pale ass was a blinding counterpart to the rest of his sunburned body. "Land ho!" he bellowed.

"There are no islands here," Brain said after taking a quick glance at the unfurled chart.

"Forget him," Doc answered. "Too much sun."

Brain studied the excitable shipmate. Beast was now wearing his underwear on his head.

"Hmm," Brain said. "And obviously not enough hat."

Face left his open copy of "Respect of Acting" by Uta Hagen on the deck and joined the au naturel Beast at the bow. "I see it," Face called out. "Dead ahead."

Squawking gulls circled above as an unpleasant aroma wafted over the schooner.

Doc took the wheel from Brain and cranked, the two catching their first glimpse of what lay ahead.

"It's an island," Doc started. "An island of…"

"Garbage," Barry concluded, appearing out of nowhere and finishing the chemist's thought. His presence had taken the two men by surprise, slipping behind them without making a sound.

The drifting eyesore was at least one hundred miles long. Plastic of various shapes and sizes had somehow bonded together to form a landscape of non-biodegradable garbage. Hills of aluminum cans jutted out from synthetic valleys of plastic that seemed to stretch for miles. A beach of Styrofoam packing peanuts undulated with the gentle current. The uncharted landmass had a strange and unsettling geography that left everyone with a cold and empty guilt over their own recycling habits.

The Guna crew went to work immediately, shoving Doc and Brain away from the wheel and seizing control of the vessel. The natives wanted nothing to do with the strange, uncharted phenomenon.

"Look!"

Beast pointed as an infant whale breached the water's surface. The frolicking calf was unaware of any danger, navigating the narrow passage between schooner and garbage.

"Humpback?" Doc asked.

"I don't think so," Face answered in all seriousness. "I think it's a whale."

Doc lit another cigarette.

"That garbage is moving," Face declared.

"Impossible," Brain answered. Despite the denial, he was witnessing the exact same phenomenon. "Must be the current."

The island rumbled, an avalanche of soda cans sliding down a hill of paper and wood. A tentacle of laundry bags, Styrofoam peanuts and assorted refuse slithered out from the mass, creeping toward the unsuspecting whale.

"Watch out," Beast shouted.

If the infant humpback heard the human's warning, it gave no sign. It bobbed out of the water, devoting its full attention to entertaining the panicking humans on board. The impetuous Beast climbed over the rail and dove into the water before anyone could stop him. The surprised calf backed away from the commotion and was now perilously within reach of the finger of trash.

The infant mammal realized instantly it had made a fatal mistake. Before the garbage poured over the top of it, it called out for help with a series of pathetic guttural moans and clicks.

"Beast!"

Fearing the worst, the three men sprang into action. Brain removed a life preserver and hurled it to Doc. The chemist continued the drill, tossing the preserver over the other's heads where it splashed into the water between stern and the living garbage. The men gathered at the rail, shielding their eyes against the intense glare.

Beast hooked an arm through the preserver, watching as his friends reeled him toward the schooner. The garbage was too fast, already climbing up over the big man's chin. "The whale," Beast sputtered desperately. "Do you see it?"

The whale was nowhere in sight. The others pulled on the line, attempting to reel in their friend. Beast splashed out at the debris with a free hand and it responded like quicksand, rapidly overwhelming the victim. The big man managed one more quick turn before the garbage swallowed him, one brutish hand clinging to the life preserver.

"Beast," Face yelled. "Get the hell out of there."

Beast's hand slipped from the preserver, disappearing under the thick layer of Styrofoam.

His friends watched from the rail in a state of shock. Each weighed the dangers of diving in after the two floundering mammals but in waiting too long had blown any chance of a rescue. Garbage now surrounded the entire schooner and was moving out of the ocean and crawling up the ship's hull.

The Guna were already hard at work. Diving equipment appeared out of nowhere, the natives stripping Barry and sliding him into a black wetsuit. The once troubled slacker was heroically rigid; a sight totally unfamiliar to his friends. They had witnessed acts of bravery before but had never seen him look as grim and determined as he was now. The aura of confidence was no longer temporary and had somehow become an integral new part of Barry Levitt's D.N.A.

"You've never used a regulator and air tank before," Brain protested. He got right to the point. "And you know nothing of the compensator, the pressure gauge or the weight belt."

"You're mistaken, Brain" Barry answered coolly. "I am now one of the leading authorities on the science and sport of scuba."

Brain's jaw dropped. He turned to Doc.

"You're not certified?" Doc blustered. He was just as flummoxed as his friend and had lit a cigarette out of pure exasperation.

Two Guna men were in the process of draping the air tank over Barry's shoulder. The only part of diver not covered in rubber was his face.

"We admire your confidence, but this is more complicated than the one class you took at the community college," Brain offered.

"I'll bring him back." Barry stated matter-of-fact. He climbed up onto the rail, his back to the growing pile of garbage.

Face remained silent through the exchange. He handed Barry the mask. "If anything happens to you, can I have the goldmine?"

The comment diffused the growing tension. Barry's determined grimace evolved into a sly grin. "Sure," he answered. "Knock yourself out."

"You heard the man," Face called out to the others. "I called it. Be nice to me or none of you are getting a penny. Find Beast and get the hell out of there." Face handed Barry the mouthpiece. He leaned close so that only Barry could hear. "I'm holding you to the whole goldmine thing."

Face slapped the tank and Barry dropped backwards off the boat. There was no splash. The garbage had snagged the diver before he broke the surface. It held him securely, keeping Barry above water. The clock was ticking, and the diver lay atop the refuse like an incapacitated crowd surfer.

His friends leaned out over the rail to grab Barry, the garbage retaliating by moving the captive away. Barry attempted to remove his respirator, the garbage closing in around his wrists.

Once again, it was up to the Guna crew to rouse the three Caucasians out of a stunned panic. Shouting in their ancient language, the seafarers were once again on deck and rushing to the side of the boat.

"What are they doing?" Brain asked.

Doc snatched a bucket and inhaled. He stopped Brain before he could challenge the native crew. "No," he said. "It's okay."

The Guna had formed a fire line, buckets exchanging hands as the contents were dumped overboard onto the sentient heap of waste.

The garbage shuddered violently, a small opening appearing next to the prone Barry. It was a temporary entry into the watery depths and the diver seized the opportunity. He shook his arms free and rolled into the water.

"Okay, what's with the bucket?" Face asked.

"Brilliant," Brain muttered under his breath. He had taken a good whiff at the remaining contents and his lean face twisted in a mix of displeasure and accomplishment.

"What?" Face repeated.

"Lysol," Brain answered.

"Kills germs on contact," Doc added with a wry smile.

"That's what I'm talking about," Face said, addressing the isle of refuse. "Now you know who you're messing with."

"Trash talking." Doc explained.

The native crew returned to their tasks, armed with a silent confidence that the man below the water had all the tools necessary to solve the underwater mystery.

Barry paddled through the futuristic thoroughfare with confident strokes, swimming toward the eerie phosphorescent lights in the distance. The tunnel was constructed of repurposed six-pack soda rings, the pinks, greens and pulsating purples in the distance marking the end of his journey. The swimmer couldn't shake the feeling that he was propelling himself directly through a ponderous sequence from "Star Trek: The Motion Picture." The bubbles belched from the respirator were the only sound and reminded him of the seriousness of his mission.

He was midway toward the throbbing lights when a gentle current took hold of his body and he no longer had to propel himself; the water gently pulling him toward his destination. With little choice, Barry positioned his hands to his side and allowed the unknown force to do the work.

It was positively ethereal and unlike any creature on earth. As he was pulled closer, the creature unfurled translucent wings of calming, undulating colors. The creature possessed a thin, tubular body with a smaller oblong head. Two oval-black orbs, placed midway on a pointed head, squinted at the approaching guest. Barry estimated the size of the creature to be well over ten feet from tip to top. As he drew closer to the alien host, the current ebbed and eventually ceased.

The tunnel emptied into a vast grotto of recycled debris. The walls appeared to be a vast, plastic honeycomb made up of thousands of individual cells. The units were stacked atop the other, each chamber imprisoning a perfectly preserved specimen of oceanic life. It was a chilling menagerie but what was the purpose? Barry paddled over to a wall and studied the closest prisoner. Inside the cell, a large seabird remained perfectly still. Veins of throbbing light blinked inside all of the cocoons and seemed to somehow link the entire collection. Barry guessed that some unknown form of energy was passing through these plastic membranes, keeping the specimens alive and perfectly preserved.

The alien's colorful wing unfolded, the tip of the appendage pointing directly behind him. With several strokes, Barry maneuvered his body and faced yet another plastic cocoon. Inside the cocoon lay the naked and unconscious body of Beast. The big man's eyes were open, his face appearing unnaturally calm and serene. Next to his friend's cage of bubble-wrap was another space of the same size and dimension. The adjoining cell was empty; waiting for the arrival of the next human tenant.

Barry fought off the impetuous urge to rip his friend out of the plastic prison with his bare hands. It was the right choice but the wrong time. If Beast were alive, the first tear would flood the plastic compartment and fill the big man's lungs with water. At this early stage of the confrontation, diplomacy was required. Barry began the inter dimensional parlay with the universal sign of "huh," his arms and elbows forming a double-u above his shoulders.

Both wings were unfurled and the colors, once soothing, took on a threatening hue of deep purple, black and blood- red. The almond eyes of the creature formed dark, menacing slits and signaled that negotiations had come to an end. An apocalyptic thrumming accompanied the sudden change in color schemes. The cavern grew dark and the noise, amplified through metric tons of seawater, pounded in Barry's head. He covered his ears, the futile action providing no relief.

An unfurled sheet of bubble wrap appeared out of nowhere and floated in the human's direction. The plastic wrap was propelled by an army of Styrofoam peanuts. The white foam halted below his swim fins, laying out the clear shroud. Barry was about to suffer the same fate as his friend, swaddled in non-biodegradable garbage and put on display by an unknown life form.

The thrumming stopped unexpectedly, replaced by a whale song that reverberated throughout the cavern of trash. It caught the alien off guard, and it turned, wide oval black eyes blinking at the new intrusion.

The adult humpback whale punched through a grotto wall on the first attempt. Lifeless specimens broke free from their cells and floated toward the surface. The adult whale raced through the water, a blubbery bullet on a ramming course with the alien zookeeper. The alternating high pitches and guttural clicks from the female mammal contained a rage specific only to mothers.

The alien attempted to flutter away but was too late. Wing color had shifted back to the softer shades of conciliation. Yellows, greens and pinks pulsated dizzyingly, in hopes of hypnotizing the rampaging whale.

The display was for naught. Alien butterfly met whale snout and the fragile being crumpled on impact. The delicate wings were ripped off in the collision and floated upward. The once benevolent alien was now nothing more than a smashed bug on a careening vehicle of unforgiving blubber. When the whale crashed through the far grotto wall on the far side, the creature ceased to exist in this dimension or any other.

The adult humpback was totally berserk. Her tail slashed, crushing one side and then the other of the cavern of garbage. Plastic cells ripped open and the specimens, awaking slowly, swam off or floated to the surface in a grateful panic. The pulsating lights flickered and dimmed as the energy that powered the zoo drained off into nothing.

Barry ripped Beast from his plastic cage. As the cocoon filled with water, he pinched the big man's nose, thrusting the regulator into his gaping mouth. Beast's eyes popped open and the freed prisoner gasped and took a lungful of air. Barry's free hand continued to excavate his friend from the plastic prison and with a few precise tears the naked Beast was finally free.

The two settled into a well-timed pattern of sharing air as they began to swim away. After only a few strokes, Beast unexpectedly thrust the regulator back at his friend. The big man pointed behind him and swam back into the collapsing grotto. Barry had no choice but to swim after the big man and into the escalating destruction.

As he drew closer, Barry discovered what his friend was up to. Beast had located an extra-large cell and was freeing the humpback calf from the plastic prison. The mother calmed, approaching cautiously, seeming to sense some sort of rescue was underway. Despite all his efforts, it appeared as if the heroic actions of Beast we're too late. Once free from the plastic cell, the helpless infant remained inert. The mother, however, was not giving up so easily. Arching her back, she dove under her offspring and gently nudged the three mammals toward the surface.

Doc, Brain and Face watched as the whale punched through the island of garbage. Humans and baby whale rolled off the top of the giant mammal as she breached. The adult whale dropped, smashing more of the island and sending a message that alien encounters in her watery world would not be tolerated.

"I don't believe it," Face managed, a wide grin spreading over his tanned face. "He did it! Hey. Hey!"

Beast and Barry did not answer. They couldn't. The unconscious calf remained in danger. Both were furiously treading water, devoting their full attention to the offspring.

"Breathe, damn you," Beast wailed.

"Hold him," Barry ordered, moving the head of the infant closer. He straddled the top of the infant and positioned his mouth around the blowhole.

"Artificial respiration on a blowhole?" Brain questioned. "Is such a thing even possible?"

Doc shrugged. As far as the chemist knew, a whale's blowhole was exclusively for expelling. None-the-less, the chemist remained fascinated by the heroics displayed by his friend.

Barry removed his mouth and spit out several Styrofoam peanuts. The baby whale gasped and shuddered, a weak stream of water dribbling out the blubbery orifice.

"There's a lesson here," Face muttered. "Somewhere."

Mother humpback watched as her offspring expelled a healthy spout of ocean. Within moments the calf had regained its strength and was nuzzling with its heroic mom.

Beast and Barry swam to the schooner. As they climbed onto the deck, they turned and witnessed mother and offspring breach, swimming away from the disintegrating island of refuse.

"What happened down there?" Face asked.

"Barry saved two lives today," Beast explained. The big man was so proud of his friend he was about to bust.

"Welcome back," Face mumbled under his breath. The big man clearly heard, and the actor was forced to change tactics. "And put some clothes on. You're making me nauseous."

Barry stared into the rising waves as if the answer to all their questions lay somewhere deep below the surface. The schooner pitched violently, the surprised men reaching for the rail. A funnel of dark clouds appeared unexpectedly, materializing directly overhead. The calm ocean had grown violent, the ship rocking from a surging tidal commotion.

"What now?" Face managed.

A sudden jolt knocked them from the rail and onto the deck.

"They're back," Beast said, pointing to the churning sea.

Bright pastel lights pulsated, shimmering from inside the lined recesses of the craft. As the obsidian pyramid rose from the water, piles of Styrofoam, plastic, aluminum, and wood slid off the alien hull and dropped into the ocean. When a giant wave nearly capsized the schooner, the Guna intervened and corrected their course. The Sea Questor slipped over the wave like a small child careening down a steep slide. The waters calmed, the spacecraft hovering overhead. The alien craft blocked out the entire sun and cast an ominous shadow over the sailing schooner.

"Erich Von Daniken was right," Beast muttered.

The five men watched as the spaceship slowly ascended into the dark sky.

"The tunnel in Redding and now this," Face said to Brain. "You realize that there's no living with the wild man now."

Brain paused, doubting his own reason. "Lucky guesses," he answered. "Much like a room full of monkeys with typewriters."

"Thankfully we've only got the one monkey," Face said, grinning.

Barry placed a protective arm around Beast's shoulders. "I give more credence to Beast's theories than most men's facts," he stated.

The ribbing ceased immediately. Barry's compliment was uttered with an authority unlike anything his friends had ever heard. Their friend had somehow been transformed. Each of them had changed, but what accounted for Barry's remarkable transformation? There was no doubt that their friend was now clearly in charge.

Preparations for the procedure had been made decades before Barry ever set foot on board The Sea Questor. The quarters, located below deck, were comfortable but cramped. Two thirds of the space were taken up with aisle upon aisle of shelved books; a scholarly collection that rivaled many of the small branches of public libraries in his hometown. The accumulated sciences were all included along with an entire history of modern warfare and martial arts. Only a few volumes seemed to be dedicated to the arts. The library had been arranged for quick and easy access. The books were organized with the end user's comprehension in mind: easiest to read to the most complicated running from bow to stern. Along with the bound volumes were oversized atlases and elaborate maps of every continent and island in the known world. With most of the cabin devoted to the pursuit of higher learning, there was only space remaining for a tiny cot, a desk and a small black and white television attached to what appeared to be a reel-to-reel videotape player.

A small folded piece of paper was taped to one of the magnetic reels. Barry removed the note, unfolded the sharp crease and read the neat, polished cursive.

"Son," the correspondence began, "I believe it is high time that I reveal myself. Connected to the television is an invention of my design. I call it the Video Playback Beta Receiver, or V.P.B.R."

Barry turned on the V.P.B.R and switched the dial on the small portable television to channel 3. The short burst of graininess was replaced by a flickering black-and-white image of a tanned man with a buzz-cut of black hair. Despite the middle-aged girth and male pattern baldness, the man appeared more than capable of taking care of himself. As the image steadied, the subject himself seemed to vibrate. Barry attempted to adjust the picture to no avail.

"My name is Rock Ravage. To my enemies, I'm known as the Ravager. I am your father." The man on the tape bore a striking resemblance to the much younger man who had been summoning him from deep inside his subconscious.

Barry's whole life had been redefined by this one statement. The entire journey had led to this one particular moment as if it had been all part of a much larger and elaborate plan. It was a father and son reunion instituted from beyond the grave.

His father continued, summarizing his entire lineage, from World War I, to the death of Barry's grandfather. The history lesson was followed by an editorial. "With the aid of science and technology, I did my best to help as many people as possible, but a hero is only as relevant as his generation. I believe this is your time, son. I am asking you to take over the family business."

Barry studied the grainy image of a man he had never met. He felt an emptiness in the pit of his stomach and a longing for a real father that the video could not quench. Still he listened, riveted to the mystery that was his own life. Before he realized it, he was two hours into the tape.

"The year is 1954 and there's a price on my head, initiated by a shadowy, criminal underworld and led by a villain named Harrison Thunder. Thunder would never be satisfied with my own death. His hatred for me goes so much deeper. I believe he will orchestrate a plot to seize control of my fortune and use my own scientific resources to wreak havoc on an unsuspecting world."

Barry's father continued calmly: "This is where you enter the story, son. You must stop Thunder before it's too late. You will not lack for resources. You are my only benefactor and, if you survive, will inherit my entire fortune. You must do whatever it takes to stop this madman before it's too late."

The tape continued with a detailed explanation of his father's view of the world and his groundbreaking theories concerning good and evil. More than once he reiterated that his part in this universal battle had ended and it was up to his only heir to continue the fight.

"For me, the days of a lone man, a protector with gifts and abilities surpassing all others, ended. There are new dangers now. With you, these heroic days may very well make a comeback."

His father became thoughtful. His tan, wrinkled brow creased, and the unmistakable, signature vibrating returned. "I blame Ayn Rand," his father explained. "I had the distinct displeasure of meeting her at a dinner party. A very unpleasant woman. Never liked her. Very bossy. And her theory of Objectivism is total malarkey."

The older man never faltered or paused, just kept on as if his life and legacy depended on it. "Here in my very own cabin, you're surrounded by volumes containing the disciplines of the known world. You will need this knowledge to carry out your destiny. I was trained from birth. You will be starting considerably later, and I have no idea at the speed in which you learn."

Barry's reading was college level, but retention had never been his strong point. Suffering from a wandering mind, he could lose an author's train of thought after only a few sentences. It was his curse. To keep his mind focused, he read aloud and now his brain required the practice anytime he processed the written word.

"And while I suspect you have no choice but to be as brilliant as me, I cannot take the chance of you not being able to comprehend as fast as myself or the man who killed me. So..."

Ah, here it comes, Barry thought. How will I ever live up to the expectations of a genius, adventuring father?

"I have created a program, perfected in one of my medical facilities for the criminally insane. What once was accomplished by a complex medical procedure can now be achieved electronically. At least, I believe so. I've never tried it. You, my son, will be the first." There was no hint of warmth or humor in the statement. It was declared with as much conviction as his father's earlier lecture on the nature of good and evil.

"Please go to the bottom desk drawer and remove the helmet of sustained learning."

Barry opened the deep drawer and removed a device weighing several pounds. It looked to Barry that its prior purpose might very well have been electronically draining pasta.

"This device, when coupled to the portable, mobile electronic brain, which I will henceforth refer to as the personal computer, will upload the accumulated knowledge of the cabin's library into your brain. It will take several hours. So, if you need to visit the lavatory, I'd go now."

Barry ignored his father's advice and placed the device onto his head. It was not a comfortable fit, the sharp probes sticking into his skull in more than a dozen places.

"The mobile electronic brain is in a storage locker at the foot of your bunk. Please remove it and place it on your desk. It's the smallest machine of its kind and is fully mobile."

Barry located the footlocker and opened it, eager to gaze upon the world's first working laptop. Taking up the entire space inside was a bulky device made from radio tubes, transistors and thousands of wires. It was too heavy to lift, and Barry dragged the entire trunk across the floor. His father must have timed out his instructions as he had paused before continuing.

"A punch card is in back of each volume in this library. You will need to remove these cards and pile them into a stack."

"Okay," Barry said. "But this may take a while,"

"Please push the pause button on the machine and resume the playback when you have retrieved and stacked the cards."

There were over two thousand books in the small library and the exact same amount of punch cards. Random holes were punched into every card and no card's patterns were alike. Gathering the requested items took a while but Barry eventually completed the task. He stacked the cards into a high, neat pile and left them to rest inside the lid of the open locker. He turned back to the Video Receiver and resumed the playback. The image of Rock Ravage wavered from the stretching of the tape before resuming with a slight audio hiccup.

"Now it's time to feed the cards into the computer. This is important, son. For the procedure to work, there must be no interruptions. The transference cannot be paused for any reason. If it is, there will be dire consequences."

"Dad, I don't have to go the bathroom."

Barry placed the pasta strainer atop his head while connecting the other end to what looked like a large earphone jack. He turned on the machine and it came alive with flickering lights and a slight smell of burning wire. One at a time, the cards were sucked into the machine with a swoosh. A series of clacking sounds followed, announcing the technology was in the process of reading the cards. The probes tickled at first and what followed was a sensation unlike anything Barry had ever experienced. A complicated inner dialogue was taking place inside his consciousness. It was the voice of his father and the communication grew increasingly rapid and beyond normal human comprehension. But for Barry, every thought, word, and equation were crystal clear as if he were processing it all by osmosis.

"Land, ho," Beast called out from above deck.

It was instinctive and happened so fast the subject didn't realize what he was doing. Ignoring his father's only warning, Barry removed the helmet and sprinted out of the cabin. The electronic brain, lights blinking and cards shuffling, was now without a human subject.

The mystery of the Island of Garbage had concluded, and an exhausted Barry returned to his cabin to finish a procedure that was designed to be carried out in one sitting. The personal, mobile electronic brain, henceforth referred to as the personal computer, and accompanying headgear were right where he had left them. There were no blinking lights and no clacking noises. It was as if he had never started the procedure. He removed the metal cap from the side of the chair and studied the intricate wiring of the headpiece. "There could be dire consequences," his father had warned him.

Barry ignored the mental reminder, once again placing the device over his head. The familiar probes stabbed into his head as the combined knowledge of the remaining volumes flooded his brain. It was no longer a peaceful transfer, the electronic pulses stabbing his brain repeatedly. Every nerve in his body was suddenly on fire. Muscles convulsed violently, and a process designed to be painless was now very close to killing him. The combined digital knowledge stabbed at the center of his cerebral cortex, an eternity of facts and figures invading his skull all at once. Barry screamed. It was the last thing he accomplished before his head hit the floor.

"What's that on his head?" It was the confused voice of Beast.

Barry opened his eyes slowly. His colleagues stood in a semi-circle, staring down at him. "What happened?" he managed.

"We heard a scream, ran below deck and found you on the floor with a kitchen utensil on your head," Face explained. "Don't get me wrong. What you choose to do behind closed doors is your business. Still…"

"What do we have here?" Doc asked. The chemist knelt beside the trunk and studied the electronic components. "A computer?"

"Hmm," Brain agreed. "A closer examination of these punch cards is warranted. There are thousands of them" Brain glanced at the prone Barry.

Barry attempted to sit up and became instantly dizzy. Face and Beast separated their leader from the floor and placed him gently in the chair.

"It's a personal, mobile electronic brain," Barry said. "And those cards contain the collected knowledge of the known world."

The four stared at the footlocker in amazement.

"A gift from my father," Barry said. His name was Rock Ravage and he called himself the Ravager. I think he wants me to take over the family business."

"You od'd on learning," Beast exclaimed.

"Is such a thing even possible?" Face asked.

"There's only one way to find out," Brain said, turning to Doc. "We will ask Barry a question that before now he'd never be able to answer."

"That's too easy," Face said with a mischievous grin. "Ask him any of our birthdays."

"The answer has to be in one of these books," Barry clarified. He was just as eager to test out his theory as his friends.

"Something the old Barry could never answer," Brain reiterated.

"Right," Doc confirmed. He lit a cigarette and looked around as if the room might provide a clue.

"Let's start with a simple one," Brain interrupted. "A train leaves Chicago for Detroit going 60 mph. At the same time, on an adjacent track, a train leaves Detroit heading for Chicago going 45 mph. Detroit is 280 miles from Chicago. How far are the trains from Chicago when they pass?"

"Are you kidding me," Barry said. "A story problem?"

"It's either that or we ask you to balance your checkbook," Doc said.

"One hundred and sixty miles," Barry answered.

"Should we make him show his work?" Brain asked.

"Check to see if the answer's written on his hand," Beast suggested.

Face stepped forward. "Who wrote the music and lyrics to 'The Music Man?'"

"Meredith Wilson," Barry answered. "Here's a little-known fact. Wilson was commissioned by President John F. Kennedy to write 'Chicken Fat,' a song used to combat childhood obesity."

"He's good," Face confirmed.

Beast raised his hand. "How many scoops of raisins in a box of Raisin Bran cereal?"

"Two scoops. However, a scoop is a nonstandard unit of volume, so the prevalence of raisins in the cereal remains uncertain. Kellogg's Raisin Bran comes in 15, 20, and 25.5-ounce boxes, all of which bear the 'Two scoops' claim."

It was now open season on Barry and the questions came fast and furious.

"Did Lee Harvey Oswald act alone?"

"Yes"

"Will man ever travel past the speed of light?"

"Signs point to yes."

"Is there a God?"

"Reply hazy. Ask again."

Brain halted the flurry of questions. "Hold it," he said in his quiet, authoritative tone. He kneeled and peered into Barry's eyes as if attempting to locate where all those answers were hidden. He cleared his throat. "Are you just giving us the options you recall from a Magic Eight-ball?" he asked.

There was a pause. "Looking good," Barry said.

Laughter filled the cabin, and the accumulated tensions of the past week were instantly erased. Things again turned serious when Barry replayed the entire video of his father.

"Physical and mental," Doc asked. "No offense but you don't appear to be any different."

"No offense taken," Barry answered. "I don't feel different."

"Ahhhhhhhhhhhhh!" It was Beast's unmistakable battle cry as the big man propelled his thick body over the small desk.

The others backed away, their eyes never leaving the attacker or the intended victim.

"We're about to find out," Brain muttered as he placed outstretched arms in front of Doc and Face.

Barry stepped out of the way, dodging Beast easily. Executing a Jiu Jitsu flick of the wrist, he swung the airborne Beast right side up and landed him firmly on both feet.

"Whoa," Beast said. "How'd you do that?"

"I don't know," Barry announced. "It came suddenly. Like I'd been doing it for years."

Beast acted before anyone could stop him. He snatched the metal helmet from a surprised Face and placed it over his head. He reached over to the electronic brain.

"Let's do this," he said as he flipped the switch.

It turned out that the greatest mind in the world had taken precautions. In case the device fell into the wrong hands, protocols and safeties were in place. A DNA match was required, and Beast didn't meet the genetic specifications. A current of powerful electricity surged through the conductors and into Beast's brain. The distinct smell of burning hair filled the cabin. Beast's eyes bulged, his mouth dropping open and emitting a gurgling sound consistent with mild seizures and Three Stooges films.

"Well I'm enjoying this," Face said.

"Maybe we should shut it off," Doc offered.

"No. No," Face interrupted. "We have to be sure."

"He seems to like it," Brain commented.

Face placed a hand on his friend's shoulder. "Who's the Ravager's son?" he teased as if talking to an infant. "You're the Ravager's son."

Barry said nothing. His mind was elsewhere. His thoughts concerned Tilly and whether he would ever find her.

"I'm sorry," he said. "What?"

"Nothing."

The current of electricity ceased, Beast flopping onto the floor. "Whoa," Beast managed, taking a deep breath after the self-inflicted seizure had passed. "Let's go again. I feel smarter already."

Tilly owed her amazing recovery to the fresh air, exhausting work detail and the daily P-monitoring administered by the redheaded, chain-smoking Commodore. She had learned that while the physical desire to re-enter the world of addiction had passed, the root causes of her problems still remained. Her taste in men and a plan to avenge the death of her mother were prime examples of a lifelong emotional immaturity and were significant barriers to a complete recovery. Tilly now understood these destructive behaviors had led her to her life of drug addiction and, unresolved, could very likely lead to something worse; psychiatry. Her only hope in avoiding such a catastrophe was becoming luminous. It had also become obvious that The Commodore had taken a special interest in her. And why not? Her newly discovered insights gave value to this organization and could help transform thousands of lives. Tilly achieved the first step of clarity off the Sea of Cortez and, shortly after, committed her life fully to the practice of Diatribe.

The new recruit had gotten past her abduction and the girl who put it all in motion. She no longer harbored any resentment. In fact, if she did happen to run into Denice with a cee, she'd thank her for helping to put her very chaotic life back on track.

After countless days at sea, The Argo 2 anchored off a stretch of the deserted Panamanian coastline. Night had fallen, a full moon floating in a brilliant star-filled sky. After mess, a spartan meal consisting of franks, beans and a plastic cup of fruit cocktail, a handful of the attractive crew were ordered to the Commodore's cabin for a top-secret meeting. Much to her surprise, Tilly had been included.

Denice was present, and Tilly noticed changes in the young blonde immediately. While Tilly had become more confident in the new-found religion, Denice had grown more agitated. The young blonde looked exhausted, staring dubiously over at three men who Tilly had yet to meet. Two women, attired in the Commodore's favorite uniform for female crew-members, short shorts and pastel-colored Polos, were included in the role call. The women clearly stood apart, standing at the opposite side of the room and never once acknowledging the others.

The Commodore chain-smoked through his third cigarette before he eventually felt the need to explain himself. "I wish I was going with you," he announced in a mucus trebled voice. "I am quite confident that this will be the adventure of a lifetime."

Everyone, but Denice, smiled. The blonde shuffled her feet, staring at the cabin deck with hollow, sunken eyes.

"The exact location of the treasure has been telepathically communicated to me by a close associate of the celestial being Zandu," The Commodore coughed mid-explanation, the hack raspy and unhealthy. "Etchmo be his name."

No one dared flinch at the obviously improvised name.

"Fellow beings have stockpiled great wealth away from the impending flood and the prying eyes of the cosmos. You brave men and women will find these treasures and report back to me." The Commodore's bloodshot eyes settled on Tilly. "Tilly will be your compass," he added. "I have chosen her specifically for this expedition. Hers, is a great honor."

Even in a state of clarity, Tilly found the remarks puzzling. Remarkable as her recovery had been, she was pretty sure she hadn't any special locating powers. She couldn't even read a map. Tilly wanted to point out the oversight but decided against it. She refused to shake the Commodore's faith he had placed in her.

"The exact location will become obvious when you reach the center of the cosmic vortex that is the beacon of Zandu's best friend."

"Etchmo," the assembled chanted.

"Etchmo," the Commodore repeated.

Under the cover of night, the band of zealots boarded the rubber raft and were lowered into the calm sea. A perfect moon reflected off the glassy surface of the bay and the only sound was the paddles, slipping in and out of the water as they made for shore.

Tilly's reticence was soon gone, and she found herself relishing her part in the spiritual expedition. The Commodore's faith was proof positive that the man's thinking was lightyears beyond other humans. There was his exemplary naval record, his best-selling science fiction novels, not to mention his ongoing holy war against modern psychiatry. To Tilly, the midnight treasure hunt was yet another jewel in the crown of the man she now affectionately thought of as her savior.

The landing party disembarked on a deserted strip of white sandy beach, a mere stone's throw from a border of thick rain forest. The chattering of unseen monkeys along with the enthusiastic cawing of exotic birds beckoned the explorers to enter this new world and begin their hunt for celestial treasure.

An intense man with a military bearing and unsightly complexion was the Commodore's eyes and ears on the mission. His name was Gary Pettijohn and he reminded Tilly of her ex, Todd Tetrus. The two men shared a common look of cruelty which made her uneasy. Tilly noticed that Denice couldn't stop glancing at the escort as if the young blonde had experienced his cruelty firsthand. There was obviously something about him that scared the hell out of her.

The other two men, good-natured jock types, appeared more than up for the physical challenge of a hike into the jungle. The two women also seemed capable enough, but Tilly couldn't help but wonder if their presence served some other purpose.

They appeared too flaky, chatty and self-absorbed for such an important mission.

As the group readied to enter the rain forest, Tilly pulled Denice aside. "Where have you been?" she asked. "I have so much to tell you."

Denice studied her with wide, green eyes. "Oh my god, they got to you, didn't they?" she whispered. "I can tell."

"The Commodore says I'm at the first stage of luminosity," Tilly proclaimed, much louder than she intended.

Denice remained preoccupied with Pettijohn. He was glowering their way and grimacing with a wide, thin mouth. His dark eyes reminded Tilly of an anxious cat stalking a neighborhood bird.

"I've been below deck," Denice stated. "Punishment detail."

"What for?"

Denise seemed anxious to change the subject. "Just watch yourself. I've been on these missions before," she whispered. The blonde peered off into the jungle. "This is not about any treasure hunt."

"What are you talking about?" Tilly asked bitingly. She was losing what little sympathy she had for the teen.

"This bunch doesn't need a map. This is my tenth expedition. We'll find nothing. You watch. This is all just an excuse to get off the ship. And something else is going on. I'm just not sure what."

The surprise must have registered on Tilly's sunburned face. "But the treasure," she stammered. "I'm the compass."

"Just stay away from Pettijohn," Denice warned. "He's crazy."

The men dragged the rubber raft to the edge of the jungle and camouflaged it with dried ferns and palm leaves. The morning sun was now peaking over the eastern mountains and, after several minutes, the seven entered the rain forest.

Tilly attempted to stay confident, but Denice's revelations bothered her more than she realized. It was the first in a series of warning signs that suggested the Commodore might not be everything she'd hoped. She attempted to ignore the alarm bells going off in her head. The observations might be nothing more than petty jealousy. Denice's reticence obviously stemmed from her own failure of achieving luminosity. Tilly made a mental note to audit her with an P Meter as soon as they returned to the ship.

The expedition had been marching several miles when they stumbled upon a fresh water pool. A mid-sized waterfall dumped an unending supply of cool, inviting water over a slick, mossy ledge. The entire scene resembled something from a tourist brochure, and it took less than three minutes for half of the expedition to shed their clothes and dive in.

Denice shot Tilly a knowing glance. "I told you," she mouthed silently.

Pettijohn was clearly upset over the unscheduled layover. He paced, glancing at his watch and sighing loud enough for everyone to hear. Obviously, an important timetable had been overruled in favor of more carnal pursuits.

Tilly was bored by the bacchanal behavior. She and Denice sat on the edge of the pool, dangling their feet into the water, ignoring the others and chatting. All the while, Denice kept a close eye on their fidgety handler.

The reluctant chaperone had climbed onto a high rock on the far side of the pool. His back was to the water as if the flagrant morals of his charges might be catching. He pulled a rusty looking revolver from the back of his jeans and studied it. Tilly watched Pettijohn flip open the chamber and eye the bullets inside. His furrowed brow signaled a concern that the ammunition might escape if he didn't keep a constant eye on it. One flick of the wrist later, the chamber closed with an ominous click.

"It's always the same," Denice volunteered. "Around sunset we'll head to the beach, motor back to the ship and report that we didn't find anything."

"Won't the Commodore be angry?" Tilly asked. She worried that she was no longer the catalyst for this excursion, the magical beacon that would lead them all to a cosmic treasure. "He's gone to an awful lot of trouble."

"Trust me. He won't be half as pissed as Pettijohn. Knowing that he's going back empty handed is when things start to get dangerous."

"Why doesn't the Commodore do something?"

You still don't get it," Denice explained. "Pettijohn is an enforcer. By the time we get back to the ship, the Commodore will have forgotten about any treasure. He's too concerned with the people chasing him."

Tilly sat up straight. "Chasing him?" she asked. "Who's chasing him?"

"The World Health Organization, the American Board of Professional Psychology and the Internal Revenue Service," Denice said. "He believes they want him dead or behind bars. That's why he faked his death."

"Oh," Tilly managed before noticing that Pettijohn had disappeared. "He's gone."

The mood of the pool's occupants changed radically at the fifth wheel's departure. Couples paired off at opposite sides of the pool and the noisy frolicking had turned to a quiet, intimate cooing.

"Where'd he go?"

"Beats me," Denice said. "Maybe he's off looking for your treasure?"

Tilly frowned over the cut. "Well I gotta pee," she announced.

"There's always the fornicating lagoon," Denice offered.

"No thanks," Tilly said, slipping off the rock and stepping into the thick foliage. "I guess I'm a bit of a prude."

Tilly wandered for several minutes before locating a discreet spot. She was in the process of unbuttoning her khaki shorts when she heard a rustling in the foliage.

"It's not safe to be wandering out here alone."

There was no mistaking the intensity in his voice. It was Pettijohn. He had averted his eyes as he scanned the rain forest for unseen dangers.

"I'm sorry," Tilly managed. "I didn't know." She pulled up her shorts and stepped out from behind the cover of a small Alzatea tree.

"Stay vigilant. You need to keep an eye out for Anacondas and guerrillas."

"Snakes and monkeys. I'll be sure and do that."

"Rebels. Not apes," Pettijohn corrected. "They say Che Guevara himself wandered these very forests."

"Is that right?" Tilly said. She was feeling uncomfortable at the revolver in Pettijohn's sweaty hands. "Well, I better get back."

"To the whores and adulterers?" Pettijohn said. "They'll meet judgment soon enough."

"They're just blowing off a little steam," Tilly said. She didn't like the direction this conversation was headed.

His stare was beyond anything resembling sanity. He was now looking at her without comprehending she was a fellow human being. It was terrifying, and for the first time, Tilly feared for her life.

"Is that what we're calling it now?" Pettijohn muttered. "Maybe it's high time I blow off a little steam."

"To each his own," Tilly said, attempting a half-assed, disarming smile. She grew more alarmed with each word out of the man's mouth. Tilly turned and took a step toward the pool.

"No," Pettijohn blurted. "I need to talk to you."

Tilly stopped but did not have the nerve to turn around. Call it a hunch but she was sure the revolver was aimed at her back. "I'm not sure the Commodore would approve? You standing there with a gun at my back?"

"Is that what you think? That I going to kill you?"

Tilly's tone was insolent. "I don't think you'd risk hurting the celestial compass." She drew a deep breath. She was shaking and fought off the overpowering impulse to flee. If she did take another step, she'd get a bullet in her back.

"Turn around."

Tilly obeyed. It was just as she'd expected. Pettijohn had the gun trained on her.

"So," Tilly stammered. "Now what?"

Denice appeared out of nowhere. She clutched a coconut-sized rock and was creeping up behind the clueless Pettijohn.

"Take off your top," Pettijohn ordered, gesturing the gun barrel at her blouse.

"You don't want to do this."

He said nothing. His nostrils flared as he pointed the gun at her midsection.

"Sure. Sure," Tilly answered. "Just take it easy."

Tilly fumbled with the top button. She needed to keep her assailant's attention as Denice was still too far away. "Easy does it," she said. "Let's take our time."

Pettijohn took a step toward her as Tilly revealed the slightest bit of cleavage. She prayed it was enough to hold his interest. She unhitched the last button, her hands clenching each side of the blouse. Denice was now directly behind her attacker, the rock clearly visible in her upraised hand.

"Here we go," Tilly said. "I hope you're not disappointed."

Denice lowered the rock full force into the back of the Pettijohn's head. The attacker stumbled forward, his eyes wide with disbelief, his open mouth emitting a faint gurgle. He dropped to his knees. The gun remained in both hands, the barrel pointed at the ground.

Denice joined her. "That's for ten days in the ship's hold, asshole," she said as she grabbed Tilly's hand. "Let's go!"

"Where are we going?" Tilly asked as the two frantically worked their way deeper into the humid rainforest.

"Anywhere but back," Denice answered. "He'll kill us. We need to hide."

"Hide?" Tilly asked. She was out of breath, anxious and her heart was thumping in her chest. "We need to get back to the ship and tell the Commodore."

"The Commodore was the one who sent me below deck," Denice explained. "How many times do I have to tell you? Pettijohn's the one who kept me there. He only does what he's told. We're not telling anybody, especially the Commodore."

Tilly stopped. She had to. She was exhausted. Could any of this be true? The blonde was lying to her. She'd certainly been guilty of that before. Tilly longed for another session with the P Meter.

"Keep moving," Denice urged, shoving Tilly forward. "He's tired and hurt. Maybe he'll turn back."

The more Denise said, the more Tilly realized the frightened young blonde was attempting to talk herself into something that just wasn't true. Pettijohn would never give up. He was wounded now, and this made him even more dangerous. They pressed on, maneuvering through the jungle toward the mountains and higher ground. Both women had no idea of where they were going but wanted as much distance from their attacker as possible.

The violence had given Pettijohn a clarity of purpose. The female gender was responsible for every slight and misfortune in his thirty-three years of life and these two would pay for all of them. His plan was simple. He'd track them down and murder them, blaming their violent deaths on the communist guerrillas.

So far, they were making it easy. The women left a trail of damp footprints in the reddish clay and the broken ferns and bent stems pointed in their direction like a compass. One unsteady step after another, Pettijohn stumbled forward. Blood oozed from the gash in his head, soaking his short brown hair and dripping into his face. The crimson mixed with his sweat, creating a horrific death mask that was a perfect physical manifestation for his tormented quest. The salty taste of his blood seemed only to add to his demented sense of urgency.

"I'm coming for you," he screamed, halting abruptly. "The monkeys in the trees will soon be skipping rope with your traitorous entrails." The threat was clearly a bluff and only added for effect. He currently lacked a sharp enough object for any gut trimming.

He continued, making his way up onto a higher vantage point. With every raspy breath, his strength returned, and his pace quickened. His senses were once again acute. The women were close. He could smell them; their damning scent as good as any map. "I'm getting closer," he howled. "There's nowhere you can hide!"

The jungle responded, and the answer was not what he expected. It started as a deafening roar and trailed off into a piercing screech. Whatever jungle creature made such a call had to be big as a house. A stillness followed the call, no other animal residing in this jungle daring to answer. His mind was playing tricks on him. Pettijohn took a single step and the beast called out again. The roar was louder and whatever made such a horrific sound was closing in. A rumbling footfall followed. The ground beneath his feet quaked and a flock of birds, hidden high in the trees, took flight. Monkeys ceased their chatter and once again the rain forest fell silent. Pettijohn scanned the jungle for protective cover just as another tremor shook the earth.

There was a sudden eclipse as the ominous shadow blocked out the afternoon sky. The panicked Pettijohn glanced overhead and saw nothing that could account for the unexpected change in weather. An eerie blackness had kidnapped the unforgiving sun.

The gaping snout was covered in gray, blue scales. Inside a cavernous maw, rows of sharp, conical teeth dripped with a slimy goo. The dinosaur's massive head lowered toward him, one yellow reptilian eye focusing on the human prey. Pettijohn fired his rusty revolver as the creature's ferocious maw closed around him.

"Keep going," Denice shouted, the two women scrambling up the side of the steep mountain.

The terrain was rough, and the dirt was littered with tangled vines. A slick moss covered the rocks and the two were now tripping or falling every third step. The climb became even more arduous and they slowed their pace. The bloodthirsty scream of their attacker along with the thunderous steps of the predator convinced them that any stop would be lethal.

"There!" Tilly shouted, pointing to a small opening in the side of the mountain. She grabbed Denice's hand and led her across a narrow, grassy ledge to a small opening in the wall of rock. Tilly prayed the newly discovered space provided enough protection from the unseen hunter.

The monster's bellow rocked the earth and the two women ducked as far as they could inside the darkness, huddling against the craggy bedrock. Seconds passed and the only sound remaining was their own raspy breaths and chattering teeth. Denice was about to speak, Tilly placing a hand around her mouth and holding it tight. The impetuous blonde understood, answering with a breathless whimper.

The sun returned, rays of welcoming daylight piercing the darkness of the cave. Still, the women refused to move. The thunderous footfalls faded in the distance, the two clinging to each other well into the first orange rays of sunset. Neither woman realized that soon it would be nighttime in the jungle and that was when the real predators came out to feed.

The predator had a distinct height advantage, looming over the humans and watching silently as one couple quenched their passion under a cascading wall of water. The remaining duo was nearby, performing their lovemaking on a patch of soft earth surrounded by yellow orchids. A chorus of moans, gasps, shudders and shrieks had drowned out the monster's approach.

One half of the meal lay on the grass with a perfect view of her own destruction. Eyes, once blinded by ecstasy, opened and focused on the predator looming over her. She climaxed at the precise moment she was swallowed, the irony of the situation completely lost on her.

The other couple stood under a rock overhang, a thick spray of frigid water adding to the sensation of their furious lovemaking. This was their first time and the enthusiastic male was doing his best to create a memorable experience for his partner. Opportunities were scarce onboard the Argo and one was forced to take advantage of any sexual opportunity. In less than six hours, they'd return to the ship, forced to pretend any exchange of bodily fluids had never taken place.

The gray blue shadow studied them from the other side of the wall of water. It followed their actions with a curiosity more associated to mammals than reptiles. But now it was time to feed and the prominent snout pierced the shield of water. The toothy jaw opened and snatched the lover's mid thrust. Accompanied by shrieks and bloodcurdling screams, the couple were hoisted skyward. Two violent shakes of the giant head later, the two humans plummeted into a gullet of darkness.

It was well past midnight and not one member of the expedition had returned. It became the duty of one unlucky officer to report this news to the founder of the world's fastest growing religion. The Commodore took the news stoically, his beady red eyes studying the young man as he stammered through his report. Another handful of their number had rejected their spiritual calling and were A.W.O.L. The Commodore, to the relief of the officer, had not flown into his customary rage, taking the news with a benevolent calm.

If there was any clue to his exact reaction, it was in the number of cigarettes consumed upon hearing the news. Since sunrise, the Commodore had smoked his way through an entire carton of his expensive Turkish cigarettes. He alone knew his reason for sending Tilly in search of treasure. The next steps needed to be executed with military precision. After faking his own death and subsequent years spent entirely at sea, he'd once again set foot on land. But first, the Commodore summoned his radio operator. He needed to make a very important call.

They anchored the Sea Questor in a secluded cove, overlooking white sand beaches and a dense rain forest. It was the middle of the day and they had encountered no other ships. A burning sun hovered in a cloudless sky as the five men gathered at the stern and gazed out over the next chapter of their adventure. There had been many twists and turns and all knew this jungle excursion would prove to be no exception. They were nearing the end, and yet no one felt any sense of accomplishment. They had been lucky, and they knew it. This jungle was fraught with unknown dangers. Even Beast was quiet, his wide brown eyes attempting to pierce the thick foliage for any sign of a happy conclusion to this crazy tale.

It was Face that finally broke the brooding silence. "Mark my words," he began. "This humidity will wreak havoc with my skin condition." He held up his hands to emphasize his point.

Barry grinned fatefully. "I'd say psoriasis is the least of our problems." He reached into his pocket and tossed his friend a sample-sized bottle of hand moisturizer. "But, just in case."

"Thanks," the actor said, snatching the bottle out of the air. Face smiled gratefully. "Where did you get this?"

"Along with an ancient treasure worth billions," Barry answered, "my dad apparently owns a chain of Comfort Inns."

"El Dorado," Doc muttered, inhaling from yet another cigarette.

"Panama," Brain corrected, peering off toward the white-sand beach.

"You say tomato, he says tomahto," Face concluded. "Let's call the whole thing off? Not a bad suggestion if you ask me."

"I wouldn't have made it this far without your help," Barry declared. "I don't know how this all ends, but there are no other people in the world that I'd rather be with right now. Thank you."

"Not that anyone had a choice," Face quipped. He glanced over at the gawking Brain and Doc. "This nonsense was their idea. I say we throw them overboard. There must be plenty of things down there that will eat them."

A small arsenal had been laid out on deck, each weapon undergoing a swift but thorough cleaning. Ammunition was assigned and placed into a nearby knapsack. It was the work of the Guna crew, and they had accomplished it all with hardly a sound.

Face felt a firm slap on his back. An old Guna tribesman, a senior member of The Sea Questor's mysterious crew, thrust a large rifle into the actor's hands. "I'd like to thank the N.R.A. for this award," he announced. "And, most of all, Melba Sparks, who never stopped teaching me about my craft.

"That's an M-4 carbine," Brain explained. "Impressive weapon."

"Thunder lizard," the aged Indian explained in excited, broken English.

"He must mean you," Face cracked to the beaming Beast.

Each adventurer was presented with their own specialized weapon and knapsack, all accepting with a grim stoicism of an uncertain future. Doc examined his 357 Magnum and slipped it into a brown leather holster.

Brain inspected his own Benelli military grade shotgun, snapping open the barrel for a quick look. He took the knapsack full of shells with a stoic nod to the Guna leader and slung it around his back. He waved his sheathed cane several times in the air as if testing his reflexes. "I'm ready," he announced finally.

Beast could hardly contain himself, waiting impatiently to be presented with his own personalized weapon. He accepted the elaborate crossbow and two slings of steel-tipped arrows with a grateful bow. The old native pointed at the stainless-steel cylinders housed at the tip of each arrow.

"Sorry, my wrinkled friend," Beast said. "No understand."

"Thunder lizard," the old man said. "Boom!"

"They explode on impact," Brain translated, examining one of the arrows. "When they are fired, it activates a short duration fuse."

"Comprende," Beast corrected, hugging the weapon as if he had just unwrapped the most important gift on Christmas day.

"My friend," Face asked. The actor gestured to the weaponless Barry. "What about him?"

The younger members of the crew answered with blank stares. The native leader grinned and pointed a crooked finger at Barry's head. There was a twinkle in the old man's eyes as if he alone knew the answer.

"They don't think I need it," Barry answered.

"Well that's just crazy," Face said. "Everyone needs something."

"I have all of you," Barry answered.

"That's even crazier," the actor muttered.

They were becoming familiar with their individual weapons as the Guna lowered the inflatable raft into the water. Canteens and ammo knapsacks had been stowed inside.

"Thunder lizard," The Guna leader shouted, pointing to the island.

"This lizard thing seems to be a theme" Doc asked. "What do you think?"

"I have no idea," Brain answered. "Giant Iguana?"

The two men remained stumped. They turned to the only person who had managed to speculate with any degree of accuracy on the entire adventure.

"You really want to know?" Beast asked. The big man was grinning, his eyes ablaze with a glee reserved for madmen and conspirators.

Everyone nodded.

"We're about to enter the Valley of the Gwangi," Beast proclaimed. "I guarandamntee it."

"Looks like someone beat us here," Barry said. He spotted the footprints before any of them had waded to shore. Such a feat required incredible eyesight. Every one of his five senses had improved after his session with the mind-altering pasta strainer. There was also a seriousness about him that none of his friends had ever witnessed. It was an entirely new purpose for a man who had been adrift for so many years.

They dragged the skiff onto the narrow strip of sand as Barry followed the tracks to the edge of the forest. The camouflaged skiff was waiting for him and he uncovered it, reaching down and removing several thick palm branches.

"Seven," Barry announced. "And Tilly is one of them."

Brain and Doc studied each other before reaching inside the raft for water and ammunition.

"The change does require a bit of getting used to," Brain noted.

"Seems like only yesterday that he couldn't change a flat tire," Doc answered.

"Ah," Face sighed. "The good old days."

"What are we waiting for?" Beast interrupted.

Barry instructed the two natives to return to the schooner. Something was not right. His hereditary alarm had now manifested itself. He felt a slight vibrating sensation from the bottom of his feet to the top of his hair follicles. The strange physical manifestation was still something he and his friends were getting used to.

"He's doing it again," Beast said, pointing out the obvious.

"It's both unique and annoying," Face added. "Can you hit the snooze button on that thing?"

"Okay, brothers. Let's go," Barry said, ignoring his friend.

"Brothers," Face muttered. "Also new but not so annoying."

Beast slapped his friend on the back. "Change good."

It was an easy enough trail to follow and they stumbled upon the pool an hour after reaching shore. What they found froze all but Barry in their tracks. Two separate piles of bloodied bones lay at opposite ends of the pool.

"Human?" Face stammered.

"Thunder Lizard," Beast managed.

"Something's not right." Barry said.

"You think?" Face asked. He cradled his rifle for comfort.

"Whatever it was, it caught them unawares," Brain offered. He probed the remains with the tip of his cane.

Doc knelt, poking his index finger into the pile. The bones were covered in a thick, sticky red goo. The chemist raised the affected finger to his nose and sniffed.

Face winced. "Is that really necessary?"

"Saliva?" Brain asked.

Doc was stymied. He knew something wasn't right but couldn't get a handle on it. "No smell," he said.

"Why don't you taste it to be sure," Face suggested. "Better yet, have Beast do it. He'll eat anything."

"Look," Barry said with authority. "Note the absence of flies or maggots."

He was right. There was no infestation. It was as if the pile of human debris had been constructed and left as part of some grisly ruse.

Somewhere during the explanation Beast had wandered off. "Over here," the big man shouted.

Face arrived last, tripping over a tangle of vines and falling face first into the mud. He pulled himself up, not realizing he was standing in the middle of the greatest scientific discovery of the twentieth century. "Well," he announced, spitting out the last remnant of muddy water. "What's the big deal?"

"You're standing in it," Brain exclaimed. "A footprint."

"Don't be ridiculous," Face blustered. "Just another jungle pothole."

"You fell in a giant footprint," Doc reiterated.

Face climbed out of the impression and backed away, studying the muddy hole for several seconds. He looked forward and spotted the matching print several yards ahead. "I think we should get back to the boat," the actor declared.

"Thunder Lizard," Beast exclaimed. "Let's go find it."

"I've got a better idea. You find it," Face offered. "The rest of us can wait on the boat."

"This could get complicated," Barry warned. A brief examination of the footprint had proved his suspicion. He'd say nothing more until he was absolutely certain.

Tilly and Denice had remained hidden in the cave for the better part of an entire day. It was now sunset, and it had been hours since they heard a sound from the giant reptile. Denice couldn't stop trembling and Tilly kept a protective arm around her quaking companion. She finally withdrew her arm and wandered out of the cave. The sun was bathing the sky in a startling pink. A full moon was rising in the west and the bright lunar orb swallowed the lesser illumination of twinkling stars that surrounded it.

"What if it comes back?" Denice stammered. "What if it's still out there?"

Tilly turned back to darkness of the cave. She could see the whites of Denice 's frightened eyes. "I don't think so," Tilly said. "I think it's gone."

"You don't know," Denice fired back. "How can you be sure?"

"Yeah," Tilly relented. "Maybe you're right and we should stay put until sunrise."

The strange voices erupted all at once. It was a language of a people who had spent centuries in these mountains, and they emerged from the thick vegetation with hardly a sound. Their distinct faces were thin, their tattooed bodies both lean and muscular. They were naked save for loin clothes that covered their midsections and each native was armed with either a primitive spear or bow.

"What is it?" Denice cried out.

Tilly watched as even more of the ancient tribe revealed themselves. All of the men sported the same pageboy haircuts, the bangs trimmed just above their dark, brown eyes.

Curiosity finally got the better of her and Denice emerged from the cave. The blonde stepped alongside the silent Tilly. "Who are they?" she whispered. "What do they want?

Several natives pointed toward the top of nearby mountains.

"Just guessing," Tilly offered. "But I think they want us to follow them up the side of that mountain."

A native stepped forward. He pointed at the two women and then to himself. The wordless conversation ended with a toothy smile. A moment later, the natives were leading Tilly and Denice away from the cave and up a steep trail.

"Flashlights."

They had been tracking the footprints for over an hour and had encountered no further sign of the gigantic beast. The collective lamps ignited, spilling much needed light on the dense, darkening trail ahead.

"Tyrannosaurus Rex is the most feared of all dinosaurs," Brain explained.

"Quiet," Face blurted.

"Even the Raptors shit their pants when he's around," Beast added.

"Shut up."

"Because he's so damn big and awesome."

"Wait," interrupted Doc. "Raptors wear pants?"

"Dramatic embellishment," Brain commented. "Or is it?"

Face's flashlight beam searched for the face of a sympathetic friend and found none. Grimacing, he aimed the powerful beam in front of him.

"A T Rex can eat more than 500 pounds in one bite." Brain explained, adding fuel to Face's growing anxiety. "It crushed and broke the bones as it ate, segregated, conical teeth piercing and ripping the flesh of its prey."

"For the love of God," Face wailed.

A very distinct roar filled the rain forest, and the men froze.

"Now look what you've done," Face stammered, slinging the rifle over his shoulder and into his perspiring hands. "His ears are burning."

"Technically, ears on dinosaurs have never been proven," Brain muttered.

"At last," Beast exclaimed. "We meet again, you magnificent bastard."

"Again?" Doc said.

"Acid flashback," Brain answered.

"Turn off the flashlights, stay quiet and follow me," Barry ordered calmly.

One by one, the electric torches clicked off, the five slipping into the thick vegetation as a thunderous footfall shook the earth.

It lumbered onto a beaten path of its own making. The distinctive reptilian snout was aimed skyward, attempting to sniff out the intruders. The Tyrannosaurus Rex was twenty-five feet from clawed toe to scaled head and lumbered onward without hesitation or fear. Halfway to the cowering humans, the jaws opened, and a thunderous growl followed by piercing screech echoed through the night. No living creature wanted to be anywhere near the source of that horrifying call. The giant reptile halted, waiting to see if anyone was foolhardy enough to respond before proceeding with the hunt.

Face heard the distinct bellow of the T Rex for the first time and it was only the collective profanity and eight hands of his friends that kept him from a full speed retreat to the beach.

Taking full advantage of his friend's vulnerability, Beast leaned into the actor and whispered, "Run for it." The big man smiled, revealing teeth stained from a lifetime of snacking on handfuls of freeze-dried coffee. "Don't listen to the others. I think you can make it."

Face studied the faces of Brain and Doc, hoping for a positive second opinion. The two shook their heads solemnly.

"I'm pretty fast when I put my mind to it." Face's addendum did nothing to change his friend's minds. Doc and Brain glanced away, focusing their attention on the location of the predator. "Still, you may need me," the actor mumbled, second guessing his chances on his own. "Maybe I should stay."

"Shush," Barry whispered.

The giant carnivore paused, turning its massive head one way and then the other. It sensed the prey was close and sniffed the night air again. Its suspicion was answered with another night shattering roar. The call was deafening, the five men forced to clamp hands over their ears.

Mid roar, Barry removed his hands, leaving his colleagues dumbfounded. "Dolby Surround Sound," he mumbled to himself. "1982." He peered over the ferns and monitored the dinosaur's enraged scream. The giant jaw, brimming with sharp teeth, closed. The head lowered and turned toward the cowering men.

"What?" Brain asked.

"Just listen," Barry ordered. "Before it takes a step."

The T Rex obliged, lifting a massive leg.

"You hear it?" Barry asked his shaken comrades.

Doc shrugged. He couldn't hear a thing save for the pounding of his own overworked heart.

The dinosaur took another step, and this time there was no mistaking the sharp blast of air followed by a slight, barely audible, mechanical wheeze. The sound was faintly reminiscent of the powering up of the jaws of life heard in their earlier adventure with the rampaging Bigfoot.

"Hydraulics" Brain concluded.

"Robotic," Doc said.

"A Transformer," Beast corrected.

"What are you talking about?" Face blurted. "What would a Transformer be doing in the middle of a goddamn jungle?

Whatever it was, it heard the frustrated actor, the mechanical marvel turning and zeroing in on the prey.

"More than meets the eye," Beast whispered. The brute seemed overjoyed at the prospect of meeting either a dinosaur or cartoon character.

"Maybe we should just go," Face suggested.

"Not yet," Barry answered sternly.

The five huddled under the cover of the bushes and listened as Barry outlined the plan. Face was not paying attention, the actor too preoccupied with the nearby predator to take part in a conversation that might save his life. Robotic or otherwise, the monster was just too damn close. Face could not get past the fact that at any second, it could very easily lean down and pluck any one of them from their hiding place.

"Okay, got it?" Barry asked.

Everyone nodded.

"Face?"

"Yeah," the preoccupied actor mumbled. "We're going back to the ship and find a bazooka."

"Just keep up," Beast offered.

"On three," Barry ordered.

"One."

The T Rex had targeted its prey. Again, the prehistoric beast thundered, lowering its massive head toward the five men.

"Two."

The imposing jaws opened, baring rows of threatening teeth evolved specifically for ripping apart prey.

"Three."

Everyone, but the actor, leapt in front of the T Rex and sprinted down the hill.

Beast glanced over his shoulder. "Anytime, Face," he screamed.

Face stood and pointed an accusing finger at the robotic monster. "Transformers," he commanded. "Turn into trucks!"

The enthusiastic suggestion failed, and Face swung his rifle behind his back and bounded onto the trail. What he lacked in speed, he made up for in determination, the actor stumbling and tripping full speed toward his colleagues. "It was worth a shot," he called out.

The T Rex let loose with another hellacious bellow. With one stride, the hulking giant gained on the fleeing actor. As it picked up speed, the upper body lowered to the ground and tunnel-sized jaws opened in anticipation of scooping up the clumsy Face.

"I thought we were going to kill it," Face cried out in a panic. "That's the plan, right?"

"Keep going," Beast cried out from the darkness. "You're almost there."

"Where?" Face panted. "I can't see you."

"Now," Barry ordered.

The vine was yanked taut directly behind the fleeing actor. The trap was stretched between two giant trees and, when the primeval beast met vine, it tripped, tons of dinosaur crashing head first onto the rain forest floor. A series of loud electrical sparks, crackles and pops followed as a thick diesel smoke streamed out between the monster's clenched teeth and nostrils.

The five set upon the giant puppet at once. Flashlights ignited, the five climbing onto the back of the T Rex and pounding on the back of the rubber scales with the butt of their weapons. Black smoke drifted out the back of the T Rex's head and the men felt an intense heat growing inside. The quick-thinking Brain unsheathed his sword cane and carved out a rescue hatch. Doc and Beast took up the cause, tearing the thick rubber off a metallic frame.

Barry leapt inside the carcass. Several seconds later, he emerged with the shaken dinosaur pilot. The blonde man was covered in thick diesel oil and was sputtering for air. Semi-conscious, the pilot was passed down to the waiting Brain and Doc, all three scrambling off the back of the remains.

"Get back," Barry warned.

Barry and Beast leapt off the puppet as the rubber skin ignited in a blue and orange flame. The explosion shook the earth and the surging fireball preceded a black, diesel-fueled mushroom cloud floating into the trees.

"She's gone," the blonde man stammered in a thick Australian accent. "I can't believe it. I spent my entire life perfecting it and now it's gone. Cranky." The young puppeteer staggered to his feet. Tears pooled in his bright blue eyes as he watched his creation sacrificed to the flames.

Barry and his crew were baffled. What was the purpose of the charade? Why was a robotic dinosaur patrolling the heart of the Panamanian jungle? Before they could stop him, Face tackled the blonde from behind and the two men tumbled onto the moist earth. The actor seized the man's head in both hands, thudding it against the mossy dirt. "You and Kermit the dinosaur could have gotten me killed," he shrieked.

"Whoa," Beast commented. "I'm not liking this side of you." Beast hoisted Face off the Australian and set him down away from the others. "Someone needs a time-out."

Face remained furious. "Didn't fool me for a minute,"

Beast turned back to the shaken prisoner. He pointed an accusing finger. "Look what you've done," he lectured. "My friend's petrified," The big man grinned mischievously and lowered his voice. "Nicely done. You have any spare Godzilla suits laying around?

Face moaned as Barry knelt beside the young surfer he had saved from a fiery death. "Okay," he said. "What's this about?"

His name was William May, the dinosaur pilot possessing the tan good looks that only came from spending an entire life on an Australian beach. The gigantic puppet was his own invention and the smoldering model was the prototype. He explained that he controlled the creature from under the breastplate, perched on a floating metal saddle. Along with the wheels, levers and gears, there was a small infrared monitor inside that served as his eyes and ears. Both feet, secured in pedals, controlled the lumbering steps. He revealed his lifelong love of dinosaurs, engineering and puppetry and that it had saved him from a drug dealer's bullet. Stranded in this humid rain forest over a year ago, the surfer and part-time inventor had been sentenced to a life of Jurassic servitude.

"I never killed anybody," May protested. "I swear. They just hired me and my dino to keep the lookee loos away."

"From what?" Barry asked.

"This is Panama, mate," came the answer. "Halfway between Columbia and the rest of the world."

"But why a dinosaur?" Doc asked.

"It does seem extreme," Brain agreed.

"Nonsense," Beast interjected. "We need to get one."

"It's always been a dream of mine," May started. He was looking at Face as if he needed the fellow entertainer's approval. "An entire arena filled with people paying money to watch my dinosaurs. I was going to call it Paleo Panic. Not bad, eh?"

"Gimmicks will never replace the magic of live theatre," Face lectured. "There's no substitute for the human imagination."

"What's his problem?"

"Never mind his problem," Barry insisted. "Go on."

"Everyone laughed."

"Except the man in charge."

"Oh sure, they had their doubts," May continued. "Who could blame them? I owed them a shit-ton of money. Hard to believe, but I once had a serious problem with the nose candy." He gestured to the burning pile of rubber. "But when they got a gander at that, he became convinced."

"Convinced of what?" Brain asked.

"That it was a bloody good way of keeping the natives and tourists away."

Barry clasped the young Aussie by the shoulders and stared directly into his blue eyes. "From what? Show me."

"There's a landing strip not far from here."

"What about Tilly?" Face asked.

Barry faced his friends. His posture was perfect and oozed confidence. His gaze was steely, full of purpose and determination. He was grinning which made his reaction all the more disconcerting. "They have her," he said, "We only need to convince them of how badly we want her back."

"Terrific," Face muttered. "Now we're going up against a South American drug cartel. There are safer hobbies that offer plenty of opportunity for exercise. What's wrong with all of us joining a softball league? We can do plenty of good on a baseball diamond."

The Aussie wilted under Barry's intense stare. "I'll take you," he agreed. "But just so you know, there's hundreds of them and only five of you."

"We'll be gentle," Beast lied.

"And there's something else," William May offered.

"There's always something else," Face countered. "You think I'd be used to saying that by now."

The victims slid down a pitch-black gullet, landing on a net of coarse rope. It was an uncomfortable digestion but far superior to the prehistoric alternative. The undigested humans cowered in the darkness and clung to the rough netting for dear life. An hour later, the trip ended with a mechanical regurgitation, each undigested course purged from the robotic maw into a pile of hay. The naked members of the bestselling religion found themselves surrounded by machine-gun toting Columbians. The captors offered no explanation and the dinosaur, having delivered the payload, plodded back into the jungle.

The victims were blindfolded and marched to a small shed where they were secured by the wrists and ankles. To discourage conversation, they were gagged with the remnants of oily "I heart Panama" tee-shirts. Now huddled on a dirt floor, there was nothing to do but question the series of bizarre circumstances that brought them to this end.

Pettijohn was the first to make the humiliating journey from dinosaur gullet to tool shed and had plenty of time to seethe over his capture. He'd taken advantage of the alone time, not by reevaluating choices but contemplating a daring escape. Once free, it was only a matter of time before he recaptured the women and exacted his revenge. Each time their attack replayed in his mind, his punishment became increasingly cruel and more severe. His body trembled over the indignities suffered, and his hands clenched into intense fists until he lost the flow of blood to his fingers. When he did manage to calm, he discovered that the ropes around his wrist had become loose. His own rage would be his salvation. While the other prisoners grunted helplessly amidst the constant noise of air traffic, the crazed enforcer for the redheaded Commodore devoted full attention to his escape.

Night fell, and the droning of propellers became less frequent. A puzzling new sound emerged outside the shed. The distinct noise grew more frequent as the minutes passed. The strange explosive swooshing sounded like a fleet of small rockets being launched in all directions.

Pettijohn ignored it. He slipped one hand free. The rest proved easy. He removed his blindfold, gag and untied the ropes around his feet. He remained silent, making no move to help his fellow believers. He crept over to the shack's lone window in and peered out. A full moon had risen over the mountains. Two rows of landing lights illuminated the dirt landing strip. He couldn't see any planes and there were no Columbians nearby. Even the sound of igniting rockets had ceased. He exited the shack and slipped into the cover of night. A border of thick jungle vegetation surrounded the entire strip, and he was back in its clutches with just a few steps. His rusty revolver had been confiscated but he no longer needed it. Not for what he planned.

Tilly and Denice had been hiking for hours. The trail continued to climb and became narrow and more treacherous with every step. Whatever their final destination, it was remote and meant to discourage anyone from ever attempting the journey. Both women were exhausted, their clothes soaked in a sticky sweat. The party came to a halt, standing at the bottom of a fifty-foot high wall of jagged rock. The entire valley stretched below. At the top of a sheer wall of granite was an even denser forest. When confronted by the rock, the native guides pointed upward.

"I think they want us to climb," Tilly said.

Denice agreed without saying a word and reached up to secure her first handhold. Minutes later, both women were making their way up the side of the mountain.

Tilly found the dangerous climb exhilarating. Occasionally, a foot slipped, and she'd send a pile of rocks and dirt tumbling. Luckily there was no one below and, as she scrambled higher, she gained an athletic confidence long since forgotten. She watched her younger companion above maneuvering through the tough climb. Tilly thought Denice must be part mountain goat. She was always ten yards above and managing the ascent without disturbing a pebble.

Tilly glanced over her shoulder to check the view. The sun had set behind the distant mountains and she noticed a tiny plane descending out of the darkness. Was the Commodore searching for the missing party? Can't be, she reasoned. Even if they had a radio, a rescue plane would never arrive so fast. She watched a moment more, following the propeller plane as it disappeared behind the canopy of forest.

If she had turned away, she would've missed it. As the plane vanished, what looked like a flock of birds took flight, navigating above the earth in a most unbirdlike way. There were several brief flashes of flame, smoky contrails trailing the creatures as they climbed higher into the sky. She peered into the increasing night for a better view, but they had vanished. "It can't be," she muttered.

"Made it," Denice announced.

Tilly turned her attention back to the task ahead. Her fellow climber scampered onto a clump of overhanging grass and smiled down at her. Were her eyes deceiving her? Had she really just seen the tiny flashes of flame and the trails of smoke? She'd ask Denice once she reached the top. Maybe the blonde had seen it as well.

The young Nazi removed his heavy gear and sat cross-legged in the dirt. The tripod mounted MG-42 machine gun was within easy reach of his sandbag protected picnic spot. The weapon's lethal barrel was pointed safely skyward as the young soldier dined on a sandwich of liverwurst and onions. His distinctive Stahlhelm helmet remained on, staking claim to the young soldier's nationality and purpose. Perched on a rocky side of a mountain, the machine gun nest was surrounded on all sides by a three-foot wall of bags. As he ate, the young soldier peered out over the surrounding jungle. His was night duty, and it was his sacred honor to keep careful vigil over the airstrip below.

Air traffic was a constant during the day but when the sun set, the Columbians vacated the strip and the real work began. This job was far too important to be left to the Narcos. The entire fate of the sacred New World Order hung in the balance. The Columbians, he thought, proved to be satisfactory partners; violent but blissfully unaware of any master plan. A plan that was far more suited for the pure blood of a master race and not the drug running mongrels who happened to be funding it.

The last plane had arrived and the landing strip lights, warding off an approaching night, were shut off. Any remaining planes had been stashed away in one of the many camouflaged hangers. The Nazi's duty was over in less than seven hours and would most likely prove to be like all the others in his two-year recruitment; uneventful.

The Nazi bit into his sandwich. He focused his attention on the air-conditioned barracks, a hot breakfast, and the brotherhood of soldiers waiting for him after his watch. A canopy of night settled, and the work had already begun. His soldier's chest swelled with pride at the thought of his fellow Aryans carrying out duties that hastened a return to the glorious days of the Reich. He crammed the remaining sandwich into his mouth and glanced over the stainless-steel apparatus leaning against the pile of sandbags. He caressed its smooth metallic surface of one of the twin tanks. With just one of these, he thought blissfully, we could have won the Great War.

"Now!"

They landed on all sides, taking the Nazi totally off guard. The soldier choked on a mouth full of liverwurst as four pairs of fists pummeled him from all directions. Three of the assailants hunkered while the other two secured the prisoner.

"Stormtrooper?" Doc whispered.

"Sturmabteilung. The black uniform confirms it," Brain answered. "These soldiers are both brutal and violent."

"Good to know," Doc craved a cigarette, but it was hardly the time. Any flame could easily be spotted from their position.

Barry, Face and Beast crawled over to the sandbags and peered out at the landing strip.

"Narcos and Nazis," Beast whispered in awe. "Pinch me."

Face slapped his companion alongside of the head. "Quiet," he muttered. "Your endless chatter is interrupting my complete nervous breakdown."

Doc and Brain took up positions on either side of the actor. The distinct swooshing was now echoing throughout the entire valley. They peered over the pile of sandbags in search of the source. The night was now alive with a dozen human-sized fireflies. Contrails crisscrossed the darkening blue and each new pattern was accompanied by a swoosh of a jet turbine.

Barry relieved the guard of his binoculars and scanned the night. He said nothing, handing the field glasses over to the excited Beast. "Jet packs," Barry whispered.

"When this is over," the big man muttered. "You'll have to buy me one."

"Why wait," Barry said. "There's one right here."

"I call it."

"Sorry, Beast." Barry said, his voice blending in with the night. "I need it."

"This is a nasty lot," the Aussie warned. "These German blokes are even more ruthless than the Columbians."

"You never mentioned Germans," Barry said. "Why?"

"It would've been nice to know," Face agreed. "Ruthless, drug-running Columbians are one thing, but I think can all agree we don't do flying Nazis."

No one addressed Face's concern. The actor watched as his friends continued to share the binoculars, too preoccupied with the flying harnesses to respond. Frustrated, he huddled against a sandbag and pouted.

Barry confronted his anxious team. "So, the Columbians leapfrog the money and drugs between the U.S. and here," he began. He was thinking out loud but welcomed any input. "But what part do the flying Nazis play in all this?"

They turned to Beast. The big man had been right on so many occasions that it no longer paid to ignore his suspicions. "Sorry," the big man said, shrugging. "I got nothing."

Face rolled his eyes. If the rest were disappointed in the big man's lack of an answer, they didn't show it.

Barry addressed the dinosaur pilot. "Okay," he said coldly. "Tell me everything you know about the person in charge of this outfit."

William May had mentioned only in passing but Barry had remembered. "I met him once," May began. "He calls himself Thunder."

At the sound of the name, the bound Nazi launched himself off the ground and onto the Australian. It was as if uttering the name had elicited the violence. Beast dragged the young soldier off, silencing him with another fist to the jaw.

"Where were we?" Beast asked, clenching his fist several times for emphasis.

"Thunder is an odd name for a bloke." The Australian's eyes never left the unconscious Nazi. "He told me we shared the same interests: science, robotics, aeronautics and telecommunication. I didn't have the heart to tell him that I know nothing about airplanes or telephones." May trembled as he continued. "On my own, it'd take decades to build one of my dinosaurs. With Thunder's resources, it was done in six months. Once completed, he moved it here piece by piece. But I didn't know nothing about Nazis and Jet packs. I swear!"

His story had concluded, leaving Barry sullen and introspective.

"What is it?" Face asked, placing a hand on Barry's shoulder.

"This man Thunder is the one responsible for the death of my father."

"What?" Doc questioned. "How do you know?"

"My dad told me."

"Whoa! This is just like Superman," Beast mused.

"Exactly the same," Face added. "Save for, I don't know, everything!"

All eyes were on Barry, watching their leader brood over an enemy he had not yet met but seemed destined to fight. Precious minutes passed, sending the lunar orb higher in a darkening sky. It was now a perfect full moon and appeared close enough to reach out and touch. The breathtaking site failed to mask the fatal cloud hanging over the five men.

More soaring Nazis appeared, crisscrossing the night and jetting packages and supplies from the sheds toward some unknown destination.

On top of the bluff, Tilly and Denice were greeted by another party of natives. The new guides immediately hustled

231

the two women away from the ledge and back into the vegetation. They arrived in the village hours later, the light of the small campfires illuminating their way through a series of thatched huts. As they continued, their escorts peeled off to unknown destinations and were replaced by laughing children, barking dogs and smiling women. The women carried wooden bowls laden with fresh fruit, flat bread, and bits of broiled chicken. Tilly and Denice were starving and snatched handfuls from the bowls gratefully, eating as they marched to a large hut located dead center of the village.

The radio tower stuck out like a sore thumb amidst the primitive backdrop. The metal structure dwarfed what appeared to be the large tribal gathering place. The base of the steel spire surrounded the long hut on all sides and climbed forty feet into the air. The primitive and future were mixed so randomly that Tilly thought she was stepping into some futuristic nightmare. She peered upward and spotted several disc shaped shadows attached at the very top.

Denice had devoted her full concentration to eating and remained unfazed over the unlikely structure. Occasionally she squealed, adding a brief comment on how good everything tasted.

"What have I gotten myself into?" Tilly muttered.

The native women and children halted just short of the hut and gestured the female guests inside. Tilly stalled. A shimmering and unnatural golden light from inside caused her hesitation. The illumination was both unsettling and hypnotic. Tilly took a deep breath, summoning the remains of her resolve and stepped inside.

"It's gold." Denice said. The teen was clearly dumbstruck by the fortune in gold bricks stacked up in the rows that surrounded them.

The gold occupied a majority of the large space. Blankets circled a fire pit in the center of the hut. The flickering flames reflected off the gold bars with such an intensity that it took a while for Tilly's eyes to adjust.

"The Commodore was right," Denice exclaimed. "It's the treasure of Zandu."

The scuffling outside the door was either their salvation or execution. For the prisoners, deep inside the Panamanian jungle, there was no in-between. Before panic set in, their gags and blindfolds were removed, the couples staring into the stoic faces of their rescuers.

"Did the Commodore send you?" the comely believer in Diatribe asked the portly gentlemen with balding head and wire-rimmed glasses.

"Commodore?" Doc whispered back. "Haven't had the pleasure. We're just a couple of guys way in over their heads." Doc located a few blankets and tossed them to the naked captives.

Brain held a finger to his lips. "Stay quiet," he ordered in a hushed monotone. "At any moment, all hell's going to break loose."

"One minute," Doc advised, checking his watch.

"Have either of you gentlemen ever taken a Singularity test?" the brunette woman offered as she draped her tanned, freckled body with a blanket. "I'd be more than happy to arrange one for you."

She was clearly flirting with the chemist and he missed it entirely. "Maybe later," Doc said, brandishing his pistol and ushering everyone toward the door. "We're kind of busy at the moment." Again, he glanced at his watch. "30 seconds."

"I still don't understand why I don't get to wear the rocket pack," Beast complained.

Face and Beast huddled by the M-13. Face checked his watch for the third time. "30 Seconds," he said. "You better be ready."

"Born ready," Beast countered.

"Your answer carries with it all the credibility of a third-rate action flick," Face deadpanned.

"Thank you," Beast answered proudly.

The Aussie, huddling in the back of the nest with the bound and gagged Nazi, contemplated his life thus far. He had fulfilled his part of the bargain. Whether he came out of this entire affair alive was still very much up in the air. These yanks were daring, he'd give them that. Wide-eyed, he watched the less refined of the two arm the crossbow with a steel-tipped arrow. "You know how to use that thing?" he asked.

"No different from the Nerf crossbow I had as a kid," Beast bragged. He aimed the crossbow toward the night sky. "Just watch me."

"This is not going to end well," Face mumbled. He clicked the safety off and pulled the hammer back, locking the first round into the chamber.

At two seconds before 8 pm, a rocket pack, without the benefit of a human pilot, swooshed high into the night sky. Beast aimed carefully, following the contrail. He held his breath, squeezing the trigger and sending the arrow soaring into the darkness. At first, the two men thought it was a miss and Beast's demeanor resembled a five-year-old who had forgotten the batteries for a new electronic toy. Finally, explosive tip met the sleek metal surface of the propulsion tank, the pack exploding in a fireball that lit up the night-sky. As Brain had so calmly predicted, all hell broke loose.

Armed Columbians sprinted into the valley, firing automatic weapons randomly into the darkness. As the white-hot shrapnel fell, Face blasted away at them from the machine gun nest, laying down a noisy covering fire.

Doc and Brain took quick advantage of the chaos, leading the four cultists toward the cover of the dense jungle. From the cover of several large trees, they hunkered down and watched the fading pyrotechnics of falling shrapnel. Soon, the authoritative shouts of the provoked Nazis joined the chaos. Several Columbians had surrounded the plane, guarding the remaining shipment with their lives. Two hopped inside the cockpit and soon the propellers once again became a whirling blur.

"Did you ask to be excused?" Beast said, arming the crossbow with another arrow.

"Get down," Face yelled, screaming over the blistering fire of his machine gun.

The Aussie was clearly in a state of panic and was now standing, covering his ears to block out the sounds of jungle warfare. "Crickey!" he managed.

Bullets whizzed past the confident Beast as he fired the crossbow. The plane was executing a sharp turn on the dirt runaway when the arrow struck. The fuselage answered with a thunderous explosion as an estimated street value of 3.5 million dollars went up in flames.

A dozen uniformed Nazis assembled inside the hanger. The attack was no longer the Columbian's responsibility and a blitzkrieg-style counter-attack was ordered. The sons of the Fatherland suited up, securing the rocket packs onto their backs. Clothed in a uniform of black leather, Bechowiec-1 Machine Pistols, tucked into holsters, they secured the last straps, sprinting out of the open hanger and launching themselves into the night.

Barry remained hidden, crouched behind a row of familiar fuel barrels that had just arrived from the Pacific Northwest. He had already deduced a good working knowledge of how the sophisticated rocket devices functioned and stepped out from behind the yellow barrels, removing a rocket pack from the rack and fastening it around his back. He was securing the waist strap when he sensed the hulking presence behind him.

"Was ist los?"

Barry turned, his hands coming to rest on the handlebar grips of the pack. The foe was a giant of a man with bright yellow hair that came courtesy of a bottle. The mechanic was well over seven feet tall, dressed in coveralls, and armed with an oversized ballpeen hammer.

"Probefahrt Ich bin auf dem Market," Barry said. It was excellent German for one who'd never spoken a word. He had just communicated to the burly German his intention of taking the rocket pack out for a test drive and the stony-faced mechanic was not amused.

Barry shrugged, his hand drifting over the throttle. With a fast flick of the wrist, the rocket ignited. Barry dropped into a belly flop and the pack did the rest, propelling his body through the air and toward the stunned grease monkey. Barry's head met solar plexus and drove the villain crashing into the far wall. The force of the impact sent tools dropping onto the Aryan's head. Barry spun the pack around and aimed himself at the open hanger door. He cranked the throttle and rocketed into the night.

Determined Nazis hovered above the machine gun nest like angry wasps. The machine gun fire was non-stop and Beast, Face and the cowering Aussie hunkered down behind the dwindling pile of sandbags. The overhanging trees of the rain forest provided some cover for their flank, but it was only seconds before someone came up with a plan that would make short work of the machine gun nest. Bullets whistled overhead, thudding into the bags and barely missing the human targets.

"This is not how I imagined my life ending," Face fretted.

"Me either," Beast pondered. "I always pictured you being strangled at the hands of a jealous husband." The big man threw an arm over his colleague. "But there's no better man to die with."

Face threw his right arm over the shoulder of his friend. "It's not really much comfort but I appreciate the sentiment," he said.

"You're a great actor, Face."

"Really? Is there a particular performance that stands out?"

Beast paused, mulling over his choices while the noisy battle continued around them. "Uh," Beast answered, clearly stalling to achieve the greatest irritation. "You were great as the singing meatball."

Face studied his comrade. "You lying sack of shit," he said. "I wasn't even called back for that commercial."

Beast chuckled in spite of the ongoing blizzard of blazing bullets. "I know that," he said. "I was just testing you."

Sand spilled out the bags at an alarming rate, their only protection nothing more than swollen scraps of burlap. It was only a matter of seconds before death would find them.

"To hell with this," Face said. He reached up and grabbed the trigger housing of the machine gun. "Let's take a few of these bastards with us?"

Beast armed the crossbow with one of the remaining arrows. "Now you're talking," he bellowed.

"On the count of three."

A bullet zipped past Face, taking with it a small piece of the actor's ear.

"One."

A bullet ripped through Beast's shoulder. Undaunted, the big man clung to the crossbow.

"Two."

The Aussie whimpered as another bullet whistled past his head.

"Three."

Beast hopped to his feet while Face grabbed onto the machine gun. It was a scene straight out of "The Wild Bunch" and neither man expected to live through the closing credits.

It was a matter of taking the pilots out of the sky one at a time and Barry was well on his way to achieving the daunting task. Only four remained of the squadron that took to the skies. One Nazi was lowering his machine pistol at the three vulnerable men inside the machine gun nest when the son of Ravage struck. Before the Nazi could squeeze off a burst of fire, Barry swooshed past, slitting the straps on the pack with an S.S. dagger and separating the Nazi from his jet-powered ride. The rocket fired up, and the Nazi plummeted, Barry flying off to take on the next adversary.

The next round of aerial combat required more forethought and some elaborate maneuvering. Barry released the throttle, dropping between two hovering Nazis. As he decelerated, he took pot shots at first one and then the other. It happened in a spilt-second and Barry was gone before they knew it, the startled Nazis turning instinctively and firing at each other. The friendly fire proved fatal, both pilots dropping each out of the sky and crashing to earth in a fiery blast of jet fuel.

In a matter of minutes, only one pilot from the elite squadron remained. The Nazi was fuming with the righteous indignation of defeat. This cowardly American had obviously been cheating. His name was Group Captain Heinrich Zimm, and he was the only member of the new Reich to be awarded the prestigious Luftwaffe Rocket Pack Flying Cross of Freedom medal. He studied the tactics of his adversary before launching and now, one hundred and fifty feet above the earth, Zimm realized he was in the fight of his military career. He had been mistaken and was about to engage one of the greatest aviators he'd ever encountered.

 Both fliers circled, preparing for the inevitable dogfight. Barry climbed higher, hoping the glare of a full moon might blind his opponent. Zimm was well aware of the old pilot's trick and was not so easily fooled. He circled the ascending pilot, giving him a wider berth with each circumference. While his adversary rocketed up, the Nazi followed cautiously, waiting for the interloper to drop out of the sky.

Barry dropped but not as expected. Somewhere high above, the engine strapped on Barry's back sputtered, spit and stalled. Fuel had run out for the hero. Fumbling with the straps, he unhooked himself, separating from the pack and plummeting to the earth. He arched his back, slammed both arms to his side and sliced through the darkness, the night air rushing in his ears.

Zimm had made a fatal mistake. He had lost sight of the enemy. The flare of his opponent's ignited fuel had vanished, and he no longer had eyes on the crafty foe. He twisted the right handle and fired full thrusters, soaring upward. He had trained countless fellow officers on how to pilot a jet pack and he drew on years of experience as he calculated his next move. His adversary was obviously attempting to mask his engine fire by the moon's light. It was a rookie mistake and would prove to be his last.

Barry collided with Zimm, sending both pilots cartwheeling across the night. The Nazi group leader had no idea what hit him. One second, he was hovering hundreds of feet above the earth, the next he was the victim of a stunning midair collision, wrestling to keep control of his own jetpack.

Zimm rolled the throttle as the two conjoined pilots zigzagged across the horizon. Rolling, tumbling, the two adversaries engaged in a life or death struggle. Barry remained acutely aware of his arms and legs. One false move and a turbine might suck in an unsuspecting limb. It was all a matter of keeping his head and the well-timed skull-butt knocked the startled Zimm senseless. Barry removed the German's hand, grabbed the throttle, and shut off the pack. The turbine stalled, and the two men dropped. With nothing but guts and co-ordination, Barry separated a floundering Zimm from his jet pack and secured the contraption over his own back.

Zimm dropped away but the two combatants remained falling at the same speed. The Nazi Ace groped and kicked as if the fruitless actions might reunite him with his adversary. Barry ignored the frenzied gestures and concentrated on the small starter switch on the side of the pack. He was now less than one hundred feet above the trees. With a final desperate click, the turbine whined and belched a blast of fire and smoke. Barry rolled into an upright position as the rocket propelled him back toward the landing strip.

Barry landed in a small clearing, removed his jetpack and met up with his friends. The anxious Aussie dinosaur puppeteer and the recently freed zealots huddled nearby. Without so much as a thank you, the young couples turned their back on the rescuers and darted back into the rain forest.

"You're welcome," Face called after them.

"They're not so bad," Beast said. "We can now take a Singularity test in the city of our choice."

Doc removed the First-Aid kit from a knapsack and adeptly dressed the wounds of both Face and Beast. The big man was lucky, the bullet passing cleanly through his shoulder. Much to Beast's delight, Doc cauterized the flesh with a magical flash of ignited gun powder. Through the entire painful procedure, the big man never complained.

Face was more vocal when it came to his mangled earlobe. "Now I'll never be able to wear an earring," he complained.

"Unless I'm mistaken, you still have one good ear," Brain commented.

"The wound's in my heterosexual ear," Face explained.

The Aussie's gaze never wavered from the direction of the cultist's exit. "If it's all the same with you, I'd like to take my chances with them," he said finally.

Barry nodded, and the Aussie darted into the rain forest, chasing after his new religion.

"My days as a hipster pirate are over," Face said to himself, rubbing his bandaged ear. "What other potential fads am I going to miss out on because of you?"

"Nazis and Columbians," Brain stated. He was thinking out loud. "I don't get the connection?"

"The former must be exploiting the latter," Barry guessed. "All of that money must be financing something. We need to find out what." He paused for a brief second, letting all the puzzle pieces fit in his mind. "I found Tilly's barrels inside the hanger. It's the rocket fuel they're using for the jetpacks. But why do they need jet packs?"

"To get high with a little help from their friends." Beast answered without the benefit of forethought.

"Now he's quoting song lyrics," the actor blurted.

"Dumb-ass. They use them to get to those pesky hard to reach places!"

"Who you calling a dumb-ass, dumb-ass?"

Barry's hand came down on the actor's forearm. "Beast may be onto something," he said. "Come on. There's a camp around here. Let's find it."

"And from what little I know about Nazis," Face offered. "They love unexpected company."

"This is all connected," Barry explained. "We're need to find out how."

His four friends had experienced more adventure in the last few days than in a collective lifetime. What new danger awaited them? They were now bound to each other by the miraculous transformation of their leader.

The elderly man stood in the entryway of the thatched hut. He smiled, oozing a sophisticated old-world charm. His face was tanned, neither ruddy or marked without any telltale spots of advanced age. He was immaculately groomed, his tan slacks and cotton shirt well pressed. It was as if the constant heat and humidity had no effect on the gentleman or his attire. Even his purple ascot, folded meticulously around his neck, was without wrinkle. "Allow me to introduce myself," the man offered with a slight bow. "My name is Harrison Thunder. Doctor Harrison Thunder. Welcome to El Dorado."

Tilly sat beside Denice on a pile of golden bricks. The two women stared at the arrival, still unsure if he were friend or foe.

"Did the Commodore send you?" Denice asked nervously. She had decided she wasn't going back no matter what.

"That charlatan," Thunder purred. "The man's nothing more than a pawn to assist me in arriving at a forgone conclusion." The villain shrugged and addressed Denice. "Young lady, your services are no longer required. You are free to go to whatever location your heart desires. It's the least I can do for you bringing Tilly back to me."

It took all of a split-second for Denice to decide. She had enough of the jungle and its dangers. Tilly's steely gaze cautioned her that leaving may not be the best idea. Denice ignored the visual cue and slid off the golden bricks.

"That's the ticket," Thunder urged. "Panama City is only a short helicopter ride away. From there you can go wherever you like."

"Even home?" Denice asked.

"If that's what you prefer."

"Okay," Denice replied without the least apprehension. "I'm ready."

The young blonde slipped past Thunder, out of the hut and into the night. "Where's this helicopter?" the excited teen asked from somewhere outside.

"Wait for me," Thunder chuckled.

The sudden shriek caught Tilly by surprise.

Thunder was not the least bit concerned. He grabbed Tilly by the arm and calmly escorted her out of the hut. "Let's see for ourselves the result of such rash and hasty decisions."

Pettijohn's animal instincts had served him well. He had successfully tracked the two women up the side of an entire mountain and now held a primitive knife to Denice's throat. The crazed zealot was sweating, crazed blue eyes darting around the unfamiliar village.

"I don't believe we've had the pleasure of meeting," Thunder offered, never losing his old-world charm.

"She's mine," he stammered. "They both are."

Puzzled Guna exited their huts and formed a concerned semi-circle around the commotion.

Thunder smiled, revealing professionally capped teeth. "My dear sir," he began. "I don't give a good goddamn what you do with that girl." His hand remained tight on Tilly's forearm. "But I assure you, you will never possess this one. We met in San Francisco and have since become fast friends."

Tilly wasn't going anywhere, and she knew it. The man holding her was the source of the terrifying, disembodied voice she had first heard in a deserted nightclub in San Francisco.

"Then I'm killing this one now," Pettijohn announced.

"No," Thunder cautioned. "You're not."

"What are you going to do about it, old man?"

"Let's just see." Thunder removed a small device from his pocket. It was metallic and only slightly larger than a pack of cigarettes. He tapped a sequence of numbers on the unseen keypad. "If I can just remember how this thing works," he cooed.

A feeling of dread swept over Tilly. The air erupted with the smell of ozone and she felt an all too familiar nausea in the pit of her stomach. Fiery crackles of static electricity appeared out of nowhere and formed a deadly crown just above Pettijohn's head. The Guna had seen it all before and, wanting nothing to do with the white man's deadly magic, scattered into the night.

Thunder sensed Tilly's apprehension and backed her toward the hut. "Do not worry, my dear," he said. "You've nothing to fear."

"What about me?" Denice wailed.

"Unfortunately, circumstances force me to throw the baby out with the bath water. My sincerest apologies."

It was the scream of a young woman who was confronting an even greater evil than a knife to her throat. Pettijohn's moan was his only protest. Both heads pulsated under the attack from the invisible electromagnetic force. Their cries of anguish were followed by two ominous pops as the victims exploded from the inside. Thunder and Tilly sidestepped quickly, missing the grizzly spray of human remains. Suddenly, it was over and the quiet of the night returned.

"You killed her," Tilly shrieked. "You killed both of them."

Thunder sighed innocently, his eyes glimmering from the eerie reflection of gold. "Me?" he answered. "How? I've been with you the entire time."

"That device," Tilly stammered. "You've used it before."

"A shrewd deduction," Thunder admitted. "All great scientific achievements come with both risks and rewards." The old man was grinning. "You just witnessed a benefit."

"She did nothing to you." Tilly was sick. She tasted the telltale bile in her mouth. "She was innocent."

"No one's truly innocent," he answered. "But left unchecked, the zealot could have hurt you and seriously affected my plans. I can't take the chance of one very disturbed young man changing the course of human history."

Thunder released her and took another step into the hut. "You, the Guna, the gold are mine. Even the son of famous Ravager can't change that."

"Ravager?"

"Funny. That was my exact same reaction," Thunder chuckled. "Surely, you've read the documented exploits of Rock Ravage, the Ravager? He's your boyfriend's father."

"I don't have a boyfriend and I know nothing of any exploits."

"You and a billion other discerning readers."

Thunder approached. His sharp dark eyes narrowed into slits. "Of course," he said, an ugly leer forming over his otherwise handsome face. "Your friend is quite ordinary. Perhaps you'd prefer someone older, significantly more intelligent and infinitely more refined."

He was close, and Tilly had no choice but to act. She raised a knee and kicked the old man hard in the groin.

Thunder uttered a slight oomph from the unexpected blow. He doubled over, and Tilly took advantage, sprinting out of the hut. Tilly wasn't sure how much distance she needed from the device in the old man's pocket and adjusted her speed accordingly. She spun away from the hut and launched herself in a westerly direction, colliding with a solid, unmovable object that stepped out of the darkness and knocked the wind out of her. The sudden obstruction seemed eerily familiar. It was not the first time she had bumped into this gigantic, foreboding presence. Her hand reached up high over her own head, settling on the cold steel of a cannon barrel.

"It might help to know what we're looking for," Face said, tripping over an unseen obstruction for the fourth time in fifteen minutes.

The moon was high in the night sky but only a sliver of light survived through the canopy of trees. Barry seemed fully accustomed to the dark, moving confidently as he forged a trail for the rest of his men.

"What are the Hun bastards up to?" Doc whispered.

"Nazis are unpredictable," Brain offered. "But I certainly wouldn't rule out world domination."

The heavy foliage opened up onto a large open space and military compound unlike anything they had ever seen. Rows of wooden barracks, two larger buildings and, off in the distance a looming tower of metal girders that climbed into the darkness.

"That tower must be twenty stories high," Brain said, pointing.

Doc hunkered and stared.

"Wow," Face whispered.

"That's a telecommunications tower," Barry explained. "And the design is at least a decade ahead of its time."

"The krauts are broadcasting to a secret base on the moon." Even in the dark, the sparkle in Beast's eyes was evident. The big man was back on track, tying every conspiracy to what the group was currently experiencing.

"What now?" Face asked of his fellow heroes. "We go back to our boat and radio for the U.S. Coast Guard?" The actor's question and answer were met with silence. "Yeah," he continued. "Because that'd be too easy."

Barry opened a knapsack, removed a Nazi's uniform and laid it across a low-lying Trumpet tree. He reached in and grabbed the matching officer's cap.

"Don't tell me," Face said. "This calls for an impeccable actor to impersonate a Nazi. A master of both dialect and mime. Someone's who's not intimidated by the mere numbers of an audience but only by the caliber of his performance. This, my friends, calls for a master thespian."

Face reached out to take the coat, a firm hand from Barry stopping him. "There's only one man who can fill this suit," Barry said quietly. "Doc, you're up." Barry turned to the disappointed actor. "Sorry, Face, but this uniform is plus-sized."

"You sure you're ready for this?" Brain asked.

"Doc was born ready," Beast volunteered. "Am I right, Doctor?"

Brain remained apprehensive. "You sure?" he asked. "You know you stammer and close your eyes under pressure."

Doc nodded. "I'll be fine." He turned to Barry. "I'll need my cigarettes."

"Those things are going to kill you," Brain offered.

"Right," Doc muttered.

As Doc dressed, Brain lit a cigarette and handed it to his friend. Doc placed the officer's cap over his balding head. It was clearly one size too big and came to rest just above the chemist's eyebrows.

"And you call yourself the Master Race." Brain teased.

"Funny" Doc said, inhaling. "Okay. What's the plan?"

"Recon," Barry answered. "How's your German?"

"One year. Freshman in High School."

"Perfect," Face quipped. "Then it's still fresh."

"We need information on that tower," Barry instructed. "Find out what it's doing in the middle of a Central American jungle."

"Sounds easy. And then what?"

"We blow the whole thing back to hell?" Beast answered. "Always a great ending to any plan."

It was early morning, the sun readying to make an appearance. The camp remained quiet, and it was at least an hour before the soldiers began the endless military drills and maneuvers that heralded each new day. Very soon a long line of hungry soldiers would line up, filing into the mess hall for their customary German breakfast of dark coffee and fresh strudel.

The elderly Anglo was tall and skinny with matted wisps of blonde hair. A round Latino woman, recruited from a nearby town, assisted the elderly baker. The two were fully engaged in their kitchen duty and paid no attention to the portly Nazi officer, in ill-fitting uniform, stepping into the mess. Both bakers were accustomed to early arrivals when authentic German strudel was involved.

A nervous Doc halted just inside the double doors, studying the two in the kitchen. He glanced down at his distinctly non-military shoes and grimaced. He wasn't sure how he'd explain if anyone asked. Luckily, it was early, and the mess remained empty.

"Where did you get those?" the old man asked in perfect German. He was pointing at the Doc's shoes.

Doc took a deep breath and proceeded inside. He grabbed a porcelain cup and poured himself some coffee from a large, metal urn. He had successfully translated the words "where" and "shoes" from the old man's sentence. He shrugged. "Herr Chuck Taylor All Stars," he mumbled with a slight stutter. His eyes remained slammed shut. "You like?"

The cook took another glance and turned his attention back to the baking sheet layered with uncooked pastry. His general demeanor hinted that he didn't care.

"For the basketball," Doc added. "Just finished a pick-up game in the gymnasium." The chemist forced his eyes open to see if the audience was buying it.

The elderly cook's assistant studied Doc with wide brown eyes as if she were hoping the conversation might save her from further work.

"You want?" Doc asked.

The plump assistant smiled.

Doc sat down at a long table and removed his shoes. "I insist," he said." Doc stood. "Now, about this tower," he continued with significantly more confidence. "Such craftsmanship. Makes my German heart swell with pride."

The gentleman wandered off with a curt nod, leaving Doc alone with the assistant. The chemist watched as the woman grabbed a tray and opened the oven door.

"Yes, sirree, Fritz," Doc continued. "If there's one thing this glorious new Reich knows how to do, it's how to build a tower," Doc placed the Chuck Taylors on the counter.

The woman turned from the oven, studied the tennis shoes and smiled coquettishly. This was his opportunity to gather Intel. Doc hadn't liked his chances with the cook. The old gent seemed both ruthless, cruel and obviously saw right through him. He was grateful he had seen fit to leave. The kitchen assistant might even have a working knowledge of English. Doc gently placed the black high-top tennis shoes into her pudgy hands.

"Deutschland, Deutschland über alles," Doc crooned.

The woman set the tennis shoes down and reached behind a large metal vat of dough. Grinning, she pulled out a Maschinengewehr 42 and aimed it directly at Doc.

"What?" Doc said innocently. "You prefer Nikes?"

The elder Aryan cook returned. He was clutching another metal bowl and a formidable whisk.

Doc smiled at what he once thought was just an innocent Panamanian. She was brandishing the machine gun like she knew how to use it.

"There must be some mistake," Doc offered. "I'm an officer of the Reich."

"Cut the crap," the woman said in perfect English. "You're a spy. We shoot spies. But, please, feel free to finish your coffee. We're not barbarians."

Doc stared down the barrel of the machine gun. This was not going as planned.

"You are a spy sent by the Zionist Rothschilds." Do you deny this?"

"Is that cinnamon I smell?" Doc asked. "Used to do a bit of cooking myself." As predicted, the chemist was stammering, his eyes slammed shut. "International House of Pancakes."

When he opened his eyes, he found his female captor as icy as the temperature inside the nearby walk-in freezer. "Small talk serves no purpose," the woman declared. "You will tell me where I will find the others."

Two uniformed soldiers entered. They were attired in full Stormtrooper regalia. The female commandant acknowledged their presence with a curt nod.

"I'm an American citizen and only required to give you name, rank and social security number."

"Firing squad," she announced. "How does this suit you?"

"I have a pack of cigarettes in my left breast pocket," Doc said with a slight stutter. "Would you mind if I had one?"

"How long?" Brain asked.

Face glanced at his watch. "30 minutes," he reported.

"Hmm."

"What are we waiting for?" Beast growled. "Let's go get him."

Face put a restraining arm in front of his friend. "No," he said. "Barry was clear. He wanted us to stay put until he gets back. He said he'd only be a few minutes."

Beast ignored the actor, loping off in the direction where they had last seen their friend. A concerned Brain followed close behind.

Face watched the two scurry across the open ground. Apparently, his friends didn't care if they were being watched. "Where the hell are you going?" he called out. After several seconds of indecision, Face took off after them. "Okay but when Barry gets back, he's going to be pissed."

The two sentries stood at rigid attention in front of the double doors. They had been on duty since 12 am and their watch was far from over. Both men looked forward to a hot cup of coffee and a piece of the wonderful German strudel that the female commandant had been advertising on the barracks bulletin board. Of course, none of this expectation registered on their bullheaded Aryan faces. Until relieved, they would remain vigilant. That's how important this particular building was.

Neither guard knew what hit them. One moment they were standing upright, a second later a shadow appeared out of nowhere, vaulting onto the porch. One Nazi was kicked, sending him stumbling into the other. The two tumbled off the landing but the shadow did not stop there. He leapt over the wooden rail, planting a boot into the neck of one guard while conducting a sleeper hold on the other. Both guards lost consciousness at precisely the same time.

Barry relieved the two of their weapons, tossing all but one into the bordering jungle. He stripped one man of his uniform and slipped into the gray tunic as he made his way back up the steps. He opened the door and entered. His senses alerted him upon first setting eyes on the nondescript wood building. His natural alarm had been activated, his body's vibration warning him of unseen dangers waiting somewhere inside.

Face and Beast hoisted Brain high enough to peer into one of the small windows. Beast shouldered most of the weight, but Face's pained grimace signaled he was the one supporting the entire endeavor. "What do you see?" the actor whispered.

"Something's definitely cooking." Brain muttered.

"What do you mean?"

251

"Thin batter containing flour, eggs, melted butter, salt, milk, water," Brain answered. "It appears to be some sort of pastry."

"The bastards." Beast countered. "Do you see Doc?"

"Do not concern yourselves with your fat friend," the female voice called out from the darkness. "We'll deal with him soon enough."

Face and Beast spun. Without the support, Brain dropped, landing onto the hard ground.

She wore a black Gestapo uniform, her jack boots refitted to support 3-inch stiletto heels. She was plump, imposing, and to Face, strangely alluring. Major Maria Elizabeth Consuela Margaret Catherine Mengele snapped a leather riding crop hard against her thigh. If the self-inflicted blow stung, she didn't seem to mind.

"So, there were more of you," she purred. "Apprehending you was far easier than I expected." She snapped her fingers and several guards slipped out of the darkness. They were quick, efficient and in a split-second had the three men surrounded.

Face raised open palms high over his head. "Don't shoot," The actor was sporting his most rakish smile. "We're Americans who got separated from our tour guide. Would you happen to know if we're anywhere near Machu Picchu?"

Beast glowered at the female adversary. The big man wasn't entirely sure, but it looked as if their captor was eyeballing his best friend.

"Oh my god," Beast whispered loud enough for everyone to hear. "She likes you."

"Shut up," Face whispered out the side of his mouth. His forced smile remained aimed at his captor. "I'm attempting to beguile her."

"We're doomed," Beast moaned.

"You're looking for your friend," Major Mengele snapped. Her scarlet painted lips curled up in a sneer. "You'll be joining him shortly. You saved me the trouble of a gruesome interrogation." As she spoke, her gaze remained fixed on Face; dark brown eyes ablaze over the chance of a private interrogation of what she was quite sure was a bottom. "You will all die together."

"I bet you say that to all your prisoners," Face cooed, smiling and winking slyly at his adversary.

Major Mengele pointed her riding crop west. "Come," she ordered. "It's only a short walk to the cooler."

"I estimate you have two minutes to charm her out of killing us," Brain whispered.

Face frowned. Even for a man of his considerable talents that would be a record. Never the less, he was determined to give it his best shot. "Lovely night for a stroll," he called out to the woman who led the detail toward the concrete structure.

If she heard, she didn't let on. She kept up the brisk march, the guards remaining stoic and disciplined while keeping the prisoners surrounded.

"Amore is in the air," Face continued. "It's a pity this all has to end with myself and my friends being tortured and shot."

"Who said anything about torture?" the captor snarled from the front of the line.

"Keep it up," Beast growled. "She's putty in your hands."

The drugs were financing something huge. The massive camp full of Nazis certainly proved that. Upon entering, Barry had found the long room completely empty. There was nothing inside but hundreds of square feet of cement floor, wooden walls and high rafters. Never-the-less, the vibration lingered, his senses remaining on edge. His nervous system was dancing a jig on a razor. Was it possible that his new gifts were failing him so soon? Maybe the Nazis knew he was coming and removed the evidence. Possible, but unlikely. Then why were the guards stationed outside? Barry strolled to the center of the room, seeking any information that might shed light on this mystery.

He was dead center in the room when he heard the audible click followed by a slight flickering of the lights overhead. The entire cement floor vibrated as if a motorized giant had awakened beneath him. The hum was next, followed by a sensation of movement. Barry glanced overhead and watched as the ceiling rafters diminished in size. The entire cement floor of the building was an elevator, and he was being transported to the center of the earth.

The unorthodox ride picked up speed, the solid rock on all four sides becoming a blur. A lesser man might have dropped to the floor. But this was the improved Barry, an all-new adventurer with unique talents and abilities. He stood fully upright, calculating the drop at well over 60 miles per hour.

The elevator slowed, and Barry finally hit the deck, dropping spread-eagle and hugging the cement floor. Whatever the devilish destination, his arrival needed to remain a secret. He had something to figure out, and it would be unwise to make a noisy, dramatic entrance.

The subterranean destination had been carved out of solid rock, the engineering far superior to that found in either Redding or inside Haystack Rock. The space was immense but eerily familiar, obviously crafted by the same engineers. The elevator came to a halt, Barry rolling until he was quite sure he was off the cement. He found himself in a storage area of some sort. To his right were high stacks of unboxed technology with a fleet of electric forklifts to move them. He glanced around quickly. His arrival remained a secret and he sprung into a crouching position behind an oversized spool of cable.

Armed Nazi guards kept watch over harried scientists and technicians as they scurried between the banks of sophisticated instrument panels. A jumbo screen on a far wall kept a video vigil of the giant tower above ground. Ravage's son had pierced the heart of this diabolical scheme and was now deep inside in some sort of mission control. Smaller monitors tracked everything from power use to fluctuating electronic waves. Barry recognized the changing yellow signals immediately. If his hunch was correct, there wasn't much time. He looked around the storage area for several items that might come in handy.

"This is your boyfriend's legacy," Thunder stated in an eloquent calm that oozed good taste and breeding. "Left by a father he'll never know. I met the elder Ravage on three occasions and, truthfully, I wasn't all that impressed."

The elderly captor and his prisoner strolled through the underground mine dug out from the side of a mountain. Electrical wire had been spooled along the entire route, flickering bulbs providing just enough light to keep visitors from stumbling or losing their way. Native Guna banged at the rich veins of gold secreted inside the red rock. The air was thick with the smell of human sweat as heavy pickaxes extracted the untold riches. Tilly watched breathlessly, dazzled over the fist-sized nuggets of gold scattered at their feet. More natives arrived, loading the rock into burlap sacks. The weighty sacks were slung over hunched shoulders and trekked to the hidden smelts located somewhere near the village.

"You made these people your slaves," Tilly protested. "And that little demonstration in the village is how you control them?"

"My dear, I'm not forcing anyone to do anything. They believe I've something to do with the legendary Ravager's return. I do, however, admit to having used that bit of information to my advantage."

Tilly paused, watching her elderly captor continue on without her.

"The tower merely serves as a subtle reminder of my superiority," Thunder continued. "They're free to live their simple lives as they always have; in ignorance. He's never coming back. And, I can assure you, killing a disappointing son will be of no great consequence to any of them."

They proceeded further into the dark depository until once again they were alone. Thunder grinned, reliving something in his devious, criminal mind. "Referring to it as El Dorado only fooled me for a decade," he said. "I found this Panamanian slice of heaven in 1967. Historians referred to that year as the Summer of Love and I certainly did all I could to change that. A grateful President Nixon even thanked me for it."

The two rounded a switchback and descended deeper into the bowels of the mountain. The air was cooler now and the smell of human sweat was less pervasive. "Of course, the sixties weren't all bad," Thunder declared after a brief pause. "I was rather fond of an article of clothing known as the Nehru Jacket. I had three if memory serves."

Tilly realized that her captor's grudge against Barry's father had blossomed into some serene sort of insanity. She was tired, but, crazy or not, the man was in a mood to talk. Her best course of action was to find out all she could. It may just come in handy. "How did you kill them?" Tilly started. "The two here and the singer in San Francisco."

Thunder seemed pleased with the question. He hummed a jaunty tune as both continued their march. "Mankind races to his future," he mused. "A future they know absolutely nothing about. And do you know why?"

Tilly had no time to answer.

"Because man's nature is to want as much as he can as quickly as he can get his filthy hands on it. Consider the speed at which technology has increased in the last few years alone? And it keeps moving faster. Smaller computers, bigger televisions, compact discs. And the poor public doesn't even know or care what it's doing to them. How it's effecting their bodies or even their minds. Frankly, humanity are brainless sheep. They just can't wait to have it. To swallow it all up mindlessly."

"I don't understand."

"In the next decade, communication will be global," Thunder lectured. He did not care whether she was following him or not. "Let's just say the ones with the aluminum foil hats were half right," He removed a pocket-sized device and held it up for his guest's inspection. "Behold the doom of western civilization."

"I've seen what that can do," Tilly managed, stifling the urge to turn on the madman. "What is it?"

"The beginning of the end," he answered. He leaned in so close that Tilly could smell his sickening sweet mouthwash. "Believe it or not, someday it will be a telephone."

Now she knew he was crazy. Mobile phones were bricks at best, some even requiring a briefcase for a power supply.

"It all started when mankind got too lazy to get up and switch the channel on their television set." Thunder laughed. He leaned over, resting his hands on his knees in an attempt to catch his breath. "Those worked with radio waves. Same principle but this device requires a more sophisticated signal."

"Don't let the size fool you," he said. "This is digital technology. Science courtesy of my enemy. His breakthroughs are responsible for all of this. Quite fitting that he'd be the one that helped make mankind fat, lazy and stupid."

The two hiked on in silence. Tilly attempting to wrap her head around the plot while Thunder gloated over his achievement.

"You've seen it work on a single person." Thunder said after the awkward pause. "Tonight, you'll witness what my signal can do to an entire population."

The cell was comprised of four cinderblock walls, one door and a wood bucket that served as the accommodation's toilet. Face, Brain and Doc sat huddled on the concrete floor. Beast had gotten his hands on an old yellowed baseball and, back against one wall, tossed the orb at the opposite side, catching it on the return bounce.

"Hey, Cooler King," Face blurted. "We're attempting to think here."

"You okay?" Brain asked Doc. It was an amazing amount of concern for the unemotional thinker. "Did she torture you?"

Doc shook his head.

"Stockholm Syndrome." Beast cautioned. "I'll keep my eye on him."

Doc studied his bare feet. He wiggled his toes. "I miss my shoes," he said.

"Queen of Hearts!" The code word from the Manchurian Candidate elicited no response from the portly chemist. "Just checking," Beast added calmly. "I think he's okay."

"I wonder what she has planned for us?" Face asked.

"Besides death by firing squad?" Doc answered. "I haven't the slightest."

"Mengele?" Face asked. "Why does that name sound so familiar?"

"Never mind," Brain lied. "Not important."

"I don't know, Face," Beast teased, bouncing the ball hard off the wall and catching it on the return flight. "I think you're sweet on her."

Face's tan turned beet-red under the two men's scrutiny. The chemist nodded as if he approved.

"What can I say?" the actor bragged. "It's a gift."

"Way out of your league," Beast offered with a mischievous grin.

"Wait a minute," Face protested. "Are you saying I can't romance a Nazi?"

Doc focused his full attention on Brain. "I'm not sure you could pull it off either," he offered. "What do you think?"

Brain studied the actor. "If he managed to push the right buttons," he said. "Perhaps."

"What does that even mean?" Face protested. "Push the right buttons. Oh, I can push plenty of buttons." The actor was growing agitated and waved his arms for emphasis. "Just sit back and watch me push the right buttons!"

"Too vanilla," Doc critiqued, keeping the clueless Face in the dark.

"I am curious," Brain continued. "How would you know the details of this particular lifestyle?" There were now two things he had never suspected about his best friend.

"I may have explored various avenues of pleasure considered off the beaten path," Doc answered. "And I happen to be a devoted reader of Penthouse Forum."

Brain's impassive face registered disdain over the unseemly confession. "He's proven to be a quick study," he said finally. "And he only needs to act the part."

Doc was unconvinced. "I don't know," he muttered. "I'm not so sure he's up to it."

"How would you know?" Face blurted. "I may just surprise you! What is it? I'm ready for anything you two can throw at me! I'm just as much a part of this team as any of you."

They had played their friend perfectly. Beast was beside himself with glee. The big man turned away so that Face couldn't see his grin.

"Okay," Doc said. "If you insist." The chemist stood and hobbled to the door. "Hey," he called. "My friend is a rat and a no-good stoolie."

"In German," Brain instructed.

"Sorry."

"Now wait just a damn minute," Face said, his agitation growing.

"The snitch wants to spill his guts," Doc continued in broken German. "He'll tell you everything!"

"Stoolie? Snitch?" Face muttered. "You two set me up."

A distinctly Aryan face appeared in the small opening of the door and waited for an explanation. "Was ist los?" the guard asked.

The three prisoners pointed at Face. "Rat," his companions accused unanimously.

The Nazi guard vanished from the door without saying another word.

"Thanks," Face moaned. "It's nice to know my teammates hold me in such high regard."

"Face, "Beast chuckled and winked. "You're the only one who can pull this off."

"We don't have much time," Brain said. He turned to Doc. "You better tell him what he needs to know."

"For the sake of our possible escape," Doc said, "I ask that you keep an open mind."

"I am so screwed."

"If you play your cards right," Beast added.

"He may need a safe word," Doc said.

"Fuck off. That safe enough for you?"

"Face," Beast offered. "Get ready to let your freak flag fly."

Barry had to get close to one of those consoles to verify his theory. The key to the entire mystery still remained several feet away. He straightened the officer's tunic and removed the safety on the MP 40 machine gun. Without a sound, he crept over to the nearest console and peered over the shoulders of the lab-coated scientist who monitored the round, green screen. There was no mistaking the familiar pattern of waves. The scientists were testing a broadcast signal.

"dBm strength at 47 percent," one scientist reported in flawless German.

"Our work shall be complete in a matter of hours," his colleague answered. "I will notify Doctor Thunder."

Barry made his way to the next row of consoles. He watched an additional pair of scientists conduct another series of tests. The computer screens displayed a dizzying amount of numbers and equations and the son of Rock Ravage understood it all. Each flashing number and symbol provided another valuable clue to the nefarious plot of his father's nemesis.

Barry stepped backwards. He closed his eyes and drew a deep breath. An abundance of encyclopedic knowledge burst into his transformed mind in one volcanic eruption. In a split-second he fully comprehended the complex principles of a simple dog whistle undetected by the human ear. He processed information gleaned from countless clinical trials regarding the cancer danger caused from radio waves and mobile transmissions. He arrived at the full scope of the evil genius's diabolical plan and his body responded with its customary biological alarm. The sound was involuntary and upon hearing the result of the exotic vibration, the scientists turned to confront the unwelcome guest.

"What the hell are you doing here?" one asked.

Barry was caught with his lederhosen down. He snapped to attention, his right arm and open palm shooting out in a perfect salute. "Seig heil," he barked.

The scientists were frozen, unsure or unwilling to respond to the newcomer's enthusiastic display of nationalism. It was the bark of the klaxon that interrupted the indecision. Soon, the sound of scrambling boot heels on concrete joined the alarm. Nazi soldiers poured out of the shadows and blocked all of the escape routes in the control room.

At the first burst of gunfire Barry vaulted over the console and rolled for cover. He peered around a bank of machines and saw that he was now outnumbered, twenty to one.

Tilly heard a series of muffled beeps and watched as Thunder removed the mobile device from his pocket.

"Yes?" he answered curtly, "What is it?"

She heard the frenzied German shouts and the exchange of gunshots. Things had gone from bad to worse and it looked like she was about to be smack dab in the middle of it. Thunder's demeanor changed drastically. An intense fire ignited in his eyes and he glared at Tilly as if she were the one responsible.

"Don't shoot him, I'm almost there," the villain barked. He grabbed Tilly by the upper arm and urged her forward. For an old man, he possessed incredible strength, her arm already numb from the perfect application of pressure.

"You're hurting me" she managed as he dragged her deeper into the mine.

He didn't answer. He was clearly in a hurry.

Face stood in the spartan room of unfinished pine walls. Two metal file cabinets were lined up against a far wall and a single, oversized desk took up most of the office space. The actor wore metal handcuffs, his wrists bound tight behind him. The metal bit into his flesh and the tips of his fingers were already numb. A second-story window was directly behind the desk and overlooked the parade grounds and camp. Face contemplated launching himself over the desk and through the glass but decided against it. His friends tasked him with a job, and he owed it to them to at least try.

While he brooded about his fate, the door behind him creaked open. A familiar female voice cooed softly, "No turning. Eyes straight ahead. Do not make a sound."

There was a sharp blow to the back of Face's knees as an unseen weapon answered with a sharp snap. The blow stung like hell, the actor faltering from the unexpected impact.

"So, the handsome charmer wishes to talk," Major Mengele purred. "Let's just see how quickly your confession charms me."

"I do my best work when I'm not wearing handcuffs," Face answered. "I find it so much easier to pledge undying allegiance when both hands are free."

The riding crop struck again. The target was the same. His legs buckled, and the actor dropped hard onto his knees.

"Silence," Major Mengele shouted. "You will only speak when spoken to. And you will address me as Major."

Face felt the smooth leather of a collar slip around his neck and heard the metallic click of the lock that secured it in place. She grabbed the collar and yanked hard, Face tumbling backwards. Major Mengele took advantage, straddling his body and snapping the riding crop against a plump thigh.

She was wearing her Gestapo jacket, and cap, the silver skull of the insignia shimmering off the lone lightbulb. Save for her stiletto boots, the Major was completely naked below the waist.

"Is it just me or does the entire room seem to be blossoming with the prospect of romance?" Face said.

The riding crop answered. The side of his face was the target and the surge of pain was so severe that the actor nearly swallowed his tongue. The skin on his face reddened immediately, his cheek swelling from the blow.

"On your knees," Mengele ordered.

Face flipped onto his stomach and raised himself slowly. His knees screamed in pain as he forced himself upward. Barely off the floor, he felt a bare leg drape around his right shoulder.

"You will now tell me why you are here," Mengele said. "And please consider that each incorrect answer will lead your friends one step closer to the grave. Make me happy with a correct response and a glorious paradise awaits."

The answer required the skills of a professional improviser. "I'm crazy about Schnapps," he said. "And I have a thing for Argentinian women."

Mengele laughed merrily. Plump fingers snatched a clump of Face's hair as her other leg straddled his shoulder. "You are a charmer," Mengele purred as she yanked a handful of the actor's hair. "Why don't I believe you?"

"I'm a very sincere guy," Face answered, attempting to maintain his balance. "Who knows how to treat a woman." He was supporting the full weight of the Nazi dominatrix on his shoulders.

One pudgy hand clutched his blonde hair, the other cupping his cheek. A long sharp, blood-red fingernail hovered beneath Face's left eye. The tip sliced into the skin and the actor felt a small trickle blood dribble down his cheek. "Your next answer must be the truth," she explained. "If not, I will cut your eye out."

Face stumbled slightly before regaining his balance. "I don't think I can," he said, continuing his attempt to rise fully.

"Up!"

It took every bit of strength but somehow, he managed. Face now supported the full weight of the camp commandant. Every muscle in his body screamed. Teeth clenched and grunting, he straightened and adjusted his feet to retain his balance. She removed the nail from under his eye and squeezed his head with her bare thighs.

"Okay, we're here, Major" Face said. "Now what?

"Who are your friends and what do they want?"

The truth escaped before he could stop himself. Maybe it's was the lack of oxygen to his brain or the surging blood to his midsection. Either way the cat was out of the bag. "We came by boat," he answered softly. "There's a hidden gold mine around here and we're going to find it. We didn't know you Nazis got here first. Honest."

There was a long pause as his captor considered the answer. "When I was a young girl growing up in Argentina," she began, "my father, the Doctor, bought me a pony. I named him Wagner. Every day I rode Wagner. For hours, we galloped through the countryside. We went everywhere together."

"Really?" Face interrupted. "That must have made it difficult for the Mossad."

The riding crop snapped against his bare flesh and Face lost his balance. The actor teetered, Major Mengele correcting his course by tugging on the handful of hair.

"Ride, pony," she said. "Ride like the wind."

Face took a faltering half step forward.

"Giddy up, faithful beast."

Face took a deep breath, summoned his strength and commenced trotting around the desk. "Wow," the actor muttered. "This is only really fun for one of us."

"Faster!"

Thunder's order was obeyed, and no further shots were fired. Despite the momentary cease-fire, the klaxon continued to blast. The jarring alarm was soon joined by the barking of German Shepherds, Barry watching the anxious dogs enter the far side of the underground control room. The canines whined and growled, pulling their machine gun toting masters ever closer to his hiding place. His mind raced through every escape senario. Eluding capture was his first priority. Second, was stopping the upcoming transmission at all cost.

Tilly Peterson arrived unexpectedly, entering from the southwest side of the cavern. An elderly man had her by the arm, holding her tightly against him. The two were met promptly by several Nazi officers and the ensuing conversation appeared formal and curt. Tilly glanced around the underground lair, taking in the unsettling mix of technology and rock. And then there were the Nazi guards, the dogs, flashing lights and klaxons. Her wide, brown eyes and tight mouth signaled that she knew all too well, her predicament was dire.

The officer saluted, and Tilly's captor failed to repeat the gesture. The old man's distinctive brow furrowed, listening to the explanation for the current chaos. The older man surveyed the complex as the officer removed his Luger from a black leather holster. Thunder took the pistol and bowed his thanks, calmly placing the barrel against Tilly's head. Even at a distance, Barry could see that the villain was smiling. The German Shepherds were nearing his hiding place and Barry no longer had a choice. He stood up, raising his hands high over his head. His eyes remained glued on Tilly as the dogs spotted him and barked their warnings.

Tilly's face betrayed the unexpected arrival of a friend and it was all the recognition the villain needed. The Luger was handed back to the officer. Thunder bowed, the Nazi Guards hustling to retrieve the trespasser. Hands on his head, Barry complied with the shouted orders, marching slowly toward his foe. Tilly was safe for the moment and that was all that mattered. His mission, however, had drastically changed.

"Son of Ravage, I presume," Thunder said, the only offspring of a persevering nemesis drawing near. "I have waited your entire lifetime to meet you."

Tilly studied the exchange. This rivalry was historic, as old as the combined ages of the two adversaries. Barry was placed in handcuffs, his steely gaze never wavering from the man who had called him by his family name. Tilly noted immediately that Barry was not the same wise-cracking slacker she had once known. He had changed in their time apart; no longer evident was the loser slouch. His usual half lidded eyes were now fully alert and oozing with intensity and even a hint of danger.

"And you are?" Barry said. "I'm sorry but we've never been introduced."

"My name is Harrison Thunder," the man answered, his eyes twinkling with glee. "I'm an old friend of the family." Thunder turned his attention to the Nazi officer. "Take them to the guest quarters. Provide clean clothes and time to rest. They'll be joining me for dinner."

The officer bowed, snapping his heels with an efficient click as Thunder addressed his prisoners. "If you two will excuse me," he said. "I have some last-minute details to attend to before making history."

Face woke up on the desk. He had been driven to the point of exhaustion by the unquenching lust of Major Mengele's perverse sexual appetites. His new Mistress was spooning him, her head buried into his bare back. She remained asleep and snored softly. Their naked bodies were covered in the Major's black leather trench coat. Face, gratefully free of the handcuffs, carefully undraped her arm and laid it on the blotter. He slid off the desk and padded over to the small window that overlooked the parade grounds. It was dawn, the first rays of daylight piercing through the jungle and onto the compound.

There was an empty machine gun nest directly below the window and Face gasped. It was bordered on three sides by sand bags, the MG 42 machine gun mounted to a tripod and aimed at a bullet-riddled stone wall. The first pangs of a guilty queasiness formed in the pit of the actor's stomach. He was now sure that the Major had only kept him alive to see this. He had foolishly believed that his prowess might spare his friends a death sentence against that very wall. Now, he realized, how badly he had been mistaken.

He watched the young Nazi appear from around a corner of the building and take his place inside the nest. The soldier confirmed Face's worst suspicion. The soldier locked a clip of bullets into the machine gun and waited. Face was too preoccupied with the preparations below and did not hear Major Mengele slide off the desk and join him.

"Good morning, Liebchen" she purred. "Another glorious day for the Fatherland."

Face was in no mood for the Major's brand of post-coital conversation. He had failed his friends and no sweet-talking dominatrix was going to change that.

"We will spend many such nights together you and I."

"Lucky me," Face mumbled. "And my friends?"

"Why don't we ask them," she answered. "Here they come."

Beast, Doc and Brain, under armed Nazi escort, marched out from around a corner of the building and toward the wall. They must have known what was coming but not one face betrayed any hint of fear of their grisly fate. Despite his deep concern, Face grinned. His friends would remain cocky to their last breath.

The actor backed into the hands of the Major who shoved him to the window. "No," Mengele ordered. "I want them to see you. Our two faces together will be the last thing they ever see."

Beast lined up against the wall, glanced up and spotted his friend in the window. The big man grinned enthusiastically and waved, seemingly clueless to his own fate. It was the last time he would ever see him, but the actor could not return the gesture. The queasiness from his inaction remained in the pit of Face's stomach. His heart pounded, and he couldn't breathe. Doc was smoking the last cigarette of his life while Brain studied the bullet patterns on the cement wall, tracing them with two lean fingers.

Having deposited the prisoners at the fateful wall, the armed escort strolled back to the machine gun nest. It was over, and the actor knew it. He had complained throughout the entire adventure. Now, his life was spared and his friends, who had put up with his never-ending criticisms and emotional tirades, were about to die.

"It will be over soon."

Face watched the Nazi in the machine gun nest yank back the bolt, locking the first bullet into the chamber. He turned away. He couldn't stand it any longer.

"No," Mengele ordered. "You will watch."

"Why don't we watch it together?" Face whispered. He reached out, placing his arm around the naked waist of the Major. She welcomed the gesture and nuzzled in. "Perhaps," he cooed. "We should get closer."

Face yanked the Major in front of him, the move clearly taking her by surprise. She lost her balance and Face took advantage, shoving with all his strength and sending the startled Major shattering through the window to the machine gun nest below. The Nazi soldier had no time to look up, the naked superior officer dropping on top of him.

The escorting soldiers scattered as the screaming Face launched himself out of the window. They raised their weapons, but Beast was ready. The big man had the first Nazi in the dirt before Face landed on the second. The Nazi broke

269

the actor's fall with a snapped neck. Doc and Brain rushed to the downed soldiers to relieve them of their weapons.

"That was unexpected," Brain clipped.

"And awesome," Beast added, helping the actor to his feet. "You okay?"

"Peachy," Face answered. "Second time in a week I've lost my pants."

While Face relieved a soldier of his trousers, his friends armed themselves.

"I take back every bad thing I ever said about you." Beast said.

Face belted his confiscated trousers and slid into the jack boots, glancing down at the prone Major. "If you love something, set it free," he declared.

"Or throw it out a window," Doc added.

"Only if they're Nazis," Face corrected.

"Damn," Beast pondered. "She fell for you hard."

"We were moving in different directions."

They couldn't help themselves. They would be dead at any minute. The world, as they once knew it, was falling apart. Besides each other, the macabre sense of humor was all they had left.

A nonplussed Face removed the jacket and threw it over his shoulders. "Let's go find Barry."

Beast slapped his friend on the back. For the big man, the adventure had accomplished one thing. It had solidified his friendship with the man he called Face. The actor was once only concerned with himself and his lack of a career in the dramatic arts. Over the past week, he had disproven Beast's theory time and time again and it made the big man proud.

"Where do we look?" Doc asked.

"Not there," Beast grumbled, pointing across the parade grounds.

As the others turned their heads, the cement wall exploded in a deafening blast of smoke and pulverized concrete. The four threw themselves behind the sandbags, covering vulnerable heads with their arms.

"Don't tell me," Face managed.

"Huh-huh," Doc muttered under his breath. The portly chemist had raised himself and was peering over a bag.

"It takes thirteen seconds to load another shell into the chamber," Brain reminded them. "Nine, ten…"

The four dashed around a corner of the building, making for the thick cover of the bordering jungle.

"Eleven, Twelve…"

Tanktop stood on the parade grounds and watched their escape. He was in no hurry. The entire Nazi brigade would soon be underground, and he alone was tasked to deal with these four. Dead or alive, it didn't matter. The long journey was nearly over. He'd take his time, savoring the hunt and the kill.

"Thirteen…"

"Go ahead," Barry suggested. "You shower. I want to look around."

Tilly studied the man she thought she knew. He had changed drastically in the short time they had been apart. For no explainable reason, he seemed more intelligent, exceedingly confident and in much better physical shape. And she realized something else. Less than a week ago, this very same oversexed smart-ass would have suggested they shower together to conserve water. An offer she'd refuse in a record-setting second. Now, he barely acknowledged her presence. He was clearly preoccupied, pacing through their quarters in search of something.

"Do you mind if I ask you something?"

"Yes," he answered curtly, gesturing to the walls as if they contained the reason for his rudeness.

The two remained underground, locked inside a well-appointed room carved out of solid rock. Priceless art, obviously the remaining booty of the Hermann Goering collection, hung on partial wood-paneled walls. The bed and chairs were early Italian renaissance, tiny but comfortable. Behind the bed was the entrance to a modern, stainless steel bathroom. If Doc and Brain had been present, they would have no doubt compared the accommodations to the early set work of Bond designer Ken Adams. The surroundings definitely gave off a comfortable but megalomania vibe; both functional and dangerous. Two sets of clothes were folded neatly on the bed. For Barry, a pair of pressed trousers and a black Polo-style shirt. For Tilly, an Asian ensemble of silk pants and cream-colored blouse.

"Who are you?" she asked. When he didn't respond, she continued. "I don't have to take my shower first," Tilly sat on the bed. "Shouldn't we talk? You know. Catch up?"

Tilly hated being shushed. And that's just how this familiar stranger reacted to her question. "Don't you dare shush me," Tilly sputtered. "I want to talk and talking is what we're going to do. I've been kidnapped on at least three occasions, brainwashed by religious fanatics and now I am being held prisoner by a man who claims to be an old friend of your family."

Barry turned from a light fixture. He ran his hand inside the shade and glass. He grinned knowingly, and this only made Tilly angrier. She was realizing that there was something more to him, adding to her growing anxiety.

Barry was now in front of a late period Picasso. "Shower," Barry said flatly. "I'm in no rush."

Tilly watched Barry slip his hand behind the painting. He was different alright. How much, she wondered? She decided to test her theory out. "We could always take a shower together."

She regretted the words as soon as they escaped her mouth. There was no response. Barry was too preoccupied by something he had located behind the painting.

"Bugged," he mouthed. "This whole place."

Eyes wide with disbelief, she sat on the bed and fixated on his refusal. Not that she wanted to. Or did she? Her confusion seemed to increase with every second. How did this onetime slacker transform himself into a curly-haired Roger Moore?

Tilly stood. What the hell? She looked Barry straight in the eye and slipped out of her clothes. Her nakedness elicited no reaction whatsoever from the son of Ravage. She was proud of this body too. It had flaws, but she still considered herself a hard eight. Why was she trying to create a moment with a man who, up until now, had only annoyed her? "Your choice," she said.

"There's most likely a camera or two as well," Barry said, ignoring her nakedness and examining the tiny microphone he had removed from behind the painting.

Tilly stepped out of the discarded pile, raising a middle finger to him and waving it around the entire room for emphasis. She snatched her clothes off the floor and covered as much of herself as possible. "You're not the same," she accused as she disappeared into the bathroom. "At least I knew where I stood with the old you."

The water was hot, the force stinging as it washed her clean. She was lathering her hair, her head thrown back to keep the sudsy shampoo out of her eyes. He slipped into the shower without making a sound. She threw her head forward, letting the water rinse her hair and stepped into the naked body of the man who had just rejected her. She gasped. Water streamed over both their bodies and before she could stop herself, her arms were up and around his neck. She leaned in, expecting a full return of the embrace.

"This is the only safe place to talk," he explained.

If there was going to be any physical relationship, she'd have to initiate it. "I understand none of this," Tilly said. "All I know is that he wants you dead."

"I know. It's an old family thing."

"Fucked up family," Tilly muttered.

Tilly drew closer. Apparently, talking was not the only thing on his mind.

A long oak banquet table, complete with formal dinner setting, awaited them in the underground dining hall. Another table, draped in a pristine white linen, held several steaming sterling silver trays containing entrees, side dishes and salads. Barry's adopted mother loved all buffets in general and J. J. North's Buffet restaurants in particular. This food was nothing more than an elaborate and expensive version of what could be found at the popular restaurant chain. An oversized globe sat atop a large computer bank directly behind the table. Blinking lights represented the major populations of the Western

Hemisphere, Europe and Asia. It was the type of display preferred by villains with dreams of conquering an entire planet. The glow from threatened populations cast a spectral glow over the dining experience.

A nonchalant Thunder wore cotton slacks, white shirt and blue sport coat. He was sitting at the far end of the table and midway through his meal when the guests arrived. He nodded to the trays and gestured for the prisoners to help themselves.

The trays were heaped with Tri-tip, broiled chicken, brown rice and both Caesar and fruit salads. Tilly sampled everything while her plus one ate nothing, preferring to sit upright and glare at the host. If Barry had a plan, Tilly couldn't see it. Thunder ate, carrying on the brunt of the conversation, gesturing with his fork while lecturing benevolently to his dinner guests.

"I have no idea what happened to him. I know it's cliché, but I loved your father," Thunder began, carving off a piece of medium-rare beef and chewing enthusiastically. "There was simply no-one in the world like him."

Barry couldn't eat. This man, in such proximity, sickened him. "How?" he asked. "What happened to him?"

"I'm not entirely sure," Thunder answered.

"You're lying."

"Your father had no shortage of enemies. Granted, they were mostly employed by me. I can assure you, it was only a matter of time before one managed to find him. He was on the run, tired, maybe even afraid. I don't know. It was hard to tell with him," Thunder explained. He turned to Tilly for validation. "You know the type, right?"

Tilly wanted no part of this conversation. "Is this anchovy in the dressing?" she asked finally.

"Why?" Barry repeated.

"I don't like anchovies," Tilly answered. She studied Barry to get his read. One look told her it was hopeless.

Both men looked at her as she took another bite. "Sorry," she said. "Far be it from me to interrupt your little pissing contest."

"Why did you want to kill him?" Barry repeated.

"He bested me twice," was Thunder's cold-blooded reply. "And no one defeats me. Ever. It's a matter of pride. Money, I have plenty. Armies and scientists, the best. But defeated by that oversized, muscle bound virgin? Twice? It was all too much to bear."

He took a sip of wine, wiping his thin mouth meticulously with a napkin. "And then it hit me," he continued. "You're only as strong as your weakest link. And with him, it was his associates. His friends were the key. I merely bided my time until they died off or left him. Most likely, he merely wasted away. Poof."

"You may not have pulled the trigger," Barry stated. "But you're the one." There was no malice in his tone, but it was said with an intensity that it removed the bluster from Thunder's explanation.

The gleam in Thunder's eye was replaced with a crazed fire. His normally relaxed face appeared gaunt and haunted. "The son," he explained. "The heir. It was one of the many things that infuriated me about the man. His unpredictability. I didn't think him either capable or inclined to reproduce. And then...."

"I found myself elated," Thunder beamed as the color returned to his face. "Unto this godforsaken world, a savior is born. It gave me something to live for." He took a sip of wine and continued. "You do have one annoying trait you share with your old man," he said.

"Is that right?" Barry asked with a mock innocence. "What's that?"

"This need to surround yourself with lackeys. Blind followers. I mean is all this male bonding really necessary?"

Barry remained stoic. "I prefer the company of my friends over that of drug dealing Nazis. Your choice seems overdramatic and trite."

"It requires money to conquer a world. And, once vanquished, it requires the strength to secure it. The Nazis had no choice but to assist me. I helped some in upper management set up new identities down south. Israel managed to locate a few but not all. Nazis, it turns out, are just as grateful as they are loyal."

"How are you intending to orchestrate this new world order," Barry asked with a seriousness that Tilly was still unaccustomed to.

Thunder pushed his chair back and stood. He was grinning, and the youthful vigor had returned. He was a young boy in possession of a great secret. "Technology," he said. "I shall hoist modern civilization on their own petard."

Barry watched his adversary grow more excited at the prospect of sharing his plan. He obviously had the villain's weakness of divulging too much information before disposing of a foe.

"Do you realize that the size of a microchip is now smaller than a postage stamp? And it's getting tinier and more powerful every day. Your father's directly responsible for making that happen. I merely borrowed and improved on some of his breakthroughs. I, alone, realized this technology would soon be affordable to everyone. And I'm not just referring to computers. I'm talking about an entire assortment of low-cost electronic devices; all linked to a common network with access to information twenty-four seven."

Thunder stood at the map and gestured at the blinking lights. "There will be a need to transmit all this information and I chose to capitalize on it."

"Cellular technology," Barry added. "And you get in on the ground floor, building the towers to transmit. But affordable mobile devices for the general public are still years away."

"I'm sure the time will go by just like that." Thunder snapped his fingers for emphasis. "In the meantime, I've discovered other uses for my towers."

Tilly had witnessed the effects of such broadcasts firsthand and had lived to tell about it. "That's how he did it," she muttered. "The towers." Her voice trembled, her words barely audible.

"Yes," Thunder exclaimed. "And I'm doing it again tonight. This time on a much grander scale." He glanced at his watch. "And we're only fifteen minutes away."

"Unless my lackeys carry out my instructions," Barry said.

"Really," Thunder replied. "And just what would those instructions be?"

"Surely my plans will be easy for a man of your superior intelligence to figure out." Barry continued, "you are the criminal mastermind."

The comment resulted in a fit of laughter. Thunder stooped over and put his hands on his knees as he gasped for breath. He recovered quickly as the globe rotated to the western hemisphere. Somewhere over Central America, a video image flickered to life, exposing sunrise over the compound. Thunder's magnificent tower was front and center.

They circled the compound for an hour, attempting to stay one step ahead of the man with the cannon head. They were doubling back once more, this time approaching the Nazi camp from the East. Beast led the way with Doc and Brain following. The constantly complaining Face brought up the rear.

"What is it we're hoping to accomplish?" Face asked, pausing to catch his breath when a distinct and recognizable whistle captured everyone's attention.

"Get down," Doc shouted.

From his prone position, Brain glanced up, his myopic lenses tracking the trajectory of the shell. It was heading in the general location of the tower and the thinker was suddenly struck with an idea. He watched as the shell exploded in the dirt, falling well short of doing any damage to the metal spire. "This is how we accomplish it," he muttered, climbing onto his feet. "But we're going to have to draw him closer."

Even Face understood. The four were going to attempt to destroy the tower. It was what Barry wanted and was now up to them to accomplish. They just had to hope that Tanktop didn't kill them in the process. "Gotcha," the actor said, joining Brain on his feet. "But who's the dumb son of a bitch that gets to lure him in?

"If I can just calculate the precise range of one of those shells," Brain explained, "I may…"

Doc nodded. "Right," he said. "He meant sons of bitches. Plural."

"Why don't we all just stay here and use that damn slide-rule?" Face asked, pointing in to the instrument in Doc's breast pocket. "It's been in your pocket the entire time."

Brain said nothing, unsheathing his sword cane and stepping onto the parade grounds. Doc followed before either Beast or Face could stop him. They were still several hundred yards away from the tower and were wasting no time.

"Hey," Face called after "What about us?"

"I got an idea," Beast said. "Follow me."

"What?" Face asked. He knew it was no use but had to try.

"You'll love it," his friend answered. "Trust me."

Beast loped through the heavy vegetation. It was slow going as the two friends were blazing a new trail, removing the tangle of vines, ferns and leaves by hand.

"Hold up a minute."

"Keep up," Beast urged, "or we'll miss our chance."

"Miss what?" Face managed. He was gasping for air and pointing over Beast's shoulder. His friend turned long enough to catch Doc and Brain sprinting toward the tower. Tanktop remained in pursuit, a cannon shot just out of range from the two fleeing men. The henchman plodded after methodically, taking his sweet time before pulling the trigger.

"He's almost there," Beast managed. "We haven't got much time."

Face fell into a sprint, passing the big man as he untangled himself from the jungle. "Now who's lagging?"

Tanktop was operating on fury and instruments. A heat-seeking digital representation of the two was now visible on the plexiglass visor inside his turret. He paid little attention to his exact location or what might be in his line of fire. This entire charade had gone on long enough, and it was high time for this meddling to be over. He'd kill them all, starting off with the fat man and his pale companion. A series of beeps and a vibrating clank signaled another shell was now housed in the chamber.

Thunder watched with disbelief as the two men approached his masterpiece. "What do they hope to accomplish?"

Tilly couldn't help herself. She pointed to metal giant as he loped onto the view screen. "It looks like they have help," she said with a smug satisfaction.

"What the hell is he doing?" The villain was clearly dumbfounded.

"You're the super villain," Tilly said. "Leading and understanding subordinates would really be good skills to have."

"It looks like he wants to kill them," Barry answered. "And he no longer cares what gets in his way."

Thunder's skin tone turned the flummoxed reddish hue of a senior citizen mid-tantrum. These inferior children were now playing in his expensive front yard. He raised a clenched fist, shaking it in the air. "No," he screamed.

"Yes," Tilly corrected calmly.

"Mister," Barry said defiantly. "May we get our ball back?"

Brain and Doc wheezed their way closer to the tower. The two men knew all too well what needed to be done. The odds of surviving were next to nothing and yet they quickened their pace.

"In case we don't make it," Doc wheezed, "I want to let you know it was a distinct honor to call you a colleague and friend."

Brain, his pale face red with exhaustion continued onward. "That's just the emphysema talking," he quipped between breaths. "Keep going."

Doc stumbled. It was a misstep born from exhaustion. "I don't think I can make it," he said.

"Not much further," Brain urged, aiming the tip of his sword cane to their destination. From the sound of his friend's labored breathing, he now doubted they'd get close enough. "Tell you what," Brain added. "We get to the base of those girders and I'll have one last cigarette with you."

Doc grimaced, his round red face focusing on the task at hand. "I hope you find the wait worth it," he wheezed, sputtering a raspy cough.

"I'm dying to find out, Brain said. He grinned, watching his friend double his efforts and pull ahead. He loathed tobacco but, for Doc, he would grant him this one last favor.

"Proceed with the transmission," Thunder barked into a microphone. "Do it now!"

Barry was eating. He chewed slowly, savoring every bite. "You're right," he said to Tilly. "This is good." The five were now a team. The image projected on the globe proved it. His friends would sacrifice their all for each other and mankind. There was no mistaking the stoic confidence in Barry's demeanor.

"DbW up 1000 percent," a robotic voice announced.

Barry knew full well the signal strength required to do significant harm to an entire population. Total exposure was only minutes away. His only hope was that his friends had enough time to destroy the tower before transmission strength was reached. "What's the intended target," he asked. "Mexico City? Miami?"

"Launch the rocket troops," Thunder ordered. "Kill them all before that steel-plated imbecile destroys everything!"

Tilly found herself smiling. Everything the old villain had worked so hard for over the decades was about to vanish in one ill-timed explosion. And by the nose of his own henchman no less. She turned from the globe and noticed that the agitated Thunder was staring at her. He had removed the device from his pocket and was entering a familiar sequence on the keypad. Tilly felt a sharp pain in her temple as a familiar smell of ozone filled the dining hall. She opened her mouth but could no longer speak. The agony spread rapidly through her brain, the tell-tale fiery wisps of electricity now dancing over her head.

"Argentinian beef is the best in the world," Barry swallowed. "My compliments to the chef."

Tilly emitted a faint sigh before her head hit the table.

The Nazis had just received their orders and time was of the essence. Four of them were removing the rocket packs from the racks when the big man and his colleague attacked them from behind.

Beast slammed one Nazi's head into the floor. He looked over at Face who was having a harder time subduing several foes who had joined forces. One Nazi was on top of the actor, both hands squeezing his neck. If Beast did not act fast, his friend was dead.

"Do something," Face managed.

Beast understood enough. He rolled onto his feet and reached out grabbing one Nazi by the rocket pack and hauling him off his friend. The Nazi's strength was no match for the big man. Face rose up off the floor, the surprised Nazi along for the ride.

"Let go of my best friend!" With one swing, Beast separated the rocket pack from the Nazi, the rocketeer and Face flying off in separate directions.

The remaining Nazis wasted no time, ganging up on the burly wild man. They piled onto him from all directions, pummeling him with angry Aryan fists. Under all this pile of flesh came a muffled battle cry and a dumbfounded Face watched as one by one the startled Nazis flew off in all directions.

Face rolled to his feet and glanced over at the big man. "Best friend?" Face said. "I don't know what to say."

"No crying," Beast bellowed as he secured the rocket pack to his own back.

"Why do I even waste my time," Face commented, eyeing the unconscious bodies on the floor.

"Let's do this."

"Must we?" asked the actor. Face located a jet pack and hoisted it over his shoulders. He secured the bottom belt. "Size 40. Regular. A little snug."

"Last one in the air is a pussy," Beast said. He placed both hands on the handlebars and ran out of the hanger.

Face watched as the thruster ignited with a bright yellow ball of flame, launching Beast with a swoosh into the air. "Hey," he yelled. "You forgot a gun."

Face located two standard MP 38s, slung them over his neck and dashed off after his friend. The actor was forced to guess how the rocket pack operated. Luckily, his first choice was the right one. Quite by accident, he activated the ignition, and the thruster rocketed him into the air with a blasting swoosh. It was not a flawless liftoff. The actor's rocket pack spun upward like an out of control top, shooting into the sky accompanied by a stream of obscenities from the unprepared pilot.

"I believe this is close enough," Brain said. "Any closer and we may get hurt."

A red-faced and out of breath Doc chuckled. Both men had spotted the oncoming Tanktop. The metal-hatted giant lumbered toward them at a methodical pace. His barrel was extending, and it appeared he was now close enough to fire.

"Why doesn't he do this?" Doc asked, removing two cigarettes and handing one over to his friend. "Do you think he knows?"

"He doesn't want to miss," Brain answered.

"Or maybe he wants to kill us with his bare hands." Doc's zippo ignited. The portly chemist lit his cigarette and inhaled. He passed the lighter to Brain who stuck the wrong end of his cigarette into the flame.

"Tobacco doesn't grow on trees," Doc commented as he tapped another cigarette out of the pack.

Two down and three to go. Targeting systems had computed velocity, trajectory and target. The two men stood perfectly still, making it even easier for the henchman to complete the job. Only the blinking of his right eye was needed to set off their destruction. The human tank failed to realize he was being setup. The slighted little boy from North Dakota was experiencing far too much rage to think clearly. The constant foiling by this team of so-called heroes was too much for him to bear. Overpowering emotion overtook cold-blooded instinct and Tanktop fired.

Barry was over the table in a flash. His only thought was to shield Tilly's body with his own.

"Two minutes until broadcast."

"Valiant effort," Thunder commented. "But cellular signals are more than capable of passing through the son of Rock Ravage."

"Stop," Barry pleaded. "You're killing her."

"That's the general idea."

"Not her," Barry begged. "I'm the one you want. The one you always wanted. We can settle this now. Take me and let her go."

Harrison Thunder considered the offer briefly before shrugging and dismissing the notion entirely. "I don't think so," he answered. "Why, you're practically family."

Tilly's convulsions grew worse with each passing second. Only Barry's strength managed to keep her still. The dancing arcs of electricity returned, and he could feel their deadly presence over his back and shoulders.

"Your girlfriend's brain is about to explode like an overripe melon," Thunder promised. "But, look on the bright side. There'll be reminders of her all over your freshly laundered clothes."

"I'll do whatever you ask," Barry vowed. "Just make it stop."

"Are you testing me," Thunder said. "Your father tested me and look how things worked out for him. Perhaps it would be useful for you to taste just a small sample of my superiority."

Thunder's fingers fiddled with the touchpad. Tilly's body went limp and Barry felt a return of brief, shallow breathing. She'd live now, and that was all that mattered.

"Feeling it," Thunder began. "That tingling sensation will soon turn into a piercing pain just behind your temples."

Barry shrieked and placed both hands on either side of his head. He fell onto the table, diverting Thunder's attention away from Tilly with his own writhing body.

"You're right," Thunder stated. "Too hell with it. I think I will kill you first."

Doc had smoked his cigarette down to the filter while Brain's smoldered between lean fingers. The growing ash was the timer. Brain glanced at the steel girders behind him. It was a little late for second guessing himself. There would be no do overs.

"Why's he waiting?" Doc asked.

The answer came within seconds. Tanktop's cannon fired with a puff of white smoke followed a split-second later by a thunderous bang. The shell whistled through the air as it journeyed unhindered toward the target. Doc and Brain faced each other for the last time. Their mutual respect required no words, the two merely nodding as the incoming projectile drew closer.

One second, they were facing a certain doom, the next, two sets of arms snatched both men off the ground and rocketed them away from the explosion. Now safely airborne, Brain and Doc craned their necks to see if the mission had been accomplished. The answer was a resounding yes; a direct hit, the shell exploding into the tower in a blast of white-hot fire and smoke.

The blast rocked the earth, sending shock-waves through the air. Face was already having a hard time keeping himself and the pudgy Doc airborne and over compensated. The rocket pack wobbled dangerously, the actor leaning hard on the right handle of the pack. Both riders plummeted suddenly.

"Don't drop me," Doc shouted over the roar of the turbine. The chemist slipped, his arms managing to find the actor's waist in the nick of time. He was now clutching onto the pilot for dear life.

Beast supported Brain's slight weight easily and maneuvered the jet so that both men saw the twisted girders of the tower collapse.

Face couldn't hold Doc much longer. He eased up on the thrusters in hopes of a landing but was still too high off the ground. The second blast sent a concussion through the air that propelled him and his passenger end over end. He reached down to secure his portly passenger but was too late. Panicked and helpless, the actor watched Doc fall.

Tilly regained consciousness, her eyes slowly focusing on the writhing Barry. A smug Thunder set the device down and focused his full attention on the display.

"Broadcast now," he barked.

Tilly reached for Barry. He was flopping on the table like a landed fish. Judging from the pain she just experienced, he didn't have much time. "Stop it," she shouted.

"It's what he wanted," Thunder responded calmly. The crazed villain was grinning sadistically. Any semblance of his old-world charm had vanished.

Her hand snaked out to grab the device but missed. Thunder expected the move and snatched it from the table. She squeezed Barry's shoulder. She wasn't sure he knew she was here. She wanted him to. He had saved her life and now she was helpless to save his. His head was facing hers and she leaned over him. She wanted to kiss him. It was a fruitless gesture, she knew. She wanted to say goodbye, thank him for coming for her. She leaned into him and as she grew closer, his eyes opened. It happened so fast she couldn't be sure she'd imagined it. Were her eyes playing tricks or had he just winked at her? She gasped and drew back.

Thunder noticed the quick withdrawal and his face betrayed his confusion. His fingers fumbled over the keyboard. Nothing was left to chance. He'd send the son of Ravage to hell.

The ruse worked. One book, mentally catalogued on board the Sea Questor, was an extensive exposition on the dangers of cellular technology. He knew he'd need protection after seeing the giant tower. Using items confiscated from his hiding place in the supply area of the control room, Barry had fashioned a set of barely noticeable, noise-cancelling in ear headphones and energy diffusers. The small devices were decades ahead of their time and would become the prototype for all of popular models of the future. Barry had now successfully diverted attention away from Tilly and was ready to strike.

He launched himself on Thunder at the precise moment the tower on the screen exploded. Thunder was facing the globe, his dream of world domination officially over. Fifty years of planning had disappeared in one ill-timed cannon blast. Barry's hands found Thunder's neck and the villain's head met the globe in a shower of glass, sparks and smoke. Thunder's body went limp, but the son of Ravage was far from satisfied. This man so closely associated with the death of his father, threatened Tilly and may have murdered his friends. He dragged Thunder across the room, slamming the old man's head against the solid rock. Thunder's neck snapped on the first impact and, revenge sated, Barry released the crumpled body to the floor.

"I'll be sure and tell dad," he muttered, "you say hello."

The klaxon sounded as the first wisps of smoke entered the dining room. The destruction above had caused an explosive chain reaction below. Barry grabbed Tilly's hand, the two making their way to the nearest door. Barry forced it open, and the two witnessed the ensuing chaos as Panamanians, Columbians and Nazis fled the destructive carnage.

"Where?" Tilly yelled.

"We've got to find the elevator," Barry answered as the two slipped into the panicked current of flesh.

"No!" Tilly announced after only several steps. "I know another way."

The two turned, heading directly into the flow of panic. It was difficult, Barry forced to shield Tilly from the frenzied horde.

Tanktop had missed. He monitored the destructive explosions with a removed stoicism. He'd pay for his failure and accepted his fate. His shoulders not only carried the weight of a turret and a cannon, but a week of overwhelming blunders. The series of blasts resulted in a blistering heat that radiated over the entire compound. And yet, the steel-plated villain refused to remove himself. If his own death was the cost of his mistakes, so be it. The metal giant stood and waited for the inferno to consume him.

He listened to the frenzied screams and shouts of the Nazis as they fled the underground lair and into the jungle. They were all cowards, but he cared little. Their attempt at world domination had ended much like the first. And, they had been thwarted in less time and by significantly less people. The Nazi Party, Central American Chapter, would never attempt world domination again.

The third explosion rocked Tanktop. Judgement was coming. It was time to walk into the flames and end it that way. He took a step toward the seething series of fireballs.

Doc dropped onto the villain's shoulders, narrowly missing the steel plated head. It was a lucky bullseye. A fraction of an inch and the portly chemist would have landed on solid steel and broken his back. But, he hadn't. He struck the massive shoulders and rolled off the back, avoiding lethal impact and saving his life. He immediately realized the identity of his landing pad and kicked out his legs to untangle himself from the metallic henchman. The giant teetered and dropped forward, his barrel impacting hard in the red dirt

Doc rolled away as Beast rocketed past, dropping Brain next to the prone villain. Before Doc could even get to his feet, Brain had his belt off and was tightening it around the villain's massive legs. The chemist's belt came next and Brain wasted no time securing it around Tanktop's massive hands. The henchman was now bound, cannon buried in the soft ground, the giant body contorted in a frozen push-up.

Beast brought the jet pack to a near-perfect landing. Shucking the heavy gear, he raced to his friends. "Nailed it," he bellowed, a direct result of his quick inspection of the prisoner. "Anyone see Face?"

The swooshing rocket passed directly overhead. The survivors turned their attention skyward, glimpsing the flare of the pack soaring out over the jungle. A split-second later, the pack exploded in a jet-fueled fireball.

"Face," Beast yelled.

The big man launched himself toward the jungle as Brain planted a firm hand on his colleague's shoulder.

Beast turned. "No," he said. "He can't be dead." Tears welled up in the big man's eyes. "He could've made it."

Doc pointed a desperate Beast in the opposite direction.

The bruised and bloodied Face stepped out of a cloud of dust and smoke. Apparently, the actor had jettisoned the rocket pack just in time.

"Face," Beast yelled. The big man ran full speed toward his friend, the actor receiving a full-on beast hug. "How?"

"Those things are dangerous," Face answered nonchalantly. "After dropping Doc, I decided it might be safer to walk."

Even Brain was smiling. They had all been through hell and somehow survived. "Let's find Barry," he said.

"And him?" Doc said, pointing to the prone Tanktop.

"Forget about him," Face advised. "As soon as we find a phone, we'll call Triple A."

They made their way slowly through the mine, Tilly taking her time attempting to explain everything she had learned. All of the gold extracted from the mountain belonged to him now; a gift from a father he would never know. She took his hand, the two continuing in silence, her companion taking in the abundance of riches with a recently acquired earnestness.

"Having money is what I've wanted my entire life," Barry said finally. "And now that I have it, I don't really care."

With all these riches came an even greater responsibility and Barry knew it. It was all part of the bargain struck with his father. The Ravager expected nothing less from the arrangement. Barry had been tasked to leverage this entire fortune toward the greater good of an entire world. Was such a thing even possible? And his friends? What about them? Would they remain as tight as they had been when he was penniless and clueless? He mentioned none of his fears to Tilly. They continued the trek while Guna workers loaded the gold into burlap sacks for the long trip above ground. A thought occurred to him and he grinned.

Tilly couldn't help but notice. "What?" she asked.

"Maybe it's time I get my own place," he said, the wise-ass grin returning for the first time in days. "I was thinking a small studio. What do you think?"

"Now you're just being extravagant," Tilly answered. "But it will make things easier when you have special friends over."

The joke was temporary and quickly replaced with quiet brooding. "This is their gold," he said. "It's always been theirs. I'm giving it back."

Tilly squeezed his hand. That was quite an offer, but she was not entirely sure the Indians would accept it. From what she saw, they seemed more than content living their lives as they always had.

Barry read her mind. "If nothing else, I can show them how to use it to keep their way of life and protect them from encroaching civilization."

The two exited the mine and strolled down the slight hill into the village where Tilly first took refuge. The Guna Indians were ready for them. They had talked of Ravage's return for generations and it had developed its own distinct mythology. Men, women and children surrounded the two and the entire throng followed them the short distance to a large communal hut where a great feast was prepared. It was a ceremony that had been planned for generations and would last for days.

Amidst all this festivity, Barry remained dour. "I'm sorry you had to go through this," he said.

Tilly slid into his arms effortlessly. "We came an awful long way in a short time," she said. "It was quite a first date."

She kissed him with a passion she had never revealed to any man. And it was in this instant that she realized that the two of them could never be together. He had other responsibilities now. Responsibilities that would take him away from her. But, for right now, in this moment, he was totally hers. The ongoing kiss passionately summed up an entire relationship.

The Native search party located Beast, Face, Doc and Brain wandering through the dense jungle and had promptly taken them under their wing, accompanying the four men up the side of the steep mountain. Tilly and Barry found their friends sitting in the thatched hut that served as the repository for the gold. Beast lay on a pile of bricks, admonished by the annoyed Face.

"You're ruining perfectly good gold," Face complained. "Now that you've sat on it, the banks will refuse to touch it."

"Wanna bet," Beast offered, his eyes closed and perfectly comfortable on his bed of hard ore.

Brain and Doc were in the middle of a quick inventory, attempting to calculate the worth of all this gold in today's market.

"Barry!"

Beast rolled off his hard cot, rushed to his friend and embraced him with his signature bearhug. The big man's brute strength might have killed him in years past, but Barry's physical endurance had changed, and he returned the embrace until the big man was forced to break it off himself.

Face was conversing with Tilly when the Chief entered the hut. There was no way to even ascertain an exact age but from the look in the old Guna's eye, Tilly had the distinct impression he had once known Barry's father. Barry greeted him respectfully and addressed him in a language that was centuries old. After several minutes, the conversation concluded, and the old Chief departed.

"There's to be a celebration," Barry announced.

Tilly slipped an arm around him. "You told him, didn't you?" she asked. "You told him you didn't want the gold?"

"What?" Face blurted before he could stop himself. "All of it? I was hoping for new head shots."

"It was always theirs," Barry explained. "They know that. My father was only paid a generous retainer to protect it. We will continue to honor that request. They are the true benefactors of my father's work."

"Mankind is their charity," Beast mused. "This shit is blowing my mind."

"What type of money are we talking about?" Face asked.

Barry stalled, studying each of them before answering. "Two hundred and fifty million dollars a year," he answered. "It will be paid as long as we continue to honor my father's agreement."

It was quiet as each adventurer wrestled with their own reasons for continuing. Only Beast was sure of his answer. "I'm in!" he shouted.

"I can't decide for you."

"Will I have time to pursue my career?" Face asked. "Righting wrongs may be my vocation but acting will always be my passion."

"I'm sure we can come up with a suitable arrangement," Barry said.

Face grinned. "And don't forget my glossies," he added. "Color's now the industry standard."

"We'll be paid equal shares," Barry added. "We are a team and we will split the money accordingly."

"That's just what the Eagles said," Face cautioned. "And look what happened to them."

Doc and Brain shrugged, no doubt thinking of the laboratories and libraries they could fund. "We're in," the two said in perfect unison.

The four's willingness to join him meant that his father's legacy would continue. Barry knew he could never shoulder such a burden alone. His new future would require the assistance of loyal friends who were willing to journey to hell and back on a moment's notice.

"Then we're decided," Barry said, pulling Tilly close. She was looking at him as if her invitation had gotten lost in the mail. "I'm sorry," he said. "You have an open invite."

"We'll talk later," she said. Her eyes betrayed such an affection that Barry never dreamed she was about to pass him up on his offer.

Tilly rose bright and early, her mind racing with the possibilities of the new day. The relationship had changed, and her decision was now all the more difficult. She untangled herself from a sleeping Barry and slipped off the simple but comfortable wicker bed. The village was deserted. The air was crisp and cool and the mugginess that was so prevalent in later hours was absent. Tilly breathed greedily, listening to the sound of the exotic jungle as it awakened around her.

"There you are," the familiar voice said, interrupting the serene calm. "I have spent countless hours and untold resources searching for you." The Commodore was attired in his dress white naval uniform, his pudgy red face sweating profusely. His naval cap was gone, replaced with an imperialist's Pith helmet.

"How did you find me?"

"There's so much more in your recovery we need to accomplish," he answered. He wiped a brow with a white silk handkerchief embroidered with his initials. "The sooner we get back to the ship, the sooner we can resume our work."

"I don't think I'm going back," Tilly offered. "I'm cured but thanks all the same."

"Not going back?" The Commodore countered. "But your PPL and KFC personality engrams are in extreme flux. It's going to take some serious work if you ever hope to achieve clarity."

Tilly studied the persistent cult-leader. She watched as he removed a gold case, took out a cigarette and lit it with the matching lighter. "You don't care about me," Tilly said. "You're here for the gold."

The Commodore grinned. "That too," he countered. "It is mine. Promised by Zandu."

Tanktop stepped around the corner of a nearby hut and made his substantial presence known.

"Allow me to introduce a new convert to the faith," the Commodore offered. "Stumbled upon the wayward soul in a spiritual quagmire of his own making. A fitting addition to the fastest growing religion in the world, don't you think?"

"No," Tilly blurted. "I'm not going with you."

"No one's forcing you, my dear," the Commodore replied. "But leaving may be better than the alternative."

"I pass."

The Commodore pointed a chubby finger at her. "Then, in the name of religion and science," he announced, "and by the powers vested in me by Zandu the divine, I place you under arrest and lay claim to the all riches in this general vicinity."

"Is this a private conversation or can anyone join?" Barry stepped out from the hut. He was shirtless, wearing only the pair of trousers that had been gifted by the villain he had recently bested. Weaponless, he offered his statement with the calm of someone not all that concerned with the sudden turn of events.

"And who might you be?"

Gyros whirred as Tanktop swiveled his turret. He recognized the familiar voice immediately. There were benefits to the new religion. Standing before him was an unarmed Zandu miracle.

"It doesn't matter who I am," Barry answered. "The gold is neither yours nor mine."

Tilly gravitated toward Barry. The situation was going south and there was no better place to be.

"The son of Ravage, I presume. All of the inferior fiction was true," the Commodore commented. "But one unarmed person is in no position to stop a world-wide movement."

"How about two?" Beast said. The big man had stepped out of the repository, armed with the explosive cross-bow. The arrow tip was aimed at the man tank. "Never been that good with numbers," he confessed.

"Two men?" the Commodore questioned. "I have an entire army of followers."

"A Navy man," Face said, strolling out from behind another hut. The handsome actor was carrying the rifle the Guna crew gifted him. He grinned, humming 'In the Navy' by The Village People. "We're a tight little band," he continued. "But, trust me. We'll grow on you."

"Such bravado," the Commodore said. "I could use people like you in my organization."

"It's not an organization," Brain said, stepping around another hutch. "It's a cult."

"A lie perpetrated by the World Federation of Psychologists and Psychiatrists. Our faith is based on certifiable science."

"Rocks and meters," Doc answered. "That's not science." The portly chemist was brandishing his shotgun and standing on top of a thatched roof. How the portly chemist managed such a feat would be discussed long after this adventure.

Tanktop was beginning to think he should have remained turret down, barrel buried in the red clay. Things did not look good for the self-proclaimed best-selling author and current employer. The Commodore was clearly outnumbered and appeared that he couldn't care less. He leered, exposing a mouthful of nicotine-stained teeth. He glanced at his gold Rolex and his shifty rodent eyes lit up as if the pricey Swiss Timepiece ticked off a countdown to some secret plan.

The soldiers poured out of the jungle at precisely the prearranged time. These were the elite forces of General Noreiga's Panamanian army, recruited to aid their newest criminal associate. The soldiers were in full, battle regalia, armed with M16 A2s supplied by American arm merchants. There were hundreds of them, and every single weapon was trained on one of the five.

"May I be of assistance," the pock-faced General said, stepping out in front of his men. He was smaller than he looked on television and most closely resembled Doc in overall body type. His skin bore the scars from a chronic case of childhood acne, his brown eyes gleaming sadistically with the delight that only comes from being an experienced bully.

"General Noriega," the Commodore growled. "You received my message."

The sound of yanking rifle bolts echoed through the village. The ominous warning signaled the beginning of a one-sided firefight. Tanktop was elated. The five who thwarted him were up against the entire fighting force of Panama. There was no way they were getting out of this and he had a front row seat.

Barry felt the weight of all eyes on him. In the last two days his friends looked to him for leadership and had been rewarded more often than not. However, a familiar feeling of low self-esteem was making its presence known. He glanced at each of them, wondering if this was the moment, they'd discover that he was an imposter.

Beast grinned. The big man seemed fully invested in Barry's unannounced plan. Face appeared anxious, the actor's eyes signaling a confidence that could only be found in the opening night of the theatre. Brain stared ahead, his oversized brain anticipating his leader's next move. Doc smoked his last cigarette, confident enough in the outcome that his last thoughts were where he'd purchase his next pack. Tilly held tight and waited. From what she'd witnessed in the past 24 hours, her new boyfriend was more than capable of handling an entire army. He had earned her respect and so much more.

Barry felt Tilly pressing against him. Her eyes grew wider as more soldiers appeared, stepping out of the jungle. That unwelcome feeling of inferiority and self-doubt had manifested itself once more. Barry found himself in the throes of another unexplained wave of panic. His father's device must have some sort of flaw. And then it came to him, his father's warning reverberating in his head. He had been advised not to remove the headgear during the procedure. And he had done exactly that. What's worse, he had taken it off and left the computer running. He had gone above deck to aid his friends in their fight with the island of garbage. He had endangered all their lives by not following his father's simple set of instructions.

These were the consequences of the blunder. He stood helpless before the half human tank, the cult leader, and the drug-crazed General from Panama. He was up against an entire army and had no clue what to do next. His mind was blank as the all too familiar panic overpowered him. His mouth became dry as desert dust and he was dizzy. His heart was racing, and he hyperventilated. His entire body was flushed as any remaining self-control slipped off into a void. He was about to lose consciousness and, in doing so, an entire fortune in gold would fall into the hands of these evangelists of terror.

His friends watched in horror as Barry crumpled to his knees and plopped onto his stomach. He passed out seconds before the formation of American military jets roared overhead. War had come to Panama and Barry managed to sleep through the entire engagement.

It was over before it began. The United States, under the leadership of President George Herbert Walker Bush, had invaded the tiny country and had been victorious. The entire forces of Panama had been crushed in a matter of minutes. The overhead fighter jets and helicopters forced a panicked Noriega and his troops to race back to the capital. It did little good. American military personnel had crashed onto the capital like an angry wave. The acne-scarred leader fled to a nearby Catholic church and claimed sanctuary. Unfortunately for the strongman, not even the Blessed Virgin could offer any lasting peace. Head banging recordings serenaded Noriega 24 hours a day for two weeks until he surrendered. Rick Astley's "Never Going to Give You Up" was the tune directly responsible for finally breaking the strongman's resolve.

Tanktop fled. He had no choice. His chamber was useless, clogged full of red clay. He was in no position to take any side. Performing a silent inventory of his life, he realized that he had made the best choice adopting the new religion. If clutching two rocks hooked-up to a box helped find badly needed answers, so be it. The first step was admitting he was powerless. As he stood there silent, chamber empty and barrel clogged, he weighed his past mistakes against the promise of a new life.

The pudgy hand of the Commodore grabbed his. "Let's go, son," the raspy voice urged. "All hell's breaking loose, and I'd just as soon miss any rendezvous with the United States Government."

The C.I.A. located the twisted remains of the tower and deserted Nazi Camp within the next twenty-four hours. It was all the proof they needed that the General was either creating weapons of mass destruction or pirating free cable. The Nazis had long since fled and only the Columbians remained. The latter were now a fixture in the small country, able to blend in with the local citizens at a moment's notice. They would reassert themselves soon.

Barry regained consciousness in the cabin of The Sea Questor. He opened his eyes, focusing on the anxious faces of his friends. Brain was in the process of removing the pasta strainer from his head.

"You missed it," Beast bellowed.

"What?"

"The ultimate in Deus ex machina," Brain explained.

"Save you the time of reading a paper," Face added. "We won."

Barry watched as Doc and Brain put away the electronic helmet. His head was pounding from the unconscious session.

"Nothing to worry about," Doc said, turning back to Barry. "Just a glitch. We ran the entire program with no interruptions. You should be good to go."

"Back to your new self in no time," Brain added.

"Tilly?" Barry asked. Despite the billions of facts and figures stored in his reformatted brain, it remained the only thing that mattered. Their collective silence spoke volumes. With or without the benefits of his new talents, he knew these men and could read their faces. She was gone.

It was Face who dared speak. "I'm sorry," the actor managed.

25 Years Later

"When did you plan on telling him?" Doc was on his third rum and the effects of the alcohol on his empty stomach were noticeable. The brilliant chemist, no longer with a scientific outlet, was drinking more and starting the process earlier in the day.

Brain was well aware of the drinking habits of his oldest friend. He nodded stoically. "After dessert," he answered curtly. "Why ruin a perfectly respectable dinner."

The event was held at a popular Italian restaurant. It was a Saturday night in mid-October, twenty-five years from the day they began their lives as adventurers. The festivities had been booked in one of the establishment's larger banquet rooms.

It was a celebration, and it was a pity that not everyone had lived long enough to join in on the festivities. Brain was there, looking not all that different than he did thirty years before. His hair had turned a salt and pepper gray and had grown midway down his back which he kept in a tight braid. His Buddy Holly-style glasses had been replaced with thicker lenses and simple wire frames. The thinker watched as his colleague consumed one drink after another, knowing full well that it was the portly chemist's attempt to calm the growing tremors in his hands.

"I'm fine," Doc barked without even being asked the question.

Face sat with his equally attractive wife Maureen. The passage of time had been good to the actor as he had spent a respectable amount of his financial resources fighting off the ravages of time. The end result was a handsome middle-aged version of his younger self. No small accomplishment, considering the appearance of his other colleagues meandering around the room.

There were some new members of Barry's crew in attendance; individuals who had slipped in with the tight band when the originals were forced to deal with other commitments. Numbers, a short, energetic Certified Public Accountant, sipped from a glass of a Napa Valley Cabernet. In his younger days, Numbers had borne a striking resemblance to Michael J. Fox. The short blonde had been active with the group since the early nineties, exhibiting a youthful cockiness that was a breath of fresh air. He soon became the group's accountant, assuring the riches that had been designated exclusively for righting wrongs were exactly where they needed to be. It was imperative that the ancient Guna Indians be protected, and that Barry's massive crime-fighting property holdings remain solvent. Number's wife, Chelsea, sat beside her husband and shared with the other spouses a common cluelessness as to their husband's true vocations.

Laser Eyes, AKA, the interrogator, was also a new member of the crew, with only two decades of adventuring on his resume. He joined the band in the early nineties and often filled in for Doc when the chemist and part-time parrot head took one of his Caribbean sabbaticals. Laser Eyes possessed the unique and unsettling gift of never needing to blink. His unending stare was piercing, enemies crumbling readily under his intense gaze. Arlene, his wife, sat next to him, the two interacting enthusiastically with lifelong friends.

"A toast," Laser Eyes announced, standing. "To the woman who organized this dinner and the only one who could ever put up with the likes of Barry, Lindsey."

Glasses clinked, the revelers grinning at the attractive wife to one of the greatest heroes of all time. The lovely Mrs. Levitt seemed embarrassed by the attention and returned the warmth, holding up her glass and gesturing to all.

Barry seemed ill at ease. He took a sip from his drink, glanced around the room and brooded. The only villain to challenge him or any of his brothers had been time. As with his biological father before him, it alone proved victorious in stopping the son of Ravage and his crew. Barry was now overweight by at least fifty pounds and his short, brown hair was gray and thinning. He wore glasses and, due to the rapidly declining vision, was forced to change his prescription yearly. The frames grew bigger and the lenses thicker with each visit to the optometrist. He could no longer see well enough to drive at night and enlisted the services of his wife whenever he needed to be anywhere past sundown. This, among a myriad of other physical ailments, proved to be a distinct disadvantage to any sort of crime fighting.

At the first notable signs of aging, Barry had consulted with Brain and Doc. He reasoned that another session with his father's brain-altering helmet to be the remedy to all ills. It might even aid in slowing the inevitable aging process. Brain and Doc proved happy to oblige but the entire experiment offered zero results. Barry continued to age and slow. Without a leader, they had all ceased to adventure, and it had been over five years since they had even attempted one.

Face's stood, a glass in his raised hand. "To Beast," he saluted. "Friend, confident and a pain in my ass for over twenty years."

"To Beast!"

Tears welled up in the actor's eyes and his wife reached up and touched his elbow. Face sat, his chin resting on his chest. He was openly sobbing.

Beast passed away earlier that summer of heart complications stemming from an undiagnosed Type 2 Diabetes. He had eaten as he had lived, the same overbearing enthusiasm that gave little thought to future complications. If there was a soul to this merry little band, it was Beast; charging in where others feared to tread. His boundless energy and constant ribbing of Face served as a constant reminder that the life of adventuring, no matter how dangerous, was what you made of it. No one needed reminding that Beast had never missed a single exploit. It was his unique brand of camaraderie that kept the others returning to this life time and time again. He was always there, willing to travel anywhere on the globe, on a moment's notice.

Maureen, an east coaster, leaned over the table to the wife of Laser Eyes. "Twenty years of nicknames," she commented. "You'd think after all this time they'd call each other by their given names."

"It makes me wonder what they've been calling us all these years," the wife answered with an agreeing smile.

The wives remained blissfully unaware, never understanding their husband's secret lives. The men had jobs and well-constructed cover stories to go along with them. The spouses assumed these jobs required a fair amount of travel. And, there were their annual Vegas trips. Boys will be boys, they reasoned. The careers had been secretly established by Numbers. Paychecks, including healthcare benefits, vision and 401K, all under the auspices of The El Dorado Finance Company.

The waiter had brought out another round of appetizers when Barry noticed Doc and Brain circling the room, quietly conversing with other members of the team. Curiosity eventually got the better of him and he excused himself, sauntering over to his two oldest friends.

"What's going on?" Barry asked. "They just served the sausage and peppers. We're going to miss it."

The two studied the leader for a moment, Doc gesturing to the bar, "We want to buy you a drink," he said.

The three made their way to the back of the room and were promptly joined by Face, Laser Eyes and Numbers. The men lined up at the bar as the bartender poured a series of bourbon shots.

"What are we drinking to?" Barry asked.

"Another toast," the actor said.

"To what?" Barry asked.

"How about your successor," Face answered.

The actor's statement was a jolt to the aging son of Rock Ravage. "Impossible," Barry sputtered. "The pasta strainer only works with someone with the same genetic patterns. There's nobody."

"Hmm," Brain muttered. "You may be mistaken. There may very well be another Ravage."

Numbers and Laser Eyes listened patiently to the elder statesmen.

"I don't understand."

It was times like this when Face missed Beast's enthusiasm. The big man would have enjoyed the complication. Right now, he'd be slapping Barry hard on the back.

"It does take getting used to," Face offered.

"What?" Barry said impatiently. With the fading eyesight, he had become increasingly grumpy over the years.

"Tilly's alive," Brain began.

"Living in Central California. She's a geologist," Doc continued. "And a very good one. I've read her work."

It was as if the last twenty-five years of his life were suddenly erased. Barry didn't know what to say. He looked over at his wife and smiled. "What are you talking about?" he stammered. "She dropped out of sight. I, we, tried to find her for years."

"We've seen her," Doc said.

"She changed her name," Face added.

"Why'd she do that?"

Doc cleared his throat. He was shaking and needed a cigarette, a drink or both.

It was Face who finished the conversation. "She has a daughter. I'm no Maury Povich, but we believe it's yours."

"How do you know this?"

Brain and Doc were embarrassed at how far they had gone to confirm their suspicions. The two men studied each other. It was just like old times.

"We stole DNA from a water glass."

"Your daughter's name is Felicia," Brain explained.

Everyone continued to stare. His days of leading had long since passed. He wasn't capable of deciding on a dinner entrée let alone something like this.

"There's more," Brain said.

"What?" Barry asked. The mention of a daughter stunned him. He stood at the bar in silence and attempted to get his head around the concept of being a father at this stage of his life.

Laser Eyes took it upon himself to deliver the rest of the news. "Someone's trying to kill her, boss."

His knees buckled, and Barry leaned against the bar for support. This was a lot to take in and he needed to remain upright.

"We've made arrangements," Numbers announced. "We're all going."

Barry's wife was mid conversation with Maureen. She had excused many things but after twenty years of marriage, it would be difficult to explain a daughter.

"Vegas?" Barry said to Numbers.

Numbers took a smartphone out of his breast pocket and finalized the arrangements. In the past he would have used the services of a good travel agent, but times and technology had changed. In some strange way, his colleagues had been part of this digital evolution.

Face held up the remains of his drink. "Once more unto the breach, dear friends, once more," he recited.

"Once more," they answered, the group of middle-aged men holding their drinks in upraised hands. They glanced over at their loving, innocent wives and wondered how they'd explain it all this time.

The Ravager Pledge

"All living creatures are sacred, save villains who are a malignant scourge on this earth. Read often and attempt to comprehend as much as you can. Use a Dictionary. Vote in all elections, not just the national ones. Respect your elders unless, of course, they happen to be villains. Strive to be your best, remaining humble only when the situation requires it. Honor the flag but never hide behind it. Don't forget, your property taxes pay for decent schools and services. Do not suffer fools gladly and suffer villains less. Recycle and take public transportation. Be kind, vigilant and, most important, prove yourself always to be a good and faithful friend."

About the Author

J.P. Linde is a writer and comedian who made his National televised debut in 1989 on "Showtime's Comedy Club Network. He wrote the libretto for the original musical "Wild Space A Go-Go," and in 2015 produced and co-wrote the screenplay for the film "Axe to Grind." This is his second novel.

Made in the USA
Las Vegas, NV
06 February 2021